Follow Me Back

Back

fight for me

A.L. JACKSON

A.L. Jackson
www.aljacksonauthor.com
Cover Design by RBA Designs
Photo by **SE Photography and Design Inc.**
Editing by AW Editing
Formatting by Mesquite Business Services

Print ISBN: 978-1-946420-10-7
eBook ISBN: 978-1-946420-09-1

Follow Me Back

More From A.L. Jackson

Fight for Me
Show Me the Way
Hunt Me Down
Lead Me Home – Spring 2018

Bleeding Stars
A Stone in the Sea
Drowning to Breathe
Where Lightning Strikes
Wait
Stay
Stand

The Regret Series
Lost to You
Take This Regret
If Forever Comes

The Closer to You Series
Come to Me Quietly
Come to Me Softly
Come to Me Recklessly

Stand-Alone Novels
Pulled
When We Collide

Coming Soon from A.L. Jackson
Hollywood Chronicles
A collaboration with USA Today Bestselling Author, Rebecca Shea

Dedication

To Susan, for your countless hours and endless insight. I wish
I could express how much I appreciate you and your friendship.
Kale wouldn't be what he is without you.

Disclaimer

Follow Me Back has the use of American Sign Language within its pages. In order to give better ease of reading, they are not written in true ASL format.

prologue

I stumbled out the sliding door and into the sunlight, which streaked like daggers through edges of the sky. It cast the last, fading moments of the day in a blaze of glittering red and blinding oranges.

Everything felt too bright. Too harsh. Too real.

Shedding the darkest light on what I'd done.

Hair fisted in my hands, I careened across the street. No destination when I no longer recognized where I belonged.

Still, a desperation took me whole, the need to get away when there would never be an escape.

With every faltering step, I felt the bond I'd thought would last forever stretching thin.

Prying and pulling until it snapped.

Until I had nothing left but the failure I held in the palm of my hands.

A mark forever left on my heart.

I'd tried.

I'd tried with every part of me, with everything I had to give.

But it wasn't enough.

The sun shimmered around me. A glowing, dissipating orb.

Dissolving on the horizon until it dwindled to nothing.

That was the moment my world went dim.

one

Kale

"Kale, congratulations! You deserve it, even if you are nothing but a pain in my ass!" Ollie shouted over the din of the busy bar, finishing his toast, which basically was a roast.

Not like it wasn't expected.

I fought an affected grin as I lifted my glass to join the ring of shot glasses that met in the middle of the round table.

I sat surrounded by my friends, who I considered more family than anything else.

Rex and Rynna.

Lillith and Brody.

Nikki.

Ollie.

They all shouted, "To Kale!" before all those little glasses were clinking together and shots were being tossed back.

Expensive tequila burned down my throat and pooled in my stomach. It landed in a splash of flames that licked and jumped, igniting in my veins.

Head to toe, a rush of satisfaction washed through me.

Contentment seeping all the way to my bones.

Smiling wide, I blew out a gratified breath as I slammed the empty down on the table. "I have to give it to you, man. That was a fine example of what your bar has to offer."

Ollie smirked. The guy was nothing but burly muscle and tattoos. A fucking giant made up of solid stone.

"Now you can't say I haven't done anything for you," he tossed out. "That was *the* best bottle of liquor in the house, asshole. Been keeping this baby stashed in the back for a special occasion or a rainy day, whichever came first. Guess the latter won out."

"Well, it's good to know my little accomplishment was deemed worthy of this level of praise."

Ollie held up his thumb and index finger, leaving a centimeter of space between. "Barely."

My body shook with laughter. "Always such an asshole."

His expression lost some of its mischief. "You do deserve it, man. Hope you know that."

Grief flashed.

A streak that blazed through me before it was gone.

Tucked back away where I kept it safe as a reminder of what I was living for.

"Thanks, man."

I let my gaze rove over the faces of my friends, who were chatting, voices elevated so they could hear each other. It was the bar Ollie owned on Macaber Street, super cool and constantly packed. People flocked through the doors to get a taste of the most popular lounge in our small city of Gingham Lakes, Alabama.

It was located about a block down from my loft, and I'd be a liar if I said I didn't frequent the place. If someone was looking for me and I wasn't at work, they wouldn't be too far off base looking for me at this bar, indulging in all the revelry it had to offer.

It was set in one of the old buildings that had been renovated during Gingham Lakes's revival. Rex's company, RG Construction, had been responsible for the restoration. It boasted red brick walls and atmospheric lights, and the never-ending rotation of local bands gave it the aura of somewhere you wanted to be.

But tonight wasn't just any night that I was out looking for a reprieve from the rigorous demands of working in the ER.

Tonight, all my friends were there to celebrate this new stage in my life, which would take me in a direction I'd been feeling the call to all along. Hoping to give back. Help the most helpless and innocent among us.

Rex tilted the neck of his beer bottle my direction as his wife, Rynna, snuggled under the arm he had draped around her shoulders. "Seriously, Kale, I'm fucking proud of you. Always knew you were an amazing doctor . . . now you've got the office to prove it. Don't let it go to your pretty head." The last came out with a quirk of his brow.

"You just wish you looked this good." I shot him my best grin.

"Cocky bastard," he returned, chuckling and dropping a kiss to Rynna's temple.

Gratefulness pulsed through my chest. Rex, Ollie, and I? We'd always had each other's backs. Together through the worst of times and the best of times. And honestly, life had dealt out some damned bitter blows.

From Ollie's sister, Sydney, going missing when she was sixteen, never to be found, to Rex's first wife leaving him to raise his little girl, Frankie Leigh, on his own, to my devastating failure.

But somehow, it'd only made us stronger. We gave each other nonstop shit, but our bond was unshakeable. Did my best to always look to the bright side for them, be the strong one they could count on even though sometimes that felt like deceit.

Truthfully, it wasn't so hard to put a smile on my face.

I enjoyed my life.

I was . . . content.

Really, damned content.

I had everyone who surrounded me tonight.

A career that I gave everything to, where my heart wholly belonged, and I did my best to make that change.

All except for the piece of my heart that belonged to Frankie

Leigh and Ryland—Rex and Rynna's kids. My godbabies.

Frankie Leigh had me wrapped around all her wily little fingers, and when Ryland was born just six weeks ago, it was instant. The way I loved that kid.

"Are you about ready to get out of here?" Rex asked Rynna.

Lillith and Nikki both booed. "No, it's early!" Nikki whined.

The guys and I had all gone to school with Lillith and Nikki. We'd known them forever, hung out now and again, but they hadn't been a part of our tight-knit group until they'd become good friends with Rynna, which of course meant Broderick Wolfe was part of the mix as well since he was married to Lillith.

"Says the girl who doesn't have to get up at five in the morning to nurse," Rynna deadpanned.

"If you stay a little longer, I promise I'll be there at five to take on the morning shift so you guys can sleep in and do whatever else it is you want to do." She waggled her brows. Pure suggestion. "And I volunteer Lillith to join."

She nudged Lillith with her elbow. "You'll come, won't you?"

"Um . . . for some Frankie and Ryland time? Absolutely."

Rex glanced at Rynna. "I do believe these two have just been promoted to my new best friends."

"Nice, write me off so easily. And on my big day," I said with a quirk of my brow, lifting my tumbler of whiskey to my mouth.

Rex cracked a smile. "Hey, man, there are few things more important in life than sleep and sex. Nikki here is allowing me both. Boom. Best friends."

An incredulous huff shot from my mouth. "Um, hello. This I know firsthand. I was an emergency room physician for the last three years, remember?"

Sleep had become my unicorn.

And sex had become my prize.

I allowed myself that pleasure. Getting lost in a willing body to forget about all the stress and trauma and horrible shit I saw every fucking day.

For a few hours, I'd let myself get lost.

Unbound and unchained.

No promises or commitments or loyalties that I couldn't make.

Just . . . freedom.

Then I'd pass the hell out for hours.

It was enough to recharge and reboot. The push of knowing I could actually make some kind of difference in the middle of a fucked-up world. A world that continually marched forward in time, meting out tragedy after tragedy.

Truth was, I'd come to realize there were just as many miracles buried beneath the rubble as there were the disasters that had caused them in the first place.

For every heart broken, one was mended.

For every life lost, there was one to be saved.

So, my life was dedicated to *saving*.

Ollie shook his index finger at me, tatted knuckles flashing under the light.

Funny, how we all looked so different sitting around this table. Brody and I in suits. Clean-cut and shaven. Rex and Ollie a little rough. Clearly, not ones to be fucked with.

"Told you, you were gonna be a doctor when I broke my ankle out by the lake when we were twelve and you set it with a damned stick and your shirt. Think you actually owe me all the thanks since I was the one with the foresight to send you that direction."

Amusement rippled across my lips. "Dude, you wish."

"No wishing about it. I expect royalties."

My brow lifted. "What, you think I'm some kind of celebrity?"

Laughter moved across his face. "Nah, man. Not even close. But they sure as hell seem to think so."

My gaze moved over my shoulder in the direction he'd gestured to. A rowdy group of women took up the entire opposite end of the bar. Five or six high-top tables had been pushed together to accommodate them, cheers and toasts going up, their laughter and voices ringing through the atmosphere.

Winding with the band that played behind them.

Celebrating and free.

With a grin, I started to turn back to Ollie, to tell him I was refraining tonight, when my attention snagged, tripping up and tangling on a girl in their party.

Like there was a goddamned chance I could look another direction.

A mass of lush red waves rolled all the way down her back. Not the kind that came from a bottle. But the kind that told me there was a smattering of freckles across her milky skin. Skin I was instantly itching to know whether it felt as soft as it looked.

From my vantage, I could see her from the side. The warm, muted lights that poured over her from above illuminated her profile—button nose and pouty lips and dimpled chin.

A knockout.

Because God knew she'd knocked the breath out of me.

But where the rest of her party was having a blast, she was sitting on a stool like she'd rather be any place than there.

My eyes traced across the cream-colored blouse, the crisscross V-neck lined in a wave of ruffles, and down the black skirt I could only imagine hugged perfect hips. Her ankles were crossed, heels hooked in the rung of the high stool. The girl was sipping a glass of rosé like she was terrified the next sip might be the one that put a hole in her rigid armor.

If anyone needed to be shown a good time, it was her.

Nikki sidled up between Ollie and me. "Looks like we're about to lose tonight's guest of honor. Look at you, drooling all over that poor girl sitting over there minding her own business."

Tsking, she shot me a teasing smile. She was always goading me about the girls I followed home, saying one of these days one of them was going to stick.

She didn't need to know that was never going to happen.

I threw a hand over my heart. "Nikki Walters . . . do you think so little of me? I was doing nothing of the sort."

"Right," she drew out, shaking her head and smiling as she gave a little shove to my back. "Well, go on, what are you waiting for? You never know, that might be the girl of your dreams waiting over there for you."

I cocked a grin. "You know me better than that. This guy is

not looking for the girl of his dreams." I slammed the rest of my drink and smacked my lips. "But I am most definitely looking for a good time." One look at the girl sitting across the haze of the dingy bar? *Bam.* The whole idea of refraining for the night had been sacked.

Nikki gave a little mock scoff of disgust. "One of these days, you're going to get tired of the games you play."

She stole a glance at Ollie. Pain pierced her expression before she covered it with a bright smile. Poor girl'd been head over heels for Ollie for all the years I'd known her. Sure, she dated here and there, but it was clear she was waiting around for Ollie to come to his senses.

I knew Ollie well enough that I wanted to tell her to move on. Live her life. Find someone who would appreciate her for who she was—this loving, free spirit who had the world to offer and deserved it in return.

Dropping a big kiss to her temple, I hugged her to my side. "And sometimes the only thing we've got time for are the games."

She shook her head. "Yeah, yeah, yeah. Married to your work. I get it."

Only she didn't. Only Ollie and Rex knew. The two people in this world I trusted with my secrets and my life and my shame.

"Go on, then. We'll just be over here polishing off this awesome bottle of tequila Ollie was so kind to share." She dragged Ollie back by the wrist. "You know where to find us . . ."

"In about an hour, it'll be with your head buried in a toilet."

She pointed at me. "Oh, dude, I'll drink your ass under the table any time. But not tonight. I'm on auntie duty in the morning."

"You're on. A hundred bucks."

"Hell no . . . I win and you go on an actual date."

I gasped. "The cruelty. And here I thought we were celebrating me?"

Her smile turned wry. "Oh, we are."

The two of them turned back to the rest of our friends, who

were laughing and chatting around the table, and I strode to the bar, got a refill of my whiskey, and asked for a glass of bubbly pink stuff.

When I turned around, I damned near stumbled again.

It was a flash.

The girl looking at me.

Eyes the greenest green.

A grassy plain.

Mossy, warm earth.

For a second, I lost my footing.

Lost ground.

Lost sanity.

Because just looking at her felt like something profound.

Before I could evaluate the feeling, I shook it off and twisted my mouth into the smile my ma said I'd always wielded like manipulation.

And I strode her way.

two

Hope

He caught me staring.

Crap.

He caught me staring.

I jerked forward, trying to hide myself in the fall of my hair.

It was no use.

I could feel him approaching.

Shivers trailed down my spine. I stiffened it, gnawing at my bottom lip when I felt the presence roll over me from behind.

Potent.

Powerful.

Persuasive.

That was what the man looked like. Persuasion and dominance and sex.

Like one of those models in a suit with a single hand tucked in the front pocket of his pants, an understated watch showing off his masculine wrist, his face hard and chiseled and angled.

If he didn't scream *all man*, he'd almost be pretty.

Turbulence shook my spirit.

I knew his type.

The type that oozed arrogance and pretension and ego. I knew to stay as far away from his breed as possible.

What made it worse were the chills that skated across the surface of my skin when he was suddenly right there, his essence a breath across my shoulder. My senses were slammed with a woodsy, citrusy scent. Like an orange zested on a pile of maple leaves and whipped up in a vat of sugar, the concoction doused with the warmth of a sweet whiskey.

Goodness. The man even smelled smooth.

A new glass of the same wine I'd been sipping slid in front of me while the man slipped into the vacant stool next to mine. "Thought you could use a refill."

I turned to face him, and I had to fight to keep my jaw from dropping right to the floor, because the glimpses I'd been stealing from across the room did absolutely nothing to prepare me for what he actually looked like up close.

So tall. So obscenely tall. Muscle packed on his long, lean frame. Blond hair short, the front a smidge longer, styled in a polished, immaculate way. Lips plush and soft and dangerous.

He looked like discord.

Chaos with an easy, arrogant smile.

A perfect, controlled disorder.

I shook my head to break myself from the stupor.

What he looked like was a damned broken heart. I lifted my chin. "Is that so?"

As if it were evidence of a crime, I glanced at my glass that was still half full.

"Mm-hmm. I'm a guy who's all about being prepared. What kind of man would I be if I ran the risk of you running out?"

"How chivalrous of you." I tried my best to force the words from my tongue like darts of sarcasm. But with the way his lip twitched in amusement, I was sure the man picked up on the way my response shook.

God, I had to be careful, or else I'd be wrapped right around his finger. My gut told me it'd be easy to do.

Round, round, round, and I'd be nothing but putty stomped beneath the sole of his expensive shoe.

I traced my fingertip around the rim of my own glass. "But completely unnecessary. I have a one-drink limit."

His brow lifted, and something playful danced around his flirty, sensuous mouth. "Ah . . . I see . . . you got wrangled into being the designated driver for your friends? Drew the short end of the stick?"

I fought the unease that welled in my chest and turned away as I admitted, "Something like that."

Truthfully, I would never consider my circumstances as a negative. The short end. A chore or a saddle. But that didn't mean I had free space to flit my days away. Especially with a man like him.

Angling his head around, he captured my attention with that potent stare. As if he'd immediately caught on to the current that ran through the center of me. I shook when I got the sense that maybe he was searching for a way to see it, to find what it was made of.

His brow drew together. "Or this just isn't your scene?" The flash of a moment passed before he seemed to settle on a conclusion, his eyes dimming in some kind of softness. "I'd put down bets on the latter."

Something about his response made my tummy twist and dragged my attention to my best friend.

Her laughter floated through the air, her voice buoyant as she talked with a few of our other friends, her smile free.

Everyone there to celebrate her.

There was no question she was having a great time. Kind of the way she'd been hoping I would when she'd convinced me to come. "It's my best friend's birthday. Jenna," I explained. I turned to look at him, unable to keep out the wobble of affection that fell into the words. "It was kind of mandatory that I show."

The flirtation rimming his lips turned to straight seduction, and he edged forward, his words a murmur two beats from the shell of my ear. "And what would she say if I whisked you away from here?"

There was nothing I could do to stop it. The attraction that throbbed in the center of me.

Its own entity.

It lit in the air between us. Heat and a lusty kind of desire.

There was no denying this beautiful stranger affected me.

But even sitting there talking with him was reckless. "*She'd* probably say go for it. *I'd* say you're wasting your time."

Almost chuckling, he rubbed one of those massive hands over his defined jaw, grin growing wide behind it. "I promise you . . . I'd make sure it wouldn't come close to being a waste of your time. I'd make good use of every second."

The other thing I didn't like about his arrogant, pretentious kind? They were also presumptuous. They thought they could reach out and take whatever they wanted without it costing them anything. Without a thought toward what it might cost you.

Ignoring the attraction that blazed at my insides, I rode on the offense and inched in a fraction. My words dropped to the hiss of a breath. "Do I look like the kind of girl who follows a complete stranger out of a bar? You might be on the prowl, but I'm here to celebrate with my friend. Give her *my* time, because she pretty much gives me all of hers. And honestly, I'm kind of tired of the idea that a man can just snap his fingers and a woman will start peeling off her panties."

He jerked back, intense blue eyes going dark. Like the sun setting on Bora Bora, tossing its turquoise waters in a glittering black. As if he were shocked by the rejection and liked it at the same time.

Or maybe he was just envisioning exactly what that might look like, because his gaze was tracing down, over my skirt, and to my ridiculously high heels I'd had to crawl to the back of my closet to find.

Slowly, he dragged those darkened eyes back up to my face. A flush pulled across my chest as he went.

His tongue licked out to run along his bottom lip while I sat there watching the flip.

The way his entire demeanor shifted into something playful and casual.

"Well then, as much as I *love* the idea of you peeling off your panties, you can see I'm not over here snapping my fingers. You just looked like you were having a horrible time, and I thought maybe I could rectify the situation."

"Which I can only imagine included the two of us ditching our clothes." I wanted it to come off as hard. Confident. Instead, it sent a rush to heat my face.

Ducking down, I bit my lip, cursing myself under my breath. I was so absolutely terrible at this. So out of my element. That alone was enough to remind me I didn't belong there.

At a bar where all the rules changed.

Chuckling under his breath, he stood, towering over me. I shivered when he leaned down, his words just a whisper at my temple. "If that was what you wanted? Me to wrap you up and steal you away from here? I'd be a fool to pass up the chance. You're wound up so tight, I'd spend the entire night undoing you. Time and again. But I would never ask you to do something you aren't comfortable with."

His response took me by surprise, and when he straightened, I was a shaky mess. The man cast me a smile and pointed at the full wine glass. "If you get the inclination, drink up. Let go. Just for a little while." He looked around the bar. "I get the feeling you deserve it more than any one of us."

Something gentle swam through the depths of those icy eyes, and my chest tightened in an almost painful way.

Kindness.

I saw it there, hiding underneath something so powerful I didn't have the strength to fathom it.

"Thank you," I said.

He dipped his head and turned away without another word.

I tried not to watch when he strode back across the bar. But I couldn't help the furtive peeks, enthralled by the way the man weaved through the high-top tables.

All casual ease and confidence.

He got right back to living it up with his group of friends, instantly laughing as if he hadn't missed a beat, slinging an arm around a big guy's shoulders as if they'd been friends forever.

At the yank on my arm, I jerked to find Jenna standing there.

Brown eyes wide and intrigued, her voice was laced with the

scandal. "Who was that tall drink of deliciousness? Good lord, if I knew what this bar was serving up . . ."

I shook myself out of the daze the man had me in and forced myself back down to reality. "He was nothin' but a train wreck avoided."

"Oh, come on, Hope." She flung my arm all around with the plea. "You promised me you'd have a good time. One night, remember?"

Peering up at her, I worried my lip. "I'm sorry. Last thing I want is to be a downer on your party. But you know I have to be careful."

"You think I don't know that, Harley Hope? But that doesn't mean you have to pretend like you're dead. I mean, look at you! You are the prettiest girl in the whole damned place, and here you are, wastin' it." She hugged my head against her chest, basically burying my face in her boobs as she petted my head as if I were a brand-new puppy.

There was no stopping my grin.

"And for the record, the only way you could possibly be a downer on my party is if you weren't a part of it. Now, get that gorgeous ass up and do a shot with me."

"Are you crazy?"

She hauled me up onto my ridiculous heels, her grin wide and her gaze hazy. "Tonight I am."

I hesitated. Sympathy lined her features.

Because Jenna?

She got it in a way no one else could.

She squeezed my hand. "It's fine, Hope. I promise. You deserve to have a little fun, too."

I shook my head, and I gave, letting myself get lost for a little while. Because I knew that, come morning, reality would be waiting for me. It wasn't going anywhere.

Two hours later, I stumbled out the front door and into the slowed warmth of the Alabama night. Streetlamps poured a dingy glow across the sidewalk, the area still busy with people moving from one place to the next, the bouncer still at the door standing guard.

Jenna had insisted she'd walk me out, but I'd refused. The last thing I wanted was to break into her fun. But it was time for mine to end. I'd already indulged in a way I never allowed myself to do.

Head down, I rushed toward the street where a small line of cabs waited to whisk away the revelers of the night.

My heel caught in a crack in the sidewalk. My senses dulled, too slow to process it. The way it tipped me and sent me fumbling forward.

I gasped, nothing I could do but anticipate the nasty faceplant.

That gasp only grew when a big arm was suddenly around my waist, hauling me back onto my feet, steadying me there.

My chest heaved, and I already knew by the time he turned me around that it was him.

Those eyes searched me, carefully, the man almost out of breath as he demanded, "Are you okay?"

I stepped back, trying to get my bearings.

I blinked so many times the man had to think I was crazy.

But Mr. Panty Dropper was right there.

Hands on the outside of my arms, the contact sending tingles flying across my flesh.

The worry in his expression shifting to a wry grin. Face so beautiful I couldn't help but stare.

Damn that shot.

Because ideas thrummed through my mind. The dangerous, dangerous kind. Ones that made me question and want and wish I could have something more in my life.

But I didn't need *more*. I had *enough*—more than enough—and I knew I had to be content with that.

"You look fine to me," he said, smirk kicking up at the corner of his mouth.

Squeezing my eyes closed, I clamored around for my senses, for something to say, mortified the second it came tumbling out. "Are you stalking me now?"

Amusement played all over that mouth. "Uh . . . you're

serious?"

I crossed my arms over my chest, trying to put up a wall, a shield, because I could feel this man everywhere. "Of course, I'm serious?"

Leave it to me that it came out a question.

A disbelieving chuckle rolled from him, and he hooked his thumb toward the door behind him. "I was standing right here when you came out. Just put my friend in the cab to make sure she made it home safe. You're the one that came blundering out, Princess. You're lucky I was out here to save you."

He took a single step forward, filling the space.

Fear tumbled through me.

Not in a way that made me concerned for my physical well-being. But for the fact this man made me feel things I couldn't. Not yet. Someday, maybe. But right then, I didn't have that luxury.

"Someone's feeling a little full of themselves tonight." It was all a rumbly tease.

"Not even close," I managed, gulping around the words.

His expression was back to doing that gentle, knowing thing. His head tipped to the side, and the gorgeous man appeared as if he might actually have the capacity to understand. As if he could see right through me to the heart of the matter.

I didn't know if that comforted or terrified.

"I really need to go," I told him.

He reached out, tender when he barely grazed my chin with his knuckle.

I gasped.

Shocked by the zing that raced through my nerves. Blooming and tugging right through my middle.

Hooked.

A tether drawing me in his direction.

A magnetic force.

Powerful and potent and somehow soft.

Tucking his bottom lip between his teeth, he seemed to contemplate before he nodded and stepped back, tucking his hands into his pockets. "Yeah. I know. Go home, sweet girl. You don't belong here. Just . . ." He wavered and then said, "Can you do me one favor?"

Unnerved, I blinked.

Waiting and unsure, because I was sure this man was so utterly different from my first impression of him. So much more than the assumptions I had made.

"Take care of yourself. Let yourself off the hook once in a while. You deserve to be happy."

I let the emotion wind to my mouth. "I am happy."

"But fear is holding some of that back."

And I knew it then.

He could see straight through me.

"There are some things important enough they are worthy of that fear," I told him, not sure why. Not sure how he made me want to split myself right open and reveal it all to him when I didn't even know his name.

His chin ticked up in a quiet kind of understanding, and I gave him a small nod before I turned and opened the door to the cab waiting at the curb.

I stalled when I heard his voice hit me from behind. "I truly hope whatever is holding it back resolves itself quickly."

From over my shoulder, I cast him a small smile. "Don't worry. My heart is always hung on hope."

Before I allowed myself to say anything else, I hopped into the backseat of the cab, slammed the door, and didn't look back when it drove away.

I gave the driver my address, my thoughts all over the place as we traveled the short distance to my sleeping neighborhood. He pulled up in front of the one-story house on the left, the grassy yard literally hedged in a white-picket fence.

My emotions warred between satisfaction and dread. This little place rang with hope. I just had to make sure it stayed that way.

I tossed a twenty into the front seat, mumbled a, "Thank you," and then stepped out. The click of my heels echoed against the walkway that cut down the center of my yard, the towering trees swaying overhead as I made my way up the two steps to the covered porch.

I already had my key out, ready to slide it into the lock as I approached the door, when I sensed the movement.

The hairs lifted at the back of my neck.

Shivers raced.

A flood of dread. A sea of apprehension.

Slowly, I turned, watching as the shape emerged from the shadows.

Ominous.

Cold.

My heart roared, an erratic crash that thundered through my body, lifting to a deafening pound in my ears.

I took a step back toward the door. "What are you doing here?"

He laughed a malignant sound.

That was what he was.

Malignant.

Set on destroying the best part of me. For years, I had kept faith that one day he would see. That the stones of anger that lined him would finally crack, and his eyes would be opened to what true beauty actually looked like.

That he'd understand the world's definition of perfection was nothing but a falsity.

Now, I knew better.

He approached, his steps slow as he moved. "I think the better question would be, what are you doing just getting home?"

"I don't think that's any of your business."

He laughed again. As if I were ignorant. Small. Foolish. "Anything you do *is* my business, Harley. Do you really think running off is going to change that?"

"Yes." I said it with as much power behind it as I could manage, the sound of the word reverberating through the dense air.

"I won't let you walk away." He edged forward. "Tell me where you were tonight."

I didn't want to give him the honor of an answer. But the last thing I wanted was to give him ammunition to feed his twisted mind. Funny, how he demanded perfection, *respect*, when he'd lost all of mine so many years ago. "You know it's Jenna's birthday. And why do you even care? I'm giving you an out. I'm not asking you for anything other than to leave us alone."

Desperation wove into the last. All I wanted was for him to leave us alone.

His eyes blinked black fury, and he inched closer, his voice dropping to a threat. "You think you can take my say away? Leave me to look like a fool? I won't allow it."

Disbelief pulled from me in a scoff. "That's all you've ever cared about, Dane. Appearances. Control. Inheriting your grandfather's goddamned business as if it were the only important thing in the world. I told you when I left that I was finished, and there's nothing you can do or say to change my mind."

I turned my back to him and pushed my key into the lock, needing to escape. Working it open, I started to push the door open but he clutched me by the wrist. I whirled around to the anger on his arrogant face.

But his arrogance was cruel.

Proud in the most twisted kind of way.

"This ends now, Harley, or you're going to regret it."

I yanked my arm free. "You've already made me regret every single second I willingly stayed in that house. That I willingly stayed with you."

I shoved away from him, quick to slip through the door and slam it shut, fingers frantic as I worked the deadbolt.

Never before had I been physically afraid of Dane. Was I terrified of him? Yes. But I was terrified of the kind of control he'd always wielded. The disgust that had only grown in his eyes with each year that had passed. The hardness that had stamped out his spirit.

I had no idea what lengths he would go to keep that power.

three

Kale

At a red light, I drummed my thumbs on the steering wheel and glanced down at the clock on the dashboard screen.

Six fifteen.

I scrubbed a palm over my face.

Early.

Way early.

But I hadn't been able to sleep. I'd spent the entire night tossing and turning. Nothing but a jumble of nerves.

Anxiety and excitement penetrating all the way to my bones.

Like a kid on his first trip to an amusement park who was terrified to get strapped into the ride.

Well aware the coaster was going to twist and swerve and flip. That it might jerk and jar and hurt.

Still, I knew it was well worth any amount of pain.

Blowing out a breath, I searched along the street that I was traveling.

Fairview—right smack dab in the oldest part of town.

The sidewalks were laid with old, gray bricks, and massive trees grew from planters, their lush branches outstretched and shading the two- and three-story historic buildings that housed businesses and apartments.

Colorful fabric awnings jutted over the doors on the bottom floors, and big windows showcased what was to offer inside.

I was up a couple blocks from Pepper's Pies, the diner Rynna ran and the trendy hotel Broderick Wolfe and his company had brought to Gingham Lakes.

The two of them had been like a straight shot to the economy. Jolting things into action.

New shops, restaurants, and bars had been popping up all over the place, much the same as the revitalization over on Macaber Street where Ollie's bar and my loft building were located.

My new office was just up the road, to the left on McAlister where a bunch of new private-practice medical offices had sprung up in the midst of the city's rejuvenation.

Admittedly, I wasn't all that familiar with everything Fairview had to provide this far down the street.

But there it was, calling out like a beacon sent to save my ass, written on one of those rustic chalkboard signs that had been set up outside a small shop.

Coffee.

Hell yes.

When the light turned green, I accelerated through the intersection, quick to jerk my car into one of the open parallel spots lining the curb right out front.

I hopped out and strode toward the coffee shop, glancing up at the mint-green awning, the name scrawled across the top in a flowy font.

A Drop of Hope.

The logo beside it was a coffee cup tipped to its side, a drop of coffee falling free.

A bell dinged from above when I swung open the door.

It was instant. The strike of my favorite aroma.

That bold scent of a fresh brew.

Damn, if it didn't almost make me lightheaded, my mouth watering with anticipation.

I blamed my addiction on med school.

My stomach was quick to catch up to the reaction, rumbling a greedy sound when I caught onto the subtler aroma—rich cream and decadent sugar—something sweet baking in an oven.

Score.

I stepped farther into the quaint shop. A bunch of round and square tables with mismatched chairs were set up in the open space.

Bookshelves, which were filled with a mess of knickknacks and games and worn hardbound books, lined the back wall.

The place rustic and quaint.

Of course, none of that was what captivated me. My attention homed in on the huge display case attached to the front counter.

Every kind of cupcake and muffin a man could hope to imagine teased from behind the glass.

Behind the counter were about ten different industrial-sized silver coffee urns.

Heaven.

I'd just stumbled upon my new favorite place.

Big chalkboards hung from the ceiling, and I looked up, checking out the specialty coffee drinks and flavors they had to offer.

Movement rustled from the back kitchen before the swinging door flew open.

A tiny gasp echoed through the air.

For a beat, I froze. Somehow knowing it was familiar. That I'd heard it before.

My attention, which had been wrapped up in the menu, was suddenly completely otherwise occupied.

Swore, my eyes had to have doubled in size.

No fucking way.

The same girl I couldn't get off my mind since Friday night, the one I didn't think I'd ever see again, stood in front of me.

All flowing red hair and pouty lips and freckled nose.

Body as mouthwatering as the cupcakes displayed in the case.

Both times I'd walked away from her that night had left me with this odd sense of regret. Something about her had just . . .

struck me. Made me want to get inside her pretty little head just about as badly as I wanted to get inside her tight little body.

She stood there staring at me with those green eyes that had to be as wide as mine, shock freezing her mouth into a perfect "O".

Tension bound the air, and that crazy attraction that had haunted my dreams all weekend was right there.

Simmering between us like one of those chaotic summer thunderstorms that gathered over the lake. The kind of storm you knew was going to rock your entire world.

Blinking, she inhaled a big breath and seemed to shake herself out of it. She ran her hands over the tiny black apron tied around her even tinier waist, smoothing herself out. Rolling back her shoulders, she plastered the fakest smile I'd ever seen across her pretty face.

"What can I get for you this morning?" The slightest country drawl tumbled out with her words.

She was fucking adorable.

One side of my mouth lifted in a smirk. "You really know how to hit a man where it hurts, don't you, Princess? Acting like you don't remember me? Come now, don't break my heart. Tell me I'm really not that forgettable."

Her eyes narrowed like she was trying to figure out what to make of me. "Actually, I'm trying to decide if you really *are* stalking me."

A light chuckle rumbled out. "Someone seems to be feeling a little full of themselves again this morning."

There was no way I could stop myself from baiting this girl.

Her eyes roamed over my best suit—the one I'd donned for the day, knowing I would be stepping through the doors of my new office for the first time in partnership with a group of physicians who had years of experience on me.

The day would be nothing but meetings with staff and reviewing cases that I'd be taking on, intermingled with the few patients they'd already scheduled me to see.

Let's just say those nerves I'd been riddled with all last night had me putting my best foot forward, because in my world, there was always, always something to prove.

Still, I felt like a king with the way she gulped as she took me in, the air flaring with the track of her gaze, her hands visibly shaking.

She seemed to swallow it all down and pasted on an expression of decided indifference. "Says the guy with the five-thousand-dollar suit."

I tsked. "Seems someone loves to exaggerate. It was only four."

She pressed her hand to her chest. "Oh my, you must excuse my naivety."

So fucking adorable.

Taking a step forward, I set my palms on the counter in front of the register and leaned in. My voice dropped. "I think there's a chance you can be forgiven. I'm not above a bribe."

So what if I injected about as much suggestion as I could into the simple words.

It worked.

Because this gorgeous girl was fighting a genuine smile as she ducked her head to the side to try to hide the flush splashed across the milky expanse of her chest.

That exquisite color rode up and lit on her cheeks.

Seemed as hard as she tried to front a brash exterior, all I had to do was peel back a single layer to expose the shyness underneath.

She barely peeked at me when she whispered back, "How kind of you."

Clearly, she was still trying to play along, but I got the feeling this girl didn't typically flirt or tease. That she felt completely out of her element.

And damn, if I didn't like that, too.

"Are you?" she suddenly asked, her question an uneasy murmur, not even a hint of playfulness in it.

Confusion drew my brows together. "Am I what?"

Her voice dipped even lower, the girl whispering out of the corner of her mouth. "You know . . . stalking me?"

Soft, amused laughter escaped, and I scratched at my temple, shaking my head.

She was something else, all feisty fire and soft-spoken uncertainty.

"Um . . . I'm pretty sure that's a question anyone would answer as no, truth or not. But for what it's worth, I promise you that I'm not. I'm starting a new position up the street this morning. I was a little early, so figured I'd check out what A Drop of Hope had to offer. Name's Kale. Kale Bryant."

A small gust of relief blew from her lungs, and she fiddled with her fingers. "Hope. Hope Masterson."

Hope.

A Drop of Hope.

That feeling was back again. It was the same one that had forced me to walk away from her Friday night. The sense that this girl was way too good to be chased and hunted and played. The game was totally unfair if she didn't know how to play it back.

She shocked me again when she asked, "So, Mr. Bryant, tell me what kind of bribe you had in mind."

She said it with the hint of a smile dancing around that soft, plush mouth.

Answer to that was easy.

Exactly the kind there was no chance this girl would entertain.

"How about one of those cupcakes?" I suggested instead, angling my head toward the case.

She chewed at her bottom lip, the hard exterior gone. Like it was so heavily fabricated she didn't have the strength to hold it up. "Do you see something you like?"

There was nothing but innocence in her expression. In her voice. She had no idea what those kinds of words would do to me. The way it sounded like she was offering herself up on a platter.

My gaze traced over her plain black V-neck tee, jeans, and flats she wore today. Her height dropped about five inches from Friday night.

Petite and delicate.

Apparently, good things did come in small packages, and I was about two seconds from telling her that she was what I wanted.

But there was just something that stopped me from saying it.

Something inside me that screamed to turn on my heel and get the hell out of there before it was too late. Warning me she was different in a way I liked far too much.

I guessed I shouldn't have been surprised the really reckless side of myself was begging for a couple more seconds.

I forced my attention from her and turned it to the treats in the display, gaze roaming across the selection, basically salivating at the sight. Each cupcake was oversized, topped with swirls of rich, colorful frosting, finished with little pieces of candies and fresh fruits that matched the flavor and names of the cupcakes.

How the hell was I supposed to choose?

A grin twisted across my mouth when I saw it. Because really, there was no other choice.

I eyed her from over the case, the girl so dainty she was barely peeking at me from over the top.

I inclined my head. "I'll take one of those."

Strawberries and cream and everything sweet.

Hope slid the door open, ducking down, hand reaching in. "Which one?"

"Strawberry Shortcake." I said it like it meant something else.

She heard it, too, and her entire being froze for a fraction of a second, and then she drew a sharp breath before she pulled one out. "Good choice," she muttered.

"I've been told I have good taste." My voice dropped low with the allusion.

She straightened, and for a beat, our gazes tangled.

Attraction wound tighter and tighter with each breath that passed.

She cleared her throat and turned to the back counter where she placed the cupcake in a clear plastic container. She spoke without looking my way. "Is there anything else I can get for you?"

Right.

What I'd stopped for in the first place.

Clearly, this girl had the power to make me forget myself.

"Just a large black coffee will do. Medium roast."

She filled a paper cup adorned with the shop's name and logo on the side and placed a lid on it.

It was at the same second a clamor sounded from the back. The swinging door banged open as someone came bustling out.

Jenna.

Instantly, I recognized her from the bar.

The sex kitten from Friday night was gone, replaced with nothing but rumpled clothes and messy bun, potholder gloves on her hands as she carried out a large tray of steaming hot muffins.

When she caught sight of me, she stumbled in her tracks.

She recognized me, too.

I stood there trying not to laugh while a completely silent conversation transpired between the two of them.

Widened eyes. Tilted heads. Purses of lips.

Got the feeling they were arguing about me, though I had no idea which side either of them was bickering for.

Jenna stepped around Hope, and I was pretty sure it was a warning glare she shot me when she ducked down to start filling the bottom shelf in the case with muffins.

There was no missing the protectiveness that blazed in her brown eyes. Though I was pretty sure that was only the half of it, and she was restraining herself from grabbing Hope's wrist, dragging her around the counter, and shoving her in my direction.

Go for it. But if you hurt her? I'll gladly cut off your dick.

I heard it loud and clear.

Apparently, all three of us were proficient in silent communication.

Hope turned back around, slid the cup of coffee my way, and put the container into a brown paper gift bag.

I dug in my pocket for my wallet. "What do I owe you?"

She shook her head. "It's on the house." She offered me the sweetest kind of smile before it turned wry. "It is a bribe, after all."

That grin on my mouth was growing wider with each second that passed. There was just something about this girl that put it there. So damned easily. Flickers of a blaze that'd been dead a really long time.

Before I went and did something stupid, I pulled a twenty from my wallet and stuffed it into the tip jar. "Thank you for the cupcake and coffee, Hope. I think this was exactly what I needed to kick off this new adventure in my life this morning."

"Kale, that's completely unnecessary," she said, eyes dipping to the jar.

Clearly, she wanted to refuse the small offering. Still, there was an undertone of gratefulness that there was no chance of missing.

"Sure it is, Shortcake. You made my day."

She just stood there, staring at me, strawberries and cream and all things sweet.

I sent her one last smile before I spun on my heel and headed for the door. All this shit on the tip of my tongue. I pulled the handle, and the door opened to the sound of the bell jingling overhead.

My guts twisted in the same second I was spinning back around, striding to the counter in a flash. Faster than I could process just what it was I actually thought I was doing.

"Go out with me."

Startled, Hope blinked in surprise, her pretty mouth trembling at the edges. "I . . ."

"Just dinner."

What the fuck?

I hadn't asked anyone to dinner in . . .

I slammed a lid on the thought, hammered it down with a bunch of rusted nails, swallowed hard. "Just dinner."

Head shaking in regret, she took a step back, like she needed to put space between us. "I'm sorry, but I don't think that's a good idea."

She was completely, one hundred percent right. It was a terrible idea. But fuck . . . I wanted it.

I let a grin tweak up one side of my lips. "How could hanging out with me ever be considered a bad idea?"

That stunning face flushed again, an affected smile wobbling around her delicious mouth. That was right before a sorrowful kind of regret took hold of her features. "I have a lot of stuff going on in my life right now. It wouldn't be right."

I nodded around the impact of the rejection, hating the way it bit and stung. At the same time, I did my best to convince myself it was for the best. I'd just dodged my own damned bullet. Because, really, what was I thinking? "All right, then."

Awkwardly, I lifted the bag and the coffee in front of me. "Thank you again for these."

She wrung her fingers. "You're welcome. I hope you have a really great day at the new job."

I didn't respond, just pushed out the door and into the spill of the bright, morning sun, the bell chiming as it swung shut behind me.

I rushed for my car, feeling all kinds of shit I hadn't felt in such a long time.

The whole way, I wished at least one of those feelings were relief.

four
Hope

"Harley Hope Masterson."

I jerked my attention from the big window that overlooked the sidewalk running the front of the shop, ripping it from the vacant spot where the sleek, dark gray car had just pulled from the curb.

The driver was nothing but a shadowy silhouette in the blacked-out tinting.

I blinked to clear the daze.

Jenna stood there with her fists propped on her hips.

Turning away, I started scrubbing down the counter where the coffee had dribbled from my shaky hands. Apparently, Kale had that kind of effect on me.

Which was just dangerous business in and of itself.

"Don't you start on me, Jenna. And you know I hate it when you call me by my full name. You act as if you're my mama or something."

"I might as well be because someone needs to knock some sense into you. Hell, I'm gonna call her down here right now so we can tag team you."

"You wouldn't dare." I shot her a death glare. Because seriously, her and Mama? That was what nightmares were made of. "And were you not the one who just gave me the we-have-a-creeper alert?"

I didn't even need to air quote it. It was an expression Jenna had patented all the way back in high school. The single look told me, *"Let's get the hell out of here,"* because she wanted to ditch some guy who was coming on too strong.

It'd recently been translated to, *"Send this weirdo packing,"* since we opened the shop together two years ago.

"He caught me off guard, that's all. I mean . . . it was kind of weird that he just showed up here after he was so clearly into you Friday night."

I shrugged it off. "He's not into me. I bet he acts like that with every woman he runs across."

"Um . . . I'm pretty sure he was picturing doing you right there on the counter." She pointed to where Kale had just had his big hands pressed beside the register. "Maybe while eating one of your cupcakes off your tits. And believe me, he sure as hell wasn't picturing doing it with me."

For a second, I got dizzy picturing it before I snapped out of it and slapped at my best friend. "What is wrong with you? Why do you have to be so danged crass all the time?"

"Don't tell me you weren't thinking about it. I mean, that man is blistering hot. One touch, and I'd bet you'd go up in flames. That boy would leave a sunburn worse than the summer when we told your mama we had a school camping trip, but we really spent the weekend at Cotton Bayou Beach with our friends."

I rinsed out the rag, wringing it a little more aggressively than necessary. "And you know that burn nearly killed me. No thank you. I've got enough pain in my life. And I'm not exactly free to go chasing after a man who smiles and asks me out."

"Pssh . . . those papers sitting on your desk say otherwise. You shouldn't let Asshat's inability to keep it in his pants keep you from enjoyin' yourself. It's his fault you're here in the first place. It's time you took time for yourself, Hope."

Turmoil fisted my heart. Every selfish betrayal meted at Dane's hand. Thing was, I really didn't care about the cheating.

"You know him stepping out on me was the least of my concerns."

I'd actually been relieved to know he'd been seeing other women except for the fact he'd continued to come to me.

It was everything else that made the coil of hate glow hot where it throbbed deep within me. A feeling that was so foreign and gross and wrong I wanted to purge it from my consciousness.

It was there, this ominous cloud that followed me day to day. Just waiting for the downpour.

I got the unsettled feeling after his unexpected visit this weekend that the storm was about to make landfall.

Helplessly, my head shook. "Besides, you know exactly what Dane would do with that information."

Really, all it would take was one rumor, and Dane's lawyers would have all the ammo they needed to bury me. Even if that weren't the case, I wasn't sure I was ready to make myself vulnerable again, either. If I was ready to open myself up. Once I did, I knew I'd be all in.

She huffed and pointed toward the door. "Tell me you aren't attracted to him."

Images flashed.

The man at the bar.

My breath gone.

My stomach twisted and twined in an overpowering kind of desire.

It was a feeling I hadn't felt in so, so long.

Too long.

I'd loved the way the idea of it had tasted on my tongue.

The way I'd thought about him when I'd crawled into the cold sheets of my bed.

The way I'd touched myself and pretended as if I were finally completely free.

The way butterflies had stormed and scattered and flapped when I'd looked up to find him standing there this morning.

Tall and confident and so damned pretty.

Polished, immaculate chaos.

An epiphany.

"I know you, Hope," Jenna continued with her badgering, all gall and exasperation. "And you haven't had a reaction to a man in years. Not since limp dick came weaseling his way into your life when you were twenty."

I started to refill the sectioned basket next to the register with napkins and coffee stirrers. "It doesn't change anything, Jenna." I lifted a droll brow. "And I'm pretty sure his dick being limp was not his problem."

The problem with Dane was he wasn't just a dick.

He had an ugly soul.

A warped kind of soul he hadn't shown me until it was too late.

"Might as well have been with the size of it. Pathetic." Jenna was fighting a smile. That was just Jenna's way.

She completely caught me off guard when she suddenly reached out and grabbed me by the outside of my arms, forcing me to face her and giving me a little shake.

"Life's dealt you some tough blows. I'm not discounting that. But I'm not about to stand aside and watch you forget how to live. That's what Dane wants. You to be so terrified you don't know how to live anymore. I refuse to let that happen. Not when you finally got up the courage to leave."

Emotion clogged my throat and tears burned my eyes. My brow pinched in a pleading way. "I've got plenty to live for, Jenna. You know that. And right now, I have to protect it. Please don't ask me to compromise that."

Grief struck across her face. "I know that . . . I just . . . the point of you leaving was so he was no longer in control. I don't want to see you give him any more."

"He was waiting for me at my house Friday night after I got home from your party," I admitted way too fast.

Shock slammed into Jenna's expression before twisting into anger. "That bastard. What did he want?"

Bitter laughter tumbled free. "What he always wants. His way.

To look like he has a perfect little wife and a perfect family. I told him there was no chance of that ever happening. Now I just have to make sure I'm smart enough to keep that promise a reality."

I was beginning to wonder if it was going to be the greatest fight of my life.

Both of us jumped when the bell above the door jingled with a new customer.

It was just past six thirty, right when it typically got busy with people grabbing coffee and a quick bite to eat on the way to work.

I angled my head and gave her a smile that promised I was okay. "It's about to get busy . . . let's do this."

five

Kale

After our morning meeting, I reviewed the few patients I would actually be seeing today. The whole time, I'd been trying to shuck the memories of Hope from this morning. Doing my best to rid myself of the impression she'd left on me, this feeling that I'd stumbled upon something significant when I knew better.

I didn't have time to allow myself to get wrapped up in someone, and if I spent any more time with her, I got the feeling that I just might.

I needed to focus on what was important.

Why I was there.

The reason I lived my life.

When I signed on at Gingham Lakes Children's Center, I already understood the load I would be carrying.

The burden I was accepting.

My patients would run the gamut, almost a reverse referral system from specialists who wanted their patients seen in-house for continuity. From easily controlled chronic illnesses that families barely considered once they walked out these doors, to the kids whose entire worlds revolved around their diagnoses.

Some of these kids? They were sick. Really fucking sick.

Looking at the scope of cases I'd be seeing broke pieces inside of me I tried to pretend didn't exist.

Quadriplegia.

Cystic fibrosis.

Cancer.

I knew this was where I'd been being called all along.

But what made me almost stumble in my damn tracks was my first patient.

My first patient.

Of course.

Life was only a test, right?

As hard as I tried to stop the onslaught of memories, it was no use. They were there.

Emergency room lights glared from overhead. Panic. Fear. Compression after compression after compression. That fucking flat line.

I swallowed it all down. Knew this wasn't even close to being the same, but it didn't mean every single goddamned time I was presented with a heart patient of any kind, I didn't crumble a little.

The reminder that I'd failed.

That I'd never be the hero.

God knew that I got up every single day and tried anyway.

I took a second to get myself under control before I gave a couple small taps to the door then pushed it open.

Josiah Washington.

An eight-year-old with a congenital heart defect. The defect had been fairly simple to treat with a balloon stent procedure when he was an infant. The boy was living without symptoms and bi-yearly cardiology visits.

See.

Not even close.

I shut down the shudder that rattled in my ribcage and put on a smile, introduced myself to him and his father, and went through the typical questions of any patient establishing care.

By the time I was in the middle of his exam, I knew without a doubt that this was in fact what I was supposed to do.

The kid so cool. Laughing. Joking. Living the happy kind of life every kid deserved.

"Are you pulling my leg right now? I think you're really just making this up because you were picturing yourself behind one of those wheels. Looks like we have a future race car driver here," I told him as he sat there telling me about what he'd witnessed last week that had definitely made an impression on him.

Josiah howled with laughter, holding his stomach as he sat on the edge of the exam table. I was on a low, wheeled stool, sitting right in front of him, basically distracting him as I did his well-child examination.

Everything seemed normal.

Especially his heart, which I'd spent an inordinate amount of time listening to.

Wasn't about to take any chances.

"Not even. You should have seen it. It was a Ferrari *and* a Maserati. Both of them floored it at the light, right here in Gingham Lakes. Who has cars like that around here, anyway? Swear, they had to be going at least one fifty. Maybe one sixty. Right, Dad?"

He looked up at his dad for validation. His dad was leaning against the wall with his arms crossed over his chest, watching protectively over his kid. "You got it, son. Right on the other side of the river at the end of town. Would have called the cops myself had they not disappeared five seconds later. Heck, they probably would have already been crossing the Georgia line by the time I made the call."

"Whew, they were faaa-ast," Josiah emphasized with a whistle.

Chuckling, I stood and grabbed the scope so I could peer into his ears. "So what else is it you like to do around here besides for dreaming about racing cars, Mr. Josiah?"

"Me and my best friend, Evan, like to go fishin' at the lake. Dr. Krane introduced us because we both have bad hearts."

Mine twisted again. I shoved it down, refusing to go down that path, and continued smiling as I listened to the cute kid go on about his friend. "He goes to a different school, our moms always take us to each other's houses, so it's no big deal. And my mom and dad *finally* let me get Snap," he said with an annoyed roll of his eyes. "So now we can send messages on our iPads."

"You know not to accept any requests from anyone you don't know, right?"

Yeah, I went there. Too many freaks out there to let that one slip by.

He sighed in exasperation. "Of course, I know. My mom told me like a million times."

"She sounds pretty smart."

"Yup. Best part about me and Evan?"

"What's that?"

Josiah grinned. "I'm taller."

Six

Kale

As soon as I left the office, I headed straight for Rex and Rynna's house. After spending the day meeting some of my new patients, I had this itchy feeling.

Needing to hold my godbabies in my arms. Feel them whole and healthy and strong.

Which was crazy, considering the day had left me feeling more fulfilled than I'd ever imagined and entirely wrecked at the same time.

I pulled into the gravel drive of the family's little house. The larger house across the street that Rynna had inherited from her grandmother was currently undergoing a full renovation. As soon as it was finished, they'd sell this place and move over there since they needed the room.

I bounded up the porch steps, Milo barking like crazy as he hopped up and pawed at the window.

The door flew open before I even made it there, Frankie Leigh barreling out. The kid was wearing the black tutu I'd given her for her birthday over a pair of shorts and a sweater, her brown hair just as wild and free as her spirit. "Uncle Kale, Uncle

Kale! Yous came to see me. What you been doing? I've been missing you!"

I scooped her off her feet, tossed her in the air as she squealed with delight. I hugged her close. "I've been missing you, too. How's big girl school?"

"It's so, so fun! I learned all my letters, and I can write my name. You want to see?"

"You know I do."

I set her on her feet, and Frankie was rounding the couch and flying down the hall before I closed the door. Rynna was bouncing Ryland by the dining room table, looking a little frazzled, the tiny baby boy facing out and releasing all these tiny, gurgled cries as he attempted to stuff his whole fist into his mouth.

Rex was in the kitchen making dinner.

I grinned at him. "About time you made yourself useful . . . what are you making me? Just don't burn it because it actually smells delicious. I mean, seriously, what miracle is this? Last time I checked, your specialty was pizza from a box."

He tossed me a middle finger with his hand still wrapped around the paring knife he was dicing potatoes with. "Don't even start, man. My family needs a good dinner, and the last thing my Rynna needs is to go worrying about making dinner after she's been taking care of the kids all day."

With an exaggerated sigh, she kissed the top of Ryland's head. "Who would have thought taking care of an infant would be a hundred times harder than running a diner all day? I'm not complaining, but I think I could sleep for a week straight. Thank God Nikki decided to take the general manager position. I don't even know what I'd do right now if I had to go in and oversee things."

Nikki hadn't been in love with her previous job and had jumped on the opportunity when Rynna had suggested she come work at Pepper's Pies.

Rynna knew she wouldn't be able to devote as much time to the diner once she had Ryland, and she wanted someone she could trust to handle the little diner that had been her dream, her grandmother's legacy.

It had been a good transition for both of them.

I approached her, dropped a kiss to her forehead, and ran a tender hand over Ryland's head. He leaned into it, the kid loving the contact, a sweet coo coming from his mouth. "No one until they're standing right in your shoes, that's who." I lifted my hands for Ryland. "Here, let me take him for a while. Looks like you could use a break."

She beamed at me as she shifted Ryland into my hold. "You're a godsend."

I quirked a brow. "You mean a god?"

"You wish, asshole." Rex was eager to supply. "And it's about time you showed up for Uncle duty."

"Hey, I've been busy, man." I held Ryland's teeny body against my chest, bouncing him lightly.

Affection went sliding through my veins. Was crazy how much I adored these kids.

"Oh, I bet you've been busy. What's her name?"

"Is there ever a name?"

Of course, there was one dancing at the tip of my tongue.

Hope.

What the hell it was about her, I didn't know. But all day, she'd been taking possession of my thoughts without my permission, my mind continually traipsing back to the heat lighting on her cheeks, that sweet shyness I wanted to dip my fingers into, desperate for a taste.

Rynna grinned at me as she headed into the kitchen to help Rex. "Oh, I'm sure there are plenty of names. You just forget them before you're on to the next one." She washed her hands, looking back at me. "And that baby looks good on you, by the way."

"Only because I get to give him back when he starts crying." I shot her a wink. "And, well, I always look good. It's kind of impossible for me not to."

Rex's expression was nothing but adoration when he gazed over at her, amusement playing around his mouth. "Can you believe this guy?"

She giggled with a shake of her head. "He's your friend. You're the one who decided to keep him around all this time."

"Hey," I drew out, fighting the laughter. "Don't be knocking my presence. Doubt very much the two of you would be together if it weren't for me. I was the one who knocked some sense into his stubborn ass."

Rynna pushed up onto her toes and pressed a kiss to Rex's jaw, her voice not meant for me. "I'm pretty sure he would have found me either way. Some people are just meant to be."

She almost did a double take when she looked back and found Ryland was already conked out in my arms.

"Oh, make it look easy, why don't you? He hasn't slept a wink all day."

"Magic touch right here. Kids love me, and you know I love them." My brow lifted. "Just as long as they aren't mine."

Frankie was suddenly right there at my feet, a box of fat markers in one hand and a frilly pink notebook in the other. A pout pursed her lips. "Uncle Kale, you said I was always gonna be your favorite girl. That means I belongs to you. You don't want to keep me anymore?"

I looked down at the adorable thing, who was growing way too fast, her sweet lisp starting to sort itself out but still evident enough to fist me right in the heart with the sweetness of it.

Swore, the kid had me wrapped around her little finger.

Rex was grinning as he was rinsing the potatoes in the sink. "Now tell me how your gonna dig yourself out of that one, my friend. And don't you dare go breaking my Frankie Leigh's heart."

"Never."

I shifted Ryland into the crook of one arm so I could rustle my fingers through Frankie's hair. "What are you talking about, Sweet Pea Frankie Leigh? Do you have beans growing in your ears? Here, quick, let me take you to the office so I can look in there, because you heard me all wrong. I said you're always going to be mine, not *as long as they're not mine*."

Giggling, she wiggled all over the place. "I don't gots any beans growing in my ears, Uncle. I think you're teasin' me."

"And you know I only tease my favorite, favorite girls, right?"

"Uh-huh," she agreed as she scrambled onto a dining room chair so she could show me how she wrote her name, completely assuaged, not another thought about me leaving her behind.

"Smooth," Rex said with a shake of his head, dumping the diced potatoes into a pot of boiling water.

"Skilled," I tossed back.

"So, tell us about this new position. What did you think?" Rynna's demeanor had shifted, all concern as she looked back at me.

I roughed a hand through my hair.

Didn't want to tell her I had to come straight from the office because I needed reassurance that Ryland and Frankie were just fine. That something horrible hadn't crept up in the time I'd been away.

It was funny because, for years, I'd given Rex crap about being too overprotective of Frankie, always rushing her to the ER whenever the slightest things went wrong. I'd continually made light of it and razzed him that he was ridiculous.

Truth was, I'd been in knots while I'd waited for them to arrive, terrified something was seriously wrong.

I saw so much bad shit come through the ER doors every single day.

Had experienced it firsthand.

Had felt death's claws tear right through my skin to rip my life apart.

Like it was teaching me a lesson.

But the last thing I wanted was to make him worry more than he already had been. He was coming to me for reassurance, not to be launched into some kind of tailspin.

So, I took it upon myself to make sure she was healthy, trying to take some of the burden from his shoulders. I would do the same with Ryland.

I pushed out a sigh, trying to find the right words. "It was amazing. Hard and exhausting and trying, and still the best thing I've ever done."

"It must be incredibly difficult . . . seeing all those sick children. Caring for them. Worrying about them. And still knowing it's worth it, making the difference that you do."

I guessed Rynna got it anyway.

Made me so happy she'd found Rex and he'd found her, two of them needing each other more than anyone I knew. She was right. Some people were just meant to be.

"You're right. It is really difficult. Only thing I can hope for is that I really do make a difference."

Rynna looked at me seriously. "Kale . . . of course, you make a difference. I think probably more than you know." She walked up to me and touched her baby's cheek as her eyes flicked between me and him. "I just want you to promise me one thing . . . no matter what you see or what you deal with . . . don't lose you. Don't let it break you. And don't ever, ever give up on hope. Because it's always there, no matter how dismal things might seem."

Emotion clutched my chest, that terror that I was right there, at the ledge I'd stumble and fall over.

Fail all over again.

I refused to ever repeat it. Because I knew that this time there was no chance I'd be able to get back up.

I forced a smirk. "Come now, Rynna, do I really look like I could be broken?"

Her expression said *yes, you do*. But Frankie Leigh was calling my name, and I was shifting my attention, her little hand scribbling across the page. "That's 'cause you're a superhero, too, rights, Uncle Kale? Wonder Woman and Cap'in 'merica, right? We're the bestest team."

"Heck yes, we're the best team."

And this little team was all I was ever going to need.

Seven

Hope

The door swung open for what had to have been the thousandth time that morning.

But this time . . . this time, my entire being took note.

The breath burst from my lungs in a rattled gasp, and my feet wanted to give out from under me.

It sent my heart taking off at a sprint, banging around in the confines of my chest like a big spoon whipping up something sweet in a metal bowl.

Jarring and vibrating.

Penetrating all the way to the bone.

I tried to swallow around it and focus my attention on where it should be—the customers lined up at the front register during our normal morning rush. Today it seemed as if the traffic had been multiplied.

Jenna, Claire, and I had been hustling nonstop, trying to keep up with the demand.

But as soon as he walked in the door, it seemed impossible. All my eyes wanted to do was get lost in the sight set in front of me.

Kale was back.

All tall, lean body and easy, casual way. His grin was pure confidence as he strode through the door. His crop of blond hair burned like white fire in the rays of bright morning sun that poured in from above him.

Lighting him up. Making him glow.

As if the light couldn't help but be drawn to him, too.

I blinked through the daze, scolding myself under my breath as I finished swirling the whipped cream on the café mocha I'd been making, quick to move on to the plain coffee that went with the order.

I was being ridiculous, wondering if he was back for any other reason than coffee. He'd told me he had started a job just down the street. It wasn't as if him swinging by would be out of his way.

Still, three days had passed.

Three days, and I'd begun to think I would never see him again. Oh, I knew the overwhelming sense of disappointment that thought left me with made me a fool.

Just asking for trouble when every time the bell jingled over the door, I looked that way.

Like a beggar who was looking for anything to hope for.

Even if it was just a spec of his time.

A moment in his day.

Because I'd forgotten what it was like to feel this way.

To have my tummy turn and my pulse race. To have someone make me toss sleeplessly in my bed, imagining what it would be like to be touched by those big hands.

Adored.

And there he was.

His fancy suit from the other morning had been ditched in favor of a crisp, white button-up, dark gray dress pants tailored to fit and accentuate every immaculate inch of his body.

A shiver traveled my spine, spreading out, drenching every cell.

No man should be that gorgeous. Or that sexy.

It was just unfair.

He shot me a knowing smirk.

I jerked, realizing I was just standing there.

Staring.

I hopped back a step to keep from spilling a cup of coffee straight down my blouse when I realized the cup I was holding had tipped to the side. The splash I'd dodged hit the floor.

"Sorry about that," I muttered to the customer, turning to make a new coffee.

From the corner of my eye, I kept watching him, the way he began to meander around my shop rather than get into line.

His fingers drummed over the displays, as if he couldn't fully appreciate something without touching it. The imported boxes of teas and packaged goods in gift baskets wrapped in clear cellophane and big bows.

The large cups with inspiring quotes.

Tumblers with the store's logo.

Not that I was paying attention or anything.

Jenna squeezed by to get to the latte machine. She elbowed me in the ribs when she did, and her voice lowered conspiratorially. "Looks like someone has a visitor. Look at all that deliciousness standing right there. Told you he'd be back."

"I'm sure he's just here for a cup of coffee," I defended under my breath, facing away as I filled a medium cup with hazelnut.

"Well, you just keep on thinking that, Harley Hope, but that man right over there is thinking about you naked."

I swatted her. "Stop it."

Her eyes went wide with innocence as she dipped into the case to get two pumpkin muffins. "What?"

"You know what. I swear that you are nothin' but a pain in my ass."

"What you need is a good kick in the ass."

"I need nothing of the sort," I mumbled, lidding the three cups. I turned and slid them to the customer waiting for her order. "There you are. Have a great day."

She uttered a thank you and moved on her way. I was quick to fill the next customer's order, trying not to pay attention to

Kale, who'd taken note of the big lollipops displayed in a pink wooden decorative box. To keep them all standing, the sticks had been stuck in Styrofoam, which had been hidden by the fake moss that covered it.

So what if Pinterest had become my lover, keeping me company in the lonely nights.

From the side, I took in the way his blue, blue eyes narrowed in curiosity, the way he pulled one out.

I bit down on my lip.

Damn it.

Normally, I wanted everyone to buy them up. But there was something about the man holding one that made a rush of unease slip and slide through my body. That achy place throbbing and needy.

As if he was holding a piece of me that was sacred.

All of them were the same. Colorful swirls with a clear wrapper and a white label on the front.

It was just my luck Jenna noticed at the second the last customer I'd been helping walked away with his coffee and half dozen muffins.

"Those are for charity," she called over the counter.

Cocking his head, he studied the label before he looked up at me. "Anything's possible if you have a lick of hope?"

He asked it like a question.

As if he were wondering if I really believed it.

Heat flooded my cheeks. The uneasy kind. The kind that had me shifting on my feet.

"Yep," Jenna said. "Hope here makes those herself. Every last cent goes to charity."

For a moment, he stared at me, something soft fluttering around his lush mouth before he tucked the stick back into the Styrofoam.

I didn't know if I was relieved or disappointed.

That was right before he scooped the entire box up under his arm. "In that case, I'll take them all. I think I have an idea of where I can put them to good use."

"If you're taking them all, you should come back and help

Hope here make some more. You know . . . philanthropy . . . not at all because you want to hang out with her or anything."

I sent a glare at Jenna. *What are you thinking?*

What? She mouthed back with an innocent shrug.

If she *what-ed* me one more time when she knew exactly what she was doing, I was going to strangle her.

I would have right then, but I was too busy trying not to shake when Kale approached the counter, filling the air the way he did.

All potent, persuasive power.

The space between us growing so thick it made it difficult to draw a full breath.

"Why do you need all those, anyway?" I all but demanded, feeling out of sorts. Hopeful and eager and awed, and that made me scared.

Because him standing there with those lollipops made me feel as if he were stepping into an area that was off limits.

As if he'd dipped his fingers in the places of my life that I protected most.

Touching on the things that were most important to me when he couldn't come close to understanding.

"Maybe I just have a sweet tooth."

"You don't be careful, and you're going to rot them all out." I tried to form it a tease, but it came out breathy and almost pleading. He had no idea just what that box tucked to his side meant to me.

He smiled a smile that pierced me straight through my center.

An arrow that nearly dropped me to my knees.

Because that knowing kindness was back. The one that made me feel vulnerable and exposed.

"I think I'll take my chances," he said.

I sucked in a breath. Set off kilter. Lightheaded. "All right, then. Is there anything else I can get for you?"

"Large regular coffee."

I swiveled away, going for the coffee urns, thankful for the moment of reprieve. Looking at him was making it impossible to stop the foolish notions from racing through my brain, especially when I couldn't help but wonder if maybe he were different.

If there were something intrinsically good at the heart of him.

Caring and . . . and . . .

Giving.

My hands were shaking as I filled the cup, my smile probably more so when I turned back to him and slid it across the counter. He already had his wallet out, pulling out a stack of crisp one-hundred-dollar bills.

He set them on the counter.

Another tremble.

"What is this?"

"For charity." The depths of those turquoise eyes deepened in a way that promised he saw too much.

Part of me wanted to refuse because something about it made me feel weak.

But the money wasn't for me.

"Thank you," I offered. "That's really generous of you."

He took out a five and placed it on top of the other bills, tapping it as he let that grin ride to his lips, which were getting more and more difficult not to reach out and trace. "And that's for the coffee, which is delicious, by the way. Though, not nearly as delicious as the cupcake."

"I'm glad you enjoyed it," I told him. A rush of that shyness pulled fast, getting all mixed up with the crazy desire that thrummed through my body.

It seemed unfair attraction was always immediate.

Natural.

Easy.

It was what came after that left your world in shambles. Battered walls and broken windows, your house falling down around you. It was taking everything I had to rebuild mine—to reconstruct and restore and revitalize. I had worked tirelessly to fill the spots that had been dredged out by cruelty, and I couldn't falter or misstep.

He hesitated for a second, as if he were struggling to find what he wanted to say, before all that easy confidence came riding back. "Thanks, Shortcake."

A short laugh escaped, and I shook my head, unable to keep up with him. "You're absurd."

"And here I'd thought you'd implied I was cocky?"

"That, too."

He laughed, though, the sound was soft. So different from the guy I'd thought I'd first run into at the bar on Friday night. This man revealing something good every time he invaded my space, making me want to dig deeper, see more.

I was drawn to him in a way I couldn't fathom.

He blinked at me, and I leaned forward, drawn, unable to stop myself from reacting to his presence.

Then he shook his head as if he needed to shake himself out of a dream.

He jarred me out of my own.

A smile was pinned on his lips, and he hiked the box up a little higher on his side, grabbing his cup and lifting it in the air. "I hope you have a great day, Hope."

I sucked in my bottom lip. "You, too."

I watched him stride across the café toward the door, hating the way everything tightened when he did. The way something like regret rippled through the atmosphere when he pulled open the door.

His or mine, I wasn't sure.

But it was there.

Heavy.

Pressing on my heart.

I couldn't stop from watching him through the big windows as he started down the sidewalk, the man a scorching silhouette in the blaze of the day.

But he didn't climb into his car that was parked at the curb.

He began to pace.

A pace that looked like indecision and turmoil.

Back and forth right on the other side of the window.

His head tilted back toward the sky, as if it might hold an answer, before he set his coffee and the lollipops down on one of the open tables, dug in his pocket, and pulled out his phone.

"You're an idiot," Jenna hissed from beside me. "That guy

likes you, and he's literally the hottest thing to ever walk through that door. And he bought All. The. Lollipops."

Maybe that was part of the problem.

"I don't get simple," was my response.

"What if he doesn't want simple?"

I would have answered her, told her that in the end, everyone did. They always took the easy way out when the going got tough. Except the café phone rang. I moved for it, thankful for the distraction, something to keep my feet from rounding the counter and running after him.

Because what the hell would that accomplish?

I lifted the receiver from the wall and pressed it to my ear. "A Drop of Hope. How can I help you?"

"Go out with me." His gravelly voice echoed through the line.

A surprised sound whispered from my lips, and Kale was suddenly at the window, his face pressed to the glass, hand shading his eyes so he could see inside. His other hand was holding his cell to his ear. "Go out with me, Hope. Just dinner. Because I can't fucking stop thinking about you. Couldn't after I saw you the first time at Olive's on Friday night. It only got worse after I saw you here Monday morning. I don't know what it is about you . . . but there's something that makes me want to figure it out."

My breaths were hard pants, my heart a jackhammer in my chest. "My life's complicated, Kale."

"And I'm offering you a night away from it. Don't you at least deserve that?"

I wanted to beg him, what then? What happened if I fell for that smirk and that smile and those tender eyes?

Fast and hard?

I could already feel myself slipping. My heart tipping his direction.

What happened if Dane found out?

What then?

But I was so tired of that man controlling every aspect of my life, even after I'd made the decision to cut him from it.

Jenna was suddenly in my face, gripping my wrist, her voice a hard, demanding whisper. "You tell him yes, Harley Hope. Don't you dare hang up that phone without telling him yes. You deserve something just for you. Just for you."

Indecision swarmed, questions and worries and want.

But it was the feeling balled in my stomach that trembled the floor beneath my feet.

The urge to reach out and touch on the beauty and tenderness that swam in his eyes. To discover if it was real.

The throb of desire that begged, a whisper in my ear that goaded—*just one touch.*

The hidden need to feel those hands skating my flesh.

I guessed I'd thought I'd never crave that again, my life fulfilled, my spirit content in knowing I was living for what was right.

Jenna squeezed tighter, my bossy best friend mouthing the word as she angled her head with the demand. "Say yes."

It was at the same second Kale fisted his hand against the window, his forehead rocking against it, his own words a petition. "Come on, Hope. Say yes. I promise you, you won't regret it."

A hint of playfulness came out on the last, but it didn't matter, because I was agreeing.

"Yes," I murmured, wanting to feel something good even though I wasn't so much a fool that I didn't know I was making a mistake. That in the end, it wouldn't hurt.

Because it already felt as if *this* mattered.

As if *he* mattered.

"Okay. One night. Just dinner," I reiterated.

He breathed out in what sounded like relief. "Just dinner."

eight
Kale

I fumbled for my phone when it dinged in my pocket. "Shit," I muttered when the damn thing nearly slipped from my hand.

Didn't help that I was all kinds of overeager and terrified like some kind of pathetic fucker begging for a bone.

That was what I'd become.

Pathetic.

Because my stomach was tied up in knots, anxiety lining my insides, nerves rattling through me like an earthquake that hit from out of nowhere in the middle of the night.

The last two days had been spent wondering what in the hell it was I thought I was doing.

What I thought I expected to pull off here.

I was so far out of bounds that I had not a single clue where I stood.

Standing around, waiting on a girl.

Wanting her.

Both her sweet little body and her sweet little mind, wondering what it was that made her reserved and shut off and shy.

What ignited that fire that so clearly burned underneath.

What brought the flush riding to her cheeks.

Why those places that had gone dormant inside me found it fit to light up when we got in the same room.

It fucking terrified me that they did. That I felt something I was sure had died with *her*. Something that had been obliterated into nonexistence that suddenly had a flicker of a heartbeat again.

Was it worth it?

I sucked in a breath. I didn't fucking know. But there I stood anyway, waiting, praying that she showed.

The guys were going to have a field day if they found out where I was tonight.

On a motherfucking date.

It wasn't even as a consequence of Nikki drinking my ass under the table.

No bets or wagers other than the one I'd lobbied against myself.

I mean, I'd made it all the way out the door of A Drop of Hope without letting the words that had been begging on my tongue free.

All the way out the damned door.

All I'd had to do was get in my car, drive away, and never look back.

Then, like a fool, I'd looked up the café on my phone.

Brilliant, right?

Taking the pussy's way out. The whole time I'd been muttering a million warnings under my breath. None of which had been heeded. I'd just gone right on ahead and pressed send.

Guessed maybe my subconscious had gone for the call since I couldn't take another rejection delivered to my face.

This girl had shot me down at every turn, and each time, I got up for another round. Something feeling like maybe she needed me to fight for her.

Like I said.

Pathetic.

Guts in knots, I read the message.

Hope: Sorry, I got hung up. I'm on my way. Be there in five.

I breathed out in relief.

I'd been doing my best not to lose my cool where I stood outside the chic restaurant on the sidewalk on Macaber. The street was all lit up on a Friday night, people coming and going, their laughter rippling through the warm Alabama air.

Waiting.

She'd insisted on taking an Uber and meeting me here. That this was just dinner. Nothing more.

Ironic.

Considering all I wanted was more.

I tapped out a quick reply.

Me: No worries. I just got here.

What bullshit. I'd been here for fifteen minutes.

This girl had me feeling outside myself.

Interested and intrigued.

Wanting to fist my hands in that lush, red hair, sure it'd be as soft as it looked.

Wondering if she tasted like strawberries and cream and all things sweet, the way I'd put down bets that she did.

Shortcake.

Couldn't help but imagine her in the shadows of my room. Wild. That sexy modesty evaporated as she begged my name.

The craziest part was I thought I might just settle for seeing that shy smile light her face.

I drove all my fingers into my hair.

Fuck.

She really had gotten under my skin.

Five minutes later, a black car pulled to the curb. I didn't know what it was, but the way my heart thundered and boomed, sped with an unsteady beat, told me it was her before the car came to a full stop.

I pasted on a confident smile, strolled that way with a hand in my pocket, and opened the back door to help her out.

I dipped down, and I swore my thundering heart came to a full stop in my chest.

On all things holy.

What the hell did she think she was doing to me?

My head spun with a rush of uncontained lust.

Fast and hot and hard.

Sloshing through my blood like an out-of-control demand.

Those knots in my stomach notched tighter, a constricting band around my chest, the easy air suddenly thick.

Heady.

Rippling with need.

That dress.

She was wearing this black dress that was super short, the backseat full of nothing but silky, toned legs. My throat went dry when I noticed the pair of black heels wrapped around her ankles.

So damned high.

So fucking hot.

Who was this girl? Because she was peeking out at me, biting back a smile that danced between shy and seductive when I reached down and offered her my hand.

A streak of lightning bolted up my arm when she accepted it.

Motherfucker.

What was happening to me?

She shifted to slide out, that fall of red cascading down around one shoulder.

I somehow managed to shoot her a grin as I tugged her toward me.

She stumbled to a stop two inches away. A gush of surprise heaved from her lungs, our bodies close to touching, the space between crackling, no doubt two seconds from catching fire.

Clearly, she wasn't anticipating me being so forward.

But if this was the only night she was giving me, I was going to make it count.

Those green eyes blinked up at me. I swore they were the same color as the moss that lined the bank of the river, deep and brimming with life.

"Hi," I told her, a smirk flitting across my mouth.

"Hi," she whispered back between her plush lips that were coated in only shiny gloss. "I'm so sorry I'm late."

For a beat, she took in our surroundings as if she was looking for someone, but then she finally turned back to face me. Her expression now held something that almost looked like worry or fear that threatened to break loose. She beat it back—buried it— and smiled at me in a way that moved through me like warmth.

"I really am sorry I'm late," she said again.

I kept her fingertips threaded with mine, unwilling to give up the connection, having the urge to tell her to trust me. That whatever the fuck was going on, she could *trust* me.

But I didn't know how to make that promise, so I tucked it all down and focused on the kind of night I had promised her.

One that was only about her. Making her feel good.

"It's fine." I arched a brow, sending her a look that told her how bad I was dying to eat her up. "Though, I thought I was going to have to track you down because you were going to bail on me. I don't think my fragile ego could take it."

A bit of that fire lit on her face.

God.

I liked that, too.

The feisty redhead ready to spar.

"You were going to track me down, huh? Tell me you aren't really stalking me." Her voice had dropped an octave, dripping with excitement and nervousness, the words a low, throaty tease.

"Is it working?"

She chewed at her bottom lip, and it took about all I had not to reach out and brush back the lock of hair that swooped across her forehead, obscuring one of her eyes. "I'm here, aren't I? Against my better judgment."

"Why's that?" I played it off as unimportant. Like I wasn't wanting to dig deeper into her. To discover all those things I couldn't get off my mind.

The low laughter that rolled from her was completely at her expense. "I already told you my life is complicated . . . hence my being late."

"Are you going to tell me about that?"

For a flash, her gaze went to the far side of the street, her profile soft beneath the glow of the strands of lights strung up overhead. Face innocent while her body looked like nothing but sin wrapped in this slinky black dress.

She was a walking contradiction.

The perfect kind of fantasy.

Sexy and soft.

Hot and sweet.

She looked back at me with a silent plea riding her expression. "Do you remember what you asked me? You asked me for one night. And this night is for me."

She swallowed and averted her gaze again, like she was gathering her thoughts, and then she set the power of those green eyes back on me. "So, no, I'm not. I just . . . want to enjoy myself and not think about anything else except for the fact I'm out with a man. A man I can't help but want to spend more time with. That, for one night, I get to experience it. Can we do that?"

Unable to stop myself, I reached out and ran the pad of my thumb across her chin, right over the cute little dimple I kind of wanted to lick.

She shivered at my touch.

"Yeah, Shortcake, we can definitely do that." A smirk kicked up at the corner of my mouth. "You want a good time? Then I promise to show you a good time."

There was almost a warning behind it. The caution that my body was already way ahead of us.

Imagining her against the wall, that short, short skirt hiked around her hips.

Back at my loft, the girl writhing on my bed.

Or maybe it was just a promise.

She must have seen every single salacious thought play out in my eyes. Because she chuckled this sound that shot straight to my dick, a hand flattening on my chest. "Oh, back it up, Cowboy. We aren't gonna be having that *good* of a time."

Grabbing that hand, I kissed across her knuckles. "Are you

sure about that? And cowboy?" My brow arched. "Come on now, do I look like a cowboy to you?"

She laughed a little deeper, her expression going light, sparking with the freedom of the moment. "Mm-hmm . . . I am most definitely certain of that."

Her tongue darted out to lick across those glossy lips, the girl cocking her head with a type of mischief I hadn't recognized in her before.

Lust knotted my insides.

"Such a bad boy. I knew it back at the bar, the trouble written all over you. And don't you know all boys from Alabama are cowboys at heart? You can dress yourself up like a city boy, but it doesn't change a thing."

A chuckle rippled free. "Actually, I was thinking more like knight in shining armor . . . you know, since I am rescuing you tonight."

"Thinking awfully highly of yourself, are you?"

I guided her into the restaurant ahead of me, mouth dipping down to brush across the shell of her ear as she walked through the door. "Hell yeah. As long as that means I get to make you my princess."

She glanced at me from over her shoulder as we stepped into the restaurant. "My hero."

She delivered it with a tone of flirtatious sarcasm.

Having no clue that statement sliced through me.

A double-edged sword.

Did my best not to reveal the cringe that jolted through me and told myself I wasn't going there tonight.

Because if this was the only one we had, I was going to make it count.

nine

Hope

Chills skated my spine, and I shivered with the slow release of his breath that washed across my jaw when he leaned in.

The heat of him took me whole.

Overpowering.

Too much and somehow not nearly enough.

"How was your dinner?" he asked.

The man was conflict.

Persuasion and dominance and sex.

Kind and perceptive and intuitive.

I didn't know what side of him was more dangerous. The only thing I knew was I could barely breathe when he set one of those big hands on my knee underneath the table.

All night, he'd been touching me. Just tiny brushes and caresses.

Flutters of fingertips that sped my heart in a needy kind of anticipation.

It was as if he were issuing little promises—assuring me I was interesting and beautiful and he wouldn't want to be anywhere else.

I took a sip of red wine, still unable to fathom I was actually sitting across from this man. "It was wonderful. I think I've had more fun tonight than I have in a long, long time. I wish I could tell you how much that means to me."

His brow quirked. "Says the girl who basically made me beg to get a little bit of time with her."

Thank God it was dim where we were seated at the back of the upscale restaurant. Because I could feel the heat rise to my cheeks. The way he managed to slip right under my skin with that easy smile, the man nothing but seduction where he casually rested in the high-backed upholstered chair.

One big hand was wrapped around the crystal tumbler he'd been sipping from all evening, the other still caressing my knee.

Back and forth.

Back and forth.

Embers flickering to life in the deepest parts of me.

I wondered if he had the first clue each stroke wound me higher. Higher and higher until it felt as if I was floating with the stars. Or maybe he knew exactly what he was doing.

"I guess sometimes we all need a little push," I admitted quietly.

His eyes crinkled at the corners. "Well, I guess it should be me saying thank you for giving you that little push."

I tucked my bottom lip between my teeth, trying to figure out what to do with the magnitude of this man. "I'm just glad you were the one to do it."

He sat back a little, head tilting to the side as he offered a casual expression. "What about last Friday? It seems like your friends don't hesitate to have a little fun."

I laughed lightly. "No, they definitely don't. Jenna is always trying to drag me out."

"Why don't you let her?"

It was the first time Kale had let our conversation traipse in the direction of personal. His eyes narrowed, studying me with a new kind of severity through the flicker of the candles that lapped and licked at the center of the table.

It cast that strong jaw in shadows, that turquoise gaze glinting in the flame.

During dinner, we'd kept to safe subjects. Reminiscing about growing up. My life in Texas. His in Gingham Lakes. I told him how I'd been a total drama geek in high school, living my life for the next play, while he'd laughed the sweetest kind of laugh and told me nerds were always the best before he'd gone on to tell me he'd won first place in the Alabama State Science Fair all four years of high school.

I guessed nerds really were the best.

Now, beneath his scrutiny, I felt compelled.

I felt looser and freer than I had felt in so long. Before I could stop it, I was pushing right past the promise I'd made to myself that tonight was just for me and I was leaving everything else behind.

The words dropped like a bomb from my mouth, my frustration and bitterness bleeding free.

"I doubt very much my husband would approve of that."

I watched as the admission penetrated Kale.

As he jerked back as if he'd been kicked in the gut.

The breath knocked out of him as he resituated everything he'd thought about me in his head. Eyes going wide before his jaw clenched tight. Slowly coming to the realization that when I told him my life was complicated, I meant it.

My life was in transition, a hard, painful transition. In the end, it would be the best decision I'd ever made. I just had to make it through to the other side.

Where I was didn't change the reality of what was happening right then, though. It didn't change the fight I had ahead of me.

I cleared my throat, knowing I'd made a mistake by telling him that way.

That was the problem when you started to feel comfortable with someone. When you started *liking* them in a way you couldn't allow. You started telling them things you shouldn't trust them with. Letting them go deeper than you should.

I tossed my fabric napkin on the table. "We should probably get going. It's getting late. The day starts really early for me."

It was stupid of me to even think this was okay when I had

no idea the lengths Dane might go to. I searched for a breath, feeling like a complete fool. All I'd wanted was one night. I should have known not even that was possible.

I pushed from the small, round table, giving him my back, unable to face him.

Not after I'd sent our night spiraling.

Ruining it with just a dash of the truth.

Warily, Kale stood, and I could sense him slowly signing the credit card receipt and then tucking the card back in his wallet.

He was probably realizing that I was no princess just as I was realizing I was an idiot to hope for a knight.

Then his hand was back on the small of my back, stealing my breath, and a tiny whimper was breaking free from my lips. His words were uttered so close to my ear that I couldn't help but cling to the security of his hold.

"Let's get you out of here," he said.

He wound us back through the lavish restaurant and out onto the sidewalk. Crowds moved around us, people darting here and there to enjoy their Friday nights, laughter ringing on the Alabama night.

I inhaled, filling myself with the calming, familiar scents of this city, the river and the trees and the thick, intoxicating scent of honeysuckle that rode the air on provocative waves.

But I guessed it was the sheer potency of him that made me feel lightheaded—drunk—when he shocked me by wrapping an arm around my waist and tugging me close.

Citrus and spice and the lingering scent of whiskey.

His lips were a murmur against my temple. "I know you're getting ready to run from me, Hope. Don't. Stay with me . . . just a little while more."

I could feel the confusion pressed into the lines of my forehead when I pulled back to look at his face. And the man . . . the man had let that knowing smirk climb to his pretty, pretty face.

My knees nearly gave when he threaded his fingers back through mine.

Tenderly.

Possessively.

"Come," he said, a glint in his eyes before he darted us across the busy street. A surprised gasp ripped from my lungs, and I struggled to keep up on my too-high heels as he hauled me in the direction of the bar on the opposite corner.

The same bar our paths had first crossed just last week that now felt as if they were being impossibly tangled together.

"What are you doing?" I demanded, the words a breathy plea.

Hope and reservation.

A giddy giggle rolled out right behind it.

Because this man made me feel so free. Unshackled after years of being chained. Years of trying to change our situation and not knowing the right answer to finding that solution. Of course, my conclusion had been swift and without question that day one year ago when I'd packed our things and left.

There are just times in your life when things become crystal clear and you know the path you need to run down, the situation you need to run away from.

Jerking open the door, Kale sent me one of those smiles that blasted through me with the power of a hurricane.

Annihilating.

Exhilarating.

Because when Kale Bryant looked at me that way?

I felt as if I were the only person in the world.

"I promised you a good time, and you're gonna get a good time."

He pulled me into the intensity of the bar. People were packed wall to wall, voices lifted above the mayhem, the vibe so much rowdier than it'd been last Friday.

Tonight, the band was the focus, commanding the attention with their distinct country flare. Tables were pushed back out of the way to create a makeshift dance floor beneath the risers that had been brought in to create an elevated stage.

My heart rate latched on to the intensity. An erratic thrum, thrum, thrum that hammered and beat.

Kale ran his hand down the center of my back.

Chills.

Fire.

Heat.

His palm hit home right above my bottom, his pinky finger just skating into the vicinity.

Oh God.

Maybe it had been too long.

Because that simple touch had me flying.

Wanting things I knew full well I shouldn't. Not when so many things were still left unresolved.

His mouth landed at the edge of my ear, voice lifted to be heard above the chaos. "Carolina George is playing tonight . . . they travel around the South, hitting cool venues and dives alike. Ollie, the owner here? He and the guitarist go way back, so once a month, they come to play here. People flock through that door in droves whenever they do."

"I take it you're a fan?"

He glanced around with a grin. "Think it's safe to say just about everyone around here is. Not a whole lot not to like."

I patted his chest, feeling bolder in his presence. "Told you all Alabama boys are cowboys at heart."

He pulled me closer. "Knight. Don't forget it."

"Whatever you say, Cowboy."

Carolina George's singer was this stunning, dainty creature, who belted out her song at the microphone. Her face was the perfect match to her gorgeous, mesmerizing voice.

It vibrated through the speakers, somehow both sultry and upbeat as it kept time with the quick rhythm that pounded from the drums.

In perfect harmony with the guitar that strummed at her side.

Clearly, it was the jaw-dropping man playing that guitar that had brought a herd of women squealing to the foot of the elevated stage.

I could feel Kale's playful smile when he saw me gawking. "Now, don't go getting any ideas. Rick seems to be a little popular with the ladies. Don't understand what they see in him, actually, when they could be looking at me."

There it was. That cocky arrogance the man wore so well, the words nothing but a tease that oozed from his mouth, which was still close to my ear.

Inching back a fraction, I stared up at his face. Because while I understood Rick's appeal, Kale was the only one I wanted to be looking at. "You don't have a thing to worry about. I'm a one-man kind of girl."

I tried to make it come out light.

Playful.

But those blue eyes saw straight through me, glinting and sparking in the hazy glow of the bulbs that hung from the rafters. Searching me for the answer he so clearly wanted to reach in and pluck out of me.

He set one of those big hands on the side of my face, cupping my jaw, making me shake. "You think I don't know that? That I can't see it shining out of you? What do you say we grab a drink, and you tell me a little about that?"

He said it as if he'd gone right ahead and sifted around inside me and found his answer anyway.

I gave him the smallest nod. "Okay."

He ran his thumb across my lips, and my tongue darted out without my permission, grabbing the tiniest taste of his flesh.

Oh God. How easily could I get wrapped up in this man?

I swore I could hear Kale's body hum with a tremor of desire. Swore I could feel every inch of him grow hard.

Ripples of lust vibrated.

They struck in the space between us, shockwaves of heat that blasted across my skin.

I jerked when a man was suddenly there, clapping him on the back.

A man who was shockingly good-looking in an intimidating, almost frightening way.

Where Kale was tall with lean, packed muscle, this guy was a monster. Nothing but hulking muscle covered in tattoos, a mess of designs running down across his arms and hands and fingers.

But his eyes. They were soft with some kind of unknown affection when they landed on Kale.

"Well, well, well, look who's here. Texted your ass fifteen

times to try to convince you to show tonight, and each time you hit me back with some kind of lame excuse about being busy. And here you are. Not busy."

Kale cocked his head, halfway toward me, his voice a little hard. "Do I look *not* busy to you?"

Burly guy laughed, drummed his fingers across his lips. "Honestly not sure what you look like tonight."

There was some kind of conversation that transpired between the two of them, the giant of a man giving Kale a look as if he'd caught him stealing from the till and was going to offer him a prize for doing it.

Gaze traveling to me, the man's eyes lit in recognition. A victorious grin pulled to his bearded mouth.

He'd seen me before.

That night.

That was right.

I'd seen him, too.

Maybe I'd been too busy stealing peeks at the splendor of the man who right then was slipping his arm around my waist and tugging me tight against his body. But it dawned on me that this guy had been there, in Kale's group that had been huddled around a back table.

Kale roughed his free hand through his hair. "Hey, just be thankful I'm gracing you with my presence tonight. I did have better things to do than seeing your ugly face, but then I thought I'd introduce Hope here to one of the best bands in the South."

"Pssh. Ugly? You only wish you could look as good as me."

"Keep dreaming, man."

The guy stretched out his tattooed arms. "I *am* a dream."

I bit back a laugh, and Kale glanced down at me with a wide smile, gesturing to his friend.

"Hope, this is one of my best friends, Oliver, but everyone calls him Ollie. Ollie here is the owner of this fine establishment. Also, as you can see, a royal pain in my ass."

Ollie's brow lifted. "Pain in your ass? Says the guy who thinks he holds the answer to every last one of the world's problems in the palm of his hands."

Amusement danced across Ollie's face when he turned his attention my way and hooked a thumb in Kale's direction. "This asshole thinks he knows what's best for everyone. Always tossing out advice like we actually wanna hear it. Singlehandedly going to save the world."

Kale chuckled under his breath at the razzing and scratched nervously behind his ear.

Part of me wanted to ask more about the whole saving the world thing, considering tonight he'd set out to rescue me, but Kale was already tossing out a hand of entreaty between them.

Or so I'd thought.

"All right, all right, man. We get it. You think I'm the smartest guy around. No need to run it into the ground. It is kind of common knowledge."

A scoff from Ollie. "Such a cocky bastard."

"Says the guy who thinks he's a dream."

"Just keeping it real."

"Right," Kale drew out.

There was no holding the laughter back any longer, amusement rolling from my mouth when I finally pushed my hand toward Ollie, feeling more comfortable than I ever could have imagined. "It's really nice to meet you, Ollie. My best friend tells me this is the place to be."

He shook my hand, gentler than I would have imagined he could manage. "Ahh, she sounds like my kind of girl. And you have no idea just how great it is to meet you."

Without releasing me, his eyes darted between the two of us. "So, tell me what you two were up to before you stepped into my house."

"Dinner," I immediately answered.

I had to wonder if it was the wrong one when Kale flinched.

Ollie's eyebrows shot to the sky. "Is that so?" This was all directed at Kale.

Kale hesitated for a second before he met his friend's demanding eye. "What, I can't have dinner with the most gorgeous girl in Gingham Lakes?"

Puddles.

God, he left me a mess of gooey puddles right at his feet.

How did he manage that?

In disbelief, Ollie shook his head. "Nah, man, it's no problem. No problem at all. Just comes as a surprise someone as pretty as her would want to hang out with the likes of you."

"Jealousy." Kale muttered it under his breath before he looked at me, mischief playing all over his striking face. "Pure jealousy. Do you see the nonsense I have to deal with?"

But there was no tension between either of them, and Ollie was all smiles when he stepped back, placating hands set out in front of him. "Sorry to cut this short, but duty calls. Need to go check on the band and see if they need anything. Cece's manning the bar. She'll take good care of you."

"Shit," Kale mumbled, rubbing a hand over his face.

Kale started to lead me toward the bar.

"What was that all about?" I asked.

"Seems you and I are both stepping out of our comfort zones tonight. When's the last time you were on a date?" he basically shouted as he wove us through the horde of people jammed shoulder to shoulder.

"Um . . . I'm not sure you want the answer to the question."

"What if I wanted you to tell me anyway?"

"Then I'd tell you I was twenty-one and naïve."

The look he gave me from over his shoulder was one filled with guilt. Maybe regret. I didn't know. All I knew was it twisted around my chest like a band.

Constricting.

Cinching tight.

"What about you?" I hurried to say, still keeping up with him as we jostled through the crowd.

"Twenty-two." Somehow it sounded like a warning.

As if he were telling me something intrinsic about himself when I'd already made my own conclusions. That I saw this devastating kindness radiating from him, and it didn't have a thing to do with my naivety.

Without giving more, he angled his way right up to the front of the bar, and the woman behind the bar sauntered right up. She was tall and curvy and wearing a leather corset, tattoos covering the flesh exposed on her chest and shoulders and arms.

Oozing sex, she flashed him a red-lipped smile. "Kale Bryant. I've missed you. You haven't been around to visit me lately."

Her eyes dropped to me when she said it. Sizing me up.

Unease spun through my senses, and Kale squeezed my hand in reassurance. "Ah, Cece, I'm sure you've been keeping yourself plenty busy since the last time we ran into each other."

She threw her head back and laughed, smile widening with a wicked sort of glee. "Oh, you know I have, but none of these other boys are nearly as fun as you. But, clearly, you aren't here for me tonight. Tell me, what can I get you."

"I'll take my regular."

No. It shouldn't have. But that stung, too. And I knew I was getting myself in far too deep, getting attached the way I would. Wanting something that just wasn't there, wondering how it was possible I wanted to claim him when I'd been the one to tell him I could give him absolutely nothing more than just one night.

And a short one, at that.

Not the kind I was sure this beautiful man was accustomed to.

But then Kale was looking at me that way again. With that tender knowledge.

The man my conflict.

"What would you like, baby?"

Baby.

Damn him. Because I was nobody's *baby*. I had to be strong.

Fierce to face each day.

But the only thing I felt then was fiercely vulnerable against the word, the part of me that wanted to be taken care of for once, adored, begging for it to mean something.

"A red would be nice."

He looked back at her. "Get my girl some red."

Cece smirked, and I knew Kale was making a statement in front of her, and she seemed to mind less than I did when she poured his whiskey into an ice-filled tumbler and pushed it his way, when she jerked off the cork of the half-empty bottle of

Freak Show and filled me a glass to the brim.

"Enjoy," she told me because, clearly, she already had.

"Thank you," I barely managed, taking a long sip while Kale tossed two twenties to the bar.

It was in that moment that I realized there was so little I knew about him.

Nothing, really.

As little as he knew about me.

And part of me wanted to push him away and keep him there while the other side was begging for him to turn around, face me, and let me see inside.

Because I kept getting this feeling that he might need me the way I was beginning to feel as if I needed him.

That maybe it was okay to lean on someone once in a while.

He grabbed my hand again, not saying a word as he led me back through the crowd. I expected him to find a table around the dance floor, but he bypassed it, heading toward the stairs that led to the second floor.

The voices filtering from above were raucous, even wilder than downstairs.

The reason for it quickly became evident as we mounted the last step and found the rows of pool tables lining the back wall, country boys and city boys alike out shooting a few rounds, beers flowing as freely as the laughter.

My mama had always told me boys would be boys. Didn't matter what fabric they were cut from.

She'd meant it as comfort.

After Dane, I'd taken it as a warning.

But I knew in my heart of hearts that no two were created alike. That no one person was a blanket statement. And someday . . . someday, I'd find the one who was created for me.

Kale didn't pause. He just led me to the far left where a wall of windows blocked off a balcony.

A sign was set on an easel in front of it declaring that the balcony was closed, but Kale wasn't deterred. He headed to the far end where the wall could be fully opened like an accordion, opened it just enough so we could slip through, and tugged me forward.

"Kale," I whispered almost desperately, feeling as if we were committing some terrible crime.

A deep, dark chuckle rolled from him, the man dripping sex when he turned to tug me through the crack he'd made. "Call it the perks of putting up with Ollie."

"You seem to have a lot of perks to offer."

The chuckle that rumbled from his chest should have been illegal. "You have no idea."

Those shivers were back, racing my flesh. There was no mistaking what was in his words.

The desire that soaked them. Drenched in gasoline. The mere brush of his hand a match.

That need was only stoked with each second that passed.

He shut and latched the partition, shutting us away from the rest of the world. Elevated above it.

The loud, boisterous voices had become a dull hum, just an echo of revelry that filtered through the glass panes. From below, I could feel the rumbling beat of the band, a vibration that traveled my legs and settled into my bones.

Only a trickle of the singer's mesmerizing voice made it through, carried on the breeze that blew through the quieted, secluded space.

I released an awed breath.

I felt as if I'd been removed. Lifted from the realities of the world and was watching it in slow motion.

The city set out below us, the river a black, twisty, shimmery rope where it snaked behind the buildings on the opposite side of the street.

I edged up to the railing, leaning against it as I took in the view. "It's gorgeous up here," I murmured, never more unsure of what I was doing than right then.

Because I could feel that power blister over me from behind.

Hot, heated energy.

Billowing in waves and wrapping me whole. His voice enveloped me from behind. "I'm sorry about what happened down there."

I almost laughed, and I bit my lip, gazing down at the couples that strolled along the sidewalk. "It's none of my business who you sleep with, Kale. We just had a dinner date. That was it. Remember?"

It felt like a lie forced through my teeth.

"Was it?" he asked, inching closer, making me shake. He ran a hand from my shoulder down my arm.

I blew out a quivering breath.

Complicated. I could feel it compounding, amplifying in the dark.

"Because every time I get around you, it feels like something else."

I gazed over at him for a long beat before I turned back to look over the twinkling lights. "My life is a mess right now, Kale."

"Are you going to tell me about him?" There was no missing the hardness that lined his words.

He eased around the side of me and leaned against the ornate metal railing. He lifted the crystal to his mouth, the amber liquid glinting in strands of lights that crisscrossed like a starry ceiling above.

But his face.

His face was cast in shadows, eyes dimmed but no less intense.

So magnetically beautiful.

I took a steeling sip of my wine and fought to keep the tremor from my voice "What do you want to know?"

"You said husband. Not ex-husband."

"I'm working on that." I shifted my gaze to study him, searching for an answer. "You knew I was married and you still brought me up here."

His head shook. "You're no cheater, Hope. I may not know you, but I do know that."

"No. I'm not," I admitted, not sure how much to give him. Because some things were sacred and should only be trusted in the hands of those who'd earned it.

"So . . . you're separated?" he hedged.

"Yes. For the last year."

I might as well have been seeking refuge in the middle of a battlefield. Because I could feel myself rushing out onto uneven, treacherous ground. Where each step was perilous. Landmines underfoot.

His comfort unsustainable. Fleeting. If I weren't careful, I'd be carving out a place for him, giving him those pieces that were sacred, the most important parts of me.

But giving him this little bit felt right.

I looked down at the red fluid dancing in my glass and wet my lips. "We're in the middle of a divorce. You could call it nasty. He . . ."

He's cruel and wicked. Appearances are the most important thing to him, but he's the one who's truly blind. The one who can't see the beauty right in front of him. The one who'd rejected the miraculous gift he'd been given.

A strained breath seeped free, and my voice lowered with the admission. "If he found out I was here with you . . ."

Anger bristled through the air. It strangled the words in my throat. I could feel it radiating from Kale. A severe kind of protectiveness I was unaccustomed to.

"Do you miss him?" he asked, something fierce barely checked when he issued the question.

Casting my attention to the street, I pushed out a weighted sigh and whispered, "No."

I lifted my gaze to the potency of his. "Is it wrong that I lost faith in him a long time ago?"

I'd wanted to believe. Believe he would come to his senses. That he was just in shock and dealing with the blow life had issued. That he would see perfection came in all forms.

But there were some lines that couldn't be uncrossed.

The smile that turned up the corner of Kale's mouth was soft. So soft, and I was trembling when he reached out and brushed his fingertips across my cheek. "No, Hope. It isn't wrong. Not if he can't see you for who you are."

I searched him in the flickers of light that danced against the darkness, illuminating the stunning lines of his face. "You don't even know me."

"Some things are just written on a person. You can't hide who you are, just the same as I can't hide who I am."

"And who is it you think you are?"

He sighed with my question, as if this time it was me who was getting too close. Digging in too deep.

Straight on, he met my gaze. "A guy who probably shouldn't be standing here doing this."

Grief.

I saw the stark flash of it take him whole, the impact of it so severe it jarred me back a step.

I blinked at him, trying to make sense of this complicated man and piece together his complex layers. "What does that mean?"

"It means I don't get close to women, Hope, and the only thing I fucking want right now is to get closer to you."

Everything inside me took flight.

Kale set his tumbler aside before taking my glass and placing it next to his. Then he pushed to his full height, towering over me, pinning me with the power of his presence.

He framed my face in both of his hands.

Gently.

Tenderly.

That conflict raged inside me.

The push and the pull.

Gravity.

"Is there any chance you'll take him back?"

"No." It flew from my mouth like a curse. "Never."

He stood there, staring down at me, rocking on his heels. "Good. Don't settle, Hope. Don't fucking ever settle."

"I won't," I promised, swallowing over the lump that had grown thick at the base of my throat.

His forehead dropped to mine, and I reached up, wrapping my hands around his wrists, the man still holding me while I clung to him.

His breaths mine. My heart reaching for his.

He groaned a needy sound before he tilted up my chin,

searching as he stared down at me.

Slow . . . so slow . . . he leaned down and brushed his lips across mine.

Fire.

Everywhere.

Racing my flesh. Hijacking my veins.

His tongue tangled with mine. Stroking, dizzying as he edged me back, deeper into the darkness that lined the far recesses of the balcony.

His kiss no longer gentle.

An all-consuming demand.

My heart rate kicked, drumming wildly.

I swore his caught, too.

Because the very air around us started to thrum.

Heads spinning and spirits soaring.

I gasped when I was suddenly propped on the very edge of a small bistro table that was tucked against the far wall, Kale's fingers sinking into the outside of my thighs as he broke the kiss and dropped into a chair in front of me.

"Kale . . . what are you . . ."

I couldn't think, couldn't speak, not when he ran his thumbs over the flesh. "You said we had one night. I want to give you this. I want to make you feel good." His voice deepened, so low it sounded like a threat. "Is that what you want? For me to make you feel good? Tell me, Hope. Tell me you want this. Let me make you feel good."

My breaths came short, needy pants rising into the dense air, my heart manic where it pounded in my chest.

"I—"

He yanked me closer, my ass barely clinging to the edge. "Do you want me to touch you?" It was a demand.

Oh God.

There he was.

The confident, arrogant man.

Dangerous and perfect.

"Yes," I whimpered.

He caressed his hands over the tops of my thighs and down

to my knees. He started gliding his palms back down the inside of my legs.

Spreading me wide.

My pulse thundered.

I wasn't sure I'd ever felt so exposed.

His thumbs traced along the inside edges of my underwear. Curling my fingers around the edge of the table, my head dropped back on a breathy moan.

I swore, I felt the ground quake.

"You are so sexy. So beautiful. Do you know, Hope? Do you have any idea the way you affect me?" he murmured, just a finger teasing over the lace that covered me. "Did you know the first time I saw you, you knocked the air right out of my lungs? For a fleeting second, I literally couldn't breathe. How's it possible you do that to me?"

I throbbed, overcome with the ache that pulsed at the juncture of my thighs.

The ache to be touched. To be adored. Just for a little while.

"I couldn't stop looking at you." My wispy admission carried on the breeze. "Wondering what it might be like to be wanted by a man like you. Wondering what it would be like to go home with you. Wishing for a little while, that girl could be me."

"She is you, Hope. I want to get inside you so badly, it's painful. But the last thing I want to do is complicate things more than they are. I get it. So, let me give you this."

Did he get it?

Because the man was so absolutely complicating things when he nudged the fabric aside, his fingers slicking through my folds.

"Oh God." Jerking forward, my fingers burrowed into his shoulders, my forehead dropping to his.

His mouth pressed up under my jaw. "Is this what you need?"

His free hand wound in my hair as he kissed down the column of my neck. He tugged my head back, demanding more.

"Yes."

His breaths came harsh when he pushed two fingers into me.

"Kale." I shook around the intrusion, fingers fumbling to

hold on tighter, my belly in knots, white-hot coils that glowed bright and blinding.

Jerking back, that dominating gaze raked over my body. Purposed when it dropped to watch where he touched me. "You are perfect. Look at you, always so shy, all spread out for me."

He drove his fingers in slow, deep, maddening thrusts, and his thumb . . . I gasped and writhed as he began to rub it back and forth across my clit.

"Please . . . don't stop."

"That's what I thought. Knew you'd like it hard and slow and a little rough. You deserve a man who'll take the time to do it right. Give me that time, baby, and I promise you, the only thing you'll regret is the fact you didn't let me take you sooner."

And God, I should be mortified, the way he was talking to me, that same arrogant, overconfident man who'd approached me last week making a reappearance.

But instead, I stared at him through the dimness. Through the shadows and questions and madness that swirled around us. As he stroked me and touched me so intimately. In a way that was one-hundred percent unlike me.

But with him . . . I felt different.

I felt confident.

Beautiful.

Brave.

Reaching out, I trembled my fingers across his lush, sexy mouth, felt the needy breath he released against my palm.

He wrapped his free arm around my waist, nearly pulling me from the table, his stare severe. "Kiss me," he demanded, and I did, nearly desperate as I wrapped my arms around his neck, our tongues coiled, winding and teasing and tasting.

While this man drove me straight toward ecstasy.

Pleasure. It gathered from the ends of the earth.

Speeding as it converged.

Tightening to a pinpoint.

Kale curled his fingers.

My frozen world ignited in a burst of flames.

The most intense orgasm ripped through my body. Unlike

anything I'd ever experienced.

Wave after wave. Crash after crash.

Staggering.

Kale continued driving his fingers as I rode them. As I let myself completely go for the first time in more years than I could remember. Flying.

I begged for him to never stop. To never let go.

But that was the thing about trusting someone. Wanting them in a way you shouldn't. You started searching for ways to make them fit into the mix of all your complicated things. Wishing there was a way to carve space for them without sending that precarious balance toppling over.

My chest heaved, and Kale held me steady, edging back to eye me with satisfaction.

While I clung to his shoulders, a gasping, heaving mess.

And just for a little while, I allowed him to hold me up before the weight of my world could come crashing back down.

He straightened my underwear and my skirt while I bit my lip and fought the creeping awkwardness that began to seep into my veins, climbing my chest and heating my cheeks.

Laughing a rugged sound, he gripped me by the chin and forced me to look at him. "You aren't going to get shy on me now, are you?"

"I don't know . . . it seems you have me at a disadvantage."

He laughed lower, pushed back his chair, his grin easy when he gestured to the huge bulge straining at his pants. "You're the one with the disadvantage? I wouldn't be so sure about that. Look what you've done to me."

His words were playful.

No expectation behind them.

My hands flew up to my face, and I frantically shook my head, the mortification finally taking hold. "I'm so sorry."

Kale pried my hands away. "I'm not."

A line pinched my brow. "You aren't?"

"No, Hope. The only thing I asked of you was to let me make you feel good."

A smile pulled at the corner of my mouth. "I think it's safe to say you accomplished that."

"Yeah?" he asked, voice winding into a tease.

I couldn't help but utter my own. "Gold medal. Perfect ten."

He pulled me onto his lap so I was straddling him. "What, you think this is the Olympics? I know you didn't get to experience my stamina firsthand, but I was thinking more like this knight deserves a promotion from his princess. Maybe then he'll get to make her his queen."

I ran my fingers through his hair and played along, though I couldn't keep the tenderness out of my voice. "I think you may already be royalty, Kale Bryant."

Because that was the way he made me feel. Special. Wanted. The girl who got her fairy tale.

But the clock was getting ready to strike midnight. "I'm sorry, but I really should get home. I wasn't planning on staying out this late."

His lips flattened, though he nodded in understanding. "Okay then, let's get you home."

He stood and gathered my hand, leading me back the way we'd come. Out through the riot of voices that shouted where they played and drank, down the stairs, and through the murky haze.

Confidently, he guided me through the crowds, which again broke for him, by the band that continued to play, the singer's sultry voice a soft encouragement against my ear.

Someday.

Someday I'll find what was meant for me.

That day you'll find me, too.

Just don't let it be too far away.

"Someday." I let the silent promise move across my lips as I snuggled into Kale's side.

He led me out onto the same sidewalk where I'd parted from him a week before. When I'd thought I'd never see him again.

My chest wanted to cave with that idea now.

With the cruelty of that distinct possibility.

But I had to protect what was important, and standing out there with him was a recklessness in itself.

He lifted his hand in the air, hailing a cab approaching from down the street.

It pulled to the curb. Kale opened the door for me.

Cavalier in his perfect, arrogant way.

"Thank you," I told him, my heart in my throat and tears suddenly burning behind my eyes.

Damn it.

This was the kind of complication I didn't need. The new kind of trouble this boy had ignited in me.

I climbed in.

Grinning, he slid in beside me.

"What are you doing?" The words were panicked.

"Getting you home. You really think I'm going to send you off by yourself in the middle of the night?" Mischief danced across his face, his brow arching high. "What kind of knight would I be then?"

I fiddled with the hem of my dress. "That isn't necessary."

"It is," he said. This time his tone left no room for argument.

Resigned, I gave the driver my address, and Kale held my hand while the car drove through the city. Night pressed down through the bottled silence, broken by the streetlamps that flashed through the windows and the loud thrum of my heart.

This was so stupid.

Giving in this way.

Because my gut had warned me that one night would never be enough.

And if Dane was waiting for me again?

Anger and a shot of fear churned in my gut because I was so tired of playing by his rules.

It wasn't fair.

Not at all.

The cab made the last left into the quiet, sleeping neighborhood. Big, dense trees stood guard over the small homes, their windows cast in darkness and wrapped in the comfort of the night.

The driver cut across the road, pulling up alongside the curb in front of my house.

I looked over at Kale, and I knew I shouldn't, that I was only prolonging the inevitable. Making it hurt a little worse.

It didn't matter.

I leaned in and pressed a soft kiss to his full lips.

So gentle beneath mine. As if they might be able to promise all the things I wanted most.

A second later, I pulled back. "Thank you," I murmured, my fingers regretfully fiddling with the top button of his shirt.

When I started to slide toward the door, he snatched me by the wrist. "Let me come in."

I sent him a small, sad smile, ran my thumb along the defined curve of his cheek. "I had an amazing time tonight. The best time. Thank you for rescuing me for a little while. I won't ever forget it."

For a moment, he stared across at me before he gave a tight nod of reluctant acceptance, his smile slight, his voice wistful regret. "Good night, Shortcake."

I would have giggled if everything didn't suddenly hurt so much.

Clicking the door open, I let myself into the vacant loneliness of the waiting night.

ten

Kale

"Fess up, asshole." Ollie flicked the bottle cap he twisted from a beer at me where I was sitting out on the balcony of my loft.

I dodged it, not surprised to see him waltzing into my place like he owned it after I'd ignored the two calls he'd made this afternoon and the ten texts that'd come in after.

Dude was worse than a stage-five clinger.

"Fuck off, man."

His eyes widened in mock horror. "Such a foul mouth for a kiddie doctor. Shame. And here I thought you'd be classier than that. You sound like some kind of lowlife loser."

I rolled my eyes and took a sip of the beer I'd been nursing for the last two hours. "Gonna blame that one on the fact I hang out with you. They say you are the company you keep."

He dropped down into the lounger beside me, kicking out his legs, crossing them at the ankles. He let out a satisfied sigh.

My brow lifted. "Make yourself at home, why don't you?"

He smirked. "What do you think I'm doing?"

"Ruining my life?"

"Oh, come on, dude. You know you were just begging me to

make a surprise visit when you ignored my calls, especially considering you showed up at my bar last night *after* you'd had dinner with the same chick who'd shot you down the week before. Far as I'm concerned, you were shooting SOS flares in the air. Man down. I came running."

He sat up on the side of the lounger, elbows resting on his knees with his beer dangling between them. "So let's hear it, because I'm pretty sure either my best friend has caught some kind of horrible disease or that heart of his is finally thawing out. Which is it?"

I exhaled heavily, eyes trained on the view that was basically exactly the same as the one from Olive's balcony. Lights stretched out across the city, the river winding behind the buildings just on the other side of the street, carefree voices lifting from the sidewalk below.

My place was just a half block down from Ollie's bar. It was located in another reclaimed warehouse that Rex's company, RG Construction, had been hired to bring back to life. I'd been looking for a permanent place to call home at the time, and he'd told me he was working on a project that might interest me.

Even though it'd been nothing but bare bones and rotted wood when I'd viewed it, I'd bought it on the spot.

Pretty much for the view alone since the unit was located on the fifth floor.

Though, I had to admit that my pad turned out to be better than I could have imagined. A cohesive flow of rustic and modern, antique and industrial.

Rex and his crew were skilled, that was for sure.

Too bad the only thing missing from the view tonight was a redhead propped on a table. Like one of those hypnotizing sirens playing you for help when you were the one who was gonna end up dead.

I roughed a hand over my face, trying to clear the vision, to purge her from my mind.

"So," he prodded.

"So, what?"

"So, why are you moping around like some kind of pathetic

pussy when you had that gorgeous girl hanging on your arm last night? Even you have to admit, she's way out of your league."

I drove my fingers through my hair. "Guess maybe she is."

"She send you packing?"

"Something like that."

I knew I'd pushed her too far and too fast last night. Touching her, thinking it was the only chance I was going to get. But it'd felt impossible not to after what she'd confessed. It hadn't even been all that much, but I could see the betrayal and hurt written all over her.

The fear.

Without a doubt, the piece of shit was the reason she didn't think she had anything to offer.

All I'd wanted was to make her feel *more*.

Treat her like the queen she deserved to be.

Ollie sobered, rocking back when he finally caught the magnitude of my mood. "Whoa . . . you actually really like this girl."

I sighed out some of the frustration that'd been nagging me all day. "I don't fucking know. There's just . . . something about her I can't shake. She owns this little coffee shop and bakery right down the street from the new office. Stumbled in there last Monday morning, and I couldn't stay away. And you know I sure as hell don't have the time or space for a girl, but I was asking her out before I could stop myself."

"So, last night was, like, a for real date?" He said it like the idea was a mystery dangling somewhere in the universe.

I rubbed my forehead before raking my hand to the back of my head. "Yeah."

"Are you going to see her again?"

"Nah, man."

One night.

It was the only thing either of us could afford.

"And why not? Because your mopey ass does not seem to be happy about it. Which doesn't fit you, by the way."

"You know why." I angled my face away from him a fraction when I said it.

Normally, I was the guy who looked to the bright side. The one who found the good buried in the rubble. But there would always be this one part of me where the sun had gone missing.

That place that had gone dark and dim.

That place I didn't have the capacity to revisit.

I could feel the weight of his frown. "That was ten years ago, Kale, and you know it doesn't have a thing to do with that girl. You've got to quit blaming yourself for something that wasn't your fault. Quit thinking you can't move on."

My laughter was hard. "Not my fault?"

It didn't matter that everyone around me had told me it wasn't my fault. That I'd done everything I could. My heart had convicted me on the spot that I was the only one who should shoulder the blame.

"You made a mistake, man."

A mistake?

"And someone died," I spat.

The girl I loved fucking died because of that mistake.

Because I'd missed it.

Because I'd been too wrapped up.

Busy.

My guts clenched in pain. In the kind of regret that would never fade.

It was right at the second Ollie flinched with my statement. A lightning bolt that ravaged his body.

"Shit," I muttered in apology, knowing where his mind had gone with the callus way I'd thrown it out there. Our situations were different, but in the end, we both were culpable for the same damned thing.

He'd sent his sixteen-year-old sister home from the lake in the middle of the night. Telling her she didn't belong.

She hadn't made it home that night.

That was the kind of guilt that could eat a man alive. Make him hard and callus and coarse.

Ollie lifted his head to the night sky. "We are a fucking pair, aren't we?"

A low chuckle filtered free. "Yeah. Guess we are."

He dropped his head back down to look at me, eyeing me seriously. "Don't let the past keep you from today, man. I know you loved her, and I know a piece of you died with her. But what about the rest of you that's still living? You're the coolest fucking guy I know. You love with all you have. You give every part of yourself to your career and still manage to give more to the rest of us after there shouldn't be anything left. You deserve to live, Kale. Really live."

That was the problem. It was those dead, dark places that didn't know how to move on. If I even wanted to.

Hope's face flashed behind my eyes, and I wasn't quite sure where the fresh bolt of regret was coming from.

The lump that rose in my throat was nothing but cragged, pitted rocks. "Doesn't matter, anyway. Hope's got her own shit."

Standing, he drained his beer and then pointed at me with the same hand wrapped around the empty bottle. "Then pull her out of it." He smirked. "And why don't you pull yourself out of yours while you're at it."

It was Monday morning, and I sat at the red light, drumming my thumbs on my steering wheel as if it might keep me busy enough not to notice where I was.

Like I could drive right by and pretend the little coffee shop wasn't tucked under the quaint, three-story building or keep the colorful umbrellas that were shading the small tables out front from singing out in welcome, begging me to stop in.

Hell, the little A-frame chalkboard sign literally read: It's a beautiful day. We're about to make it better. Come on in.

Motherfucking sunshine.

I accelerated through the intersection, a war going on inside me, knowing she was fighting one of her own. I tried to convince myself to let it go. To just man the fuck up and get to the office because God knew I had plenty to do.

Leave all this nonsense behind.

Because all Hope had given me was one night.

I kept my attention facing forward as I passed, the logo calling out to me where it was printed on the large plate glass window.

A Drop of Hope.

"Fuck it." I whipped my car into an available spot and jumped out into the warm Alabama morning, probably a little quicker than necessary.

Like I said, pathetic.

My insides were nothing but a jumble of nerves, but I pasted on a smile and roughed an easy hand through my hair as I jerked open the door, figuring what the hell.

Some things were just worth a second try.

The bell jingled overhead, and movement rustled in the back. The door swung open, and Jenna rushed out while drying her hands on a dishtowel.

A little too eagerly, my gaze jumped around the small space, across the tables littered with people enjoying their morning coffee and a muffin rather than taking it on the go.

"You lookin' for someone?" The question was delivered with an undercurrent of laughter.

I jerked my attention back to Jenna, who stood there grinning.

Like she didn't know exactly why I was there. It was written all over me. "Just wanted to grab a cup of coffee before work."

It wasn't like I was going to admit it, either.

"Is that so?"

"It is the best coffee in town. It says so right there." I pointed at the little plaque proudly affixed to the wall.

She grinned. "I guess it does, doesn't it?" She turned away and grabbed a large paper cup, talking as she did. "If I remember right, since you seem to just keep stumbling in for our award-winning brew, you prefer a regular ol' cup of Joe. Nothing fancy." She shot me a look from over her shoulder. "I mean, unlike your clothes and your car and that face."

My chuckle was two-parts unease and one-part amusement. "Hey, I was born with this face."

She turned back around, head angled in scrutiny as she slid

the coffee across the counter in my direction. "Really. Here I was thinking it might have been cosmetically enhanced."

"I don't know whether to take that as a compliment or not."

Her eyes went wide. "Well, probably depends on who you're talking to."

I laughed again, this time lighter. "Which would you be?"

She leaned against the counter. "Depends."

I pulled a ten from my wallet and passed it to her. "On what?"

"On what you're really doing here."

I pushed out a breath, eyes darting around, searching for that fall of red. "Is she around?" I asked. Clearly, Jenna already had my intentions pegged.

"No, she has an appointment this morning."

Disappointment.

It was there in the way the anxious tension in my shoulders slumped in some kind of defeat.

That should have been warning enough.

"I love her like a sister, you know? So you probably should be aware I'll happily cut your dick off if you hurt her."

Apparently, I really was fluent in silent conversations. I'd gotten that one spot on.

"She's the one who said she could only give me one night."

"Did she?" Jenna handed me the change, looking at me like I was dense. "Or was that her asking you to be careful with her because she's terrified of getting herself mixed up in another situation that isn't healthy? But you need to know that when she tells you her life is complicated, she isn't exaggerating or feeling sorry for herself. It's because her life is really that damned complicated."

I pushed out a sigh. "Last thing I want to do is hurt her."

A puff of air shot from her nose. "That's what they all say in the beginning, isn't it? It'd be nice for a guy to actually prove it for once." She headed for the back, sending a flippant wave over her shoulder. "See ya around, Sir Bryant."

Laughter burst from my chest, and I pressed my fist over my mouth, shaking my head as I tried to keep it contained.

But with the thought of Hope talking about me to her friend? It made hope come bubbling up inside.

Because maybe Ollie was right.

Maybe it was time for me to move on. And maybe Hope needed help moving on, too.

White lights glared from above. Blinding. The emergency room stark and barren and cold.

Arms aching.

Compression after compression after compression.

Desperation bursting in my blood.

Sweat ran down my brow and soaked the back of my shirt.

And I tried and I tried and I tried.

A flat line . . .

I sucked in a breath against the phantom hum of the machine.

That fucking flat line.

I gave a harsh shake of my head to clear the pictures from my mind and forced myself to focus on the chart I was studying on my laptop.

Telling myself not to freak the fuck out. This wasn't the past trying to test me.

Taunt me and tease me.

This was shit that just happened.

Uncontrolled.

While doctors did their best to control it.

I'd come to accept it was cases like this that got me most, but that didn't mean it didn't shake me to my bones.

My eyes moved over the screen.

An eight-year-old boy who'd been born with a genetic defect that had required a heart transplant when he was an infant. That genetic defect had also affected other organs and caused complete deafness.

It wasn't like I hadn't constantly dealt with life-threatening issues in the ER.

But when kids had come through those doors, I either patched them up and sent them on their way or referred them to someone who specialized in what they were going through.

Or in the worst cases, which thank God were rare in this town, a child was rushed in, already so far gone there'd been nothing anyone could do.

Twice, I'd lost a kid on my table in the ER.

Both times, I'd thought I might lose myself.

That was somehow different. Part of this boy's permanent care was being placed in my hands when I'd signed up to become a part of this team.

Evan.

Josiah's best friend with the "bad" heart.

But I didn't think Josiah understood the full extent of what that meant for Evan.

Another swell of dread tumbled through me, and I knocked it down, refusing it. Seemed the more time I'd spent with Hope, the more unearthed that feeling was becoming. That girl making me face the reasons why I couldn't give myself wholly. The reasons I couldn't risk it.

Why I had to keep my focus on what I'd devoted my life to.

But knowing it didn't seem to make a difference. Not with the way I'd gone running into her shop earlier today. Not the way I just kept wanting more.

Because fuck.

Ollie was right. Maybe it was fucking time, and that scared the shit out of me.

Pushing to my feet, I forced myself to leave my office and get this over with. I knew that no matter how much this was going to affect me—make me remember—I was still going to pour myself into this kid and his case.

When I stepped out into the hall, my nurse was calling over her shoulder as she flew by. "Vitals are all logged. He's ready for you."

"Thank you," I mumbled before I lightly knocked at the door with my knuckle, mentally preparing myself. I pushed open the door, ready to meet him and his family for the first time.

And my own heart . . .

It stalled in my chest.

Before it bottomed out and spilled onto the floor.

Breath gone.

Shock racing my veins.

Eyes wide as I tried to process the scene in front of me.

Because there was this adorable kid, sitting on the exam table, legs swinging over the side, kicking the heels of his shoes against the metal drawers.

Massive grin on his face like he didn't have a care in the world. Or like maybe he had every care, and he embraced what life had given him, anyway.

He wore these thick glasses that made him look like a cute little bug because his sight had also been affected by the congenital malformations.

But his eye involvement hadn't been nearly as severe as the defect of his ears.

His hearing loss complete and profound.

As profound as the deformity of his heart.

His chart had told me he'd had his heart transplant when he was six months old. The last-ditch effort that had saved his life.

When he sensed my presence in the room, his attention snapped my direction, his messy red, wavy hair flopping over with the action.

Attention landing on me, he grinned even wider.

The sight of it clutched me everywhere.

I had this instant, overwhelming sense of affection.

And fear.

So much damned fear I didn't know how to process the two.

To make sense of the two of them together.

Because there was also his mother.

She was standing in the middle of the room. Like she'd barely just made it to her feet a second before I'd opened the door.

Gasping for air and backing away.

Clutching the business card with my contact information my nurse had undoubtedly just passed to her, the same way she did with every new patient I'd taken over for Dr. Browning.

Her horrified gaze bounced between me and the card and the fucking lollipops that were still in the basket, left like a tease or a prize or maybe an outright bribe, on the counter at the back of the exam room.

"Hope," I breathed, my hand still clutching the knob, frozen in the middle of the doorway.

God. In all my hunting for crucial information in Evan's chart, I hadn't even taken note of his last name.

Everything came crashing down.

The things she'd said, and everything she'd implied. The fact she had nothing left to give and no time for herself because she was giving all her time to this little man who needed her most.

She swallowed hard and blinked at me as if she were begging me for something.

Problem was, I didn't exactly know what that was, and I thought maybe she didn't, either.

We stood there staring.

Held.

Bound.

The air between us alive. Thick and tense and aching.

Fuck. What was I supposed to do?

Finally, she broke the connection. She dropped her gaze and sank back into the chair.

Every single thing about her movements were riddled with anxiety. It was as if she was teetering between reaching out and stopping me and heaving all her hope and trust into my taking care of her son.

Because all those amazing things I'd been thinking about her?

They were suddenly right there.

Brought into the light.

Whole.

Flickering with the goodness I saw surrounding her every time I got in her space.

Her *reason.*

And that reason was right there, grinning this bright smile that lit the whole room.

Clearing my throat, I moved the rest of the way through the door and snapped it shut behind me. "I'm Dr. Bryant," I said, feeling totally off-kilter.

Hope made a little choking sound, and my attention darted that way. Trying to tell her I was sorry for putting her in this uncomfortable position. That I had been caught just as much off-guard as she was.

Fuck, I had this intense urge to tell her that her son was everything that terrified me the most. What made me question and made me fight to be the best damned doctor I could possibly be.

"Dr. Bryant," she whispered, as if she were processing that fact.

Cautiously, I went to the little wheeled stool and dropped down onto it, sucking in a breath as I used my feet to wheel closer to Evan.

I felt the frantic movement off to the side and behind me. For a flash, I cut my eyes that way.

Hope.

Hope was signing, her hands and fingers moving in this choreographed dance. The sight of it pierced me somewhere deep.

God. It was beautiful.

She was beautiful.

And I had no fucking clue how to process the turmoil raging inside me.

Evan smiled a wide smile at her, nothing but adoration and belief, before he was looking at me, freckles speckled across the bridge of his nose and his cheeks. He lifted his hand, fingertips to his temple, drawing it out to the side in a wave.

"He said hello." A hoarse explanation from Hope.

Which I got because my own throat had grown thick. I offered an awkward wave to this adorable kid.

And Evan.

He laughed.

It was a quiet sound that scuffed from the depths of him, a laugh from his belly that shook his entire body.

He reached out, all excited like, and grabbed my wrist, pulled my hand up, and showed me how to do it right.

I repeated it.

He smiled again, touched his chin, fingertips coming out toward me like he was blowing a kiss.

"Good." I saw the word form on his lips when he did.

GOOD.

He was telling me I did a good job.

But I knew that was the furthest from the truth.

Because everything inside me was screaming that I'd already fucked this up beyond repair. Of all the people I couldn't get involved with, Hope owned the number one spot.

Goddamned forbidden.

Because my insides were clenching and all those fears and inadequacies were rushing back.

A smile tweaked at the edge of my mouth, and I eyed him carefully as I spoke. "I bet you are way better at it than I am, though, yeah?"

He nodded enthusiastically, green eyes glinting beneath the lights.

A mossy, earthy green.

Just like his mom's.

His hands suddenly went wild, speaking a language I was ignorant to. Somehow, it made me feel like some kind of illiterate asshole.

Tinkling laughter filtered from Hope, the woman so in tune with her kid that it sent a tumble of affection through the center of me. She shifted forward so she could look at me, her expression so damned soft as she said, "He said there's no way you can keep up, but he might be nice enough to let you try."

I turned back to him, cocked my head, mouth moving with the tease. "Is that a challenge?"

Another emphatic nod, the kid's grin so wide I could have counted his teeth.

"Oh really . . . I'm the doctor here. You don't think I can beat you at your little game?"

He made a gesture across his body, a swipe of his hand as he pinched his fingers together, his mouth moving in time.

NO WAY.

I hefted out a breath. That was what I thought.

Evan could read lips.

Of course, he could. This sweet kid who oozed love and faith and intelligence.

A kid whose chart promised he was fragile and breakable and weak, when really his spirit was big enough to fill the entire room as he prepared to outwit me.

"Well, then, I'll do my best to keep up. How's that sound?"

GOOD, he signed again.

And my insides were twisting again because I had no idea how the fuck I was going to get through this. But I had to suck it up, act like the man I'd been trained to be. How I was going to pretend I hadn't had his mother propped on a table a mere three days before, touching her and wishing things could be different, was beyond me. One thing at a time, though.

Because this was the reality.

I was Evan's doctor.

His doctor.

The one responsible for his care.

And I wasn't about to fuck that up.

Stark lights. Cold. Barren. Flat line.

I jarred against the sudden vision, blinking the cruelty away, voice rough when I said, "All right, then, Evan. Let's check you out."

If I wasn't paying such close attention, I probably wouldn't have noticed the way he flinched.

Wouldn't have noticed the fear that went racing beneath the surface of his skin.

Or the way his mother cringed in sympathy of it. Swore, I could feel her having to physically restrain herself from reaching out and gathering him into the safety of her arms.

This amazing woman so clearly desperate to shield him from the things she didn't have the power to protect him from.

No doubt, he was no stranger to needles and pain or being poked and prodded.

Even though I knew he couldn't hear me, I kept my voice soft, filled with assurance. "I already checked out your records, Evan. You don't need any shots, and you did all your heart tests for Dr. Krane last month. That means, I'm going to give you a really fast checkup. Make sure everything's going just right. No needles. How's that sound?"

His trusting face flushed with relief, tension draining from his body.

While mine curled with the yearning to be able to take everything from him.

Make it better.

Promise him he would never hurt again.

Wishing I could be the hero I could never be.

Another part of me wanted to tease him about monsters growing in his belly. Make him laugh the way I did Frankie Leigh and my younger patients, but the boy was eight years old. If I did that, he would probably demand a new doctor because the one he'd been assigned had lost his mind.

Sounded about right.

"I'm going to take your shirt off, okay?" I made sure to keep my mouth in view of his eyes when I asked it.

Without any reluctance, his arms flew over his head.

I chuckled, reached down, and worked it over his head. Had to beat down the urge to ruffle my fingers through his hair when I did. "There we go," I said, setting it beside him.

From behind and to the side, I could feel the weight of his mother's stare against the side of my face.

Could feel the weight of her burden and her fear that I was sure never went away.

The anticipated prominent scar ran from the top of his sternum to about two inches above his belly button. I ran my fingers across his breastbone, palpating the area and familiarizing myself with his scars and the way his surgical wound had healed.

I moved back to make sure he could see my mouth. "Do you ever have any pain in this area? Anytime you're playing or trying to sleep? Anything that makes you feel funny?"

He'd had a cardiology checkup with Dr. Krane recently. His

chart affirmed his transplanted heart was functioning well. But as his primary care, I would cover all the bases.

That was what the clinic was all about.

Ensuring nothing was overlooked. If one doctor missed a sign, chances were, the next would pick up on it. And I sure as fuck wasn't going to miss it.

Evan gave an assertive shake of his head.

Clearly, he knew the importance of that answer.

"That's good. Why don't you lie back so I can check your belly?"

He didn't hesitate. He shifted and laid on his back, and I stood over him, my fingertips checking his abdomen for any lumps or bumps, examining all the quadrants, watching his face for any kind of reaction. "Anything feel funny when I do that?"

He smiled when he gave another shake of his head.

And the examination continued that way. Like he was any kid who walked through my door. Which of course, I cared about every single patient I saw.

They were the reason I lived.

Why I devoted my life.

But this one . . . this one left me with a lump the size of a grapefruit in my throat and my heart battering my ribcage.

I stood over him, pretending like I didn't want to drop to my knees and tell him I'd make it better if I could.

Pretending I didn't want to say a million things to his mom and demand a million things of her in return.

Instead, I carried on like this was perfectly normal while tension I hoped Evan didn't notice bounded through the tight space, ricocheting from the walls and echoing in the air.

Swore, I could taste the woman on my breath and hear her moan in my ear.

God. This was brutal.

I patted his knee when I finished. "All done."

Rolling the stool to the counter, I set my laptop on it, cleared my throat, and tried not to really look at her when I started going over all the shit I normally did first with the parents but had been too shocked to focus on when I'd found her there.

I asked Hope about his diet and exercise and if she had any concerns while thousands of unsaid questions roiled between us.

I told her he was at the fifth percentile in height and weight, to be expected for his condition, that as long as he was eating well, it was nothing to worry about.

Right.

Nothing to worry about.

Because worry surrounded her like a dark, ominous cloud. But with a simple glance at her kid, that storm was obliterated with the force of a thousand suns.

"Thank you, Dr. Bryant," she said, eyes downcast as if she couldn't physically bring herself to look at me.

She stood, took Evan's hand, and helped him down. She ran a tender hand through his hair and then signed something I didn't understand.

He beamed up at her.

Clearly, she hung the little boy's moon.

Watching it felt like I was being shredded in two.

I looked at him, trying to loosen my jaw. No doubt, he'd recognize if I was grinding my teeth.

"It was great to meet you, Evan. I . . ." I hesitated, suddenly feeling like a fool. Like maybe I was the brunt of a cruel, sick joke. So out of sorts, I had no clue how to decipher up from down.

Still, I didn't want to treat him any different from anyone else, so I plucked one of the lollipops from the box and bent at the knees to offer it to him. "Here. This is for you . . . if your mom says it's okay."

His face lit up, and Hope choked over a tiny sob that I knew she was doing her best to hide. I paused, reluctant to turn and look her way. I'd told Hope that night that I didn't know her all that well, but some things a person couldn't miss. And I knew without a doubt that Hope was at her breaking point.

She'd warned me her life was complicated. I guessed I couldn't really grasp what that really meant until right then when all those threads I could sense her hanging by started to weave together. Taking shape in my mind. The fact she was in the middle of a nasty divorce.

Dread settled over me like a sheet of ice, awareness taking hold. Suddenly, I was sure all that *nasty* had to do with the well-being of this kid.

Evan yanked at her arm, signed something quickly. Casting him a soft smile, she nodded, and he took the candy, grinning at it like he was in awe before he pushed past me toward the counter.

Hiking up onto his toes, he grabbed the pen and the pad with the clinic info at the top, tongue sticking out at the side in concentration as he scribbled something across the paper.

When he was finished, the beaming was directed at me, the kid getting under my skin as quickly as his mom had as he stood there with the pad of paper lifted up to me like an offering.

Unsure what to do, I glanced at Hope.

Her voice scratched. "He wants to be able to talk to you himself. Not through me. He said it's a secret."

My throat was nothing but sheers of broken glass when I accepted the pad. My eyes moved across the messy marks scored deep on the page.

> *I helped my mom make those. She said a nice man came in and bought them all so we need to make more. We gave all the money to the babies with bad hearts like mine. Was it you who bought them all?*

My nod felt like a confession of a crime.

He grabbed it back and scribbled some more.

> *You are nice. I'm glad you're my new doctor. If you think I'm going to die, don't tell my mom. I don't want her to be sad.*

Emotion screamed through my throat. Racing the length. Winding down to fist my heart and crush my ribs. With a shaky hand, I took the pen from him and wrote my own message below his.

I'm glad I am, too. Really glad. And you aren't dying, Evan. Not even close. I promise I won't let that happen.

I thought he might be more alive than anyone I'd ever met.

His grin lit up the room when he read my answer. He gave me a thumbs-up. Apparently, he thought that was simple enough for me.

When I'd never felt so *complicated* in all my life.

Hope gathered him by the hand. She cast me a remorseful glance, those green eyes telling a million secrets that I knew she wouldn't allow her tongue to speak. The two of them started out the door. Evan dashed out ahead of her.

Before she could make it all the way out, I snatched her by the wrist, unable to keep it back.

"Why didn't you tell me?" It came out harder than I intended.

An accusation. A demand.

I didn't know.

She spun around, all that red hair swishing around her like a red, violent wave. It was almost terror that rippled across her gorgeous face.

It wrenched through me.

Tripping me up.

Bringing me to my knees.

"What was I supposed to tell you? I told you what you needed to know. I told you my life was complicated, and I didn't have room for anything else."

"You could have at least told me you had a kid."

Disbelief pinched her eyes together. "And what then? What difference would it have made? He's my priority. My only priority."

Her tone swung into desperation. "And right now, I'm fighting for him. I've *been* fighting for him since the second he was born, Kale. But this fight I'm in the middle of right now? It's one I didn't see coming. One that's going to take all of me to win. *Sacrifice.*"

Instead of releasing her, anger tightened my hold, none of it directed at her.

"What does that mean?" The question hissed between my teeth as all those threads had suddenly laced together became clear.

Venom seeped into my veins.

The implications of her confessions.

"He wants to take everything from me."

I suddenly understood what kind of fight she was talking about.

Motherfucker.

I could feel the emphasis of it twist across my brow. "He's trying to get custody?"

Fuck. I didn't even know who *he* was. But I hated him. Hated him more than I thought I'd ever hated anyone in my life.

And that shouldn't be possible.

Her entire being winced, her chin trembling before she gave me a small nod. "The suit is asking for joint."

She pressed her hands to her chest. "Which I know sounds fair to most people, but if you knew . . ." She inhaled a sharp breath. "If you knew how unfair that is to my son . . ."

I gritted my teeth, fighting the rage that bloomed in my blood.

She swallowed hard. "Do you get it now? Why I can't do this? Why I can't risk it?" Those green eyes moved across my face, searching for understanding.

And I got it.

I got it on every level.

That didn't mean I wasn't seething inside. Wanting to hunt the piece of shit down.

She blinked, like she was trying to break the connection, the band of understanding that stretched and pulled between us.

"We never should have done what we did, Kale. I shouldn't have. That's on me. It was selfish, but I wanted to experience it for a little while. Being with a man like you. But it was a mistake."

It was.

I knew it was.

But I wanted to counter her claim.

Refute it.

Tell her I'd just been getting started.

But Evan was my patient.

My fucking heart-transplant patient.

"Shit." Dropping my hold and the power of her gaze, I ran a frustrated hand through my hair.

"Shit," I mumbled again.

What had I done? How could I have let myself get into this position again? But that was the way it happened. Without your knowledge. Without your permission. You got caught up, and before you even knew it, you were in deep.

Swept away.

Hope reached out to caress my jaw with her fingertips.

Sweet.

Soft.

Heat.

Her lip trembled as she traced across my chin before she tilted her head and looked up at me with the warmth of those green, earthy eyes.

Need and something else I didn't want to recognize tumbled through my body, a flare in my spirit that lit.

"I told you I'd never forget that night. I meant it. But now . . . now I'm going to walk away and pretend it didn't happen, and I'm going to trust you to take care of my son."

eleven

Hope

"You've got to be shittin' me."

I glanced over the back of the couch and toward the hallway to make sure the coast was clear before I turned back to Jenna, who waited impatiently, legs crisscrossed under her and hugging a frilly throw pillow to her chest. She looked seconds away from pressing her face to it and releasing a frustrated scream.

Or maybe that was what I was imagining.

Because it was the truth. I wanted to scream.

Or maybe cry.

I wasn't sure.

So, I opted to clutch my wine glass in my hands.

Maybe it wasn't healthy, but tonight, it was my lifeline.

"Do you really think I'd joke around about something like that?"

"You'd better not. Good God almighty, Harley Hope. He's a doctor. I should've seen it all along." She fanned herself.

My eyes narrowed, my voice dropping to an incredulous whisper. "Why are you acting like this is a good thing?"

Hers widened, her brows disappearing behind her bangs.

"Um . . . have we not established that man is nothin' but straight deliciousness? He's sex on a stick and should be licked up and down. I'd eat that boy with a spoon. Hell, you could name a cupcake after him and put one of those little stakes in it with a picture of his face. *Bam*. Bestseller. *And* he's a doctor. Honestly, the only thing I'm seein' here are the positives."

"He's *Evan's* doctor."

She shrugged. "So."

"So I'm going to have to see him for basically all of forever."

It was hard enough to resist him when he kept coming into my store.

Seeing him care for my son?

Those puddles he'd left me in during our date had up and boiled at the sight, leaving me a shaking, quivering mess of awe and desire. I'd sat there watching him from behind, my stomach clenching in need and my heart doing wild, wild things.

My subconscious had been quick to offer up all kinds of excuses to convince my mind why seeing him again would be just fine. A whisper that urged me to reach out, caress his striking face, to run my fingertips across that magnificent jaw.

And maybe, just maybe, it would be okay to reach out to touch on the beauty of his kind, genuine heart.

Shivers raced my spine.

That was definitely going to cause all kinds of problems I wasn't sure I knew how to deal with.

"You don't see the complication?" I asked.

She huffed. "You and your *complications*. What it seems to me is *convenient*. One-stop shopping. You *are* the one who's always sayin' she doesn't have time."

"This isn't about having time, Jenna. You know that. This is about Dane."

"Who you need to stop letting control you."

"I'm not letting Dane control me. I'm trying to protect my son."

"That's it? You're not going to see Kale anymore?"

I gave her a resolute nod that made a rush of sadness billow through my spirit.

Someday.

But as of right then, I had to make the sacrifice. This wasn't about me, and I had to put my son first.

"That means you wouldn't mind if I went for him then?" Jenna tossed out, sipping her wine as if I shouldn't reach out and smack her just for suggesting it. "You know, I wouldn't mind a little of that *royal treatment*."

She waggled her brows. Goading me.

God, I never should have told her that. I was never gonna hear the end of it.

"You're disgusting and crass and no longer my best friend," I told her as petulantly as I could.

She laughed, set her glass down, and then scrambled across the couch, hugging me to her side. "You know you love me. Just like you know I love you. Which is why I want you to take care of you, too. You give and you give and you give, and you never know when that giving is finally going to bleed you dry."

Tears pricked at my eyes, and I rested my head on her shoulder. "Evan is enough for me, Jenna."

The only thing I needed, at least for a little while. Until life sorted itself out. Until we were free, and we could move on and leave the ugliness behind.

All I wanted was a safe, secure home for my son. That was what I'd strived for all along. I was determined to give it to him. The rest would fill itself in. I had faith that it would.

Jenna ran her fingers through my hair. "I know. I just want you to promise me you will remember that it's okay to love, too, especially if you're doing it because you want to instead of because you have to. You deserve it."

"I know that. But right now, with Dane showing up here, I need to be careful."

Honestly, I shouldn't have been shocked when I'd received the papers that he was going after joint custody.

It was nothing but a show, I knew that. The vile man wasn't doing anything but keeping up appearances and then turning right around and hating me for having the *audacity* to actually leave him.

I should have left him as soon as he'd reacted to the news of Evan's heart the way he had, our son only a couple days old.

But I'd believed in him, in the man I'd thought I'd married, and had been certain it was only shock and grief and fear making him behave the way he had.

Rejecting our precious child as if he were a stain.

The years had whittled away that faith until there'd been nothing left before the proverbial final nail was driven into the coffin, the one that still made me sick to my stomach.

"Not all men are pricks, Hope. You just happened to marry one."

"He definitely set the bar, didn't he?"

"Yeah, so low the snake couldn't even slither under it."

Light laughter escaped me, and I let her hold me up for a little bit. When I heard the clatter of footsteps smacking the floor behind me, I shifted, turning to look back over the couch.

Evan stood there, dripping wet and making puddles on my wood floor, clutching the ends of the towel, which he hadn't taken the time to actually dry with, to his chest.

He was grinning that smile that decimated me. My heart so full I was sure any second it would burst.

He hooked his towel under his chin and chest.

FINISHED, he signed.

GOOD BOY, I signed back.

Jenna shifted all the way around. "Come give Auntie a hug good night."

Evan scrambled around the couch, throwing himself at her. My best friend squeezed him and wiggled him around. She roughed a hand through his wet hair. "Who's my favorite little man?"

EVAN THE GREAT! he signed.

"That's right," she said. "Because You. Are. Great."

Grinning from ear to ear, he nodded emphatically.

My miracle boy.

They say there is no love like a mother's, and I'd never claim to love my child more than any other mother loved theirs. But what I did know with everything inside me was I couldn't love mine more. That I'd never know a love greater.

He'd been written on me.

In me.

For me.

I knew I'd been the one created specifically for his care because I loved him in a way that no one else could.

In a way that was ours.

Whole and complete.

I pushed from the couch and set my wine on the coffee table. *TIME FOR BED.*

He made an *oh-man* face, before he was trotting off toward his room, and by the time I made it there, he had already pulled on his underwear and tee. He jumped into bed, and I dimmed the light, crossed the room, and lowered to my knees beside him.

He pulled the covers up to his chest and wiggled beneath them.

COZY?

A nod, Evan still oozing love and smiles.

GOOD.

I hesitated, considering what to say. If I even should. I bit my lip as I stared down at my incredible son.

WHAT DID YOU THINK ABOUT TODAY? I finally asked.

In the dim light, his green eyes danced, his lips and hands quick with their reply.

ABOUT MY NEW DOCTOR?

We always mouthed the words to each other when we signed since Dane had refused to learn. He'd claimed we were only giving Evan a crutch. If he worked *hard* enough, *listened* better, if we didn't coddle him, he might be *normal.*

What an asshole.

YES, I gestured.

I THINK YOU WERE RIGHT.

I frowned. ABOUT WHAT?

THAT HE'S NICE.

BECAUSE OF THE LOLLIPOPS?

He didn't hesitate with his response. *YES. THAT, AND HE'S GENTLE, AND HE DOESN'T WANT TO HURT ME.*

My guts clenched. *I DON'T THINK ANY OF YOUR DOCTORS WANT TO HURT YOU. SOMETIMES THEY HAVE TO. TO KEEP YOU HEALTHY.*

With honesty, he blinked up at me. *BUT SOMETIMES THEY GET USED TO IT, AND THEY FORGET TO BE CAREFUL.*

My son saw things in a different way.

As if he were years older.

Insightful.

Quick and keen.

Kind and knowing.

Maybe it was because the constant noises most of us were inundated with were silenced for him. Because he could observe people without having to listen to the things they said. Actions always spoke so much louder than words.

I WISH YOU NEVER HAD TO HURT, I told him. *IF I COULD, I WOULD TAKE IT ALL AWAY.*

I KNOW, M-A-M-A. He signed *Mama* instead of *Mom*, which he only did when he wanted to make me feel special. I could feel the affection in it, his love as he spelled out the letters.

I smoothed my hand out over his chest, felt the steady thrum beneath my palm. *My heart,* I mouthed.

Evan reached out and set his on mine. *My heart,* he mouthed the same.

Smiling down at him, I brushed my fingers through his hair, leaned up, and pressed a lingering kiss to his forehead.

I leaned back so he could see my mouth. "I love you."

I LOVE YOU THE MOST, he signed.

ARE YOU SURE ABOUT THAT? I teased.

Because it wasn't possible.

Not when he was my center. My earth, moon, and sky.

****

Night seeped in through the window and branches scraped at the eaves in the slight breeze. The tiny lamp on my nightstand cast my bedroom in a golden glow.

Basking it in warmth.

I lay propped against the white fabric headboard, surrounded by pillows and huddled under my comforter, reading some smutty novel Jenna had shoved at me and insisted I read.

It wasn't helping things. Not with the riot that had been ignited in my body. Not after Kale had taken me to a place where I'd touched on the most intense kind of beauty.

My phone lit up on the nightstand, vibrating on the wood.

Unease slammed me when I glanced at the clock.

Twelve thirty-three.

It wasn't all that late, but . . . still. I hated that I was instantly on guard. Continually on watch. God, how I was counting the days to that court date circled on the calendar. Two months and all of this would be over, and then Evan and I could finally fully move on.

But Jenna was right.

It was time I stopped tiptoeing and allowing Dane to control me in the way only he could—through fear and apprehension. The asshole knew my weakness.

And my weakness was my son.

Taking in a steeling breath, I prepared myself to fight another battle in this war and swiped my thumb across the screen.

The air left me on a shaky exhale.

Not Dane. Emotion pulled tight across my ribs when my eyes moved over the text.

Kale: Your son is amazing.

That emotion climbed my throat and trembled across my lips. My tongue swept out to wet them, unsure of how to respond, wondering what good any of this would do.

Still, I found myself tapping out a reply.

Me: He's the best thing that's ever happened to me.

I almost jumped when my phone buzzed in my hand.

Kale: He looks like you. He has your eyes. Your hair. Your smile.

Kale: Your heart.

That one came in a few seconds behind. As if he'd hesitated to say it.

Hands shaking, I replied.

Me: If I could, I would give him mine.

Time spun on, me staring at my phone, wondering why the man made me feel as if I could tell him anything.

It was probably stupid that I'd even returned his text. Because we'd already established that we couldn't do this. That the timing was all wrong. And even if the timing were right, I really had no idea what Kale's intentions would be. If he even wanted to date a woman with a child. Because Evan and I? We were a package deal.

But that didn't mean my heart wasn't fluttering in its confines, legs trembling with the rush of excitement that stampeded through my body, warming my flesh.

I sucked in a breath when he responded.

Kale: I think you already have.

A wistful smile lifted my mouth. Gratefulness a shaky heave from my lungs.

It was as if he got it.

Understood the sacrifice.

I should have shut the conversation down, but instead, I was typing out another reply.

Me: He likes you.

His response was instant.

Kale: I like him, too. A lot.

A second passed and then another text came in.

Kale: Problem is, I like his mom as well. Not sure what to do about that.

Butterflies scattered.

God, what was I doing? But I couldn't stop the way my bottom lip quivered, the way my belly flipped, or the way my fingers were all too eager as they tapped across the screen.

Me: Then I guess it's an even bigger problem that his mom likes his doctor, too.

I bit my lip, knowing I needed to rein this in, so I sent a second behind it.

Me: But we can't do this, can we?

I didn't know if it was a question or a plea. Because my mind was back there, on that balcony where he'd made me feel like a woman for the first time in years. As if I'd been exactly where I was supposed to be.

As if maybe I'd belonged there all along.

His breath on my neck and his hands on my body.

My name on his tongue.

A shiver rolled down my spine and need became an achy appeal in my core.

Kale: What? Text?

I could almost see him lifting that strong brow, biting his lip as he fought a mischievous smile. It took everything I had not to imagine him doing it on his bed with his shirt off.

Me: This isn't a joking matter.

Kale: No?

Me: No.

Kale: You're right. It's not. But tell me one thing. What's the second-best thing that's happened to you? I'd bet my bank account it went down on that balcony.

Redness flushed my cheeks, and I typed out my response and hit send before I could think better of it.

Me: No man has ever made me feel the way you did.

Kale: That's because you deserve a man who will treat you right. Guessing that fucker didn't come close.

Wow.

I shouldn't have been surprised.

I'd seen it in Kale's eyes when I'd watched him come to the realization in the office earlier today. When it dawned on him exactly what was at stake.

Rage had burned across his face and tightened his hold, as if he didn't want to let me go.

Then he'd realized he had to. That we might be drawn to each other, but our paths couldn't connect.

Me: I can't do this with you. There's too much on the line.

Someday.

Someday, I could let myself get lost in the sea of a brilliant, beautiful man. Swept away. No need for solid ground because he would be my footing.

It took the longest time before a response came through.

Kale: I know. I know better. I'm sorry. I keep crossing that line when it's clear neither of us are allowed to have what's waiting on the other side.

But you make it really damned hard not to try to jump over it.

Neither of us.

I frowned at that, wondering what he meant. What would hold him back—his own circumstances or my baggage? Maybe he didn't have the capacity to be with someone like me.

Even if I weren't in the middle of a divorce, my life would always be hinged on the most perfect complication.

The center of my world a red-headed, freckle-faced boy.

A bunch of texts blipped through in quick succession behind it.

Kale: Shit.
Kale: I'm sorry.
Kale: I'm fucking this up.
Kale: I just wanted to check on you both. Tell you, you have an amazing kid.
Kale: See what you do to me? You make me lose control.

An affected smile lit on my face. I had the unsettled feeling this man could be the completion of my joy.

I let the feeling take me over, gaze moving back over his words, wishing for a way.

Then I did what I knew I needed to do.

Me: Good night, Kale.

Kale: Good night, Hope.

I started to set it aside, but it blipped again.

Kale: Good night kiss?

Oh, this man. I was right all along. He really was trouble.

Me: I don't think that's a good idea.

I hoped it came across as stern and he couldn't tell there was a giddy grin threatening to light on my mouth.

Kale: Boob shot? I'll reciprocate.

It was no longer a threat, affection racing out, twisting my lips in a ridiculous smile, my heart beating overtime.

Me: You're out of your mind.

Kale: I was thinking more along the lines of blowing yours.

Sitting in my bed, I laughed, out loud. It was as if I could actually feel his playfulness behind it. That easy confidence that had slipped into his tone.

Me: Go to sleep.

I was still wearing that silly grin when I hit send.
If only Jenna could see me right then.

Kale: If you won't blow me a kiss, tell me you'll at least dream of me?

I would not be admitting to that, though, the chances were good.

Me: Stop it.

When the next one came through, my heart grew heavy.

Kale: You're beautiful, Hope. Seriously. That's the last thing I'm going to say. Now I'm gonna back away.

I held his message to my chest and looked toward the ceiling, cherishing the words, fighting the urge to beg him not to.

Finally, I forced myself to set my phone aside.

I flipped off the lamp and curled on my side, hugging the comforter to my chest.

And it shouldn't have been possible.

Not with everything that was going on.

But that night, as I drifted to sleep, I did so with a smile on my lips.

twelve

Hope

I tucked a receipt into the register and glanced up to the next customer in line. "Can I help you?"

The man stepped forward. "Harley Hope Gentry?"

It was instant.

The apprehension that bolted through me, forcing me back a step. The fact that he used *that* last name, the one I was trying to purge from my conscious and my life and my reality, set off a deafening scream of warning sirens in my ears.

Still, I was nodding, a painful lump growing up in my throat, obstructing any words that might have passed. He shoved a large envelope my direction. "You've been served."

Tears burned, and the room spun. Violent trembles rolled through my body because this was so much like that day six months ago when Dane had rocked my world, contesting my divorce claim that would grant me full custody without support.

All I wanted was to cut ties.

Be done with it.

Give Evan the life he deserved.

I could barely clutch the envelope, my hands were shaking so bad.

"Jenna," I tried to call but my voice cracked, coming out as little more than a whisper.

She was in the seating area wiping down tables, and she jerked her attention to me. As soon as she caught sight of my expression, she started moving toward me.

What had to be fear and dread and hate contorting my face in pain.

"Can you take over for me?" I all but begged, angling my head toward the long line of customers waiting at the counter.

"What's going on?" she demanded instead.

"I don't know . . . I just . . . I need a minute so I can find out."

Her attention dropped to the envelope. Her brown eyes turned sharp as daggers, as if her glare might set it on fire.

I could only wish.

"Excuse me," the lady called at the counter, patience clearly not her strong suit.

Jenna gave me a regretful look. "Go on. I'll be right here."

With a jerky nod, I fumbled through the swinging door and staggered toward the small office area set up at the very back of the kitchen.

Barely able to stand.

I set my hand on the desk to steady myself, drawing in a few deep breaths before I forced myself to rip open the letter. My eyes raced over the words drawn up by Dane's attorneys.

Terror ridged my spine, that dread igniting in the worst kind of horror.

"Asshole," I gasped, choking, my vision turning black.

Scrambling for my purse I'd left on the desk, I dug for my phone. I could barely get my hands to cooperate enough to pull up the number I needed.

I squeezed my eyes closed as I pushed send.

I didn't have to wait long.

Dane answered on the first ring. "Ah, I see you got my present."

Present.

What did he think? That this was a joke?

Fun?

A competition?

I swallowed around the razors that lined my throat, forced out the words that scraped and ground. "Why are you doing this?"

"I told you I was finished playing your games, Harley. I warned you that if you didn't come home and stop this foolishness, you were going to regret it."

"This *isn't* a game, Dane. The furthest from it. I'm giving you an out. You and I both know you don't want Evan."

I flinched just saying it.

The years of silent abuse.

The rejection.

The disgust.

Everything was hoarse and choppy as it flooded from my mouth. "And now you're asking for full custody and a review of his medical records? Stating I'm an ill-fit mother? You don't have the first clue what his care requires."

"Hiring help has never been an issue, Harley. I think you know better than that."

Sickness roiled. "Help."

He wanted strangers to raise my son.

God. Knowing Dane, he would probably lock him away. Hide Evan and pretend he didn't exist. Put him in some institution as if he were shame.

Humiliation.

When my son was beauty and life and joy.

"When you married me, you promised you would be mine for all your days, and be clear, all your days belong to me. You think I'm actually going to let you walk away from me? You knew you had a role as my wife . . . now stop being foolish and fill it."

"I didn't marry you for that role. I married you because I *loved* you. And you promised to cherish and love me in return. In sickness and in health."

The words crawled from my throat, venom and a plea. Not for him to have a change of heart. But for him to let us go.

Dane laughed a morbid sound. One that echoed with his own grief. "I never stopped loving you."

"And you never started loving him."

Silence moved through the line, and the tears I'd been holding broke free. Hot veins streaked down my cheeks. Years of holding out for this man and the hatred that loss had left in that void.

I could feel the shift, the detached control that filled his voice. "You know how to resolve this, Harley."

Bitter laughter rumbled somewhere inside me. The disbelief. "Do you not know me at all? Do you think I will ever give in? Allow your disgusting, vile demand?"

The final stake had been driven into my faith in him that day a year ago when I'd opened our front door to find a mailman, holding out a certified letter. One that had to be signed for.

A DNR that had been drawn up for Evan. Without my knowledge or consent.

"It's time to stop propagating his suffering."

That was what Dane had said when he'd tried to force me into signing it.

Evan and I were gone the next morning.

"Why fight the inevitable?" he said indifferently, as if it didn't matter at all.

Pain leeched into my pores. Because I knew he wasn't talking about my losing Evan to him. He was talking about me losing him forever.

"I will never, ever give up hope on my son. Never. I'll die first."

I rushed to end the call, unable to listen to him for a second longer. Slipping from my shaking hands, the phone clattered to the desk, my weak knees finally giving. Back pressed against the wall, I slid to the ground. My face in my hands.

It didn't matter how hard I tried to contain them.

Sobs broke free, ripping from my throat, fed from my soul. And I swore, I was right back in the hospital on the day my entire world was ripped apart.

I shivered when the door to the private room we'd been whisked to on the maternity floor edged open.

I had no idea what was happening, though every cell in my body warned it was bad.

I'd been waiting for hours. Days, I thought. I wasn't sure. The only thing I knew was my world had stopped the second they'd taken away my infant son.

The doctor who came through the door was older, hair gray and thin, his expression stoic. Yet, I could read people well enough that I could see beneath it.

To the grim lines that had been checked. Held. As if it might make the delivery of horrible news more bearable.

Slowly, he sat next to me.

My husband was on the other side of me, the heel of one of his expensive dress shoes bobbing incessantly.

Waiting silently. Swimming in his own turmoil.

"Mr. and Mrs. Gentry . . ." the doctor broached.

I clutched my trembling hands on my lap.

"I'm sorry I don't have better news. We've discovered a severe abnormality of your son's heart."

Dizziness whipped through my head, whooshing through my body. A vortex of dread and fear and grief. The man continued to speak, attempting to explain the deformity.

But the only thing I could hear was my soul screaming, "No, no, no!"

"What does that mean?" I finally whispered through the anguish.

"We are going to have him transported to Camden Children's Hospital in Tennessee. One of the best in the nation. He'll need to undergo surgery as soon as possible. We hope to repair the abnormality, which may make it so a heart transplant isn't required."

I blinked as the term penetrated.

Heart transplant.

I jarred forward.

Unprepared.

How could this be happening? It couldn't. It couldn't.

The doctor continued speaking, "Not all of the tests are back, but we believe this is due to a genetic defect. If he survives, this will most likely present itself in other ways in the future."

If he survives.

Horror burst in my blood, and I curled in on myself, no longer able to remain upright, the overwhelming joy and love inside me shattering.

Splintering out.

I squeezed my eyes closed as the tears fell. And I issued up a million prayers. Begging for this not to be real. To go back to hours ago when I held my tiny, healthy baby boy in my arms.

"Evan," I rasped, clutching at my chest as I whimpered his name.

"I'm sorry," the doctor offered, pulling himself back to standing. "A case manager will be in to talk with you about making arrangements to get him transported by air to expedite his care."

The door swung shut behind him.

Dane jumped to his feet, the first reaction out of him since the doctor had begun speaking. But I was unprepared again, jerking in fear and surprise when I heard the crash.

The punch of his fist against the wall and the sound of his guttural shout. Then his dark head of hair dropped between his shoulders as he gasped for the air that had been sucked from the room.

I forced myself to stand. To go to him. I set my hand on his back, needing to comfort him, desperate for it in return. Needing him to hold me, support me, whisper that it would be okay.

We had to have faith. We had to. Otherwise, we'd have nothing left.

But he shocked me again when he twisted away from my touch, spinning into the middle of the room and facing me. Hatred glinted in his eyes. "Don't fucking touch me."

"Dane," I gasped, eyes pinching, a terrified kind of confusion sinking like lead to land with the fear and grief.

He hesitated for a moment before he pointed at me. "Don't fucking touch me."

He whipped away, anger and fury in his stride. He flung open the door and didn't look back before he disappeared down the hallway, leaving me standing there by myself. Knees weak. Foundation gone.

I slid down the wall and onto the ground, my hands clutching my chest that ached and moaned.

And I was sure, never in my life, had I ever felt so alone.

"Finally got the last of the customers out of here," Jenna said as she blew through the swinging door.

Shaken from the horrible memory, I jerked my head from my hands. Through bleary eyes, I stared at her. The second she saw my state, she rushed for where I was crumpled on the floor.

"That asshole. What is he spoutin' this time?" she demanded, sinking onto her knees beside me.

Unable to answer, I gasped over another sob.

"Fuck," she muttered, shifting to sit on her butt. She pulled me to her chest, wrapping me in her arms. "What did he do now?"

"He's trying to take him from me." It left me on a coarse, whimpered cry.

Anger ripped through her body, and she hugged me tighter, her mouth at the top of my head. "What's he sayin'?"

"That I'm not a fit mother. That he wants full custody." The last broke. "Oh, God—" I choked, burying my face in her neck.

"That's not gonna happen, Harley Hope. I promise you, there is no way any court is going to give that man custody."

"Why is he doing this?" I whimpered.

She squeezed me. "Because *he's* scared. Because he knows you have the upper hand. He's a pathetic rat bastard who's scared he's gonna look bad. That you're gonna expose him for the kind of man he really is. That, for once in his life, he's not gonna win. You know he can't stand the thought of that."

Unease spun through my spirit. I couldn't escape the feeling that it was more than that. That his intentions were different from what I could see.

Crueler.

Uglier.

He wanted me back in that house, and I didn't know why. Not when I knew he wanted us gone.

Swallowing hard, Jenna drew me closer. "I promise you that those courts are going to see him for what he is. You have given up your entire life for that little boy, and that piece of crap hasn't given up a damned thing. And every single person who knows is gonna sit up on that stand and testify to it, including your son. And where do you think he's gonna want to be?"

I knew it. I knew all of it.

"What if he finds out what we did?" The words were nothing more than the gasp of a breath.

Wisps of terror that spun through the atmosphere and clawed at my spirit. My spirit that burned to be set free. Gone to a place where I might land in the arms of a man who would hold me up rather than beat me down.

God.

It was stupid for me to even be thinking about another man when I was in the midst of mayhem. But every day that'd passed since Kale had last texted me made me wish for him a little more.

Someday.

Someday.

"He won't," she said vehemently, though there was no missing the spark of fear in her eyes. "He won't. Okay?"

"I've always had to be the strong one, Jenna. The one who had faith." I fisted both my hands over my heart. "I never stopped believing my son would live when everyone else had. And somehow . . . somehow this time, I'm petrified I'm going to lose him in a way I never imagined."

"That's because you're being attacked. Your heart and your faith and your family, all your beliefs, everything you've worked for . . . it's being attacked. But this is a battle you and Evan are going to win. And we're gonna fight it however we have to."

I pressed my fingertips into my eyes and gave a sharp shake of my head. "I can't even stand the thought of Evan having to spend one night in that house."

"He won't have to. And seriously, this is Dane we're talking about. He'd probably have Evan for one hour, and the pussy would send him home to you. Evan always did put a cramp in his style. Honestly, I don't think he ever thought you'd let it get this far, and he's just trying to put the pressure on you. I'd bet my life he's too much of a coward to see this through."

Anger blew out of me on a rigid huff. "Or *Mommy Dearest* will pay to have someone come in and care for him full-time." Locked away like some modern-day flower in the attic. "Or send him away like she suggested we do when he was born, you know, because Evan is a 'bad representation of the Gentry name.'"

I could feel the consequences of what we'd done barreling forward, the memory of the moment I'd felt so helpless I'd been left without a choice.

"That's crazy," I had said.

But it didn't matter how crazy Jenna's suggestion had seemed, my heart had screamed it was the only way. That I had to take action and do it then. I could no longer sit around and wait.

"How?" I'd begged through my tears while I'd peeked over at my precious son who'd been fast asleep on Jenna's couch since we'd gone to her house to find escape.

She'd grimaced. "I might know a guy who can help."

I'd started down a path I thought I'd had to take. My actions illicit as I tried to hide Evan away from the clutches of Dane.

Illegal things I never could have imagined myself doing a few years ago.

Getting myself in deeper and deeper each day that passed.

But protecting my son was worth any crime or sin on my part. But Dane was asking for the records.

Dread coiled and twined. A downward spiral.

God.

What was I going to do?

"Hey. This doesn't change anything. You don't let him beat you down or scare you, because that's what he wants. You and Evan are gonna keep moving forward. Do you understand what I'm saying?"

I nodded minutely, the tweak of my lips thankful. So grateful for my friend who'd stepped up, my rock when I'd needed to be Evan's.

She brushed back the hair matted to my face. "Okay, then. It's settled. No more tears. What do you say we go pick up Evan the Great? I'm taking you both to dinner. My treat."

Sniffling, I nodded again. "Okay."

thirteen

Kale

Willpower was a tricky bitch.

Out of the gate, you felt strong in your resolution. Confident. Insolent, even.

You could so absolutely do this.

No question.

It was in the bag.

Easy-peasy.

Whether you had committed to quitting smoking or cutting your calories in half or giving up the bottle, that first moment you made that promise to yourself?

You were almost on a high. On top of the world. A champion.

Your only focus was why you should do it and why it would benefit you and the people around you.

No thought given to how hard it was actually going to be.

You hadn't considered that when you woke up in the morning, it'd be the first thing on your mind or that it'd track you through the day. No deliberation of the niggling sensation at the back of your brain, constantly whispering that you were missing something.

And you definitely hadn't given thought to the reality that when you tried to go to sleep at night, it'd be the only thing you could see when you closed your eyes.

But I did it.

I drove past that little shop every damned day for nearly two weeks and barely gave it a glance. And by the time I passed by it in the evening, I'd gun the accelerator, flying right on by, jaw rigid and teeth clenched, refusing to look that way.

Not allowing myself to wonder if she was still behind the doors. If she was smiling. If Evan was with her.

When I crawled in bed at night, I pretended she wasn't the only thing I could see. Pretended I didn't wonder if she was wet and thinking of me.

It was for the best.

It was stupid to even want her, anyway. It wasn't like I was going to make something with her and that kid. A life like they deserved.

If I could even if I wanted to.

Just being around them had dredged up too many memories. Made me *remember*, and remembering fucking hurt. Gut told me if I got any deeper into Hope, any deeper into Evan, it just might ruin me.

So, I shoved that little obsession aside, buried it with the flickers of worry that kept flaring up when I thought of her shit-pile of a soon-to-be ex-husband, who was probably still giving her a hard time.

Restrained myself from looking him up so I could pay him a little visit.

None of my concern.

Right?

Right.

And then . . .

Then there was this little girl.

Five years old.

Tiffany.

Fucking adorable, black curly hair that was all kinds of wild around her chubby face.

She'd returned for her second visit with me, being worked up for intermittent high fevers that we couldn't pin down the cause of.

The whole time, she'd been completely cooperative, smiling, following my requests.

In hindsight, maybe she'd been a little too cooperative.

Because the second we'd finished, she'd looked up at me with wide, hopeful eyes and told me she'd been a good girl during her examination and she wanted to know where her lollipop was.

Of course, she did.

With my mouth flopping all over the place, I'd finally managed to tell her I'd run out.

You'd think I had single-handedly taken down the entire Disney franchise.

That'd been my breaking point.

At least I was blaming it on that.

I scrubbed a hand over my face and looked to the Alabama sky, so blue with the day. "You're an idiot," I mumbled beneath my breath before I spun on my heel and moved the rest of the way down the sidewalk.

I didn't hesitate at the door. I pulled it open and stepped inside.

Hoping I was making the right choice.

But I had no idea what else to do.

The bell chimed above when I stepped into the small shop. The second she saw me, Jenna grinned like she'd won the lottery.

But she wasn't who held my attention.

It was Hope whose mossy gaze snapped up to meet mine when she felt my presence, those full lips parting in surprise.

Hope.

Fucking Hope.

The air got thick, and I felt a little dizzy while I was standing there just inside the doorway, looking at this girl who had to be the best thing I'd ever seen.

Red hair twisted into a loose braid and pulled over one shoulder, pieces falling out everywhere, those eyes so damned green. And she was wearing this floral dress that did funny things to me, twisting me up in knots of need.

Fuck.

I wanted her.

I wanted her so damned bad I could taste it.

"Kale."

"Hey," I said, taking one step in from the door, feeling flustered and hot. So unlike me, but this girl had me outside of myself. My attention darted to the spot where the lollipops had been, a bunch of coffee mugs filling the space. "I'm out."

Hope frowned in confusion. "What?"

"I need more," I stammered.

Her frown deepened.

Brilliant.

If only Ollie could see me, he'd be giving me shit for the rest of my life.

I drew a circle in the air with my index fingers, starting at the top and meeting at the bottom.

She looked at me like she was concerned for my sanity.

Yeah.

Me, too.

"The lollipops. I'm out of the lollipops," I finally managed.

"Oh." Disappointment or surprise, I wasn't sure, but she blinked like she was rearranging the idea of why I was there around in her brain.

I guessed maybe I should have been doing that, too. Too bad all I could think about right then was stalking around the counter and propping her on it.

Kissing her and touching her and sinking inside.

All the reasons why I couldn't slammed against the visions.

Cold, stark lights. That fucking flat line.

My heart shivered in my chest, and then I was thinking about why this was bad for her, too. The fact she was fucking terrified of whatever that dickhead was demanding of her.

I'd seen it. Written all over her when she'd made that admission in the examination room. When she'd told me what she had to lose, which was so much more than I could even

132

comprehend or imagine. Knew I wasn't even close to understanding what she was going through.

The thought of that sent a fresh round of rage rushing through me.

I had this intrinsic need to know what that asshole was demanding of her, of Evan, all the while I was contending with all these images of what their lives might have been like when he was in them. If it was good or bad. If she missed him or was glad he was gone.

If he'd *hurt* them.

My nerves zapped with the threat of rage.

Fuck. I couldn't even tolerate the thought.

She smoothed her hands over her apron nervously. "I'm still out. I was planning to make some over the weekend at the house. If you want to come back on Monday, I'll have them ready for you to pick up."

Right then, the swinging door to the kitchen swung open and Evan came bounding out.

Joy.

Life.

Hope.

It swirled through the air. Filling the space.

Radiating and vibrating and confusing.

It made it difficult for me to stand, the solid ground suddenly unsteady, those memories trying to press themselves into the forefront.

His entire face lit up when he saw me, and he pushed his glasses farther up his nose with both his hands like he was making sure it was really me he was seeing.

God, the kid looked like the cutest little bug when he blinked at me from behind the thick lenses.

Heart squeezing in a fist, I lifted a hand to wave at him.

HI, he gestured. Now that I could read.

He gestured a bunch more while he mouthed, *Dr. Bryant.*

All of a sudden, he darted back into the kitchen, the door swinging behind him. In a flash, he was bursting back through, holding a big spiral-bound notebook and a marker. He went straight to the counter and started writing on the notebook.

He held it up.

What are you doing here?

Hope fidgeted beside him, her expression nearly unreadable because it said too much.

Why are you really here?

You're only making this harder.

I wish things were different.

Stay.

Carefully, I edged across the space, eyeing Hope as that energy lit between us. That insane attraction I felt when we neared.

Flares.

Fire.

Flames.

I wanted to lick her up and down. Touch her and fuck her and maybe hold her afterward.

That right there was the reason I should hightail it out the door.

Among a million others.

Instead, I accepted the marker Evan offered.

I'm out of lollipops. All the kids love them. I need more.

His attention dropped to read it and then he looked back up at me.

I swore the magnitude of his smile knocked me back a step.

REALLY? he gestured. I got that, too.

"Really," I said.

He went back to writing.

That's good because me and mom and Aunt Jenna are going to make a lot. How many do you want? Maybe we'll sell enough that there will be no more bad hearts.

I rubbed at my chest, having to wonder exactly what it was this kid was doing to mine.

That depends on how many you can make.

Lots. Do you want to help? I bet we can make a million.

Hope cleared her throat and touched his shoulder to get his attention. Apparently, she'd been watching the interaction over his shoulder. "I don't think that's a good idea. The kitchen is already going to be pretty crowded with the three of us."

She didn't even sign. She was talking to me. Expecting her son to pick up on what she was saying.

"That's okay. I get it."

Jenna made a dramatic gasping sound. Her phone was held out in front of her, her eyes wide in an exaggerated way. "Oh goodness, Harley Hope, I am *so* sorry . . ."

Harley Hope.

A smile edged my mouth at her full name, and I tucked away that information for another day.

Jenna continued without pausing, "But I just got word Maw-Maw needs her hair done up real nice for bingo tonight, and I'm not going to be able to help like I promised. Apparently, there's a man she has her sights set on. I'm afraid I'm going to have to bail. I feel so bad."

Hope shot her a look that promised she *was* going to be sorry before saying, "Evan and I can handle it. No worries."

Jenna's brow twisted in horror. "Are you sure? That is a lot of work."

"Completely sure. We have all weekend."

"Oh, I have a good idea!" Jenna turned her gaze on me, forged innocence written all over her face. "Why don't you help? You're the one who needs them, after all. Plus, Hope here is gonna have all these supplies she needs to carry in, and they're super heavy, and she's had a really long day here at the shop. It might be nice for her to have a big, strapping man help her out."

Could the girl be more obvious?

She shot me an exaggerated wink.

Apparently, she could.

Hope hissed something under her breath and smacked Jenna's hip. Clearly, she thought I couldn't see it, so I stood there trying not to laugh.

But it was Evan who was suddenly jumping up and down and waving his arms, the nod of his head about as overdramatic as the ridiculous story Jenna had just told.

That was what nailed me to the spot.

The little lip-reader.

Had the feeling he always knew more than people gave him credit for.

I rubbed a hand over my mouth.

Not knowing what to say.

Because there was Evan basically begging me to, and Hope begging me with her eyes to stay away.

I glanced around at all three faces that were waiting for me to respond.

It didn't seem all that hard to figure out.

How could devoting a Friday night to helping out a single mom ever be considered bad?

I had been the one who walked through the door, asking for the favor. The one who'd come here after I'd committed to stay away and put Hope on the spot, telling her the kids needed more candy.

I'd lend a hand. Help out. Put a smile on the kid's face and make a fat contribution to their charity when we finished.

That was it.

Nothing more.

Easy-peasy.

Because just like that willpower?

Right then, I was riding a high.

Resolved.

Confident.

I could do this . . . said every addict trying to give up a vice.

fourteen

Kale

It was five after six when I pulled up in front of Hope and Evan's house.

The sun was a blazing halo that hung low on the Alabama horizon. Hazy rays glinted through the leafy trees and cast the air in shimmers and shadows.

The second I stepped from my car, the overpowering scent of honeysuckle hit my senses, the muggy summer in full bloom.

My heart rate kicked. A jumble of nerves and uncertainty.

That didn't stop me from heading for the white-picket fence that enclosed the perfectly hedged lawn.

Still, each step wound me tighter, ribbons of anticipation and greed.

I opened the short gate and strode up the walkway that cut through the center of the front yard, passing by the two massive trees on either side of the sidewalk that stood like proud soldiers guarding the quaint house.

Never slowing, I bounded up the two steps and onto the white porch. Potted plants were set up all over the place, vines growing over the railings, the door painted a bright red to give it a splash of color.

The little house screamed charm and comfort. It was the kind of place where you liked to imagine a happy family rested behind its doors, all of them curled up on the couch where they watched a show together.

My chest tightened, my mind wandering with questions, knowing I didn't really have the first clue about their lives. Wondering if it was good. If they were really happy.

This antsy need lit up my veins with the drive to offer them some of it.

Fuck. I really was losing my mind.

I rapped at the door.

A riot of footsteps thudded on the other side, frantic fingers flying through the locks. I thought maybe I had some of my answer to that when what had to be the happiest kid in the world grinned from the other side when the door swung open.

Wavy red hair and freckled nose and hopeful green eyes.

HI, he signed, bouncing on his toes, putting all kinds of emotion into that simple gesture.

My heart did that wobbly thing in my chest. Like it no longer fit. I gave an awkward wave. "Hey, Evan, how are you?"

He gave me a thumbs-up, and I had no idea why I found that so cute.

Felt like he was trying to make things as simple for me as he could—because God knew I was the one who had no clue what the fuck he was doing—the same as when he waved his hand in the air, indicating for me to follow.

I glanced around, quick to take in their home.

The front door opened to a small foyer that faced an arch that led to the living space, which was lined by crown molding.

An overstuffed couch covered in pillows and throws took up most of the room, two armchairs situated on either side, and a plush area rug covering the dark hardwood floors. All three pieces of furniture were angled so each seat had a good view of the television.

But none of that was the focus. No, because it was abundantly clear where all Hope's attention was aimed.

Pictures of Evan as far as the eye could see. Every surface and wall. A mismatch of frames and sizes.

Organized like art.

Like praise.

Evan darted down a short hall to the right, and I tore myself away from the scene in front of me and followed.

My stride easy until I damned near tripped over my feet when he led me through a smaller arch and into the kitchen.

Because Hope was bent over, wearing that same lust-inducing dress she'd had on earlier at the shop. She was digging into a bottom cupboard, her perfect, round ass swaying from side to side.

That ass I wanted to sink my teeth into.

Mouthwatering.

Every bit as much as whatever that insanely delicious smell was that filled the air.

Hearty and thick and warm.

She jerked around when she heard us walk in behind her. Green eyes went wide in her own kind of shock, like even though she expected me, she was still unprepared.

And that unbridled connection I felt to her every time I was in her space . . .

It surged.

Free and fast.

Rushing across the floor before either of us had the chance to find our footing.

Invading and penetrating and capturing.

Attraction and need.

This insane desire that threatened to get the best of me.

But that wasn't why I was here, so I tamped it down.

Clearing my throat, I pinned on an easy expression. That was the only way I was going to make it through this without having her on that counter, her legs around my waist, mouth devouring every inch of her.

"Hey, Shortcake." I stretched out my arms, the sleeves of my button-up rolled up my forearms. "I'm here and at your disposal. Whatever fits your fancy. Don't be shy. Use me up."

For a few beats, she breathed deeply. Like she needed to find her axis the same way I just had to do.

Beating the attraction down.

Both of us coming to the same place. The reason I was there.

To give something back when these two so clearly gave and gave.

I watched as her shoulders relaxed and amusement fluttered across those plush, pink lips. "Watch yourself, Dr. Bryant. You call me Shortcake one more time, and I'll have you out back mowing my lawn."

"Is that a threat? Come on, tell me you can do better than that."

She grabbed mitts and opened the top oven, because even though the girl's house was modest, the kitchen was not.

Gourmet might have been an understatement.

She had one of those huge industrial refrigerators and a double oven to match. Everything white and country and oozing the same kind of charm that seeped from her pores.

She leaned over and pulled out a casserole dish.

Good God. I almost blacked out.

Lush red hair falling around one shoulder as she leaned down, back arching just a fraction, the profile of her face revealing that button nose and pouty lips and dimpled chin.

She glanced at me from over her shoulder. "Oh, Dr. Bryant, you are heading into dangerous territory . . ."

My eyes raked over her body. Didn't I know it.

"I just might have a to-do list that is begging for attention. Considering I have no 'Honey,' it's grown about fifteen miles long," she teased, and I realized how much I liked it when she did.

When she felt comfortable enough to let go of a little of her worry when she was in my presence.

I flexed my arms. Satisfaction lined my insides when her attention went there, her breaths coming shorter and shorter. "Are you asking me to rescue you again, Shortcake? Bring it on, baby. Sir Bryant, remember? I'm obligated to do anything for my princess. And believe me, I won't consider it a burden."

Evan was suddenly right in my face, holding his pad up for me to see it, jarring me back into the reason I was there.

Which was absolutely not to flirt with his mom.

With all his stealth lip-reading, I could only pray the kid couldn't pick up on innuendo, too.

He jabbed at the page with his forefinger, brows rising high.

Hey, I thought we were making lollipops?

Forcing myself to stop looking at his mother, I chuckled at the way Evan was staring up at me like he'd be all too happy to put me in my place.

This time, I didn't even try to stop myself from ruffling my fingers through his hair.

Grabbing his notebook, I headed over to the island. He scrambled onto a stool right beside where I stood so he could read as I wrote.

Don't worry, buddy. I am here to make lollipops.

Knew he could read my lips, but something about communicating with him this way made me feel like I was talking directly to him.

I looked up, made sure Evan wasn't paying attention, and said, "But if your mom wants to put me to work after we're finished, she totally can. I'm all hers."

Fighting laughter, she narrowed her eyes at me. "I'm pretty sure these lollipops are going to keep you plenty busy. They are a lot more time-consuming than you can imagine. By the end of the night, you'll be regretting agreeing to come help. Begging for someone to put you out of your misery."

"That's where you're wrong. I can go all night."

Damn it all, I just couldn't help myself. Not when it came to her. Not when I knew that redness would go flushing up her neck and splashing on her cheeks.

Sweet.

Heat.

"Awful sure of yourself, aren't you, Dr. Bryant?" The words fell from her lips, throaty and low.

As she rounded the island, my attention swept from her legs, to the swish of her hips, and to the sway of her ass. She hiked up on her toes and grabbed three plates from a high cupboard.

"I'm one-hundred percent confident in myself, Ms. Masterson. I wasn't granted *knighthood* without reason. And I believe we've already talked about my stamina."

This time, she did laugh, shaking her head. "You are the cockiest man I've ever met."

She glanced back at me. Playful and sexy and the best thing I'd ever seen.

This woman was a vision. The kind of face that hit me right in the gut. Because there was no question she was stunning.

But it was the sheer goodness radiating from underneath that absolutely made her glow.

"Don't ever mistake confidence with arrogance. They are two very different things," I told her. Tension throbbed, clinging to the air and rippling with unspoken things.

Like she was issuing a secret, saying she'd really like to experience what that might be like.

"Shall we get to work so I can prove it?" I asked, not even sure what I was asking anymore. Knowing I just kept getting myself deeper and deeper. But I didn't know how to stop myself when I was around her.

She walked back to the island. Evan had his head down, scribbling something across the page. She set the plates on the counter and pressed her hands to either side of them, the swell of her tits just peaking over the neckline of her dress.

"Dinner first. You're going to need your energy."

Favorite food?

Reading his question, I pursed my lips in playful contemplation before I said, "Pizza."

I made sure Evan, who was sitting next to me at the table,

could see my lips clearly.

Favorite car?

"Uh . . . foreign or American?"

He studied me through his thick glasses, so damned cute I was having a hard time focusing on making the candy. Having a tougher and tougher time keeping it at bay, the affection for this kid that just kept growing and growing.

American.

"Well, that's easy then. A 1968 Shelby Mustang."

Whoa, he mouthed, nodding his agreement. *Mine, too.*

"Really . . . are you sure you're not just trying to copy me?" I would have written it down, but I was wearing plastic gloves that were covered with melted sugar.

Across the table from us, Hope was over there, grinning this affected, sweet grin as she worked.

Her expression beneath the light pouring in from above shot straight through the center of me. The girl looked so damned happy while she listened to the interrogation Evan had been giving me for the last twenty minutes.

I'm not a copier!

He angled the pad of paper in my direction before widening his eyes and giving me a little shake of his head.

Like I already should have known.

I grinned at him. Of course, I did.

My expression must have assuaged him, because he was tapping the end of the marker on the pad, considering his next question.

Favorite ice cream?

"Strawberry."

It was out without a thought, and my gaze immediately darted to Hope across the table.

Maybe just so I could catch the blush heating up on her cheeks.

Obviously, she knew exactly the direction my thoughts had gone spiraling.

To strawberries and cream and all things sweet.

The way I wanted to lick her up and down. Go back to that night when she'd been in the palm of my hands and my name had been a whimper on her tongue.

A curl of lust threatened, and I tamped it down, refusing to go down that path, yet somehow, feeling like *going there* was inevitable at the same time.

Evan's hand flew across the page.

Are you my mom's boyfriend?

Okay, then. Apparently, I wasn't doing that bang-up of a job keeping my thoughts to myself.

I stopped what I was doing and shucked off the gloves, eyeing him as I grabbed the pad.

Why would you say that?

His answer was swift and honest.

Because when you look at her, you smile like you think she's pretty.

Damn, this kid saw things in a way unlike no other kid I'd ever met.

Keen and smart and discerning.

I hesitated for only a second before I wrote out my response.

That's because she is pretty.

Evan was grinning when he looked over at her before

scratching something on the pad.

My mom is the prettiest mom in the whole world.

"What are you two over there gossiping about?" Hope asked, leaning farther over the table so she could sneak a peek at our private conversation.

That subtle blush blossomed when she saw the truth of what her son and I had been discussing.

"Oh, you two stop it. Every eight-year-old boy thinks his mama is the prettiest in the world until he gets to be a teenager, and then he decides to pretend like she doesn't even exist." It was all a gentle chiding.

NO WAY, he signed. *MY FAVORITE* was as close as I could get to figuring what he'd said.

Which made perfect sense, considering her smile turned so damned soft I felt something inside me melt just looking at the two of them.

MY HEART. That I got, without question, Evan's little lips moving as he looked at his mother, his little hand fisted over his chest.

Hope gestured the same, touching her chest, her gaze adoring.

My insides clenched almost painfully. Something that beautiful was hard to take in. The bond they shared. How was it possible I was goddamned terrified of it and drawn to it at the same time?

Evan looked back at me before he scribbled quickly.

Is she?

Was it regret I felt when I took back the marker and started to write?

No, Evan. We're just friends.

Another pass of the marker.

Are you my friend?

This kid.

Yeah, Buddy. We are definitely friends.

Sitting there, I didn't know why that didn't seem like enough.

I shoved the feeling off and poked him gently in the side. "Now get to work, little slacker."

He laughed, that rasping sound coming from his mouth, his smile so bright, his lips moving between the juts of laughter as he wrote.

I'm not a slacker.

No.

Not even.

But if I spent more time in their space, I was going to be a goner.

And I wasn't sure *my heart* could take that.

"You were not joking." I glanced over at Hope, who was standing hunched over the table and carefully winding the long ropes of colored candy into circles before she pressed sticks into their bases.

Why I was whispering, I didn't know.

But somehow it fit the mood the long night had slipped into.

The quiet vibe that had taken over the space.

"Where's that stamina you were bragging about a few hours ago?" It might have been a tease if the words hadn't have been so strained, so weighted in her own exhaustion.

A light chuckle rumbled out. "Guess I shouldn't be so sure of myself, after all. Some things are harder than they look."

She flinched with the double-meaning of it.

Both of us painfully aware of the other.

Like each of our movements barreled across the table.

Ricocheting and compounding.

We'd been at it for hours.

My fingers were sore, and my back hurt from leaning over for so long.

Heating the sugar and corn syrup on the stove.

Adding the flavor and the colors.

Rolling it into ropes.

Twisting them into circles.

Pressing the sticks into the bases.

It was tedious and time-consuming, and we most definitely hadn't come close to making the *million* Evan thought we would.

Still, we'd made a ton. Trays of them sat on every surface in varying degrees of readiness. Cooling before they could be wrapped in clear wrappers so the ribbon and stickers could be affixed, which was actually Evan's job on this makeshift assembly line.

Evan, who was fast asleep on the couch. Three hours before, he'd claimed he needed a break. Thirty minutes later, I'd tiptoed to the living room to check on him, only to find him curled under one of the throw blankets on the couch, his glasses askew, mouth open as his small breaths filled the air.

I'd taken his glasses and set them on the coffee table, somehow knowing I was crossing far too many lines when I pulled the blanket over his shoulders, affection so thick in my chest I could almost taste it.

I couldn't stop it.

Not after having what had to be the most amazing night of my life.

Hours spent with him and his mom. With his trusting smile and open, incredible mind. With their amazing connection. Their love so free. Unconditional.

With Hope's heart shining so bright, her body a stunning distraction.

Light and life and belief.

Yeah. I loved seeing it with Rex and Rynna. Their happy family. Didn't know of many people who deserved it the way they did.

But that experience was always me on the outside looking in. Doing my best to be there for them when they needed me.

Tonight, I'd felt right in the middle of it.

A partner to it.

A part of it.

It was stupid.

I hardly even knew them.

But standing there looking down at him, I'd been wishing things could maybe be different. I'd been wishing that fate wasn't such a cruel bitch to send me these two when I couldn't keep them. Shouldn't keep them.

Because everything felt too close and too raw and too real.

Besides, I knew Hope was struggling to deal with something bigger than I fully understood.

My bones howled with the warning that I shouldn't even be there. But my spirit was demanding I stay. That I explore whatever was happening between us. It felt too important to ignore.

The awareness of it had seeped into the atmosphere when I'd come back into the kitchen and told Hope he was asleep.

All the playful easiness from earlier had been erased.

In its place was an intensity that slowed the atmosphere. The room echoing with what-ifs and questions and hunger. This blinding need that tugged and pushed and bound.

"It's really late, Kale. You should go home. I never expected you'd stay this long."

I glanced at the clock. "It's barely one a.m. on a Friday night. That's still early."

I attempted a smirk that fell flat.

She gave a little huff. "I bet. Though, I'm sure you are much more accustomed to putting that stamina to better use on Fridays in the middle of the night. You regretting it yet, Cowboy?"

My mind blazed right back to that Friday two weeks ago.

I could hear her.

Taste her.

I angled my gaze her direction, pinning her with my stare,

voice going deep. "My only regret is you not having the chance to experience it yet."

"Kale," she whispered, her fingers fumbling as she wound the candy. "Don't do this."

"I'm not the one who's doing it, Hope. Seems to me it's already there, whether we give it permission to be or not."

She blinked, trying to concentrate on finishing one of the last lollipops. I still could see the small tremble on the corner of her delicious mouth. "You're right. It's there. I just wish it would have come at a better time." I could see it, the fear that suddenly blistered across her flesh, the way those eyes glinted beneath the light with the moisture that had instantly gathered.

Rage.

It burned.

Immediate.

Hardening every place inside me. The sudden, consuming need to wrap both of them up and protect them.

"What is he asking?" I pushed out through gritted teeth, trying to keep myself cool and composed.

Impossible.

She exhaled a harsh breath, eyes moving to the archway to ensure Evan was still asleep before she looked back at me. "I'm not sure I should be telling you any of this."

I blinked, swallowing back the fury, something that was typically so foreign for me. I was the laid back one. The one who found the good in all situations.

But whoever that piece of shit was had the power to obliterate that.

My teeth gritted. "Why not?"

A small gesture of her chin as she said, "For starters, you basically look like you want to up and murder someone at the mention of my ex."

"That only seems natural."

"What's that?"

"Wanting to protect you."

She dropped her gaze back to her work, and I reached out, touched her hand from across the table. "I want to know, Hope.

You can trust me."

Her eyes squeezed closed, like she wanted to disagree, or maybe like she wanted to run and hide, obviously struggling around the fear that had taken her whole.

"He wasn't a good dad?" Obvious, I knew, but I needed the verification. Her proof. Because I was feeling things I hadn't ever felt before.

A wild kind of protectiveness.

A savage kind of possessiveness.

She rasped a hoarse, unamused laugh, as she peered over at me.

"No, Kale, he wasn't a good dad."

Violence curled my fists. The itch to get up. Hunt him down.

"And I know what you're thinking . . ." she rushed. "It wasn't physical. It was . . ."

I attempted to keep my voice steady, but it tremored with barely contained fury. "What? You can tell me anything."

Fuck.

Deeper and deeper.

I couldn't stop.

She looked over at me.

Hopelessly.

Which just about fucking killed me.

"He rejected him as his child the second we found out about his heart condition."

My curled fists tightened. The tight rein I had on my anger slipped, just a fraction. "How could he do that?"

It wasn't even a question. I just couldn't fathom a father rejecting that kid.

That amazing kid.

An old kind of sorrow shook her head. "At first, I thought he was in shock. Processing it in his own way. But time wore on, and it only got worse and worse. The only thing he cared about was inheriting his grandfather's company, working day and night, his life consumed with earning that spot. Wanting the *money*. That became the only thing his life was about. I tried to hold out faith until there wasn't any faith left to hold on to."

Her tongue darted out to wet her lips, and she pressed the stick into the last lollipop, sinking into a chair from where she was standing.

Like she couldn't remain on her feet anymore.

"He—" She slammed her lips together and harshly shook her head, like she was about to admit something and then stopped herself. She hesitated for a couple seconds before she tentatively cut her gaze my direction, admitting what she thought she could, "It all finally came to a head a year ago, and I knew I couldn't keep my son in that house for a second longer."

Without a doubt, she was keeping the details veiled. Hidden. But I wanted to know it all. Every element. Fuel for the hatred that coursed and raced.

She cleared the thickness from her throat. "I packed our things and left. We were hiding out at Jenna's house, and of course, he showed up there demanding for us to come home. She threatened to call the police if he tried to get through her door. I petitioned for divorce. I asked for full custody and nothing more. I'd saved enough that I could put a down payment on this little house. I didn't want his support or his time or anything because he has never wanted anything from Evan. All I wanted was a quiet separation and our freedom."

Lines of pain tweaked all over her face, her voice rough. "I did what I thought I had to do, Kale."

There was so much in that statement. Something she wanted me to know and couldn't bring herself to say.

Anger swelled in the room. A swilling wave threatening to take me under.

Because this? I didn't know if I could handle it. Hearing about someone doing either her or Evan wrong.

Her inhale was sharp. Cutting. "He fought me from the beginning . . . saying I would regret it if I left him. I told him the only thing I wanted was my son free of his influence, so he did the one thing he knew would hurt me most . . ."

Head dropping, she choked as tears streaked down her face. When she finally looked up at me, her eyes were nothing but devastation. "This last week, I received a counter to my divorce claim. He's asking for full custody. The whole point of my leaving was to remove Evan completely from his life, protect him, and now he's trying to take him away from me."

My teeth ground as that rage clattered around my ribcage, and I couldn't remain sitting any longer. I was moving around the table. My discarded gloves hit the floor a split second before my knees did, and then I was cupping her face, urging her to look at me. "There is no chance on this earth that any court would declare you an unfit mother, Hope. None. I don't want you to worry about that."

Sniffling, she gave me one of those believing smiles, the kind that made her glow.

Sunshine.

Could feel it heating those vacant, dead places inside me. That place riddled with fear when all I'd ever wanted to be was the one who was brave.

The goddamned hero.

Or maybe it was the hatred that flamed. Hate for a man I hadn't even met. A man who was the one who was going to be feeling all the *regret* if we ever crossed paths.

"That's what Jenna keeps saying, and I'm trying to cling to that belief."

I ran my thumb under the hollow of her eye and then dropped my hands. "Good. Believe it. Hold on to it. Don't ever, *ever* give up on hope."

She smiled this wistful smile. "My heart has always been hung on hope."

My chest squeezed. Because I got it. She was an incredible woman who carried her entire world on her shoulders. And, fuck, I wanted to bear some of that weight.

I knew I didn't deserve the jealousy that raved through my insides. But it was there. Alive and thriving. "So, if he rejected Evan, why the hell would he want custody?"

A shrug of her dainty shoulders and a tug of her bottom lip between her teeth. "Part of it is because I left him. Because of his pride. But I can't help but feel it's more than that. He says he still loves me, but then he always blamed me."

"That Evan was sick?"

Her nod was shaky. "We didn't know anything was wrong until Evan was two days old. He was this perfect, tiny thing. Small. So small. But the doctors didn't seem to be all that concerned. Until the nurse listened to his heart on his final check when we were being discharged from the hospital."

Her voice trembled, taken back to that day. "They flew him to Memphis to the big children's hospital there. He had his first heart surgery when he was five days old. *Five days old.*"

Hope clutched her chest. "I've never been so scared in all my life. They tried to repair his abnormality, hoping it would be enough for him not to need a transplant, but they didn't give us a lot of reassurance that it would. They told us to prepare for the worst. They told us his condition was typically caused by a genetic defect, and that if he did live, then we should expect it to also present in other ways."

Images flashed. My greatest loss. My biggest regret.

I sucked in air against the memories, trying not to compare the two. But it was so fucking hard. So close. Too similar. Still, it didn't seem to fucking matter because all I wanted was to move closer, hold her, take the turmoil away.

"Hope," I murmured, shifting farther around so I could see her better, see the brilliant love that shined on her face.

Really, I didn't even have to look.

Because I could feel it.

Bounding from the walls. She gave a soggy smile. "I didn't accept what they said, Kale. I knew my baby would be just fine. That he would grow and love and live. And that the world might see him differently, but he was exactly how *he* was supposed to be. I won't lie and say it was easy, because those were the most difficult, terrifying months and years of my life. But never—not once—did I give up hope."

"And that hope shines right out of him," I said.

Her face pinched. "But his father . . . his father didn't get the perfect son he demanded. He refused to be tested to see if he carried the gene. Telling me it was bullshit. That we should *let him go* and try again."

The last tore from her throat on a cry. On the hurt and wounds the bastard had inflicted.

That rage.

It blistered.

Blinking through her tears, she dropped her gaze, her chest heaving, before looking back at me.

Destroyed.

Her expression was nothing but desolation.

"I took Evan away because he wanted me to sign a DNR. If Evan falls ill again, he doesn't want us to fight to save him. I can't let that happen. I did what I *had* to do." She begged the last. Like she was pleading for me to understand.

I choked out this sound that verged somewhere between horror and the threat of revenge.

"Fuck," I muttered, trying to process. To make sense of what all of this really meant.

Monster.

That vile bastard was nothing but a monster. I hated him.

But I didn't know how to say it. How I would get out of it if I stepped in the middle of it. But that was what I wanted to do. I wanted to get in the ring and beat the piece of shit bloody.

Her expression shifted into one of stark vulnerability. "But you've probably already read all of this in his records, haven't you, Dr. Bryant?" She said it like she wanted to attempt a tease, before she fell back into somberness. "You probably understand it better than I do."

I let a small smile tweak the corner of my mouth. "Well, I knew some of it. But his records never said anything about his father being a douchebag who needs to be taught a few lessons about being a man."

She stumbled over a small laugh. "Well, I wish they did. I could use it in court."

"Done," I said, forcing a grin before I sobered again, studying her expression.

"So, really, he's just doing all of this to threaten you? To force you into doing what he wants?"

He wanted her.

But not Evan.

What a sick fucker.

A tremor raced her throat when she swallowed. "I have no idea what he really wants, Kale. I don't even think he knows. And the only thing I want is him to leave us alone. Let us live."

I took her face between my palms again, making sure she was looking directly into my eyes before I said, "You are, Hope. You are living and giving your son the best kind of life. He's the happiest kid I've ever seen."

"He's the best thing that ever happened to me," she whispered. I did my best to tame the overwhelming feeling that raced my veins.

Possession

Greed.

Not because I wanted to control her the way that prick tried to keep her under his thumb but because the need to protect her was almost a riot where it clamored to take hold inside me.

Raging and growing and stirring.

"Don't let him scare you. I know that's simple for me to say, but I promise you . . . you don't have anything to worry about. No judge would ever find in that bastard's favor. And if you need me to sit up on that stand and claim it, as Evan's doctor, I will."

Fuck.

This was getting messy.

So damned messy.

Because all those lines were blurring and crossing and tangling.

A fresh round of tears streaked down her face. "Thank you, Kale, but I don't know if I can ask you to get in the middle of this mess. It goes deeper than you know." Grief and fear struck on her face. "When I told you my life was complicated, I meant it, but I refuse to regret a single choice I've made in my life that I've made to protect my son. No matter what it costs me"

"Maybe you should stop questioning the lengths I'd go to in order to protect the both of you."

"You don't know what you're getting yourself into," she

whispered softly.

It was like a zap to the air.

Energy.

Need.

That tether of awareness cinching and cinching, pulling us closer until it felt like there was no space between us at all.

My fingers slipped into the silky strands of her hair.

I wanted to kiss her.

God, I wanted to kiss her so damned bad, and I knew if I did, there would be no going back.

I thought maybe she saw the hesitation in my eyes, because she cleared her throat and inched back to put some space between us.

"Let's call it a night. The rest of these need to cool before they can be wrapped, and I need to get Evan into bed. He and I can finish them in the morning. I'll drop them off to you so you don't have to bother on Monday morning."

I quirked a grin. "What, you don't want to see me walking through your shop's door on Monday morning. What if I'm having a terrible craving for A Drop of Hope?"

I let my voice twist with the tease, a distraction from the chaos staging a war in my spirit. The selfless war raging in her.

Heat rushed across her cheeks, and she peered at me, that vulnerable expression laying siege to her face.

Faith and belief.

The girl was so gorgeous that it was hard to look at her.

She let her fingertips roam the collar of my shirt, staring at the action before she met my gaze again.

Words a breathy confession. "Am I a fool to admit that the favorite part of my day is watching you walk through that door?"

"Think maybe both of us are guilty of that . . . being fools," I told her, gentling my fingers through a long strand of her strawberry hair. Through the silky softness.

Relishing.

Wanting more.

Something darkened in her gaze, and I knew she was about to dive deeper than I was ready for her to go. That she was getting ready to ask me things I wasn't ready to answer.

Because the girl could read me, too.

I edged back, hating being the asshole who shut her down after she'd just completely opened up to me. Trusted me.

But I wasn't ready to bring the darkness that lived deep inside me out into her light.

"I should go," I told her.

She nodded. "Okay. But please . . . let me bring the lollipops to you. It would make me feel better after everything you've done."

For a moment, I just stared, blinking, assaulted by the urge to ask her to let me stay.

But I had to go. I knew it. I needed to get the hell out of there before I did something I couldn't undo.

"All right then," I told her, smiling slowly as I pushed to my feet.

I stretched my hand out for her, and she accepted it.

Need.

Just that small touch had need racing through my veins, careening and curving and compelling.

My jaw clenched, and I forced myself to let her hand go once she was standing.

Hope followed me down the hall. Her presence covering me all over. Skating my skin and spinning my head.

Intoxicating.

I tried to hold my breath because I swore this girl floated on the air.

So damned sweet.

I paused in the doorway to the living room, hesitated for a beat before I went for the couch.

Before she could stop me, before I could stop myself, I scooped the kid into my arms. He made a grumpy, grumbling sound as he looped his arms around my neck and snuggled closer.

Shit. Shit. Shit.

"Kale." More fidgeting from beside me, Hope anxious and restless.

"Let me help you get him to bed," I managed, no longer able to see how the lines holding me back made any sense.

Resigned, she nodded, and I followed her when she headed through another arch and down a separate hall that led to the back of the house. We passed by one small room that was set up as an office, and she turned into the last door at the end of the hall.

I followed close behind, unable to stop myself from grinning when I saw his room.

Decorated in everything comics. From Marvel to Conan to the completely obscure.

It so utterly, completely fit this adorable kid that my heart was thumping again.

Mind spinning with impossibilities.

I laid him on his bed and stepped back so Hope could pull his covers over him. She pressed a kiss to his temple and then ran her fingers through his hair. Neither of us said anything as we tiptoed out of his room, back down the hall, and through the living room.

For a flash, my gaze darted to the far back of the living space. To the double doors I knew had to lead to Hope's bedroom.

I wanted to take her there. Lay her out. Treat her right.

Lust curled my guts. Almost painfully. No question, Hope knew exactly where my thoughts had gone. Hers right there with mine.

Desire a flood in the room. Rising so high that there was no doubt we were getting ready to drown.

Both of us going deeper and deeper into that territory where it was so abundantly clear we couldn't go.

Fisting my hands in restraint, I forced my feet to move the rest of the way across the room, back through the foyer, and out the front door.

When I stepped out onto the porch, I inhaled the cool air that brushed my heated skin and prayed it might stand a chance of dousing the fire.

I pulled in a couple deep breaths, letting the sounds of the night calm my racing heart, the bugs trilling in the trees and the leaves that rustled in the light breeze.

I turned around when Hope came out behind me and quietly snapped the door shut behind her.

Moonlight poured down on her face. Milky skin a translucent glow.

"Thank you so much for helping out tonight," she whispered, her arms crossed over her chest like she didn't know how else to protect herself.

"No, Hope, thank you. For dinner. For taking the time to make all those lollipops. For letting me experience the best night I've had in a long time."

For being you.

Her head shook, and her brow pinched. "I don't know what to make of you, Kale Bryant."

I let out the tiny huff of a laugh. "When I'm around you, I don't know what to make of myself, either." I smiled at her. "Good night, Harley Hope. Tell your little man I had the best time tonight. And you tell his mom that he's lucky he has her, just as lucky as she is to have him."

Her expression turned almost pleading.

Want and desire and that unbridled hope that radiated from her like it was a second skin.

It took everything I had to force myself to turn away and start across her porch. My footsteps echoing on the dense night.

She retreated, standing in the doorway. I could feel her staring back at me.

"Kale." I heard it at the same time that intensity swept through the air.

A bolt of lightning.

Combustion.

I turned around just as the girl spun in the doorway, coming for me.

I was already moving back that direction.

We collided.

Fire.

I hoisted her up, and her legs wrapped around my waist as our mouths crashed together.

Her tongue swept against mine.

That sweet, sweet tongue.

Frantic.

Needy.

Desperate.

Laps and licks and frenzied strokes.

Winding a hand in her hair, I kissed her just as wildly as she was kissing me. Without breaking it, I carried her back across the porch and into the foyer. Held in the protective shadows of the short hall, I pressed her against the wall.

Ground my hard-on against her center, her skirt riding up, just her underwear and my jeans separating us.

Her pussy as hot as her fingers that sank into my shoulders.

As hot as her tongue that tangled with mine.

I had no idea how I was going to make it back from this. How I was ever going to stop craving it.

"Fuck, Hope. One touch, and you are already killing me. I want to disappear in you. Sink deep inside. Get lost in your body. Tell me you want that."

God. What the fuck was I saying?

I rocked again.

Hope moaned. "Kale. Yes. Please."

"What do you need?" I mumbled against her mouth, and she was mumbling back, "Make me feel good. You make me feel good. How is it possible you make me feel so good?"

"Because I know how to take care of you. You deserve a man who will treat you right."

And I pressed myself harder against her, rubbing and rocking and driving her mad.

Which was the best kind of torture.

Complete, utter torture as she writhed and pitched and begged, the urgent thrust of her hips against my jeans and the delicious sounds from her mouth as she kissed and begged, bringing me to the edge.

That greedy, selfish place inside me roared, telling me it would be fine if I ripped open my fly and sank right in.

That she was right there.

I shoved the urge down and gave her what I knew she needed.

My hands moved to her hips, and I rode my palms up, cupping her ass so I could angle her just right.

Hitting her clit with each roll of my hips.

I was so hard I swore I was going to lose it right there.

Her nails cut into my shoulders and scratched at the back of my neck, and she whimpered, her back arching off the wall. "Kale, oh God . . . again."

I dipped down and bit her tit through her dress.

Harley Hope caught fire.

Trembles rocked through her body, vibrating through me.

Her pleasure.

The sweet, sweet heat.

I could feel it radiating from her body and into mine. And I didn't even care that I was in physical pain or that I was going to go home with the worst case of blue balls I'd ever endured.

Because watching her glow?

For a moment, the girl free and riding on ecstasy?

That was all that I needed.

She whimpered and moaned these tiny, perfect sounds, trying to keep quiet as she flew.

A stark reminder that we needed to hide.

That there was some pussy bitch out there who wanted to hurt them. Maybe not physically. But the kind of wounds he wanted to inflict cut just as deep.

I was right there to catch her when she came back down.

She was gasping tiny, uncontained breaths, her chest heaving from the wall as she struggled to find her control.

Swallowing hard, she stared at me through the shadows with a mix of awe and regret. "I lose myself when I'm with you. I am so sorry."

I think I'm already lost.

I didn't say it. I just peeled myself from her body and carefully set her on her feet. I touched her face. Softly. Hoping she got it. "For once in your life, Hope, I think it's time someone took care of you."

She set her hand over mine, pressing it tighter into her face. A blaze of affection smoldered in her eyes as she looked at me. "It feels good, Kale. You feel so good. You make me want things I know I shouldn't ask you for."

A smirk ticked up at the corner of my mouth. "I certainly hope it feels good. Wouldn't want my knightly duties to be lacking, would we?"

The redness bloomed, the freckles across her cheeks sparking against her soft, soft skin.

I ran my thumb over her swollen lips. "And believe me, Hope. You have me wanting things I know I shouldn't ask you for, either."

I looked around the enclosed space, the house blanketed by the deep, deep night. "I don't want to do anything that hurts you."

And I didn't even know what I was referring to. Putting her in a situation that might cause trouble with her ex or putting her in a situation where I bailed.

Because there I stood, tempted to tell her that her son terrified me but that I wanted to wrap him up and protect him anyway. Wanted to tell her I was terrified of failing again. That I might not be enough when I'd been struggling to be that man for all my life.

Instead, I backed away, still looking at her, my smile gentle. "Now go . . . sleep. Rest. You deserve it."

She gulped around the emotion that rippled between us.

I shoved my hands in my pockets so I wouldn't reach out and take more and headed back out the door.

"Thank you, Kale," she whispered, her soft voice riding on the night, hitting me from behind where she'd followed me out.

From the gate, I glanced back at her, at her silhouette on her porch.

The girl the best thing I'd ever seen.

"Good night, Princess," I called quietly into the night.

Then I turned and forced myself to get in my car, start it up, and drive away.

Hope

I didn't even have to look to know who it was when I heard the rustling in the foyer.

"Oh, now you decide to show up," I called, glancing at her when I felt the force of energy burst in the room.

Jenna stood in the archway to the kitchen, arms stretched out and braced on the jambs, grinning from ear to ear. She glanced around at the disaster that had become my kitchen. "Looks to me like you had it all under control."

Under control.

Right.

I didn't think I'd ever felt so out of control in all my life.

Without an invitation, she waltzed in and went straight for the coffee maker. "Besides, some people need a little nudge in the right direction."

I eyed her as I slid the wrappers over the lollipops. "And just what direction do you think you're sending me?"

She poured coffee into a big mug and then grinned at me from over her shoulder. "With the way that man looks, I'm hoping to the moon. Or maybe the stars. He does have big hands, after all . . . you know what that means."

She wiggled her fingers out in front of her.

"Jenna," I hissed. My eyes darted to Evan, praying he hadn't been paying attention. I'd already been feeling itchy this morning, unable to believe I'd let that man bring me to orgasm right out in the open.

Twice.

This time in my foyer.

A shiver blazed a path down my spine, landing in that well of desire in my belly that was getting fuller and fuller. I had no idea how much more I could take before it overflowed.

Thank God, Evan was completely occupied where he sat in the built-in booth at the breakfast nook that curved under the big window.

His focus was trained on his iPad and whatever goofy pictures he and his friend Josiah were sending back and forth over Snapchat.

Their favorite way to communicate.

"What?" Jenna defended, giving me that look. "I already checked to make sure he wasn't paying any attention."

"But still."

Her brows lifted as she dug into my fridge and pulled out the creamer. "But still, you need to lighten up. You're strung up so tight that I bet one touch really would send you rocketing for the moon."

A rush of heat flushed my skin. My thoughts were back there. To last night. God, I didn't recognize myself around that man.

Jenna cocked her head, eyes going wide before she squealed in vicarious delight. "Oh my God. Did you two do the deed? Give me the details. I want them all. Don't leave anything out. Please tell me it was right here on this counter." She smacked it with the palm of her hand. "So hot."

I shushed her, waving my hand in her face, my voice dropped to a manic whisper. "We did not do the *deed*."

It wasn't as if Evan could actually hear, but that didn't mean he wouldn't *hear*. My son was about as clever as they came and could read body language almost as well as he could read lips.

"But you did do *something*. You would not be lookin' like that otherwise, so don't try to lie." She circled her finger around me, her expression pure glee.

For a second, I hesitated before the muted words tumbled from my mouth. "He kissed me."

Okay, so he'd kissed me before. But this kiss . . .

This kiss.

There was something between us last night that hadn't been there before. Something beyond the attraction. Strong and fierce and overpowering.

My insides shook and, suddenly, I couldn't breathe. I reached a shaky hand out to steady myself on the table.

Jenna loosed a knowing smile before taking a sip of coffee. "Whoa. That must have been some kiss."

I nodded. "It was some kiss."

Kale had kissed me in a way I hadn't ever been kissed before. As if I was beautiful and right and he wanted me more than anything else.

With respect.

With adoration and desperation.

As if maybe I could be everything.

Was it foolish to want him to be that for me in return?

I sank into a chair. "I've never felt anything like it."

Jenna washed her hands and plopped down beside me, sliding on a pair of gloves so she could help me put the wrappers on the lollipops.

Her voice was quiet. "You like, *like* him?"

I nodded slowly.

I liked him.

"So much." I gave a harsh shake of my head before I peeked over at her. "Why do the best things have to come into our lives at the worst times?"

"I know sometimes it feels that way. But in the end, it turns out things happen exactly when they're supposed to."

In contemplation, I bit down on my bottom lip, wishing it were true. "Maybe. But I . . ." I glanced over at my son, my reason for living. "I just can't do anything that would put Evan at risk."

Jenna rolled her eyes at me affectionately. "Newsflash, Harley Hope, I don't think you could do anything that would put Evan at risk. Your make up just wouldn't allow it. He's always come first, and he always will. And the fact that you are even considering something with that man should tell you something."

"My instincts weren't exactly spot on with Dane."

"Dane lost his ever-loving mind, Hope. Seriously, that man was himself one day, and the next? *Poof*, he was unrecognizable. I don't think your instincts could have warned you about him."

I blinked, knowing what she said was the truth. Not that it was even close to an excuse, but I'd always known Evan's diagnosis had somehow sent my husband over the edge. Sparked a cold, cowardly wickedness in him that had been nonexistent before.

Jenna eyed me. "What about him bein' Evan's doctor."

A sigh pushed free. "I don't know. I would think . . . I'd think he'd have to stop seeing him as a patient if he were to get involved with us in any way. And the records . . ."

I gulped, fighting the sick, clawing feeling that took to my blood when I thought of the consequences of anyone finding out.

"No one's gonna find out. We're gonna make sure that divorce is final and then it won't matter, anymore. It was just temporary, Hope. You know that."

I did.

But I realized the closer Kale got, the more he knew, there was a chance I might be putting his career on the line, too.

Besides that, I hated the idea of Kale no longer caring for my son.

He was a *good* doctor.

I'd seen it the second he sat on that stool in front of Evan in the exam room.

We'd been through enough physicians that I instinctively knew when they actually cared. When they felt for their patients and would do everything possible to keep them healthy rather than treating them as another number or dollar sign.

"But honestly? My biggest concern about all of this is what Dane would do with the information if I started seeing someone. He wouldn't hesitate to use it against me. Call me a cheater."

Not to mention, the unease and obscured fear I couldn't help but notice flicker in Kale's eyes. A part of him I couldn't really see. A demon of his own. Gone before I could establish exactly what it was. As if that sea of blue suddenly went murky, muddled with questions and reservations and panic before he forced it down into a secret place.

Maybe we both were complicated.

"Pssh . . . that asshole has been cheatin' for years, Harley Hope. If he tries to use it against you, it won't take much to dig up evidence to throw down your own accusation. Maybe you returning the favor and calling him out on in it court is exactly what Mr. Limp Dick needs."

A wry grin took to Jenna's face. "Hopefully his *mama* will be there for support so she can have a front-row seat. Dane Gentry III. Heir to the Gentry fortune and lousy cheater shoots himself in five seconds. Every. Single. Time. Poor boy wouldn't know a clitoris if it smacked him in the face. Think we can bribe anyone to add in those few minor details? They may not be admissible in court, but I think it's about time someone brought that horrible *obstruction of justice* to light."

A giggle slipped free. "Could you picture his mama's face?"

Jenna made a face like she was sucking on a lemon. "Well, I never," she feigned the rich Southern accent, her hand pressed to her throat.

"I bet she never." It slipped out before I could stop it, and my eyes bugged as my hand slapped over my mouth.

Jenna busted up laughing. "Oh my God, what has gotten into you, Harley Hope?" She leaned in closer. "Tell me it's a big, huge, yummy dick."

This time I did smack her, unable to keep myself from laughing. "Jenna. What is wrong with you?"

"The question is, what is wrong with you? A man like that wants you, and you're sitting over here wrapping lollipops on a Saturday morning? Here we went through all that trouble to hire a manager to run the cafe on the weekends so we could have them off, and we are both still working. You should be spending this time *wrapping* something else."

"Oh, I think I have plenty of *wrapping* to do. We need to get all of these packaged by noon so Evan and I can drop them off at Kale's place."

She jostled her shoulder into mine. "Swapping addresses now, huh?"

I sent her a playful scowl. "Yeah, because of your meddling."

And because of the meddling, the few evenings I'd spent with Kale Bryant had come to feel more profound, more *important*, than all I'd spent with Dane combined.

"Give that man a chance. You really need to move on and find what's right for you and Evan."

The concept of that flared in my chest, pressing out, wrapping me in warm, perfect ribbons. But I had no idea what Kale really wanted. Why he kept coming through my door, shaking up my world, tempting me with the kind of pleasure I'd never known before.

And if he did want it? Us? Would it be me who hurt him in the end?

"I'm not even sure he wants a chance. He said it himself when he asked me out. He wanted one night."

"Yet, where was he last night? Here, with you, working on lollipops for your son's charity, on a Friday night nonetheless. Doesn't sound like a one-night thing to me."

Warmth fluttered in my belly.

Wings of hope.

Still, my reservations were like an updraft. "And you know me dating isn't only about me. Especially when Evan gets involved, which he already is. That man is his doctor. And Evan and I are a package deal."

"Maybe he likes the look of your *package*."

"Jenna." It was pure exasperation.

"Just sayin'."

I looked up when I felt the movement from the side. Evan was scrambling out of the nook, eyes wide with excitement as he bounced over to me, already signing frantically.

CAN I GO TO THE PARK WITH JOSIAH? PLEASE. PLEASE. PLEASE.

My phone started ringing before I had the chance to answer him. I held up a finger for him to give me a second, picked up my phone, and smiled when I saw the name on the screen.

"Chanda, hi, it seems our boys have been scheming again," I said warmly.

Chanda laughed on the other end of the line. "Well, Josiah has been begging me to get together with Evan for the last week. Richard and I thought we'd take them to the park and then have a sleepover, if that's all right with you?"

Evan was jumping around, flapping his arms, begging me. I smiled at him. "I'm thinking Evan is excited by this prospect."

I could hear Josiah shouting in the background, "Can he, Mom, can he?"

"Put me out of my misery, Hope. Tell me Evan is free today," Chanda said, nothing but affection in her voice for her son, who had to be just as eager as mine.

Light laughter tumbled out, and I ran a loving hand through my son's hair. "Of course, that would be great. I have a project I need to finish up really quick, but I can drop him off at your house in an hour."

"Sounds good. See you soon."

I ended the call, my hands quick as I spoke with my son.

PACK YOUR THINGS. YOU'RE SLEEPING OVER, TOO.

YES!

He gave a victorious pump of his fist before he was flying out the kitchen, the entire house shaking as he banged down the hall and into his room.

"Someone must be excited," Jenna said, taking a sip of her coffee.

I angled my head when another clatter echoed through the walls. "Apparently."

Jenna grinned. "I wasn't talking about him."

sixteen

Hope

I pulled into the parking lot tucked behind the rows of old buildings that ran the length of Macaber Street.

An anxious shiver ran my spine.

Nervously, I glanced between the address Kale had texted and the copper-hewn letters affixed to the back entrance of the building.

This was it.

Opening the door to my Suburban, I hopped out, doing my best not to shake like some kind of giddy fool as I rounded to the back and opened the hatch.

But that was what I felt.

Giddy.

Jenna was right.

Someone was excited.

And it was me.

He lived in a building that had to be more than a hundred years old.

Gorgeous.

Stoic.

Proud.

It was five stories high, the red bricks aged to a roughened, blackened patina. It was obviously one of the old, historic buildings that lined this street that had been reclaimed and repurposed into trendy, downtown living spaces.

Trees grew up all around its perimeter, thick trunks and spindly branches stretched wide as they lifted toward that blue Alabama sky, the everlasting scent of wild honeysuckle wafting through the warm, heated air.

I felt flushed beneath it, but I was sure it didn't have a thing to do with the sun.

I grabbed the big box, which held five hundred lollipops, balanced it against my stomach, and pressed the fob to lower the hatch.

My heels clicked against the pavement as I walked toward the building.

Yep.

I was wearing heels.

After I'd dropped Evan at Josiah's, I told myself I was just hopping into the shower to freshen up since I'd gotten a little hot and sweaty. Of course, since I was in there anyway, I shaved just about every inch of my body. Then I spent way too much time on my hair and another hour standing in front of the mirror deciding what to wear.

God, I really was in deep. Getting reckless and eager and hopeful in a way I wasn't sure I should be.

But it was there. Spinning around me. The need compelling me to step forward and take a chance. Urging me in a direction that might be foolish.

I knew I had to be careful.

But I refused to live my life walking on eggshells. A prisoner to Dane's will. I was living for Evan. I was living for myself. I was living for *us*.

At the security door, I situated the box onto my left hip and punched in the code he'd given me. There was a buzz and the metal lock gave. The door popped open an inch. I pulled it the rest of the way open with the toe of my shoe and angled through.

Inside, the bricks remained exposed, and a bunch of leather couches were set up in a common area that took up a good amount of the bottom floor.

An old-style elevator with a half-moon dial waited behind the sitting area in the middle and an open-well staircase zigzagged back and forth against the right wall.

Elevator.

Definitely the elevator.

When the door slid open, I stepped in and hit the button for the fifth floor with my elbow. The elevator lifted, bouncing and jerking as it climbed, grinding on its cogs, winding me tighter and tighter the higher it went.

By the time the opposite side of it opened at the top floor, I was a shaking mess.

I didn't know why.

But coming there felt like taking a leap.

Stepping out on a limb.

On faith.

Landing on this shimmery, fluttery feeling that promised Kale was intended to be something special to me.

Even if it might be dangerous.

I advanced into the quiet, dimly lit hall. Choking on my nerves, I turned right, passing the first apartment and heading to the second and only other one on the floor.

I paused, gathered my wits, and shifted the box to my hip before gently rapping on his door.

Two seconds later, it flew open. The sight of Kale standing there made me take a stumbling step back.

The man so beautiful.

So tall and commanding.

Jeans snug and his T-shirt tight.

Arrogant.

And somehow so fundamentally sweet.

It was written all over him when his confused gaze bounced around me, searching the hall for my son. "Where's Evan?" he asked when his attention landed back on me.

"He's spending the night at a friend's," I answered, the words rough as they pulled from my throbbing throat.

Kale's expression transformed, disappointment melting to something severe when he realized I was alone.

Seductive.

"Ah, my princess has made it to the tower. All by herself. Awfully brave."

A shy, affected smile tweaked the edge of my lips, and I peeked up at him. This man.

He made me feel . . . different.

More beautiful than I had in a long, long time.

Wanted in a way that was right and not filled with cruel intentions.

I did my best to play along with his ribbing, widened my eyes. "Um . . . I think you might have this backward. Isn't it the knight who's supposed to save the princess who's locked in the tower?"

He grinned that grin that made me weak in the knees. "Who said I'm not about to lock her up and keep her here forever?"

My tummy tightened, affection pulsing from within while I tried to maintain the playfulness this boy exuded. "Should I be scared? Here you promised you weren't stalking me. *And* I thought you claimed to be the one who wanted to save me? I'm confused."

"Yet, here you are, standing at my door, searching for a way to break into my castle and looking like that while you do it."

His gaze swept me from head to toe.

It elicited a rush of heat that climbed into the thrumming air. Awareness spun like an exotic dance, twisting through the motes that floated in the rays of sunlight that speared through his door and lit him up from behind.

A spotlight.

Undoubtedly, that was where he belonged.

Everything about him was distracting. That body and those eyes and his giving, beautiful heart.

That was the part that had me snared. Happy to get caught up in his trap.

"Touché." It played from my mouth on a flimsy, shuddered breath.

He edged forward, voice growing darker. "And don't you worry yourself, Princess, I'm all about the saving. Why don't you come inside, and I'll show you exactly what that's like? I think you might have been misinformed."

That well of desire in my belly sloshed, threatening to overflow. A few fat droplets splashed out like a drenching tease, fuel for the ache that begged for more at the juncture between my thighs.

Because he was right. All these years, I had been brutally misinformed. He'd showed me just how much so that first night out on the balcony. Again, last night. And I had no idea how much more of that education I could take before I completely belonged to him.

Before he owned me in every way.

He felt so much bigger than my tiny world. As if he were expanding it. Filling it with possibility.

So obscenely tall. Overpowering in his casual, confident way. Lean muscle that bristled when he worked with those big, big hands.

Lips full and soft and lush.

So lush my mouth watered standing there looking up at his provocative face.

I'd been right at the beginning.

The man was discord.

Chaos with an easy, arrogant smile.

A perfect, controlled disorder.

I could almost feel that broken heart already making its first, tiny crack.

A splinter that creaked through me like a warning.

Because I could resist a pretty face.

But it was the tenderness and care lined beneath his gorgeous exterior that made him truly dangerous. What had drawn me to him all along.

"I don't think that's a good idea. I think you already showed me plenty last night."

Kale pressed his hands to either side of the doorjamb, leaned in close, and whispered, "Oh, Shortcake, that was me barely getting started."

Tingles spread. A flash fire of need that raced through my veins.

That was the thing about Kale Bryant. He knew exactly how to get to me.

I pushed the box his direction. "Here are the lollipops. Thank you so much for helping with them. I wish I could express just how much that means to me."

I wished, too, that I could express to him how I was feeling more. How I felt desperate to explore and test and tease him the way he'd been teasing me.

He took the box and set it on the floor just inside his door, one of those smoldering smirks lighting at the edge of his alluring mouth when he straightened to his full, towering height.

Oh, he was dangerous to me when he got that way. Steadily winning me over. Second by second. Grin by grin. The heart beneath that chipped all the brash away.

"I can't believe I left you standing there holding that. I'm really slacking on my knightly duties, aren't I? Letting you stand there with that heavy box. The atrocity. Have to admit, I was a little distracted by the very stimulating conversation I was having. Let me make it up to you."

It was all mischief and mayhem from between those flirty lips, because he knew as well as I did that box didn't weigh all that much.

His eyes glinted in playfulness while his pupils dilated in a distinct kind of wickedness.

His expression alone invited me to partake in a thousand scandalous acts.

I wavered, rocking back on my heels. "I think I should go."

Before I fell.

It was instant, the way his hand darted out to cup my face, his voice gruff. "I think you should stay."

I watched the plea play out in his eyes.

Let me touch you.

Let me take care of you.
Let me be your hero.
Just for a little while.

A tremble ripped through my body. His touch gasoline.

Instant.

The inferno raging inside me.

My tongue darted out to wet my suddenly dry lips. "If I sleep with you, there won't be any going back for me, Kale Bryant. Don't make me fall in love with you. I don't think either of us are ready for that."

There was zero provocation in the words, no hint of a tease, just my stark vulnerability. I wrung my fingers in front of me, waiting for his reaction. The air thick. So thick I couldn't breathe while Kale stood there staring at me as something flashed across his gorgeous face.

Both vivid and obscure.

And I couldn't stop myself from letting the words tumble free. "I know what I deserve, Kale. I know who I am, even though it's only been the last couple years that I've finally stood up and demanded it."

I inhaled a harsh breath, my eyes darting across his face to make sure he understood. "What I'm afraid of is you leading me down a path I'm not sure I can travel. Because maybe I *am* the fool who loves too easily. The one who sees the best in people. The one who sees what *they* deserve. Evan's dad didn't leave me jaded. He left me knowing exactly what it is I want. And what scares me most is I see so much of what I want in you, and I'm not sure you see the same in me."

My heart clenched, and I felt another piece of my world shatter when he stepped forward and pushed his fingers into my hair. His hand weaved all the way around to hold me by the back of the head, angling me back as he pulled me closer.

Holding me up. As if he'd never let me fall.

"God damn it, Hope. You really think I don't see that in you? I have no idea how to make sense of this. How to understand what it is you make me feel. What you make me want. But it's there. Haunting me. Chasing me. Demanding more."

He gathered me closer, his nose brushing mine, his words quiet and rough. "I don't know how to stop thinking about you. About Evan."

A tremor rolled through him, and his hold tightened. "I want you in a way I've never wanted anyone. Not ever. But I'm afraid I'm not capable of being the man you see because there isn't a whole lot of that guy left. I lost him a long time ago. I live for the people around me. For my job. My friends. Their families. *My patients.* I've walked that line for a long, long time. The straight. The narrow. Never veering from my path. But as hard as I try to stop it, colliding with you feels unavoidable."

God. This incredible man.

So beautiful and giving, radiating a selfless kind of devotion behind that stunning, devastating exterior. Haunted by something he wouldn't allow me to see.

Staring up at him, I let my fingertips trail across the sharp curve of his jaw. "What about living for you?"

The chuckle that rumbled in his chest was almost dark, words back to flirting with a tease, skirting that subject that hovered around him like a dark, condemning halo. "How about I just keep showing you what you've been missing out on?"

"That hardly seems fair," I whispered, the words wisps and tendrils that got hung up on his seduction that spun around us.

He gently plucked the pad of his thumb across my bottom lip. "Just getting to touch you feels like the best thing in the world."

My heart shivered.

In affection.

In want.

In something that almost felt like despair.

"Kale." It was a murmur.

Praise.

A spark.

Because his mouth crashed against mine.

His arms wound around my waist, and he pulled me into his apartment.

He kicked the door shut behind us without breaking the kiss.

Hot hands explored. Gliding down my back. Palming my bottom. Roaming up my sides.

A moan rippled up my throat, and his tongue swept into my mouth, tangling with mine.

Needy and desperate.

Overpowering.

Overwhelming.

My head spun, and I was suddenly in his arms.

My legs wrapped around his narrow waist.

Second nature.

Exactly where I belonged.

"Hope," he mumbled at my mouth as he carried me through his massive, open loft.

The floors echoed with his heavy footsteps as they thudded across the worn, dark planks and toward the massive leather couch set up in the middle of the living space.

Pure masculine style and impeccable taste with the need for comfort at the root of it all.

Just like the man.

Setting me down on the dark cushions, he dropped to his knees on the plush white rug.

Expression predatory.

No doubt, he was preparing to devour and destroy.

He palmed my knees. The simple contact made me arch and gasp.

"It's getting harder and harder to resist you," he murmured, voice scraping and raw.

"Then why are you trying?"

Because I was already so far beyond that point. The second I stepped through his door, I knew it was over. That there was no longer any resisting.

I was tumbling.

Plunging.

Falling.

He groaned, as if my statement caused him physical pain, his blond hair striking in the late afternoon light, the curves and lines and definition of his striking face bold.

His expression enough to tear through me.

Flames licked across my skin, and just the sight of him had need coiling inside me so tightly I could barely see.

"Fuck, Hope. I want to give. You make me want to fucking give." He blinked, sucking in a breath. "Let me make you feel good. Please. I want to make you feel good."

I arched. "Nothing feels better than you."

That smirk resurfaced, whatever reservations that had lingered in his eyes eradicated, that brazen confidence riding back.

Taking hold.

"This dress. What are you wearing, baby?" He ran his hands up the outside of my thighs, under my flimsy, beige dress, the material loose but the skirt short. "God, you are the sexiest thing I've ever seen. What do you think you're trying to do to me?"

He dipped down and ran his lips along the inside of my thigh as he whispered the words. "Showing up at my house looking like this?"

I whimpered, threaded my fingers through his hair while I sank back into his couch, head rocking on the cushions as he made a delirium-inducing path upward.

Kissing up my bare thigh.

Shivers.

His mouth continued its assault, traipsing over the top of the material while his hands moved under it. He grabbed me by the outside of the thighs and dragged my bottom to the edge of the couch as he edged up, kissing higher and higher.

Over my belly that shuddered and shook.

Nose running across the top of one of my breasts.

Dipping between.

He kissed a path over my heart, which thundered and roared, until he buried his face in my neck and carved out a spot for himself between my knees at the same time.

I could feel his heat where he pressed eagerly at me.

The outline of his cock where he nestled between my legs.

Desire tumbled.

A violent twist.

Because I had never wanted a man the way I wanted him. I wanted to beg him to put me out of my misery. To release the ache. Wholly trusting in him that he would.

He leaned back down on his knees, taking me by surprise when he kissed across my belly.

Something about it so erotic that desire flooded, the feel of his mouth moving over the material driving me wild.

Both of my hands were in his hair, tugging lightly and caressing gently.

A whimper tumbled from my mouth.

"I don't know what this is, Hope." His mouth kept moving higher, whispering into the thin fabric.

My heart kicked. Bucked against its confines.

"What's happening between us. All I know is that you're making me feel things I haven't felt in a long, long time, and it terrifies me."

He pulled back and looked at me. His expression grim.

As if saying it brought him some kind of physical torment.

I wanted to ask him to show me what was hidden in his eyes. Trust me with it. Why this flirty, easygoing guy would suddenly lose himself to a place where it was dark and dismal.

I traced my fingers along the prominent curve of his powerful jaw. "Take me, Kale. Show me."

A tremor rolled in his throat, and he shook his head, dipped his face away so I couldn't see his expression.

As if he were pulling himself together. Getting himself back on that line he walked. When he looked back at me, his eyes glimmered.

Lust and need.

"You know that isn't what you really want, Harley Hope. I refuse to become your regret. But I am going to set you free. Make you scream."

He burrowed his face up under my jaw. He nipped and kissed at my pulse point, his body pressing deeper between my legs as he edged up higher.

My head rocked back, and my fingers sank into his shoulders.

A dark chuckle rumbled from his throat. "Look at you. Barely takes a brush of my body and you're already about to go off."

My arm curled around the top of his head. "That's because you make me feel something, too."

He inched back and set his hand over the thunder that beat at my chest, the intensity of his gaze meeting with mine. "Hope."

I gulped around the emotion that suddenly felt prominent at the base of my throat. "When did you lose yours?"

Because that was what came in flashes.

From the depths of this man.

Grief.

I wanted to hold it, the way he was holding me.

He groaned almost painfully before he was back to kissing between my breasts, giving me no answer, hands riding back up the outside of my thighs.

He tucked me close. Rocked against me.

Sparks and shimmers lit up behind my eyes.

He kissed across the V neckline of my dress, inching it lower with each pass. Licking across the top swell of my breast. His fingers adept as he undid the three little buttons. He showed no hesitation when he pulled the fabric down, exposing me.

Cool air hit my sensitive flesh.

I gasped.

Kale glanced up at me with a smirk, running his thumb around a nipple that pebbled with his touch. "Perfect, Hope. Fucking perfect."

"Kale."

He was going to ruin me. Save me. I didn't know. The only thing I knew was he held me in the palm of his hands.

To crush or protect.

"Hmm?" he hummed as he bent down and blew across the delicate flesh before he bit down lightly, tugging it between his teeth.

"Oh," I whimpered, arching toward him. He must have taken that as an invitation because the next second had him sucking and lapping, and both my arms were curled around his head, hugging him to me, begging him for more.

For the kind of *more* I'd had no idea I needed until Kale

swaggered into my life.

He was right.

That was exactly what this felt like.

Like I was colliding with what had been missing all along.

He released my nipple with a *pop*, his thumb back to circling the tight bud before he eased back and set both hands on my knees.

I sat there panting toward the ceiling, eyes cut down so I could take him in.

Blue eyes gleamed as he slowly ran his hands up the tops of my thighs. This time, they disappeared beneath the fabric.

Like a warning.

A promise.

Because the dress gathered on his forearms the higher he went before he hooked his fingers at the sides of my underwear.

Deliberately slow, he dragged them down.

"Shit," he hissed.

His thick throat bobbed, lust radiating from him as he watched himself peel them off.

Lace grazed my legs, tingles sprinting across my flesh as he pulled them down.

Shivers skated my skin, and my breaths turned ragged as he unwound the fabric from my ankles and heels.

He peered up at my face when he did. "You are perfect, Hope. Sweet, sublime perfection. The first time I saw you, I knew it. Had this feeling like I'd been struck. Like maybe I wouldn't ever be the same. Know now that I never will."

Then there was that grin. That wicked grin as his tongue swept across his bottom lip. "Not sure I really want to be."

Then he spread me. Pressing my knees apart the way he'd done that night at the bar. But this time, there was no barrier.

My body completely exposed.

And he was diving in without further warning, his hot, hot tongue sweeping into my folds.

I yelped and desire tumbled.

Pleasure spiked on all sides.

Magnified.

Compounded as he licked through my sensitive, engorged lips, dragging up and circling around that achy spot that throbbed and glowed.

"Kale." A whimper.

"I know, Hope," he rumbled. "I told you I know what you need."

But that was where he was wrong. Because I needed all of him. Every inch and every word and every smile.

A flicker of a warning rose up in my consciousness, telling me I was spiraling too fast, tripping into a free fall while Kale continued to drive me higher.

Higher and higher and higher.

His kiss so intimate I would have blushed if my skin weren't already covered in a flush of heat.

Red from the flames that licked up inside me. Flames that spiked and flared and grew hotter with each decadent stroke of his mouth.

Igniting into a full-body blaze.

Blistering.

He tucked me closer, his hands on my bottom as he lifted me from the couch, his thumb doing magical things to the most private part of me.

Circling.

Teasing.

Easing into my ass.

"Oh, God. Kale . . . what—" The words were thready. Thin with the rasp. My fingers slipped frantically across the leather of the couch, searching for something to hang on to.

"Relax, I've got you," he murmured. His low command reverberated through me. "I've got you. Trust me. I've got you. Want to make you feel good. Let me give you this."

"I trust you."

I did.

I trusted him with every part of me.

With the recognition, the *acceptance*, my heart clattered in my chest, and I whispered, "Please."

Though I knew he didn't know I was begging for so many

things.

I gulped for the nonexistent air when he dipped his head back down and burrowed back between my thighs. With his other hand, he pressed two fingers into the well of my body. He moved in perfect sync with his thumb.

My walls clenched around him.

With his tongue, he laved at my clit, suckled and licked and tempted me into a boiling frenzy that gathered to a pinpoint.

It was unlike anything I'd ever felt.

An avalanche of sensation riding on every nerve.

Filling every crevice.

My head swished back and forth on the back of the couch, pleasure gathering fast.

Flashing of bliss. Flickers of ecstasy.

Then everything split.

Breaking wide open.

Streaking and spinning and spiraling.

Euphoria.

I wanted to stay there for all of forever, and I couldn't help but whimper as I tumbled back down.

A weightless dive through limbless bliss.

When I landed, Kale was right there, placing gentle kisses along the inside of my thigh, holding me steady as my body twitched and jerked with the most powerful kind of aftershocks.

There was nothing I could do, my hands were on his face, pulling him up to me.

His jeans ground against my bare center, and I almost went off again.

I kissed him. Kissed him frantically. Maniacally. A frenzy that had taken hold. "Kale. Take me. I'm yours. I want to feel you. I need to feel you. Please."

He groaned a sound of pain as he kissed me deeper, and his eyes squeezed shut before he palmed the side of my face and pried himself back. "You know you don't want that."

"I do."

"No, Hope, you don't. You told me you couldn't afford another complication. And you know that's exactly what I'd be."

But he already was the most intricately exquisite complication.

I kissed across his jaw and up to his ear. "What if I want to take care of you, too? Make you feel good?"

Another groan, but it was one of those belly-flipping smirks that hitched up at the corner of his sexy mouth when he pulled back. "What exactly did you have in mind, Shortcake?"

This time, I did blush. Heat rushed to my cheeks. But I tried to remain bold, confident as I nudged him back. He eased onto his knees.

Fumbling beneath the hem of his shirt, I pressed my hands up under the soft material, inching it up.

My palms gliding over carved, defined muscle as I went. "I want to see you," I confessed.

He shuddered and shook, but he was grinning when he lifted his arms over his head and let me draw his shirt from his body.

I blinked when I dragged it free.

Stunned.

Struck dumb.

Left in staggered awe.

Holy crap.

Jenna may let a ton of nonsense roll out of her mouth, but she'd had one thing right.

This man was delicious.

I let my fingertips run up his chiseled abdomen, fluttering across his huge, bulging pecs, running over both of his shoulders and down his arms, watching the path I made the whole time.

Sucking on my bottom lip, I peeked up at him. "And you said I was perfect."

"You are, baby. So goddamned perfect. Just looking at you makes my guts hurt. Nothing should be that beautiful. But you are."

My blush deepened, my hands shaking, unsure of where to go from there.

But Kale, he knew when he needed to take control.

When I wanted him to.

He slowly pushed to his feet, straightening to that towering height of security where he stood right in front of me.

Potent.

Powerful.

Persuasive.

While I still sat on his couch, nothing but a fumbling mess of need.

"You want to touch me?" he grated.

I could barely get out a spastic nod.

Staring down at me, he started flicking through the buttons of his jeans. "You sure?"

He almost grinned, but it was weighted with his own desire, held back by the tight clench of his jaw as he freed the last button.

Oh goodness.

My insides trembled.

A tiny earthquake.

"Yes," I whispered.

He pushed his jeans and underwear down over his hips, and the little air I had left in my lungs jetted out on a panted heave when his cock sprang free.

Massive, thickened, and throbbing with his need.

Pointing toward the sky, it bobbed in front of my face, swaying just to the right, just as arrogantly confident as the rest of this mesmerizing man.

"This is what you do to me, Hope. This. Every time I see you. Every time I think of you. *This.*"

A shiver rocked me to the core.

My core, which had been sated to a simmer, was stoked into an all-out blaze again.

My tongue darted out to wet my dried lips, my fingers shaking and shaking when I reached out and tentatively traced them down the velvet skin.

His hips bucked, and his stomach clenched.

"Hope, baby, are you trying to embarrass me?"

I peeked up to find him gazing down at me, as if he were riveted by the feel of my hands on him. Touching him.

"I don't think that's possible, Kale Bryant. I don't even know what to do with you." It came on the huff of a breathy laugh, a tease and the utmost truth.

The truth was, my stomach was twisted in a million intricate knots when I took him in my trembling hands, circling him at the base. The crash in my heart an uncontrolled bang, bang, bang.

A groan jutted from his mouth. "I think you're doing just fine starting right there."

"This is okay?"

"Yes." It was a long moan when I ran my hands up and back down before I picked up a slow pace, letting one hand glide over his dripping head each time.

"Just like that," he said.

Leaning forward, my tongue darted out, flattening across the tip.

Tasting him.

"Or that. Yes, that. Fuck, Princess. I think it's me who doesn't know what to do with you."

But he did.

Because his hands landed on either side of my face, and I held him while I looked up at him.

The man lit up in the blaze of the sun.

A conqueror.

A champion.

"Suck me, baby." It was a grunt, his tip nudging at my lips. "Let me have that sweet mouth."

I wanted to tell him I would give him anything, but he was already tugging me forward, begging his own plea.

My lips parted, and I drew him into my mouth.

My insides clenched.

Why did I love the feel of his flesh on my tongue? Why did I ache with the impact of his soft grunt?

He drove his fingers into my hair. They dug in deep, spreading out, all the way over the back of my head until his fingertips were brushing the back of my neck.

"I'm going to fuck your mouth, Hope. Hold on, baby." His hips surged forward, my hands and mouth and heart full of him.

Overflowing and somehow wanting more.

More.

I whined around him, trying not to gag as my trembling hands spread out to clutch his hips.

He drove deeper and deeper with each of his slow thrusts. As if he were carefully claiming me while I felt frantic to demand all of him.

"Fuck . . . so good, baby. Just like that. Your mouth is perfect. So perfect. Just like the rest of you." It was a muddled jumble of pleasure that tripped from his tongue.

His wicked, delicious tongue.

More.

My spirit sang, and those hidden places that Dane had beaten down danced.

Freed.

There was some kind of magic in touching Kale this way. Power in making him moan. Power in hearing his pleas rumble from somewhere in the depths of him.

Both of us unchained and unbound.

His stomach tightened just the same as his fingers tightened in my hair. He gave a little yank, and I tipped my gaze toward his magnificent face.

I was literally brought to my knees by the magnitude of what I saw there, my body slipping from the edge of the couch to kneel on the floor.

Held by the raw, unbridled possession.

The passion and the need.

Hunger.

Never before had it been so fiercely directed at me.

"I'm getting close. Can you take it?" It was a warning that pressed between his lips, grit and lust and desire. Every inch of him trembled in restraint, muscle rippling and twitching as his own pleasure gathered.

My hands moved to his chiseled ass, gripping him, my eyes wide, begging him to let me be the one to give him what he needed.

To be the one who believed in him. To hold all his secrets and hidden desires. To be the one to cherish him in the highs.

To stand beside him on the lows.

Because I wanted him to be a part of all of mine.

"Sweet girl," he murmured. So softly. As soft as his gaze that traced over my face.

Riddled with affection.

Lined with fear.

One second later, Kale let go.

I let him possess me as his hips began to snap, desperate in their play.

His thrusts wild.

Unhinged and uncontrolled.

And maybe I was a fool, thinking I could have stopped it. Kept it away. The chaos that rose and lifted and shivered in the bright, blinding light that poured in behind him.

But I should have known better.

Because I was already lost.

The room spun and the ground shook and lights flashed where I knelt before him on my knees.

An offering.

His.

Kale gripped me as if he were determined to never let me go. His beautiful, glorious body stretched taut. Muscle keening, twisting, covered in a light sheen of sweat.

"Hope, baby, oh . . . fuck . . . yes."

His hips surged forward, and I took him as deeply as I could. Tears pricked my eyes as he pressed all the way into my throat.

He throbbed and jerked and poured in my mouth.

And that spinning room canted, my axis knocked.

I felt almost frantic as I swallowed around him.

Because all I could see was hope spread out in front of me.

seventeen

Kale

Struggling for a breath, I stared down at her staring up at me, my hands still twisted in that perfect mass of red, lush hair.

Affection.

It pulled and taunted and teased. Stretched tight across my chest. The squeeze in my lungs was almost painful, already lacking breath and looking at her stealing more.

I had no fucking clue how to make sense of what I was feeling. How to understand how this woman had singlehandedly made me question everything.

What I wanted and where I was going and what I stood for.

I wasn't supposed to need anyone, my devotion all locked up on the fact my patients needed me. My fate sealed the day I'd failed.

Yet, there she was, looking at me like I might be something better. Something more than just the *Dr.* tacked to the front of my name.

Fear tumbled through my spirit.

Because I couldn't—wouldn't—allow myself to fail.

Not ever again.

And I'd molded myself into accepting being a doctor was my only identity, but this girl was making me wonder if I might have a chance to find something more in the middle of it. Something good and right that might be meant for me.

Or maybe fate really was a cruel bitch. Teasing me in the worst of ways. Putting this woman and her kid in front of me. Knowing I'd never make it through a repeat.

Hope's chest heaved as her tumultuous green eyes watched me like she wanted to crawl around inside me to discover all that I was. Though, hidden deep, flickering right on the recesses, was a spec of that shyness, that uncertainty of where to go from there.

She dropped her gaze and gathered the top of her dress, covering herself and fumbling with the buttons because those exquisite tits were still exposed.

All it took was a glance of her, and I was kicked in the gut with a fresh bolt of lust. Didn't help that her panties were crumpled on my floor, the memory of getting my first real taste of Harley Hope Masterson forever ingrained on my mind.

Strawberries and cream.

Sweet, sweet heat.

The girl was calm and a raging fire.

Peace and a hurricane.

Modest and demure with straight shot of vixen.

Quickly, I pulled up my jeans and readjusted myself, figuring the last thing I needed was to be standing there looking like some kind of pathetic fucker caught with his pants around his ankles.

Not when she kept stealing peeks at me. Wondering where we stood when every time we crossed paths, we just got deeper and deeper. Running faster and faster down that path she wasn't sure she should follow me down.

I had no answer, but I no longer knew how to stay away. Wasn't sure if I wanted to.

I stretched my hand out to her. "Come here."

With an affected smile, she accepted it, and I helped pull her to her feet. She wobbled on her heels and shaky knees.

I tucked her against my chest, wrapped my arms around her,

and pressed a kiss to the top of her head. "You just blew my mind, Harley Hope. Where exactly did you come from? Because if you disappear, I'm pretty sure I'm gonna have to hunt you down."

"Stalker," she mumbled on a breathy laugh.

My own laugh was full. Hearty. Happy.

Because right then? That was exactly what I was.

I wrapped her even closer, swaying her slowly in the pour of light that tumbled in through the windows behind us.

Those dark places inside me light.

She released a contented sigh, her breath lifting chills that sped across my chest.

"I liked doing it," she finally whispered like a confession right over the thunder that was my heart.

Another chuckle rippled free, my lips murmuring against the crown of her head. "Have to admit, I liked you doing it, too."

She glanced up to meet my eyes. The warmth held in that mossy green swept through me like a caress. "Are you sure you aren't just telling me that because you don't want to make me feel bad?"

"Uh . . . considering I'm probably going to be begging you to do it again in about ten minutes, think you can safely assume that was no platitude." Then I glanced around my loft, eyes going wide with the tease. "See . . . no blowing of smoke anywhere." I hugged her back to me. "You're the only fire around here, Shortcake."

I could feel the force of her smile, and she gave a fake cough. "Oh, I smell smoke all right. Seems as if someone is trying to butter me up."

Fantasies flashed, and I grabbed her round ass in both of my hands, giving her a good squeeze. "Don't tempt me, Hope. You have no idea just what I could do with that."

She choked over a surprised laugh. "I swear, you are worse than Jenna. I think maybe you should be hanging out with her, instead. She'd probably handle you a whole lot better."

I gathered her close, her heart beating against mine.

Wild in its content.

Filling me with more of that joy that spun through the center of me. Winding up and taking hold.

"Sorry, Shortcake. That isn't gonna work for me. Seems I've acquired a taste for you. Don't want anyone else."

I meant for it to be playful, but it hit the air like a sonic boom. It thundered and roared through the sudden silence. Dense and deep and heavy with questions.

Her blunted fingernails scratched across my chest, inciting a new kind of storm that was building inside me. "I don't want anyone else, either."

For a few minutes, we just stayed there, lost in the other.

Swam in the possibilities.

Finally, I cleared my throat, stepped back.

"I'm starving."

Really. We needed a distraction. Because I had none of those answers.

But what I did know? I wanted her like I wanted the sun to keep rising in the morning. And if I didn't put some distance between us in the next five seconds, I would have her tossed over my shoulder and laid out on my bed.

And going there would change everything.

For her.

For me.

Since I'd lost Melody, I'd spent my life living casually. Easily. But there was nothing casual about this girl, and if it went there, it was going to mean something.

And I didn't want to be that asshole.

The one who took and took and took when I wasn't sure what I could give in return.

What I could offer.

I mean, fuck, if I kept seeing her? I was going to have to write a report. Have Evan's care transferred.

But if I was being honest, that was the easy part. Not a big deal except for the fact I hated the idea of not being able to treat him. Relinquishing the kid's care to someone else.

Trusting his health to them.

Unease slithered through my senses. Hooks and lines,

drawing me closer to the realization of how much I fucking cared.

Problem was, I didn't know if I wanted to protect him because I couldn't stand the thought of missing something again or if it was simply because it was this kid.

I was getting attached to him just as swiftly as I was getting attached to his mom.

Fuck.

I was.

I was falling.

Ripping myself from her, I locked down that train of thought because none of that needed to be entertained right then. I cleared my throat and started for the kitchen. "Are you hungry? Let me feed you."

A moment's hesitation brimmed around her, her gaze jumping around my loft before she gave a quick nod. "Sure. Something to eat would be nice. I'm never quite sure what to do with myself when Evan isn't around."

I glanced at the spot where we'd just been tangled, letting a smirk climb to my mouth. "I'd say I approve of your most recent choice of activities. Great use of your time, Shortcake."

She tucked her bottom lip between her teeth, like she didn't know whether to be embarrassed or laugh. "I bet. It seems you really do have me at a disadvantage, Dr. Bryant. And here I thought I'd finally graduated to princess and ditched the whole Shortcake thing."

"Ah, there's no ditching the whole Shortcake thing . . . not when you're so damned sweet."

She stood there with that blush riding to her cheeks while I stepped up to the sink to wash my hands.

She angled her head toward the hall. "Do you mind if I freshen up a little bit?"

"First door on the right. Make yourself at home."

She gave a slight nod before she reached down and covertly snatched her underwear from the floor. She tucked them in a ball to conceal them in her hand, like I hadn't been the one just peeling them from her body.

I chuckled, shooting her a grin. "Feel free to leave those here if you want."

"Kale," she admonished, flustered, as she shook her head and fought a smile before she bolted down the hall. The door slammed behind her, shaking the panes of the windows.

And my smile?

My smile was wider than I thought it'd ever been.

Giggles floated through my kitchen. Wrapping around me like soft, lulling waves.

I smiled back at her from over my shoulder where I was digging something out to make for an early dinner.

Hope was propped up on my island, that dress bunched up around her thighs, her lush legs swinging over the edge.

Feet bare.

Sun shining all around her from behind. Lighting up that red hair. Setting it aflame.

Swore, the girl was like curling up in front of a fireplace on a cold winter's day.

I pulled an onion, fresh garlic, and tomatoes from the crisper. Spaghetti was the one meal I cooked well, which wasn't surprising since that shit was what I'd lived on in medical school.

I rinsed everything, set a cutting board beside her, and started dicing so I could start the sauce.

I glanced over at her. "If I make you dinner, that means you're making me dessert, right?"

"Oh, I see how this works. A favor for a favor, huh? And here I thought you were making me dinner out of the goodness of your heart."

She sat up there like her weight had been lifted. The girl was lost in the mood, relaxed, catching on to the vibe of the sun slowly sinking in the sky.

My phone was synced with Spotify and set to one of my favorite playlists. Mellow and gritty, the guitar-driven beats pumped quietly from the speakers set up all through my loft, the hypnotizing lyrics setting the mood.

I feigned an offended gasp. "This is out of the goodness of my heart, Shortcake. But, seriously, have you tasted your cupcakes? You can't blame a man for trying. Call it self-preservation. The instinct to survive kicking in. Because I might die if I don't get another taste."

"The dramatics," she teased.

"The truth," I shot back.

Amusement flitted across her features, and she placed her palms on the stone counter behind her, leaning back, hair swept over one shoulder. She stared at the ceiling like she was really contemplating what she was going to say. "And what flavor would you pick if I was kind enough to make you something? On my day off, mind you."

She dropped her gaze back to me, that mesmerizing green swallowing me whole.

My brow lifted. "Do you really need to ask?"

My eyes raked her. Head to toe. Not even attempting to hide the fact I was already ready to devour her again.

Strawberries and cream and all things sweet.

A soft giggle floated from her delicious mouth. "You haven't even tried anything else. Strawberry shortcake might be your least favorite and you don't even know it."

"Oh, there are some things a man just knows." I leaned in closer to her, letting my nose graze her jaw, my voice rough. "And this I know. Don't need to taste anything else when I already know I've got the fucking best thing sitting right in front of me."

Truth was, I'd *tasted* enough in my lifetime to know when I'd never stumble on anything better.

Goose bumps spread across her flesh, and a shiver rolled down her spine as I pressed a gentle kiss behind her ear. "Got it?" I murmured.

"Well then, I guess I'd better stock up on strawberries." A tremor rolled out with her wispy response.

I chuckled, swiveling around and digging out a large saucepan from the bottom cupboard and placing it on the stove. "I like the way you think. But I have to wonder if you're thinking big enough. Not sure simply stocking up will suffice. I'm thinking maybe we need to invest in some stock in one of those fields up north. Maybe buy it outright."

While I spoke, I flicked on the burner, a ring of blue flames jumping to life, and tossed some olive oil in the pan. I let that heat before adding the onions and garlic.

"You think so? Sounds to me like someone is getting a little greedy."

Filling a pot with hot water, I smirked over at her. "Hard not to be when I want it all."

There I went, running down that path, not sure how to stop myself.

Knowing if I reached out my hand, she'd be right there running along beside me. Or maybe it was the girl who was out front, hair flying all around her as she looked back at me from over her shoulder, smile so wide and welcoming.

Tempting me into chasing after that blinding, blistering hope. Wanting the striking, stark beauty of it. Hungry for something I've always wanted for the people around me, but never thinking I could keep any of it for myself.

I focused on getting the pot on the stove instead of all the thousand thoughts and temptations dangling right there.

Within reach.

The whole time, knowing if I were to grab on, every single one of them might be covered in spikes and spurs and barbs.

The onions and garlic began to sizzle. The thick aroma rose in the air.

"God, I love that smell," Hope murmured, her head dropped back and her eyes closed.

Savoring.

Lust twisted my guts.

So tightly, I could feel it climb all the way to my chest and squeeze my heart.

"Yeah?" I asked as I dumped a can of premade sauce into the pan, tossed in the diced tomatoes to add a little extra texture and flavor.

"It's my favorite."

"Onion and garlic?"

She laughed that mesmerizing sound.

Sex and innocence.

The score of this girl hypnotic.

"No, spaghetti. It's my favorite."

A short chuckle rumbled deep in my throat. "Good. Because that's about the only thing I know how to make."

She hummed softly, lost to some kind of memory. "When I was a sophomore, my grandparents took me to New York City to see one of the Broadway shows. They said they were feeding my love of the theater. I think what they really were doing was feeding my love for Italian food."

A gentle smile pulled at one side of my mouth as I poured the noodles in. "And how is it my little actress turned into a baker?"

A giggle slipped free, hair swishing around her as she shifted. "Sometimes dreams are only meant for a moment. They mean the world to us, and then sometimes something takes their place, and they're not quite as important to us anymore."

Slowly, I turned and rested my back against the counter facing her. "What happened to that dream?"

She shook her head, her shoulders lifting in the smallest shrug. "I can't really pinpoint exactly when it happened, but somewhere along the way, it stopped being a burning need inside me. I loved theater in high school. I think it was an outlet. A way to express myself. And I guess I got to a point where I no longer needed to express myself that way."

"So . . . how did you end up here?"

Lines crossed. I wasn't even jumping over the hurdles set between us. I was barreling right through them.

The hint of a smile edged her mouth, made up of regret and honesty. "In college, I fell in love, and I followed him here."

I flinched.

A stake driven through the center of me.

God, that was stupid, but just her even mentioning the idea of that dirtbag, the thought of another man touching her, made my skin crawl.

Unable to tolerate the distance, I slowly crossed the space, awareness thrumming between us. I took in a shuddered breath when I planted myself between her knees, staring at her through the glittering rays of lights that glowed against her gorgeous face. "Do you ever regret it? Not going to New York? Not following that dream? Chasing it even after it was gone?"

Her head shook. Zero reluctance behind it. "No. I don't. Because Evan *is* the reason I dream."

I set my hand against her cheek. "Hope." It was praise from my mouth. Sure a girl as selfless and giving as this one didn't exist. "You are amazing. The most incredible woman I've ever had the honor to meet."

Redness flushed up her delicate neck, splashing on her cheeks, and she pressed deeper into the well of my hand. Hungry for the touch. Relishing in me. "I think I could say the same thing about you."

My brow pinched a little, not sure how to handle a girl like this saying something like that.

Catching it, her eyes narrowed, and she was reaching up and softly trailing her fingertips down the side of my face. "Who are you, Kale Bryant? Because you *are* the most incredible man I've ever met, but there's something inside you that you try to keep hidden. And I wonder if that's the part of you that I'm drawn to the most."

Eyes falling closed, I swallowed around the painful lump that was suddenly prominent at the base of my throat. Throbbing and tormenting.

And I wanted to lay it all out.

Tell her everything.

"You can trust me, Kale," she whispered.

I blinked at her. "But I'm not sure if I can trust myself."

She searched me. Gently. In all that belief. "How is that?"

I gathered both of her hands between mine, forcing the tweak of a smile. "I always wanted to be a doctor. My dad was a general practitioner. I basically idolized him my whole life. Couldn't wait to walk in his shoes."

A wistful smile pulled at her mouth, her eyes tracing over me like she was trying to imagine what I was like when I was little.

Drawing an image in her mind of a blond-haired boy who wanted to be just like his father.

"He must be so proud of you. You are the best doctor I know. And I'm not just saying that. The second you sat in front of my son, I knew what kind of doctor you were."

I winced, the words flooding out before I could stop them. "I try to be, Hope. I try to be the best damned doctor I can be. Making sure I never get so wrapped up inside myself, distracted, or focused on things I shouldn't be that I start missing or neglecting the things that are most important. And what's most important are my patients."

Something flickered through her features.

A kind of understanding I wasn't sure she could possess. A tiny sound fell from her tongue, and she was back to caressing across my lips.

Sadness and grace rippled through her.

"You're scared of getting involved with someone." She didn't even ask it as a question. It was just a statement. An awareness. No judgment. Just her quiet compassion.

That didn't mean I didn't see the tiny flame of hurt in her eyes. Her want for something more for me, *from* me, was clear. Only, I didn't have a fucking clue if I could be man enough to offer it in return.

Thing was, I was wanting to. Fuck. I wanted it more than I'd wanted anything in a long, long time.

"I . . ." For a moment I wavered before I surrendered, giving her a little of what I could. "When I was in med school, I fell in love for the first and only time in my life."

My mouth tweaked up with the old memories. Before they were horror and regret and shame.

Hope's almost matched. That green glinting.

This girl.

I could feel her cracking me wide open.

A small puff of air jolted from her lungs, but she looked at me, filling me with silent encouragement.

"I met her at a fundraiser on campus. It was before I even started my clinicals . . . basically spending my time in books and labs."

My head slowly shook as I was assailed with the memories, my lips pulling with the old affection. "She had the biggest spirit. She lit up any room she stepped into. She kept . . . complaining that she didn't feel well. That she was tired. I should have known. I'd learned enough by that time that I should have known." The words scraped from my throat.

Emergency room lights glared from overhead. Panic. Fear. Compression after compression after compression. That fucking flat line.

"She was sick, Hope. She was fucking sick, and I didn't even see it. I thought she was just tired. Exhausted from classes and studying and always wanting to be a part of everything. I missed it."

I was unable to admit to her why Evan petrified me. Why the situation was so fucked up. Why it was different and still felt so goddamned much the same. That I was there. That I tried to save her.

I tried.

I tried.

"You lost her." Grief rang from Hope's tongue. Spinning through the room. Wrapping me in her warmth.

Those dead places flickered, and I dropped my head to her chest, nodding against the steady thrum of her heart as I struggled with the crushing wave that slammed into me.

The regret and remorse and the old feelings I'd done fine at keeping locked down, all being unleashed at once.

"Oh, Kale, I'm so sorry," she whispered, fingers gentling through my hair.

I buried my face in her neck.

Ashamed.

Stricken.

She hugged me to her for the longest time, her scent all around me, strawberries and cream and calm.

It felt like an eternity before she edged back. She framed my face in her delicate hands. Sympathy and that stunning understanding ridged every line of her expression. "You still love her?"

Oh fuck. This girl was going to destroy me.

eighteen

Hope

My hands trembled where they rested on his striking face.

But it had shaken me.

Being able to finally see all the way past the gorgeous exterior. Down, deep inside this miraculous man with his huge, beautiful, bleeding heart.

To the man who had lost, who remained terrified and hurt. The one who had somehow taken on some of that responsibility when it clearly didn't belong to him.

The one who was so clearly scared of repeating it again.

And my son.

He was sick.

I understood it in a way I wasn't sure I wanted to.

I wanted to ask him so many things.

How?

What happened?

I wanted to tell him it would be okay.

That it was all right to hurt.

That I understood.

Instead, I just sat there, waiting for him, needing this answer, knowing if I had it, I might be able to understand him on a level I hadn't before. That maybe we could make sense of what was going on between us.

He peeled himself away and looked at me. Grief swam in that turbulent sea of blue. "Part of me will always love her, Hope. But what torments me is she didn't get the chance to experience life. That I missed her symptoms and took that chance away."

Sorrow clenched down on my chest, sorrow that he could possibly think he was responsible for his first love's death.

His Adam's apple bobbed heavily as he swallowed. "Then the other part of me wonders . . . wonders what my life would have looked like had I been able to save her. Would we be married? Would we have kids? Would she be an anesthesiologist like she'd wanted to be? Or would her dreams have changed, too?"

His voice cracked as he continued, "She deserved to experience everything life had in store for her, and I stole that from her. Failed her when she needed me most."

I could feel my heart splintering under the devastation in his expression.

"I've been told that sometimes it's the what-ifs that hurt the most. What haunt us the longest. But there is absolutely no chance you were responsible for her death, Kale. You have to let that go. Live and find joy. Because I promise you, you deserve it, everything life has in store for you."

He flinched as if he wanted to refute my claim, so I was quick to add, "Believe it. I do."

He took my hand and pressed his face in to my palm, kissing the flesh before he moved to kiss the inside of my wrist. "Incredible. Told you, Hope. You are incredible. And I don't know how to make sense of it."

"Do you want to try?" I asked him. Stepping out, that limb teetering beneath me, threatening to splinter.

And God . . .

The smile he sent me?

It rocked me to the core.

Confidence and naked vulnerability, the contours of his face lit up in the glow of the fading sun.

"I do . . . but the last thing I want to do is fail you. Fail Evan."

I blinked at him, my chest tightening, and I started to tell him I didn't think it was possible for him to do that.

Fail us. But then the sizzle and hiss of water boiling over onto the stove hit our ears.

"Shit." He spun away and rushed that direction. He drove a pasta spoon into the pot, stirring quickly to settle the roil down.

I almost giggled when the sauce started to bubble and spit all over the place.

"Shit," he said again, this time with an amused huff that came at his expense, his strong back bare as he worked to salvage our dinner.

Cute.

Confident.

Chaos.

He glanced back at me, the heaviness from moments ago gone. "Can't even get spaghetti right."

I ignored the questions still looming around us and slid off the counter. I slinked up behind him and pressed a gentle kiss to the warm, bare flesh at the center of his back.

He shuddered, the quiver of an arrow straight through the center of me.

"You are the most incredible man I have ever met, Kale Bryant. I am so sorry you had to go through that. I hate it for you. If I could take it away, I would," I whispered against his spine, which stiffened the barest fraction.

I knew I needed to give him space, let him process. He had probably shared more with me than he had with anyone in a long, long time. I moved to stand beside him, nudged him with my hip, and sent him a smile. "Here, let me help with that."

Kale laughed. "What? You don't trust me in my own kitchen?"

I widened my eyes up at him. "Should I?"

He hesitated for a second before he busted up laughing. "No . . . no, you definitely should not."

I shot him a grin. "That's what I thought." I snagged the

spoon from his grip. "Give me that before someone gets hurt."

He took his turn knocking me with his hip. "Fine. I relinquish these duties. Thinking they're not so knightly, anyway."

I gasped a horrified sound that was completely feigned. "And just what is it you're implying?"

He laughed again. A bellowing sound that came from his belly, making his abdomen ripple and flex. "Absolutely nothing, Princess. Nothing at all."

I poked him in the side. "I'll let you off the hook this time. Just because I like you."

His eyes smoldered when he looked down at me, the edges brimming with something brilliant.

Something beautiful and whole. "You like me, huh, Shortcake?"

I didn't know why I adored it when he called me that. That coaxing tease that clearly meant so much more.

I kept my focus trained ahead, stirring the noodles, the confession a breath on my tongue. "Yeah, Kale, I like you."

I think I'm in love with you.

Sitting out on his gorgeous balcony, we shared our meal beneath the blaze of the setting sun. Engines hummed from below and voices carried on the breeze. The Alabama air thick and warm, comforting in a way I didn't know it could be.

Or maybe it was just Kale.

The man who steadily stole more and more, each laugh and tease and smirk shackling another piece of me.

"That was delicious," I told him, sitting back in the chair, my stomach so full it was close to painful.

He arched an eyebrow. "And just who are you complimenting?"

A giggle floated out on the air, every shield and guard ripped away, my ribbing so easy. "I was complimenting you, but I guess I really should give the credit where it belongs."

"Is that so?"

"Mm-hmm," I drew out.

Flying from his chair, he lunged for me, and I squealed, jumping to my feet and racing through the open doors.

He chased me. And God, I loved it.

Loved it when he caught me from behind. When he lifted me from my feet. When he hugged me against his bare chest.

Loved it when he kissed the back of my head. Loved it more when he started leaving dizzying trails of kisses down the side of my neck, nipping at the corner of my jaw, his cock growing thick against my bottom.

Oh.

He was undoing me.

My phone rang from within my purse, and I held back the groan at the interruption.

He set me back on my feet.

"Don't think just because you have a phone call that you get a free pass. I'll be waiting for you."

I glanced at him from over my shoulder, putting an extra sway into my steps when I moved toward my purse, grinning wide. "Is that a promise?"

"Oh, Harley Hope, you are in so, so much trouble."

I was.

I already knew it.

And I loved that, too.

I was grinning when I dug into the side pocket and found my phone. I glanced at the screen. A frown pulled across my brow when I saw Chanda's name.

Quickly, I answered it, sure it was nothing.

But it took only the flash of a second before I knew it was something.

Dread curled through my insides when I heard her voice coming through the line. Frantic. Words so rushed, I couldn't make out what she was saying.

"Evan . . . breath . . . hurry."

My insides trembled. Panic blew through me. Pummeling and beating.

A gale force.

"What?" I asked, eyes pinching shut as my fingers drove into my hair, yanking, struggling to process what she'd said. "What are you saying? Where are you? What happened? Slow down and tell me what's happening."

Chanda sucked in a breath. Trying to calm herself. "We're just pulling up at the ER. The boys were tossing the football with Richard. The same as they always do. He was fine, Hope, he was fine, and then all of a sudden, Evan said he couldn't breathe."

A hand landed on my shoulder, grabbing hold, maybe holding me up.

Tension wound tight. Round and round and round.

"Is he okay?" I didn't know if she could hear me, the words choked where they locked in my throat, not prepared for what she might say.

"I think so. I think so," she rambled. Frazzled. Frenzied.

Or maybe all that frenzy belonged to me. Because I could feel it shaking through my system.

Speeding through my veins.

Seeping into my spirit.

Penetrating to my bones.

"Okay, we're here. We're here. I'll call you back," she said.

The line went dead and dread pressed down on my chest.

Too heavy.

Too much.

I couldn't move.

Frozen.

Kale spun me around and pried the phone from my hand, setting both of his on my shoulders. He gave me a tiny shake, trying to snap me out of the daze. "Hope, what is going on? Who was that? Tell me what's happening."

"Evan."

His name.

It was a plea.

A prayer.

Kale's face blanched.

White as a ghost.

Or maybe I could only see what was reflected in me.

Tremors rolled beneath my skin, my muscles trembling as the

freeze finally thawed.

It gave way to a raging river. Sweeping me away. Taking me with it and shooting me into action.

I fumbled into my shoes, grabbed my purse, and jerked open the door.

I could sense the torment of the presence behind me. The anguish in his silence. And maybe I did understand him better. His walls higher than mine. Why he couldn't do this with me.

I didn't pause to look back when I floundered with the latch and flew out the door.

The only thing I knew was I needed to get to my son.

nineteen

Kale

The door slammed closed behind her.

I gripped fistfuls of my hair, staring at the spot where she'd just been.

Air gone, my lungs squeezed tight.

What the fuck was I supposed to do?

Fear spiraled. Slammed and howled. It beat against this overwhelming sensation that welled.

Growing bigger—more powerful—than anything else. Constricting my chest and shattering every reserve.

I was moving before I let myself think through the consequences. Because the consequence of standing there like a worthless piece of shit were so much greater than going after what had just fled out my door.

Bolting into the living room, I nabbed my shirt from the rug. I was pulling it over my head at the same time as I was grabbing my keys and wallet from the entry table. Not wanting to take the time to go to my room, I shoved my feet into some ripped-up Vans and then went racing out.

I didn't bother with the elevator.

I pounded down the stairs, taking them three at a time. I blew through the big metal back door and flew out into the lot.

Twilight had taken hostage of the sky, the heavens streaked with darkened clouds, a single star blinking on the horizon above the copse of trees.

My eyes hunted.

Immediately, they landed on Hope. She was across the lot, stumbling through her panic as she tried to run in her heels.

She jerked at the door handle of her big SUV, fumbling and shaking as she struggled to get inside.

Sprinting her direction, I caught her just before she was all the way in. "Hope."

She gasped a pained sound. "I've got to get to him."

My voice was grit at her ear as I hauled her back from around the waist. "I know. I know. But I can't let you drive like this. Come on, baby, let me help you. It's going to be okay."

She gasped another sound. This one a guttural cry, her terror that had been bottled spilling out.

"I've got you. It's going to be okay," I told her, anxiety gripping me like a vise.

It is going to be okay.

He'll be okay.

I promise I won't let anything happen to him.

I shifted her around, slamming her door shut as I did. Quickly, I guided her to my car parked two spaces over. Opening the passenger door, I helped her in, darted around the front, and hopped inside.

The second the engine turned over, I threw it in reverse and whipped out of the spot. Half a second later, I had it in gear and was gunning the engine, tires squealing when I skidded out onto the street.

Teeth gritted, I weaved in and out of traffic, trying to remain calm.

Cool.

Which was impossible since my heart was a fucking throbbing mess where it was lodged in my throat.

When all I could think about was that kid.

That kid.

I struggled to focus, to breathe in the dense, dark air that had taken hold.

Hope fisted her hands on her lap, choppy pants heaving from her shuddering chest.

Terrified.

Doing my best to keep it together, to be there for her, I reached out and set my hand on her leg. I gave her a soft squeeze. "He's going to be okay, Hope. I promise you, he's going to be okay."

The oaths I'd kept silenced before came tumbling out.

Her nod was jerky. She set her hand on top of mine, squeezing so hard I was sure she was drawing blood.

Leaning on me.

Relying on me.

Silently begging me to keep that promise.

Five minutes later, I skidded into the parking lot at the ER.

The same ER where I'd been a resident for the previous three years.

I jerked into a vacant spot, killed the engine, and was already out and at Hope's door by the time she had it open and was climbing out.

"Thank you," she rasped, clutching my shirt. She was shaking all over, so I wrapped my arm around her waist to support her.

Together, we rushed for the entryway doors.

They swished apart as we approached.

Once we got inside, I let Hope run ahead of me, feeling like a complete asshole for dropping my arm.

But I felt so tied.

Those memories too close. Too real. Too much.

I rubbed an anxious hand over my jaw, watching Hope as she went for the triage station, her son's name a plea from her tongue.

The door leading into the back buzzed and swung open. Hope went right for it.

And I stood there like a chump.

Fuck it.

I hurtled after her, barely grabbing the door before it closed. I hurried to catch up to her where she raced down the hall that was lined with curtained exam spaces, a big nursing station in the middle.

She headed straight down the hallway and toward the room number she'd been given.

This place was so familiar. So much of my time had been devoted to this emergency room. But it was always me caring for the patients that came through the doors.

My complete dedication given to them.

But this time . . . this time it was different. The tables turned.

I passed familiar faces, and a couple of nurses offered confused hellos as I passed.

Frantically, Hope jerked open the door of one of the enclosed exam rooms reserved for higher-risk patients. Equipment at the ready for testing and treatment that might need to be rendered urgently.

And that chaotic world spinning around us?

For a moment, it completely froze.

It gave Hope a second to catch up.

A chance to take in her son, who was in the middle of the room, partially propped up on an elevated hospital bed with an oxygen mask covering his nose and mouth.

He was alert, those green eyes scared, but they shimmered with relief when he caught sight of his mom.

For a beat, Hope was locked in that suspended moment where only her son existed.

Then she jolted forward. "Oh . . . God . . . Evan."

Her hand was on the side of his face, the other going straight for his heart.

My heart. My heart.

From behind, I could see her shoulders sag in relief when she felt it beating.

When she felt the life that pounded through his veins.

And there was nothing I could do but step up behind her, touch Evan's cheek, his forehead, fingers trembling as I felt along the steady pulse in his neck.

It was the furthest from an exam. It was simply a man needing to be reassured that someone he cared about was okay.

From under the mask, Evan smiled his wide smile, and I ruffled my fingers through his hair, barely able to mouth the words, "Hey, buddy."

He was okay.

He signed *HI.*

A breath pressed from my lips, a million pounds of worry let loose in the sound. I glanced at Hope, touched her cheek, praying she could see it in my eyes.

He's fine. I promise. He's fine.

A throat cleared, and my attention jumped up to meet the confused gaze of a woman I'd never met, but knew had to be Josiah's mother. She stood on the opposite side of the bed, watching over him, dried tears still staining her cheeks.

She tore her eyes away from me and turned them on Hope. "Hope . . . I'm so sorry to scare you this way. I think . . . I think he just got out of breath, and I panicked—" She fumbled, hesitated, her worried gaze turning to Josiah, who was huddled in the corner, sitting on his father's knee.

Josiah's eyes were wide and terrified and confused. Worried about his friend.

"You know . . ." She said it like an apology riddled with empathy.

Because Josiah's mom understood all the things Hope was feeling perfectly.

"It's okay," Hope managed, stare still locked on her son. "It's okay. I'm just . . ." She forced herself to look at Josiah's mom, offering a soggy smile. "I'm so grateful you brought him here, Chanda. It isn't worth the risk. I would have done the same thing."

Chanda gave a reassuring tip of her chin, her eyes flitting to me before they jerked away. As if she thought she was invading on something private.

At the exact same time, her husband's brow was pinching together in his own confusion, clearly working to figure out where he'd seen me before.

I roughed a hand over my head, blinking, calculating, trying to figure out what the fuck to do. I had no idea how Hope would want me to handle this.

How I wanted to.

That was right when I noticed Dr. Laurent Kristoff standing just off to the side, studying the readout on the portable ECG machine, checking the rhythm of Evan's heart.

In all the upheaval, I hadn't realized the emergency room doctor I'd worked next to for years was right there. Seems Hope wasn't the only one with tunnel vision.

Laurent did a double take when he noticed me. "Dr. Bryant?"

Nodding, I forced myself to give him a cordial smile, but I didn't get anything out before the door opened behind me.

Dr. Krane, the cardiac specialist at GL Children's Center, stepped inside.

Obviously, he was the pediatric cardiologist on call this weekend.

Shit.

He grinned when he saw me. "Dr. Bryant, I didn't realize you were on call."

That's because I wasn't.

I grimaced. "Not on call," I admitted.

His expression shifted for a flash, morphing into confusion or concern, I wasn't sure, before he shrugged it off, moved across the floor, and turned his attention on Evan.

The reason we were all there.

That didn't mean I couldn't feel the weight of Josiah's dad's stare. The questions that were coming from everyone.

Because I was responsible for the care of both of these boys.

They were supposed to be my single focus.

No distractions.

I'd lived my life on that rule.

And here I was, so goddamned distracted my insides were in knots and my spirit was roaring, wrapped up in a way I'd never let it before.

Sure. I'd examined Frankie Leigh. But always on the side. As a bolster for Rex. A second opinion. Reassurance. Her pediatrician was the one who was truly in charge of her care.

Hope sent me an apologetic glance.

I shook my head.

Don't be sorry.

Because the truth of it all?

I wanted to be there.

I wanted to be there for her.

And goddamn it, I needed to be there for him.

twenty
Hope

"Ms. Masterson, I would think it would greatly benefit you to apply for our state health care program."

I blinked at the woman behind the desk, who was speaking to me about the fact my son had been rushed into the ER. Uninsured.

What she didn't understand was that he had to be, for just a little while longer.

My head shook, and I fought the new kind of panic that clawed through my spirit. "No, I'll be paying out of pocket."

She looked at me as if I were crazy, which admittedly, was exactly how I felt, never having imagined I would ever go down a path such as this. But my son was worth it.

He was worth any debt. Any sacrifice. Any lie.

It was only for a year. Until the day I could ensure Dane would never be a threat to Evan again.

"You're looking at, at least five thousand for this visit alone, Ms. Masterson."

My throat constricted at that number, but I managed to force a bright, fake smile. "It's fine, I have the funds."

Or really, I would find a way to get them.

Another loan taken out against the coffee shop.

A rush of guilt made me cringe. I hated that I was putting Jenna in this position. A Drop of Hope was every bit as much her dream as it was mine. But she'd promised me she was willing to make any sacrifice she had to. Promised she was in this with me. Whatever it took or cost.

The woman pushed out a confused sigh. "Okay, then, but I'm including these pamphlets for you to look over. I'm sure there's a plan that's a good fit for your son."

I reached over the desk and took them from her. "Thank you, I'll look through them," I promised, telling another lie, tossing it right on the mounting pile. The shorter the paper trail, the better.

Pushing to my feet, I left her office, feeling shaky all over as I went. Adrenaline dumping from my veins, leaving me drained, the remnants the fear of this day had evoked almost too much to bear.

My emotions precarious. So close to breaking me.

Desperate.

That was what I was.

Desperate for my son to be okay. Desperate for this charade to go away and Dane to leave us be so we could live our lives.

Rounding the corner, I peered into the examination room through the small window in the door, just needing to get a peek at my son.

A buoy to give me the strength to keep fighting. To gain the confidence that he was really okay. The doctor had spent a half hour trying to reassure me that he'd just overexerted himself. That it was typical. That there wasn't anything to worry about.

Still, Dr. Krane had made an appointment for him to follow up in two weeks to do a thorough workup of his heart to make sure it was functioning fine. Covering all the bases.

My frantic spirit eased when I gazed in, taking in the sight in front of me.

Evan was fully propped up in the hospital bed, his mop of messy red hair flying all around as he laughed.

Laughed because Kale was sitting at the end of his bed,

angled with his knee under himself so he could face Evan, scribbling something on the pad one of the nurses had brought in for ease of communication.

My heart clenched.

Painfully.

Beautifully.

Because my son looked so free and content and comfortable with Kale at his side. And Kale was looking at my son the way a child deserved to be looked at.

Protectively.

Adoringly.

And now I knew the source of Kale's unease. His fear of loving someone and taking the chance that they might be violently, savagely ripped away. The barriers and shields he struggled to maintain to protect himself from that chance.

And he had stayed.

That meant more to me than he could ever know.

Kale met my eye through the small window.

That protective possessiveness extended out to me, searching through its own confusion and uncertainty. The man holding me up with a simple glance.

I'm here.

I blinked, swallowed, no steel left around my heart. Because in that blink. I was right back in that day. The day I'd been left alone . . .

"Mrs. Gentry, has your husband returned?" He looked around the room where I sat alone. Clutching my arms over my chest.

Rocking.

Trying to be strong.

Jenna had just left to get coffee, and my mama was on her way from Texas. Promising she would get there as quickly as she could.

"No." I swallowed around the ball of agony cinched tight in my throat. Cutting off circulation. Shutting down belief. I didn't know how much more I could take.

The doctor who'd first given us the news tried to hide his surprise when I told him I was still alone, but it was there. He shook his head in what I knew was supposed to be sympathy. "All right, then."

He sank to the chair beside me. "We would like to have your blood drawn so we can try to determine the exact genetic defect your son suffers from."

Jerkily, I nodded, rushing my hands over the chills that lifted on my arms. I was cold. So cold.

"Of course."

I would do anything.

Give anything.

The doctor paused, as if he were waiting for me to snap. Break. Then he issued almost carefully, "It is important we get your husband's as well."

I blinked, trying to stay upright against the force of the walls that spun and spun. "He's not here," I said, somehow feeling as if that statement was on repeat.

The words leaving me through the stark numbness that echoed from that hollow place inside.

He hadn't been there since he'd stormed out the day before when I'd refused to leave.

Refusing food.

Refusing sleep.

"Just as soon as it's possible is all we ask."

I nodded again. "I'll do what I can."

I couldn't understand it. How he could leave us there. He'd doted on me through my entire pregnancy. I could never forget the amount of pride on his face and love in his eyes when we'd found out we were having a boy.

Then he had just . . . disappeared.

Abandoned us.

But Dane was the least of my worries right then.

"The arrangements have been finalized for his transfer, and the heart team will be ready to perform his surgery as soon as he arrives. Transport is scheduled for three this afternoon."

I nodded again, clutching myself tighter.

"You can go in and see him now, and I will send someone to come to draw your blood while they prep him for transfer."

The only thing I could process was that I could see him. I could finally see him.

"Thank you." The words left me on a gush of air.

Kindly, he patted my knee. "I know things look bleak right now, and I know you're scared, but don't stop praying. I've seen a lot of miracles in my lifetime."

Gratefulness pulsed through my being, thankful this doctor had taken the time to step outside of his duty and offer me kind words when it felt as if the world only had cruelty to offer.

"I won't," I promised, though I was terrified it might be a lie.

When he stood, I followed, my knees weak and my body swaying.

I followed him out and down a long hall and then another before I was cleared through a set of imposing double doors.

I was taken to a preparation area and instructed on how to wash, before I was led into a darkened room. The large area was only illuminated by dim, unobtrusive lights, sections curtained off, concealing the isolettes behind each.

Some of the curtains were opened where I could see mothers nursing and fathers cradling their babies in the rocking chairs.

I gulped again when the nurse led me toward another sectioned off area. My heart raced in its confines.

Fear and grief and hope.

They constricted and squeezed, my chest so tight I thought my heart might be physically crushed.

The nurse drew the curtain back slightly so I could slip through.

At the sight in front of me, a tiny sound climbed from my throat.

Love.

The impact of it was staggering.

My infant son lay riddled with tubes and lines, attached to monitors, tape concealing the lower half of his face to keep the oxygen in place.

But I saw none of those things.

I saw the child that'd been given into my care.

I saw a little boy running on a playground.

I saw a future.

Slowly, I edged forward. Tears blurred my eyes as I looked down on my son. Hand shaking, I reached out and caressed my thumb across the back of his tiny hand.

Those tiny fingers searched, tightly wrapping around my finger.

He stared up at me.

I was certain that connection was greater than anything I'd ever felt.

My mouth trembled, overwhelmed with affection. With my free hand, I *reached up and softly ran my knuckle down his plump cheek.*

"My heart," I whispered, and the little boy stared up at me as if he'd known me for a million years.

The little boy who would forever hold my heart.

And I murmured a million of those prayers into the air.

Believed.

And knew, right that second, with every part of me, I would never, ever give up on hope.

Blinking out of the reverie, I ran my fingertips over my eyelids, clearing the tears. Refusing to allow myself to spiral into hopelessness.

I just needed to focus on the fact Evan was okay. Spend this time in gratefulness.

Knees shaky, I opened the door.

Instantly, Evan was frantically signing my way, his eyes still dancing with his laughter. *DR. BRYANT SAID HE WAS A NERD IN SCHOOL. DID YOU KNOW THAT? HE SAID NERDS ARE THE BEST. THEY GROW UP TO BE DOCTORS.*

Nerds are the best.

The memory of him teasing me about being a nerd that first night hit me.

This man. He had completely demolished me in the best of ways.

A sound that was half a sob and half laughter tripped from my mouth. It originated somewhere in my spirit.

The sound made up of the remnants of terror I'd felt this afternoon.

The astounding relief when I'd found Evan was really okay.

The million emotions Kale had taken me through earlier at his loft. The need and the desire and the beauty.

The pure adoration I felt then.

It was all there.

Compounding.

Kale stood from the bed, and I sucked in a shattered breath.

"Come on, let's get your little man home."

I felt him in the doorway behind me.

His presence thick and potent and powerful. It surged into the room, a crashing wave, taking me whole.

It was late, close to one in the morning.

I'd been kneeling in the same spot on the floor beside Evan's bed for the last three hours. Watching him sleep. Just . . . feeling the beat of his heart.

My amazing son, who'd fallen asleep on the way home from the hospital.

Kale had carried him in from the car and laid him in his bed. The way he'd done the night before.

Only this time, he'd stayed while I'd changed Evan into his pajamas, brought me hot tea when I'd refused to leave Evan's side, and then paced my house for hours as if he were searching for a purpose when I knew he could already feel his purpose echoing from the floors.

Footsteps shuffled behind me, quiet and subdued, before the man knelt next to me. Fingers ran the length of my hair, massaging into my neck, as his nose pressed into the locks as he inhaled.

I shivered with the whisper at my ear, "You need to get some rest. You're exhausted."

I glanced back at him, gazing into the depths of those caring, kind eyes that glinted and shone in the muted light that glowed from the lamp on Evan's nightstand. My mouth trembled, my lips soaked with the silent tears I could no longer hold back.

As if I was purging every negative thing from the day and casting up a million prayers of gratefulness at the same time. "I don't know how to leave him after a day like today."

We'd been assured he was fine.

Still, I felt chained to my son's side. Unable to move.

Kale wrapped his strong arms around me, pulling my back to his chest. I could feel the thrum, thrum, thrum of his magnificent heart. The sound reverberating and seeping into me.

"Let me take care of you. Let me take care of him," he murmured.

Shifting, he pushed to his feet, bringing me with him, sweeping me from the floor and cradling me in his arms.

I held on, sinking into the staunchest kind of security, and pressed my face up under his chin, feeling the warmth and the life. Inhaling the woodsy, masculine scent.

"I've got you," he said for what had to be the hundredth time that day.

And I trusted that he did.

He carried me out of Evan's room, through the house, and into my bedroom.

A room he'd never seen.

I could feel it when his sight landed on my massive bed, the heft of the breath that pressed from his lungs.

He moved through my room and set me down on one side. He didn't say anything, just quietly worked through the buttons of my dress. Though this time it was different. This time, it was with care and deference.

He slowly lifted it over my head. Cool air skated my skin. His gaze swept over me, but there was no smirk. No tease.

He moved to my dresser and pulled open the top right door, as if he already knew what he was looking for. Silently, he moved back through the space, his hands winding the silky soft pink nightgown over my head, gliding it over my body where it barely landed at the top of my thighs.

Everything felt so intimate.

Our breaths and his touch and his care.

"Kale."

I didn't know what I was asking for.

He cupped the side of my face and ran his thumb along the hollow beneath my eye. "I know."

He kissed my forehead once, twice, and then lifted my covers. "Get in, sweet girl."

I sank back into the comfort.

Not just of my bed.

But the feeling that swam through my spirit. The promise that everything was going to be all right. He pulled the covers over me, and his fingertips danced across my cheek. "Sleep well,

Hope."

Exhausted, I slumped into the welcome of my pillow, my body relaxing beneath the blankets, only a fluttered breath before I was asleep.

I jolted awake to the silence. To the thick darkness of my room.

I reached over, switching on the lamp on my nightstand. I blinked, adjusting to the shadows before I pushed off the covers and slid from my bed.

Barefoot, I padded across the wooden floors. Drawn. Silently moving through the living room and back down the hall.

At Evan's door, I paused.

Kale lay on the hard floor next to the bed, a pillow from the couch under his head and a tiny throw barely covering his torso, still in his shirt and jeans.

His arm was slung up onto Evan's bed, his palm resting across my son's heart.

And that feeling—that affection that compounded and churned and swelled—it burst.

I'd known this man was *more*.

Now I knew he was everything.

I tiptoed over to the side of Evan's bed and gently ran my hand over my son's forehead.

He sighed from the depths of his sleep.

Content and safe and perfect.

And Kale's hand that was on Evan's heart? I gathered it in mine and threaded my fingers through his. Those eyes popped open, twilight on the sea.

He looked up at me before he climbed to his towering height.

He followed me without a word.

Without a sound.

The only voice the energy that rumbled beneath our feet.

twenty-one
Kale

Silently, I followed behind her. Our footsteps subdued as we waded through the tension that climbed into the atmosphere, amplifying the closer we got to her room.

Energy lapped, mounting and building in the dense, dense air. Severe.

Intense.

That storm I'd felt coming for weeks was suddenly overhead. Battering at the walls and howling at the windows.

Hope didn't look back at me as she led me through the living room, her head bowed, her motions somehow deliberate. Like she was moving through honey.

The minutes set to slow. Like we didn't have to rush.

But there was no doubt, no hesitation in her decision.

I could feel it galloping ahead of us. This girl already riding toward a divine destination.

Inviting me to join her.

Part of me screamed and raged, tearing at my insides, shouting at me to go. To tell her this was a horrible idea. It was four in the morning and our walls were down.

I needed to leave because I had no idea where this path was going to lead us, and if I hurt her, I wasn't sure I'd make it through this time.

Because she brought every old feeling back. Ones I'd never thought I'd feel again. Then she multiplied it by something that was brand new. Bigger than anything I'd felt. Not once. Not ever.

Only her.

Blips of the day flashed through my mind. The girl blowing my mind. Confessing to her that I'd lost the first and only girl I'd ever loved. The sheer terror I'd felt over Evan. The fact I hadn't been able to walk away when I'd brought them back here.

And I knew.

I knew.

I wanted to try.

God. I wanted to try. Hope's breaths turned shallow when she guided me through the threshold of her doorway and into the dimmed, shadowy glow that clung to her bedroom.

Golden shadows and a lusty haze.

Just inside, she dropped my hand. Slowly, she swiveled around to face me, her chin lifting on a lurching breath. I saw the offering just as clearly as I heard the plea.

Her legs were bare beneath that tiny slip of a gown.

Every damned inch of me grew hard at the sight, my chest tightening and my dick thickening, begging at my jeans.

I shifted to quietly latch the door shut and flicked the lock.

The promise of it hit the room like a sonic boom.

I stepped forward, erasing the distance between us, my fingertips reaching out to flutter along the delicate column of her neck.

Her pulse thrummed an erratic, reckless beat. I trailed them back up, over the divot in her chin, and ran them across the pout of those lush, full lips. "You are so beautiful, Hope. So beautiful that I think I have to be dreaming right now."

"I need you, Kale," she whispered across my fingertips.

It sent a spiral of need curling through me.

Lust.

Greed.

Possession.

"I need you," she whispered again.

Every muscle in my stomach clenched when she stepped back and gathered the hem of her nightgown in her hands. Slowly, she peeled it over her body.

Exposing herself. Inch by delicious inch.

After tugging it over her head, she dropped it to the floor.

That mass of hair fell around her bare shoulders, caressing over her collarbones. Kissing her tits.

Pink, pert, pebbled nipples peeked through the long strands like the most brutal kind of tease.

Her belly flat and her waist narrow, hips flared and wide, thighs full.

Pussy covered by the same scrap of underwear that had earlier been on my floor.

That felt like a lifetime ago.

Like everything had changed. Like time had shifted and I no longer knew where I was.

A shudder took to my spine, lighting up my insides.

I ran the back of my knuckles across one peaked nipple.

She emitted a tiny moan.

"Is this what you need? You need me to touch you?"

She looked up at me. Baring herself. "I just need you. The only thing I need is you."

"Hope," I murmured, knowing exactly what this girl was saying.

Her heart and spirit soaring through the room.

Spinning around me.

Sucking me in.

I gripped her by the back of the head, my fingers splaying wide, drawing her to me.

I kissed her slowly. Deeply. Because right then, I got that this girl needed to be treated delicately.

Carefully.

That in her amazing strength, she was fragile and vulnerable, and she needed someone to hold her up. Treat her like a queen.

And I wanted to be him. That guy she said she saw when she looked at me. The guy who might make her better rather than destroy her a little more in the end.

"I need you," she muttered again, a sigh against my lips.

"I need you, too, Hope. Fuck. I need you, too."

There was so much in that statement. Things that burned in that cold, dark place. Impaling the numbness I'd surrendered it to.

Her light threatening to bring that dead place back to life.

My kiss was a slow claiming, as I backed her across her room until she butted against the bed. She didn't hesitate to crawl on top.

Our breaths heaving into the dense air when we broke apart.

The girl watched me through the shadows that jumped and danced against her bedroom walls while I stood there, taking her in, all lush milky skin and fiery red hair and hopeful, trusting eyes.

So damned gorgeous where she rested on her elbows with her knees bent and feet planted on the bed.

Rocking softly.

Touch me.

Love me.

Protect me.

Body singing with the appeal.

"If I sleep with you, there won't be any going back for me, Kale Bryant. Don't make me fall in love with you."

Another shudder ripped through me at the thought because the way she was looking at me promised it was already too late.

"Are you sure this is what you want?" I asked her, gritting my teeth, hands fisting in restraint.

"You already know my life is in turmoil." Her words were wispy tendrils that left her sensuous mouth. "I hate that I'm dragging you into the middle of it, not knowing what's going to happen. But if I'm sure of one thing? I'm sure of you."

Heart clattering with her words, I tugged my shirt over my head and ticked through my fly, shoved down my jeans and underwear, shrugged them free of my feet.

Lust knotting my insides.

A needy sigh puffed from her lungs when she looked at me, those eyes wandering with a greedy awe as they roved over me. The girl doing her own claiming. Raking my chest. Moving down my abdomen, muscles flexing and bowing, taut with need.

Her attention dipped lower, those pink lips parting when she let her heated gaze trace over my cock.

I was hard.

So damned hard.

Harder than I'd ever been.

Because this felt different from anything I'd ever felt.

Her eyes flicked back up to mine, her words soft adoration. "How is it possible you're standing there? You are magnificent, Kale Bryant. Better than any dream. Better than any fantasy. Inside and out."

I didn't know what it was about those words. But they crushed my reservations and made me forget any old devotion and any lingering fear.

Without thought, I was reaching down, fisting her underwear in my hands, dragging them down her gorgeous legs as I dipped over her to kiss at her belly.

She squirmed and sighed.

Body reaching for mine.

And I was wondering what it really meant to dream. To hold them and possess them and never give them up.

If she and Evan could possibly become the reason for mine.

Because my heart was careening in my chest, knocking at my ribs like some kind of beast when I climbed over her, when I made a spot for myself between her thighs.

Her pussy bare. Fire against my cock that barely kissed through the slick warmth of her lips. I hesitated for a second before she whispered, "I'm on the pill."

I brushed my fingers through her hair, staring down at her. "Princess," I murmured.

Her expression shifted, so soft and tender, voice sweet affection. "Hey, Cowboy."

And fuck. I wanted to tell her I'd be her anything. Her

cowboy or her knight when the only fucking thing I wanted was to be her hero.

She looped an arm around my neck, our chests pressed together, hearts beating wild against the other.

Little pants of anticipation escaped from her mouth.

"Are you ready for me?" I asked.

She blinked at me through the shadows, the fingertips of her free hand running the line of my jaw. "I think I've been ready for you my whole life."

I grabbed the hand tracing my face, kissing her fingertips, her wrist, the inside of her forearm, hoping she knew that this meant something to me. That it was *more*. Then I hooked that arm around my neck, too. "Hold on to me, sweet girl."

I edged back a fraction. Just enough that I could watch her while I began to tuck myself deep in the tight, clutching grasp of her body.

Her walls hugging my dick perfectly as I spread her.

Sweet, sweet heat.

"Fuck . . . Hope . . . baby." It was all a guttural rasp from my mouth.

Heaven.

Didn't think I'd ever touched on it until right then. Because she was warm and snug and felt a little too close to home. Like maybe this girl had been meant for me. Like right here . . . with her was exactly where I was supposed to be.

She sucked in a sharp gasp, and her chest arched into mine.

"Kale." It was a shaky, unstable prayer.

Slipping my arms under her back, I gathered her tighter, wrapping her whole. Holding her as close as I could get her.

Our hearts battered against each other's, almost frantically, and I swore, I could feel the beats catching time. "I know. I've got you. I've got you," I told her.

And that energy—that feeling that had made me stumble the first time I'd caught the full impact of her face back at the bar—it combusted.

I should have known it that night that she had the power to change everything.

Because it spun the room and my head, licked through my veins, and knocked something loose inside me.

My spirit thrashed when it touched those dark places. Kindling and sparks.

Pushing up onto my hands, I pulled almost all the way out, until the tip of my dick was just hanging on.

My eyes swept over her sweet, sweet body where she was laid out beneath me, and her knees hugged my hips eagerly. Her nails sinking into my back. "Kale."

I pressed back into her heat.

Slow and sure.

Deep and promising.

Until I was filling her, the girl taking all of me the same way I was taking her.

Wholly.

"You are perfection. So goddamned perfect."

She whimpered, her perfect tits jutting toward me as she arched.

Demanding more. Emotion thick as it washed across her gorgeous face.

My hips dragged out then surged forward.

Possessing.

I quickened with each thrust, and Hope met every one with the needy roll of her body. Her hips lifted from the bed to meet mine, my name a constant prayer from her lips.

I dropped back to my elbows, every inch of us pressed together because we no longer knew how to be apart.

I fucked her and consumed her and murmured her name. Kissed her mouth. Her neck, her jaw, her tits. My lips everywhere I could reach.

She whimpered and begged and moaned, nails scratching deep into my skin. Sinking in until we were a blur of rocks and moans and twined bodies.

And I wanted to make a million promises.

Promise it all.

Pleasure threatened at the base of my spine, my balls tightening as I drove deeper and madder and faster.

Hope grasped at my shoulders as her moans and pleas increased.

Until she was begging, "Please. Kale. Oh, God, I'm close . . . please."

I edged back, pushing up onto a hand, giving myself a second to let the other smooth over her unforgettable face.

Then I dipped my thumb into the well of her mouth. She sucked it, tongue grazing the flesh, nearly sending me flying right then.

Tugging it free, I cupped her round, full breast and ran my thumb across her nipple.

She mewled a tiny plea.

Slowly, I dragged it down the valley of her stomach, winding her up, before I slipped it lower and against her clit.

I circled and flicked and teased as I climbed to my knees. The new position let me take her deeper.

And this time . . . I took her hard.

Her head rocked back on the mattress, and her hips lifted from the bed.

Every fuck of my hips drove her higher.

Higher and higher and higher until I could see it.

The second it split.

The orgasm ripping through her being.

Hope tried to mute her scream. To control the way the quivers of bliss ravaged her body.

It was the exact same second that ecstasy went streaking through mine.

The most intense kind of pleasure rocked through my body. I held back a roar when I came, pouring inside her, not giving a single thought to consequence except for the one where I might get to keep her.

I panted over her before I slumped down, resting most of my weight on top of her. Hope wrapped her slender arms back around me and held on as I rolled us to our sides.

She smiled at me.

Smiled this smile that demolished me.

"Are you okay?" I asked her.

Her fingertips danced across my brow, my jaw, my lips. It wasn't shyness that blossomed on her cheeks, just soft, sweet affection. "I think you ruined me."

There was a tease in it, mixed with a heavy dose of awe.

I let the smirk ride to my mouth and pulled her naked body flush with mine. "You think *you're* ruined?"

A giggle slipped between her swollen lips. "Really?"

I ran the palm of my hand over the top of her head, cupping it from behind. "Yeah, really, Hope. That was . . . I don't know how to properly describe what I feel when I'm with you. And getting to be with you like that? Inside you? You own me, Princess."

Redness flushed her cheeks, and she drummed her fingers over my bare shoulder. "I'm pretty sure it's the other way around, Kale. I've never experienced anything like that."

I ran my nose down her face, nuzzling up under her chin. "So, you're telling me you like my stamina after all?"

Another giggle. "If I tell you I do, will it go to your head?"

I laughed, pressing my hips to hers in a playful way, my dick already perking up with the contact. "Uh, I'm thinking that's a possibility."

Smacking at my arm, she laughed, keeping it quiet, so much easiness floating through the air. I gathered her closer and locked my arms fully around her, loving the way she felt against me.

All warm, silky flesh and lush curves and tender spirit.

Light.

Rolling again, I pulled her on top of me, and more of those giggles slipped free. And fuck. I loved being her haven. Giving her some reprieve.

She pressed her palms to my chest and pushed up, red hair falling all around her, lighting up in the dawn of the day that was barely breaking at the window.

She stared down at me, all that belief shining around her like a halo.

And this gorgeous girl?

Looking up at her?

I was gone.

Incinerated.

"What you did today, Kale . . ." Sincerity took hold of her expression, and she chewed at her bottom lip, like she was searching for what to say. "I want you to know how much that meant to me. You staying with us."

"I wanted to be there," I told her, threading my fingers through the fall of her hair.

Her eyes searched mine. Honestly. "I wanted you to be there, too."

A heavy sigh pressed between my lips. "I hate that I have to, but I'm going to need to put in a transfer of care for Evan. It isn't a good idea for me to see him as my patient if you and I are together."

It was a tweak of joy that pulled at the corner of her lush mouth, though concern swam in her eyes. "Is that what we are . . . together?"

I bucked up a little. "Sure feels like it to me."

Heat bloomed on those sweet cheeks, her freckles prominent in the wash of the sunrise that glowed against her face. Hesitation rimmed her words when she said, "But you do this all the time."

I shot up to sitting, framing both sides of her face in my hands. "No, Hope. I don't do this all the time. Not like this."

"It feels different, doesn't it?" she asked, voice almost whimsical as she chanced meeting my eyes.

I cupped the side of her neck. "Yeah . . . it feels different. It feels better."

It feels right.

A sad smile tweaked her mouth. "I hate the idea of you not seeing him. You're a good doctor, Kale."

"I want to be."

"Does this scare you?" There she was, once again, so goddamned open. Vulnerable and honest and real. No games.

I refused to play them, either. "Yeah. It fucking terrifies me."

"I don't ever want to put you in a position you don't want to be in, Kale. I'd never back you into a corner. But you need to know, Evan is my life, and every choice I make affects him. I have to be careful, especially with what's going on with his father right now. Most of all, I need you to know I will do whatever it takes to protect him."

There was almost a warning in her words.

Anger flamed, and I pushed it down, refusing to let that bastard come into our sacred space.

Instead, I wrapped my arms around her slender waist and tipped my head back so I could read her expression better. "I'm not here to yank you around, Hope. You already made yourself perfectly clear, and I knew what I was doing when I followed you into this room. I get it. I know what's on the line."

With her, I wanted to walk it.

She wrapped her arms tighter around me, pressed her mouth to my neck. "I didn't expect you, Kale Bryant."

I hugged her body against mine, our hearts synced, beating in time. "I definitely didn't expect you, Hope."

I glanced at the clock on her nightstand. "I should go before Evan wakes up."

"Yeah," she agreed, albeit reluctantly.

I shifted so I could toss her onto her back on her bed. Giggling, she bounced, red, red hair splayed all around her, her smile brighter than the sun that rose through her window.

My chest clenched. Never thought I could feel this way.

I climbed off her bed, feeling the heat of her gaze as she watched me dress from behind. When I turned back to her, she had her sheets pressed to her mouth, blushing all over the place.

God. This girl.

I leaned over and planted my hands on her bed, kissed her mouth. "You can ogle me any time you want, Princess. You don't have to be shy about it. I've been ogling you since the second I met you."

"It's just . . . you're gorgeous, Kale. Such a beautiful man. Inside and out. I don't think I ever want to stop looking at you."

I dipped down closer. "And you're the best damned thing I've ever seen."

I let my gaze rake her body. "Fair warning . . . next time I get you in bed, I'm not gonna be so easy on you."

Because there I was, wanting to climb right back onto her bed and take her again. My mind running wild with fantasies. The ways I wanted to have her. Wanting to incite that sweet little vixen.

Redness splashed those cheeks when she grinned. "Is that a promise?"

I growled, buried my face in her neck before I pushed back, smirking down at her. "You are in so much trouble, Harley Hope."

She ran her fingers through my hair. "Figured as much. I knew you were trouble the first time I saw you."

I pecked her mouth again. "I'll swing by later, if that's okay? Check up on Evan?"

Her expression grew soft. "Yeah, that would be nice."

"Why don't you try to get some more rest? Yesterday was a long day."

She tucked her bottom lip between her teeth, gave a nod. "Okay."

"Okay," I told her in encouragement before I straightened. Wavered.

Looked around her room, not really wanting to leave but knowing I needed to.

She was right.

We had to be careful with Evan. Their lives were riddled with complications, and I definitely didn't want to make a single one of them worse.

I headed for her door where I slowly and quietly released the lock. The door barely creaked when I opened it. I tiptoed out, leaving it open a crack behind me, heading for the door.

I froze when I saw the mess of red hair sticking up all over the place from over the top of the couch.

I wondered if it'd make me a horrible person if I tried to sneak out, taking advantage of his disability that way.

But he'd already noticed the movement, anyway. His eyes keen and knowing, the kid always picking up on more than I thought he would.

He scrambled from the couch, going for the pad that was on

the coffee table like he'd been waiting for me.

Furiously, he scratched something on the top sheet, and I slowly eased around to the front of the couch. I sank down onto the edge of it, the coward's side of me wanting to bolt.

Somehow sitting there made me feel like I was fifteen and had been caught sneaking out the window of my girlfriend's bedroom in the middle of the night, her dad standing with a shotgun on the lawn, waiting for me.

Which was ridiculous.

Or not.

Because my eyes bugged out of my damned head when I saw what he'd written.

Did you and my mom do it?

Evan's green eyes were hard and demanding behind his thick-rimmed glasses, his demeanor a little mad when he shoved it at me.

I roughed my palm over my face. Apparently, that feeling hadn't been so off base.

Warily, I eyed him, watching him carefully when I took the pen and wrote out a response.

How do you know what that is?

He seemed annoyed when he snatched it back.

I'm 8. Almost 9.

"Exactly," I said, knowing he was reading my lips.

He scribbled more.

Do you even watch TV?

A disbelieving laugh jolted free, nerves and caution and unease.

He scribbled again.

Did you sleep in her bed?

How the hell was I supposed to answer that? I didn't want to lie. Fuck, I didn't want to lie to this kid.

Because I saw it all over him.

He thought he was the one who was supposed to be protecting his mom.

Looking out for her.

The man of the house.

And I didn't think he really knew exactly what he was asking me, but I knew it was wholly important to him.

My chest tightened, and I swallowed around the lump in my throat, leaned over, watching him as I wrote.

That's private between your mom and me.

I knew in his expression that answer brought him to his conclusion.

In a flash, he was on his feet in front of me.

Tears of anger and frustration glistened in his eyes when his hands frantically signed.

No. I couldn't read it.

But I knew exactly what he said.

BUT DO YOU LOVE HER?

Everything clenched and crushed, and I was rubbing my mouth again, dropping my hand to make sure he could see.

"It's complicated, Evan," I said.

He was back to the pad, the pen cutting deep into the paper.

You have to love her if you live here. That's the rule.

And God, he was so innocent and wise. Smarter than I was. Seeing the world so simply.

I reached out and grabbed him by the outside of the shoulders, dragging him a step toward me, wishing with all of me he could *hear* me. That I could communicate with him better.

That I could make him understand something that I didn't fully understand, either.

"I care about your mom, Evan. I care about her so much. And I care about you. Okay?"

Without warning, his tears were running free, and I had him in my arms, hugging him against me.

I suddenly realized so many things about those complications that Hope had warned me about.

This kid and his mom had been through hell, and he was terrified of a man taking them there again. I pulled back, dried his eyes. "I won't hurt her."

He swiped his forearm under his nose. "Promise," he said. His lips formed the word, but the sound he forced from his throat was unintelligible.

But I heard.

I heard.

"I promise."

He stared at me for a beat before he nodded. *OK.*

Okay.

I huffed out a breath, hit with a distinct rush of relief.

I grabbed the pad and wrote out the question.

How are you feeling?

Hungry.

I chuckled.

All right then.

Breakfast.

I stood and offered him my hand. And there weren't a whole lot of things in the world that felt better than when he took it.

twenty-two

Hope

It was early afternoon when I heard a clatter in the foyer. The front door banged open then slammed shut. Two seconds later, Jenna stumbled through the kitchen archway.

Hair a mess. Clothes splattered with dough and streaked in frosting.

Frazzled and unnerved.

Her gaze darted to Evan, who was sitting on his knees on the stool next to me with his elbows propped on the counter as he Snapped with Josiah.

As if he hadn't been through the trauma of yesterday.

Jenna had been at the coffee shop this morning when I'd called to let her know what had happened. The weekend manager had been short-staffed, so she'd gone in to pick up the slack.

She went right for him, hauling him into her arms, hugging him tight and peppering a bunch of sloppy kisses all over his head and face.

"Is he okay?" she asked, her eyes cutting up to me from over his head.

I nodded, fighting that rush of terror I was struck with when I thought of what might have been. Instead, I forced myself into focusing on the fact he was here.

Whole.

Healthy.

"He got a little out of breath. Chanda and Richard were concerned, so they rushed him in. He was fine by the time I got there."

No. It hadn't been our first urgent trip to the ER, and I hated to accept that it certainly wouldn't be our last. But it was the life we lived. But it sure didn't ever get any easier. Terrified that one day the diagnosis wouldn't be so simple. That our worlds might be rocked once again.

"Thank God," she said, squeezing him tighter. He pulled back, sending her a huge grin, shaking his head as if he thought she was being ridiculous.

She set him back on the stool and ruffled his hair before dropping down low to be sure he was watching her face. "You have to stop scaring me like that."

He gave her an indulgent nod, signing, *I DON'T MEAN TO SCARE YOU, AUNTIE.*

Jenna only signed well enough to pick up on whatever my son was trying to say.

She ran a tender hand down the side of his face. "I know, sweetheart. I know."

Evan immediately went back to his iPad.

Straightening, she ran both her palms over her face and blew a big puff of air between her lips.

She gave me that look, the one asking if I was okay.

I grimaced, not sure how to answer that question. Yesterday had been horrible, bad enough to drop me to my knees, and still one of the best days of my life.

I was struggling to process all the emotions roiling inside me.

I could still taste Kale on my breath and feel him on my skin.

"Yesterday was rough," I told her, "but I promise I'm okay. I'm just thankful it turned out the way it did."

I turned to make sure Evan couldn't see me speaking before I set my attention back on Jenna. "You know I'm going to have to borrow more money to pay for that visit."

We'd figured paying out of pocket for Evan's medical care for a year was going to be steep. But we hadn't prepared for any emergencies, praying we could eke by on the bare minimum, going with it, riding on the hope that it would all work out in the end.

"Don't you dare mention money, Hope. I told you from the start, I'm in this with you."

I blinked, pushing out the words around the heavy emotion in my throat. "I just hate that I'm putting your livelihood on the line, right along with mine. It isn't fair to you, Jenna."

"Pssh." She waved me off with a wry grin. "Don't give yourself so much credit. Who do you think the criminal mastermind is around here? If I hadn't have come up with the idea, you never would have been in the middle of this. Just be thankful I'm your BFF—best friend felon."

My brows lifted. "Best friend felon?"

"Um, I did go into a dark alley to make that happen. Doesn't get more gangster than that."

"So hardcore," I teased her, letting myself latch on to her mood. Because she was right. It was all gonna work out. I just had to hold out a little longer.

"Hey, that dude was scaaaary," she drew out, before she fanned herself. "And hot. On all things holy, that man was hotter than Hades. Hell, he might have been Lucifer himself."

Only Jenna.

She dropped her smile. "But seriously, the last thing I want you worrying about is money. We'll figure it out, no matter what. We're almost to the end. We've got this, okay?"

"Okay."

"Good."

Shucking off the heaviness, I grabbed a coffee mug from the cupboard and waved it toward her. "You want?"

Her eyebrows disappeared behind her messy bangs. "After a day like today? That cup had better have wine in it."

I laughed, shaking my head. "Wine it is."

Ducking into the fridge, I pulled out a chilled bottle of rosé. I hunted in the drawer for the opener, focused on tearing off the foil and popping the cork.

"So, why didn't you call me yesterday?" she asked. "You know I hate the idea of you having to go through something like that on your own. One call, and you know either me or your mama would be there in a flash."

There was a hint of hurt in her tone. A little bit of conniving, too.

Because Jenna knew me so well that I was pretty sure she'd waltzed through that door and saw everything about me was different.

That my insides had been rearranged to make room for something new.

Something beautiful and wonderful.

Magical.

I could feel the flush race up my neck, and I dropped my face toward the floor, trying to conceal what was probably written all over me, anyway.

"Harley Hope Masterson, you better fess up right now . . . because I see that pink hitting your cheeks, and you haven't even had a sip of your wine."

I peeked up at her. "I didn't have to go through it alone."

"And who might it have been at the hospital with you?"

Evan caught my attention in my periphery when he sat upright, nonchalantly signing, *K-A-L-E*.

Little stinker. He had a knack of knowing exactly when to start paying attention, picking up on the little bits I might want to keep hidden.

But there had been no hiding what I felt this morning when I'd gotten up and could hear the deep tenor of Kale's voice echoing through my walls.

After I'd thought he was sneaking out when I'd wanted to beg him to stay.

I'd tiptoed out to find the staggering sight of the man in there with my son. Cooking for him. Laughing with him. Caring for him.

After the night we'd shared together, seeing him there like that had almost been too much.

Triumph glinted in Jenna's eyes as they slanted from Evan toward me. "Oh, really."

Evan was back to divulging all my secrets. *YUP. AND HE SPENT THE NIGHT AND MADE ME BREAKFAST. HE'S HER BOYFRIEND.*

The last he said with a little shrug.

No big deal.

Jenna choked, sputtered over her laugh, that original triumph shifting to an all-out celebration of victory. "You little slut."

"Jenna," I hissed, glancing at Evan, who'd decided we were boring after all, his attention wrapped up in watching Josiah dancing around the screen with his face the center of a flower.

She stalked toward me, a gleam in her eyes, and then turned so her back was toward Evan. "Was he good? Oh, God, I bet that doctor is amazing with those big hands. I told you all you needed was a big, yummy dick and all would be right with the world."

Her words deviated from a salacious secret to a breathy wisp to the worst kind of tease.

"A lady never tells," I tried to defend.

Though I might as well have been shouting it from the rooftops with the way heat went flushing over every inch of me, the memory of the way he'd touched me. Bringing me to ecstasy as if he were the one who'd always possessed my pleasure, the one sent to deliver it.

"Oh, come on, Hope. That's a total crock, and you know it. You've at least got to tell me if the man knows where the clicker is."

How she and I were friends, I didn't know. When I didn't answer, her grin just grew, yet, her voice turned soft. "At least tell me he knows how to treat you right. That's the only thing I want for you. Don't ever settle. Not again."

I cracked, whispering, "He definitely knows how to treat me right."

In every way.

We were all hushed secrets behind the corner Jenna had backed me into. "How right?"

"So right." My tummy flipped at the thought.

"Like . . . how . . . how right?" She angled her head, prying the truth out of me.

"Like, so very right. Like I've never felt anything close to the way I do when I'm with him. Not in all my life."

She squeezed me in her arms like a miracle just had happened. "Praise Mary."

Then she pulled me back, staring at me as all the prying tease left her voice. "Are you okay?" she asked me again. Though this time, the question was entirely different.

Because when I said she knew me, she knew me. She knew I'd never have slept with him if it didn't mean something to me.

I searched around inside myself for what to say. How to express what it was I really felt. "My life is crazy with Dane right now . . . I feel like I'm running faster and faster, trying to outrun him, praying he doesn't catch us."

All the while not fully understanding why he was chasing us in the first place.

My words started to become breathy, the horror of what Dane might actually do, what he might actually want.

"I'm terrified of what's coming. But somehow . . . that world? Right now, it feels like it's stronger than it has ever been. Like maybe Kale is holding some pieces together I might have lost if I had to do this alone."

"He's good with Evan?"

"He's amazing with him."

She rubbed her thumbs where she was still holding me by the arms. "But you know it's got to be more than that, Hope. This can't just be about Evan. And I know you live for that boy, as you should, but you deserve to find happiness in the middle of that, too. Real happiness."

I knew she was prodding. Digging deeper. Forcing me to evaluate everything. That was Jenna's way. Goading and coaxing and shoving me toward something she might think I needed and then urging me to look at it for what it was.

Playing devil's advocate. "It's so much more than just that."

I glanced at Evan before turning back to her. "Evan will always be my first priority, and I'll never allow a man into our lives who doesn't care about him. But this . . . what I feel?" I splayed my hands flat across my chest. "It's overwhelming and wonderful and terrifying, and what happened between us last night? It was bigger—more powerful—than anything I could have imagined."

Magical. A fantasy that shouldn't have been real.

"I want to feel like this, every day, for the rest of my life. And I want to get to do it with him."

She huffed an affectionate breath and edged back. "Oh, Harley Hope. You're already in love with him."

Maybe it made me a fool.

Naïve and unsuspecting.

"I don't think I could have stopped myself from falling for that man if I'd tried."

She quirked a playful brow. "He is delicious. Sex on a stick. Tell me we are naming a cupcake after him."

"Watch yourself," I tossed at her with a small laugh.

My phone chirped on the island. I went for it, unable to stop the force of my smile when I read the text.

"Look at you over there, grinning like you just swallowed a big ol' canary," Jenna teased. "Don't think I need to ask you who it is. What's he sayin'?"

"He wants Evan and I to go over to his place for pizza and a movie this evening. He said he'd pick us up since my car is still over there."

"Oh, Harley Hope. I think that man just might be a keeper."

"I know."

He was so, absolutely a keeper. I could only pray he was really ready for it. For us. That he understood what being with us would be like.

Because Evan and I? I knew we were a big decision. What I knew would be a huge change to his life . . . his previous lifestyle so different than the kind of life we had to offer.

But I knew, with all of me, that Evan and I could fill his life

247

with so much joy. The kind of joy he had evoked in me.

And my heart?

It was always hung on hope.

And all I was hoping was Kale could see it, too. That he really wanted it.

That he would take a chance on us.

twenty-three
Hope

A rim of light blazed at the edge of the horizon as the day sank away. The twinkling lights that were strung between the buildings sparked to life and spilled in through the bank of windows that overlooked Kale's balcony and the bustling city below, casting his loft in a warm glow.

Or maybe the warm glow was actually radiating from Evan and Kale where they sat facing each other on the expansive plush rug on the floor.

We'd just finished eating pizza, our bellies satisfied and full.

I watched them from where I was curled up on the same couch, in the very spot Kale had undone me yesterday afternoon.

God, that seemed like a lifetime ago. Another world. As if a stake had been driven into time, segmenting and dividing it, giving us a new direction and a new day.

A new chance.

A chance that maybe the three of us could become one.

A rush of nerves streaked my spine. Hope and a niggle of fear. Because Kale and I were moving fast. So fast that I was still struggling to wrap my mind around the fact I'd given myself to him last night.

Fully.

Wholly.

But somehow, despite everything that was going against us, every worry and every complication, I knew this beautiful man with that huge, magnificent heart was meant for me.

Because there he sat, grinning at my son, his right hand lifted as he attempted to copy the sign language letters Evan was trying to teach him.

"Like this?" he asked aloud, concentrating and still getting it horribly wrong.

Emotion pulsed in my chest, lost to the adorableness of it all. The man, who was larger than life and seemed as if he could accomplish anything, couldn't seem to manage to get his fingers to cooperate.

Evan rapidly shook his head and reached out and tried to move Kale's hand into the correct position.

Like that, Evan mouthed.

Kale's hand curled into some kind of deformed ball as he struggled to keep the position. "Got it!"

I bit back my amusement at his fumbling because he *so* didn't have it. Honestly, it seemed downright absurd, considering I knew firsthand the type of *magic* those fingers could evoke.

Evan laughed that scraping sound. I could feel the echo of it ripple across the wooden floor. Joy and life. Vigorously, Evan shook his head while he leaned over to write on his notepad, all too eager to hold it up for Kale to see.

Dr. Bryant, you're not even close.

"What?" Kale defended playfully. He sent me a roguish wink that made my tummy tumble before he let his expression wind into a goofy face that he directed at my son. "What are you talking about? That was perfect. I mean, how hard can making an 'A' be?"

Evan wrote some more.

Too hard for you!

In mock horror, Kale's mouth dropped open. "Hey, I thought you told me the first time I met you that you were going to let me try to keep up with you?"

Evan's little hand flew across the page.

I said you could TRY to keep up with me.

"And you think you're too fast for me?"

A downpour of love flooded me as I watched Kale interact with my child. These overpowering, stunning emotions hitting me from every side.

They were feelings that were foreign, though, I intrinsically knew I'd been missing them all along.

Emphatically, Evan nodded, grinning big enough to fill the room.

"Oh, little man, you better run, because I'm about to show you just how fast I am," Kale warned.

Evan's eyes widened in both surprise and delight, and he scrambled to his feet at the same second Kale leapt to his. Evan darted across the living room and Kale was hot on his heels.

Always *just* missing him as they zigzagged and weaved.

Evan's sock covered feet slid on the slick floor as he rounded the island in the kitchen and came running back for me, arms thrown above his head and face tipped toward the ceiling, silent laughter pouring free.

I stretched my arms out for Evan. "Hurry, Evan. Mom's home base!" I called.

Right before Evan made it to me, Kale scooped him up from behind and tossed Evan onto his back, galloping around the room with him, Kale's deep laughter ricocheting against the walls.

Both of them were smiling these smiles that blasted through me.

So wide.

So happy.

So right.

I pressed my palm over my mouth. Overcome. Because I'd had no idea I'd wanted this so much.

No true idea how much I'd been lacking until Kale had filled that vacant place. I had to wonder how much my son had been lacking, too. I'd spent years trying to compensate. To fill all the holes Dane's rejection had to have carved into his innocent spirit.

Suddenly, I hungered for it, this feeling of completeness that took me over and set me free when Kale looked at me that certain way.

As if I were his everything and he would always crave more.

Added and multiplied to that was the way he treated my son.

Accepting his disability and still acting as if it weren't there to begin with.

Adoring him in spite of it.

Loving him because of it.

Love.

Is that what shone when Kale grinned up at my son, holding him in the security of his arms and still allowing him to fly?

"Got you," Kale sang.

Evan kicked and flailed and laughed before Kale settled him on his feet and ruffled his fingers through my son's mess of red, red hair.

Somehow, I understood exactly the way Kale felt in that moment. Evan was eight, yet still so vulnerable. I always had this incredible urge to pick him up and hold him. Protect him forever and never allow anything to happen to him.

I could see the exact same feeling written all over Kale's face.

Evan began to frantically sign, hands flying in front of him.

Kale looked over at me for help, and a shiver raked across my flesh when the power of his gaze landed on me.

"He said you're stronger than Superman," I told him, trying to keep the needy tremor from my voice.

Kale chuckled and looked back at Evan. "Superman, huh? My goddaughter, Frankie Leigh, would argue with you. She insists I'm Captain America."

Evan signed again.

"He wants to know who she is," I said, emotion tightening my throat.

Kale widened his eyes in emphasis. "Wonder Woman, of course."

Evan grinned, his own eyes going wide with excitement. This conversation had definitely taken a turn down Evan alley.

WHO AM I? he signed and mouthed at the same time.

"That's a no brainer. You've got to be The Hulk. Smart as a whip and look at these muscles."

Kale squeezed Evan's tiny bicep.

Evan's whole body rocked with his glee, and he forced out the rasping words, as if he couldn't hold back his praise. "Dr. Bryant."

Slowing, Kale's gaze turned tender. "What do you say you start calling me Kale instead of Dr. Bryant?"

Affection burst in my chest.

Evan signed quickly, his head cocked to the side with the question.

"He asked if that's because you're his friend now." My words were choppy.

A warm smiled pulled to Kale's lips, something so genuine and sincere. "Yeah, buddy, because you're my friend. Because I care about you."

Evan signed, *OKAY*, beaming at the man who continued to weave himself deeper and deeper into my skin.

Into my heart.

"Good," Kale said as if what he'd just done didn't matter all that much. "I think it's movie time. What do you say we put us on some superheroes, and we can decide exactly which we are? I have just about every Marvel movie ever made."

YES! Evan signed, giving a little fist pump in the air.

A small giggle fluttered from my lips, but my tone was coated with the emotion that gathered thick. "Careful, Evan won't ever want to leave."

My insides fluttered when he began to stalk toward me.

Potent.

Powerful.

Persuasive.

That was what the man looked like. Persuasion and dominance and sex.

Most of all, right then, he looked like he was mine.

I sucked in a breath when he leaned over me, his mouth coming to my ear. "Maybe that's my intention."

"Don't say things you don't mean," I whispered.

He pulled back and stared down at me, those blue eyes intense. "What if I do?"

That crazy attraction I felt around him climbed to the air. This time fuller. Denser. Brimming with *more.*

So badly that I wanted to lean forward so I could press my mouth to his.

Touch him and claim him as mine.

But we'd decided to take it slow in front of Evan. Working him into the idea of us, especially since Kale and I hadn't quite established what that meant.

But it was Kale who pushed it further, inching closer, the words a breathy murmur that sent a shiver down my spine. "I can't wait to be inside you again. I've been dying to touch you since the second you walked through my door. Second I get the chance? You're mine."

Oh.

Butterflies scattered in my belly and desire pooled. There was nothing I could do but press my thighs together.

Kale edged back with a smirk. "That's what I thought, Princess."

As if he hadn't just made my knees knock, he stood straight and shifted his attention back to Evan.

"So, what movie do you want to watch?" Kale asked. He grabbed the remote, flicked on his big television, and switched it to the long list of his downloaded movies.

He hadn't been joking when he said he had about every Marvel movie ever made.

Boys.

Evan grabbed his pad.

We have to take a vote. That's the rule.

An affectionate chuckle rumbled from Kale. "You are just full of all kinds of rules, aren't you, little man?"

Only good rules.

Contentment seeped into my pores.
More so than I'd ever been.

Darkness swam through Kale's loft, broken by the flickers and flashes from the television as the movie played on.

We were on the second Avengers movie, and my son lay across Kale's couch, still facing the screen, his breaths soft snores as he slept the movie away.

His head was on Kale's lap and Kale was running his fingers through his hair.

I was on the other side of Kale, curled up so I could rest on his shoulder.

He pressed his lips to my temple, his voice a rough murmur. "I'm so glad you're here."

Shifting to face him more, I peered at him through the shifting light. "I'm so glad I'm here."

He traced his nose down the curve of my jaw. "You'd better be."

A tiny moan left me when he kissed down the slope of my neck. "Is that so?"

I could feel his grin against my skin. "You know it's so."

"Stalker," I whispered with a smile fluttering at my lips, the word nothing but affection.

"Knight, Princess. Knight. After last night, tell me I get to be your king."

My head tilted back, and the smile that had been threatening lit in a full bloom. "Hmm . . . I don't know," I teased, my fingers twining in his soft hair.

"Ouch, Princess. You know exactly where to hit a man where it hurts, don't you?" It was all mischief on his tongue as he kissed and nipped. "I guess you don't need me after all."

A giggle slipped free before I pulled back and cupped his face, sincerity weaving into my tone. "Yesterday was terrifying, Kale, and somehow . . . somehow you turned it into the best night of my life."

Those soulful eyes glinted in the light, his throat bobbing as he swallowed. "I don't think I've ever felt the way I felt last night," he admitted his voice gruff.

I tucked my bottom lip between my teeth before I asked, "What are we doing, Kale?"

His fingertips fluttered across my cheek. "I think we're needing each other." He blinked. "I had no idea I needed anyone or anything until I met you."

And that need . . .

I could feel it compounding and expanding and shifting.

Restoring.

"Stay with me tonight," he said.

My gaze moved to my sleeping son. "I don't think he's ready for that yet. Plus, I need to be up early to get to the shop in the morning, and Evan has his summer program."

The words flooded out like excuses I didn't want to have. But they were there, and they were real.

"I have a guest room. You both can sleep in there. I just want you near me. I need to know you're safe. I have to be at work early, too. I'll wake you first thing."

"This is getting so very complicated."

A grin tweaked his striking face. Goodness, no man should be that pretty. It just wasn't fair.

"I promise that if you stay, I'm going to take you in my room and really complicate you."

Oh, and neither was that. Not at all.

Desire exploded in the air.

Hot, heated energy.

But it was bigger than ever before.

Because I could feel it.

The love that shined all around me.

Powerfully. Brilliantly.

But looking at Kale? I was too scared to let it escape from my tongue. Afraid to put it out in the world. I knew once I said it, it was going to ring so true that I'd never be able to hear anything else.

"Stay with me," he coaxed in that magnetic way.

There was nothing I could do but relent. I guessed I'd been relenting all along. Giving and giving because I couldn't stay away. Last night, I'd fully succumbed. I should know any reservations would be futile.

"Okay," I whispered.

"Need me after all, huh, Princess?" That tease was back.

"I think I'll always need you," I murmured.

A soft smile fluttered across his sexy mouth, before he shifted around so he didn't disturb Evan. He climbed to his feet and carefully pulled my little boy into the well of his arms.

Kale hugged him to his chest.

And it spun and spun.

The love that whipped through the room like a hurricane.

The strength of it was so massive that a slice of terror cut through my center.

Awed by its beauty and intimidated by its force.

Kale started for the hall, and I climbed to my feet and followed him through the darkness.

Angling Evan a bit, he dipped down so he could turn the knob.

The room was obviously reserved for guests. The ceiling high, coffered and finished with crown molding and massive windows that overlooked the city beyond.

A rustic, four-poster bed, covered in plush, luxurious bedding, sat against the right wall.

Kale went right for it, dragging down the covers and nestling my son in its safety. He ran his fingers through Evan's hair and pressed a tender kiss to the top of his head.

Evan sighed and sank into the comfort.

I swore that I felt the ground shake beneath my feet, felt the tangle of emotion lodge in my throat.

Tears threatened to strangle me.

Overwhelming. The way Kale's aura was suddenly everything. Wisps that wound.

Vapor.

Kale headed back my way, the softest kiss pressed to my cheek. "Hold on one second, I'll be right back."

He slipped by me, disappearing for a few moments into his bedroom before he returned with a baby monitor. "I have this for Rex's kids. I know Evan's not a baby, but it will make me feel better that we can hear him if he wakes up and needs us. I set up the speaker in my room."

And that love?

That was the moment it shattered me.

He plugged in the monitor and then slowly moved back toward me. He threaded his fingers through mine and led me back into the hall, leaving the door open a crack.

A breath jutted free when he shifted and moved toward me. My back hit the opposite wall of the hall.

He pushed his fingers into my hair, his nose back to running along my jaw. "I haven't even gotten to kiss you yet. I've been going out of my mind thinking about last night. About you spread out under me. Your sweet body. Want to get lost in it, Hope. Get lost in you."

A whimper left me, and I fisted my hands into his T-shirt. "I will never forget feeling you for the first time . . . the way it felt the moment you took me."

That piece that would always belong to him.

He lightly swept his lips across mine.

Fire.

I swore that one brush was all it took for this man to set me on fire.

My phone blipped from my back pocket.

Kale dropped his forehead to mine. "Someone has awful timing."

"Whoever it is can wait because I'm not sure I can."

A sexy chuckle rumbled from his chest. "Ah . . . there she is . . . my little vixen hiding under all that sweet. I love it when she comes out to play."

My phone blipped again.

"Shit." He pulled back, those blue eyes glimmering, hovering somewhere between playfulness and lust. "If that's Jenna, you'd better get it."

The smallest laugh jolted free. "Don't tell me you're afraid of my best friend."

A smirk ticked up at one side of that delicious mouth. "Not scared. Terrified. You know she threatened to cut off my dick."

"No," I wheezed, embarrassment riding to my face.

She had no shame.

Kale ran a thick lock of my hair between his thumb and forefinger, flirty play moving across his features. "It is my best asset. I don't think I can risk it . . . for your sake."

He grinned one of those earth-shattering grins. The kind that was cocky and arrogant and did funny things to my insides.

Heat flashed to my face, flutters lighting in my belly and making my hands tremble. I fumbled to reach for my phone, the words a wisp. "You're ruinin' me, Kale Bryant."

He nuzzled under my chin, leaving a trail of kisses across the sensitive skin. "Oh, baby, trust me, I plan on it."

Oh God.

This man.

I quickly slipped my thumb across my screen, sure Kale was right and it was Jenna checking on us. Hell, knowing her, she was probably wanting a play by play.

When I saw what was on the screen, it was instant. The way fear cinched down on my chest like the tightest band and sickness clawed at my spirit.

Nausea churned in my gut.

Unknown: Last chance, Harley, before I see to it that you never see your son again.

Kale edged back, eyes slanted down so he could read me in

the darkness. "What's wrong?"

Anxiety climbed my throat, clotting and suffocating. I tried to force it down. Play it off. "It's just my ex."

Anger.

In a flash, it had taken Kale hostage. His entire being vibrated with rage.

Fierce and brutal and savage.

His voice was grit. "What does he want?"

I had a feeling if I told him the whole truth, he would go flying out the door. Set on destruction. Intent on crushing anything that might stand as a threat to Evan or me.

But I couldn't hide this from him. Not when I'd already dragged him into the middle of it. I turned my phone toward him so he could see what it said.

Fury.

It ignited on Kale's face.

Kerosene.

This was not a knight dressed in shining, unblemished armor. Not the kind fairy tales were made of.

This was the kind that filled history books.

The kind that fought to the death for what they believed was right.

Kale pressed a fist to the wall at the side of my head as if he was barely holding on, coming unhinged, words gravel as they scraped from his throat. "I want to erase him, Hope. I want to hunt him down and destroy him. Make sure he can never hurt you or Evan. Not ever again."

"I hate him," I admitted over the clot of horror and fear bottled like acid in my chest.

Kale dropped his forehead to mine, this time in a tortured, rattled rage. "Who is he?"

I blinked, pressed my mouth to the roar of his heart that pounded through his shirt. "You can't do something crazy, Kale. You can't. You have to trust me that I'm doing everything to end this and end it for good."

I'd already gotten myself in deep enough without drawing more attention.

I needed to do this quietly and swiftly.

And God, I wanted to tell Kale, admit it all. But he was still Evan's doctor, and I wasn't sure I could risk putting him in that position.

Endanger him that way.

It wasn't fair.

It wasn't right.

So instead, I pushed my phone into my back pocket and wound my hands back into the fabric of Kale's shirt. Clinging to him. Hoping he could hear the beat of truth in my words.

"I'll do whatever it takes to keep him away from my son. But the next months are going to be difficult. I'm up for the greatest fight of my life. I need you to know, I will do anything, sacrifice anything, to make sure I win that fight."

I was gathering evidence.

Each text.

Each message.

Each threat.

My attorney was sure that would be all the proof of abuse we needed. The callousness and carelessness.

Kale groaned, as if it caused him pain. "And what if I want to be the one to do it? Protect him. Save him." His big hand slid to my face. "*Save you.*"

My words were a breath. "You're already savin' me. In so many ways."

Kale groaned again. But this time, it was in need. "God damn it, Hope. God damn it, what have you done to me?"

His mouth slanted over mine.

Commanding.

Demanding all of me.

Tangles of tongue and nips of teeth.

He didn't break the kiss when he hoisted me from my feet and pressed me deeper against the wall, his hands on the outsides of my thighs as he made a place for himself between my legs.

He rubbed himself at my center, his cock hard, as desperate as his touch.

I ached and whimpered, my fingers sinking into his shoulders.

As if I might be able to hold on to him forever. "Kale."

"I won't let him hurt you. I won't. Not you or Evan. You're mine."

Need tumbled through me. A raging storm.

This man too much.

Too perfect.

He pulled me from the wall and carried me the rest of the way down the hall and through the double doors at the end of it. He stepped inside, nudged the door shut with his foot, and fumbled to click the lock behind him.

He pulled back, staring up at me as he carried me into the center of the enormous, darkened room, the only light filtering in through the wall of sliding doors that overlooked the city below.

His room luxury and peace and comfort.

Masculine.

Sexy.

That was what I felt when he kneaded his big hands into my bottom, kissing me again and murmuring, "I'm losing myself."

I framed his face in my hands. "And I'm finding myself." He carried me toward his bed, which was massive and imposing, just like the man. Slowly, he slid me down his body, my feet unsteady when he set me on the floor.

He pressed a hand on either side of my neck, and I was sure he could feel the raging thunder of my pulse beating through me.

The way my heart went pound, pound, pound. "I want you, Hope. Want you in a way that scares me."

I searched his face. "Fear never negates hope. It just means we want something badly enough that we're terrified we might not get to keep it."

A groan rumbled in his chest, and he was pulling me flush against all his hard and heat. "Sweet girl."

"I need you," I returned.

The air stretched taut around us. Pushing and pulling and demanding.

That attraction alive.

A thriving, breathing entity.

We panted through it. Sucking it into our lungs, inhaling each other as all our pieces fell together.

Forming something complete and whole.

Kale stared down at me. Eyes that intense, fathomless blue.

It felt as if I were jumping into the coolest waters, floating in the deepest sea, soaring through the warmest sky.

He gripped me tight. "Told you next time I had you, I wasn't going to go easy on you."

His voice grated with the warning.

Desire boiled my blood. "Don't you know what they say . . . nothing good in life is easy."

There was no longer any question about what had gotten into me. It was this magnetic man. Seeping into my skin. Dripping into my veins.

That was the only invitation he needed. Kale was on me in a flash. His mouth swooping in to capture mine the same way he'd captured my heart.

Swiftly.

Madly.

Wholly.

Plundering—body, mind, and soul.

I felt beautiful in his arms.

Bold and sexy.

My mama would call it risqué.

She'd be right because, with Kale, I was ready to take every risk.

He flattened his hands under my shirt, running them up my back and lifting it higher and higher.

"Strawberries and cream. So fucking sweet," he murmured.

Those words sent a rush of chills skating down my neck and scattering across my flesh.

He tore my shirt over my head and dropped it to the floor before he flicked the hook of my bra and dragged it free of my arms. His eyes swept over me. Head to toe. "Look at you, Hope. You are a vision, baby. I think every fantasy I've ever had was of you, and I didn't even know it."

My spirit danced, and I was pressing my hands under his shirt, running them over the hard, defined planes of his abdomen, needing to discover him, expose every inch of smooth, tanned skin.

He stepped back and yanked it the rest of the way over his head.

A sharp breath left me at the sight. "I close my eyes, and this is what I see. You, Kale. Beautiful you. I never thought it would be possible to want a man the way I want you."

I leaned forward and pressed my lips to his chest right over his beautiful heart that thundered and sped.

Every part of this man was stunning.

Captivating.

Kale suddenly dropped to his knees in front of me. Adept fingers were quick to work free the button and zipper of my jeans. He pulled them down a fraction and dragged me forward to kiss me on the lace fabric that covered my center.

He inhaled. "So, so sweet."

My fingers twisted in his hair, and I swore I couldn't breathe. "You undo me."

The air grew thicker when he peeled both my underwear and jeans down my legs. My legs that shook as he stripped me, leaving my clothing a discarded pile on his floor.

The way he looked up at me was staggering.

He nudged my legs apart and dragged his fingers through my lips, spreading me.

I gasped.

"So sweet and wet and hot. Your pussy is perfection. Want to live in it. Fuck you day and night."

A blink of that shyness gathered on my chest and climbed to my cheeks. A part of me was shocked that I was turned on that he was talking to me this way. Shocked that I was standing there letting him touch me this way.

My world flipped so quickly.

No longer recognizable.

But those thoughts were chased away when he slowly drove two fingers into my body.

So deep that I shuddered, my knees giving, close to buckling.

The man knocked me from my feet.

Kale pushed to his and set me on the edge of his bed. Free hand smoothing up the inside of my thigh, he spread me wide for him while he continued to pump me with the other.

"Kale," I whispered like a plea.

He dipped down and licked against that spot where I needed him most. Where I felt needy and achy and desperate. My fingers dug into his covers. "Kale . . . that feels so good. How do you make everything feel so good?"

I whimpered when he pulled his fingers free, and he edged back, leaving me a wet, quivering mess where he had me lain out on his bed.

He sent me one of those smirks as he began to shrug out of his jeans and underwear. "I'm just getting started, Princess."

He kicked free of his clothing.

An earthquake rocked me to the core, looking at him standing there that way.

Arrogant and bare and bold.

His cock jutting for the sky.

He stroked himself once.

I swore, I nearly lost it right there.

"On your hands and knees, baby."

Oh.

Oh God.

My insides trembled and shook.

Watching him, I slowly rolled over and climbed to my hands and knees. I started to crawl toward the middle of the bed.

Hot hands landed on either side of my waist, and Kale hauled me back to the edge. "Not so fast, Shortcake."

Standing behind me, he smoothed his palms over my bottom. He groaned. "Perfect."

And I knew I'd been right all along.

I was in trouble.

So, so much trouble.

Because from behind, the man licked through my crease.

I jumped then moaned, pushing back, my body begging for more.

I had the errant thought that I'd never been so exposed.

Had never given myself so freely.

Had never been so vulnerable.

But then that thought was gone, overpowered by the sensation of his tongue.

His tongue that was working the most mind-blowing bliss as he suckled and lapped, his thumbs running up and down my slit before he was easing his big fingers back inside me.

I shook, his name a whimper as he worked my body into a frenzy.

I wanted to cry when he pulled away, unable to make sense of the way this man made me feel. What he made me need. "Kale, please."

I couldn't seem to keep up, never knowing if he was coming or going, my head spinning.

Desperate for him.

His chest was suddenly plastered to my back, his penis nestled against my bottom.

This time it was two of his fingers that were pressing deep into my mouth, his mouth at my ear. "Suck, sweet girl. Taste how delicious you are . . . everything about you."

I did. I sucked them into the well of my mouth.

Unsure why it sent a rush of euphoria ripping through my body when my taste hit my tongue.

Why I felt so powerful when I was pinned.

Why I felt so confident in his hands.

Cool air hit my back when he again jerked away.

I wiggled and squirmed, my hands fisting in his bedding, not even ashamed when I panted a frenzied, "Please."

His hands were back on my bottom. Caressing and kneading. Winding me higher. "I love this sweet ass, Hope." He gripped two fistfuls in his hands.

He started running his thumb around that sensitive spot.

"Kale," I whimpered.

"Need you to know, I'm an ass man, sweet girl." His thumb pressed into that tight hole, and I clenched around him. "Not tonight, but I'm going to want to fuck it and lick it and bite it."

He shocked me again when he leaned down and sank his

teeth into the flesh of one cheek. Not enough to hurt. Enough to send my stomach tumbling with the decadent, dark threat.

From over my shoulder, I looked back at him, floored by the sight of him. My spirit reeled with the impact.

Winding us. Wrapping us. Bonding us.

I gave him my truth. "I'm yours."

He groaned, and I could feel the fat head of him broaching my lips, nudging in, spreading me. "So sweet. So fucking sweet."

Then Kale slammed into me.

Filling me full.

So full.

All other sensation lost. Nothing but him.

Taking me. Owning me the way only he could.

He clutched me by the hips when he pulled out and then took me again.

I jolted forward, my heart frantic, my need escalating as I gripped at his comforter to keep myself grounded.

Fearing I just might float away.

He began to pound into me, his cock so massive he stole my breath with each powerful thrust.

He fucked me exactly like I knew he would when I'd seen him that first time in the bar.

Arrogantly.

Confidently.

Relentlessly.

And he still felt like a broken heart. Because I had no idea what I would do if I lost him.

It was true.

I needed him.

Needed him not because I would fail without him but because he perfectly fit that hollow spot that had been carved out inside me. Filled it till it was close to overflowing, the way he was filling me right then.

Stroke after stroke.

Too much, and somehow, I wanted more.

Pleasure glowed all around me, this needy feeling that was desperate and shaky.

Sweat slicked my skin and light flickered behind my eyes.

"Is this what you wanted, Hope? Is this what you wanted? Tell me."

"Yes," I rasped, rocking back to meet every dominating thrust. "Yes. I want this. I want you."

Everything sizzled and sparked.

Kale's palm slid around to my chest, and he pulled me up, my back against his chest. I reached up and hooked my arm around the back of his neck.

Our bodies pressed together.

Sweat slicking our heated skin.

Through the reflection in the plate glass window, I met his eye. "Look at you, Hope. Look at you . . . what I see every time I look at you."

I gasped a tiny sound when I did, my body all stretched out, my breasts heavy and peaked. Flesh flushed and hair a mussed-up mess.

Kale's stunning, chiseled face gazed at me from over my shoulder. The man so gorgeous I felt the earth shake.

And I was sure I'd never felt so wanted in all my life.

So sexy.

So adored.

Kale fluttered his fingertips down over my trembling belly, before he strummed them where I throbbed, rolled those magic fingers around my clit.

He continued to drive into me from behind.

The angle almost more than I could take.

Thrust after obliterating thrust.

He spun me into the tightest knot.

And the light.

It was brilliant when it shattered.

Crashing, crushing waves.

Radiating through me. Taking me under.

I writhed and pitched and begged as the most tortuous kind of bliss flooded my body.

Kale grasped my breasts in both hands as he bucked into me.

Hard.

Desperate. He buried his face in the fall of my hair to cover the roar of my name when he came.

He pulsed and I soared.

We rode through ecstasy. The two of us lost to each other.

He held me against his shuddering body until I slumped facedown onto his bed.

"Stay," he told me. Naked, the man walked into the en suite bathroom and flicked on the light.

His gorgeous body was set on display, the sight of him sending a fresh round of shudders through me. He grabbed a washcloth, wet it under the sink, and sauntered back out.

Leaning over my back, he kissed my temple, brushed back the damp hair from my face, and pressed the warm cloth between my legs.

"Are you okay?" he asked, crawling up and lying on his side facing me. Those blue eyes swam, all his goodness pouring out, darkened pools of adoration.

This man.

This man.

I let my fingertips trail down the side of his face. "I don't think I've ever felt better than I do right now. Right this minute. With you."

He grabbed my hand and kissed across my fingertips. "Good. Because I don't think I can let you go. Not ever."

His tone was playful, but his expression flickered with something serious and sincere.

"Stalker," I let myself rib, though I knew there was no way he missed the soft affection that tripped from my tongue, knowing I was exposing everything I was feeling right then.

Love.

It sang all around us.

Whispering and thrumming and spilling into the sanctity of his room.

He wrapped an arm around my waist and pulled me flush against him, fingers brushing through my hair, the peace that echoed through my body swift and whole. "If that's what it takes for me to get to keep you. Keep Evan."

A knot grew heavy at the base of my throat, and I searched him in the shadows. "You can't keep saying things like that if you don't mean them."

His voice was rough. "What if I mean them, Hope?"

Hesitation billowed in my spirit. All the things we didn't know about each other suddenly felt like a chasm between us.

Bottomless.

Fingers fluttering across his full lips, I let my whispered question hit the air. "What do you want from your life, Kale? Before you met me . . . where did you see yourself tomorrow? In five years? Where do you picture yourself when you're growing old?"

Awareness filled his expression. Clearly, the man knew exactly what I was asking. Words faltered on his lips before he got a distant look on his face.

When he finally spoke, his confession was hoarse and choppy. "I think we need to go back to what I used to want, Hope. Not yesterday and not a year ago."

He grimaced in pain. "But ten years ago? I'd pictured that by now, I'd be married. Have a horde of kids who'd come running out of the house to meet me at the end of the day."

A sad smile kicked at the corner of his mouth, and his voice turned wistful, as if he were lost to the image in his mind. "They'd be shouting 'Daddy' and tugging at my pant legs and driving me crazy in the best of ways."

He swallowed hard, his gaze filled with longing when he set the sincerity of those eyes back on me. "I thought I'd have a wife, who'd be waiting on the porch after her own long day, and we'd meet in the middle. Our lives would be chaotic and busy, but they'd be perfect because we were living for the right things."

A tremor ran his thick throat. "Then that picture was shattered. And it destroyed something in me. From the day I lost her, I thought I'd be going my life alone. And I was okay with that."

No longer was his gaze distant, but he was right there, with me. "That lonely picture remained the same until the day I met you."

My heart pressed and thrummed and battered at my chest. Agony.

The words caught, and I had to force them from my lips. "You know I can't give you that . . . a horde of kids."

He blinked in confusion. It only took a second for the man to come to understanding, and I thought maybe it was anger that flashed through his features. "I know what his records say, Hope. They don't know where his disorder stems from."

I blinked my own tears. "And you know I can't take that risk."

He rolled me to my back and propped himself on an elbow, staring down at me as he wound a lock of my hair around his forefinger. "And if you knew . . . what would you want?"

Wetness seeped from the corners of my eyes. "I'd always dreamed of a big family . . . but Evan will always, always be enough for me."

His smile turned tender. "You think the two of you aren't enough? You two are more than enough. So much more. Which means I can't help but want to give you everything."

Dreams and faith. They spun around me, wrapping me whole.

Because to Dane, Evan and I had never been enough.

And I swore, right then, Kale Bryant had become everything I needed.

twenty-four
Kale

I glanced at her from the corner of my eye.

Sitting in the front seat of my car like she'd been meant for that spot.

My chest clenched in an almost painful way. Reverberating with a deep-rooted sort of pleasure. The kind that promised it might last forever and, still, you were terrified of letting it slip through your fingers.

That didn't mean my muscles weren't knotted in anticipation.

I was heading in a direction I'd never gone. Taking a girl to hang out with my friends, who I considered family.

I'd asked Hope and Evan to go to Rex's with me for a barbeque.

Not since Melody had I invited someone into our intimate circle, and even then, she'd only hung out with them once or twice because I was attending medical school in Birmingham.

That was where I'd met her.

Where I'd lost her.

I clamped down on the morbid thoughts that threatened to rise from that dark place inside me and, instead, focused on

Evan, who was bouncing with excitement in the backseat, his smile bright as he strained to see out the windows.

Funny how all those questions and what-ifs were rambling around me, and I still felt completely at peace.

It was like that frantic lust and greed and want that had flamed inside me since I'd met Hope had become aware that feeling was actually an everlasting need.

An undying devotion.

And it wasn't ever going to go away.

I felt the weight of her questioning stare burning into the side of my face. I took a right-hand turn, and I let myself peek over at her for a second as I accelerated down the road.

Fuck.

She was gorgeous.

So goddamned gorgeous.

All that red hair aflame, a halo of fire where it was lit up in the streaks of light that blazed through the passenger window.

Body tight and skin soft. Pale with that smattering of freckles.

Like she was sprinkled in some kind of fairy dust and she held her own special brand of magic.

Enchanting.

Entrancing.

That was what she was.

"What?" I asked, word scraping from my throat.

She bit down on that plump bottom lip and fiddled with the skirt of another one of those sundresses I was pretty sure she'd figured out were the ruin of me.

"I'm nervous," she admitted in that sweet, shy way.

"Why are you nervous?"

She laughed a disbelieving yet hopeful sound. "You're taking me and my son to meet your friends . . . the people who mean the most to you. You've got to know that's kind of intimidating."

I arched a brow. "As intimidating as your best friend?"

Her laughter rippled through the cabin of my car.

Swore the sound made me glow.

She tried to hold back a grin. "She's not that bad."

"Oh, believe me, Shortcake. A girl starts threatening the most important parts? That ranks her up there with arsonists and serial killers."

She laughed outright, her gaze so soft. "So dramatic."

I sent her a reassuring smile. "Seriously, though. They're amazing. You're going to love them just as much as they're going to love you and Evan."

Tenderness moved through her expression, that feeling rising high between us.

Alive.

I think both of us knew we were embarking on something new. It was no secret I wouldn't be inviting anyone to meet my family unless I intended for them to become a part of it, and it was palpable in the air, the fact that everything was getting ready to change.

Truth was, my world had changed that night at the bar. I'd thought it was simply because I was changing careers. Taking the partnership at the children's clinic. Maybe all along, that coming change had been Hope.

I made a left into Rex's gravel drive, my tires crunching on the rocks as we came to a stop.

The houses in his neighborhood were spread out and elevated from the ground by several steps that led up to the porches of the modest homes.

Yards hedged in towering trees, which gave them a private feel.

Secluded and quiet.

Like they were in the middle of the woods and might not have a neighbor for miles, when in reality, they were in the middle of the town.

I killed the engine. "This is it."

Hope sucked in a breath, and Evan freed himself from his seatbelt. Grinning, he scrambled to poke his head between the two front seats. That innocent gaze darted between us, excitement rolling from him in waves.

My chest tightened. Affection and that fluttering feeling. The one I was terrified to give a name.

I turned so I could face him. "You ready, little man?"

An energetic nod, and then he was yanking open the back door and flying out. Chuckling, I was quick to follow, wrapping his hand up in mine, running my thumb over the back of it.

Giving him the encouragement he didn't seem to need but I wanted to offer anyway.

He and I wound around the front of the car just as Hope was ducking into the backseat to grab the container of cupcakes she'd insisted on bringing, her sweet ass swaying in the air, sending all kinds of thoughts and ideas skating through my head and licking across my skin.

She whipped around. A blush rushed to her cheeks when she caught what had to be the salacious expression on my face.

Busted.

"You are nothin' but trouble, Cowboy," she said with a jittery giggle, smoothing her rumpled self out.

Affected.

I let a smirk climb to the edge of my mouth. "Don't act like you aren't begging for it. Wearing those dresses that you know are gonna drive me straight out of my mind."

Hope was shaking her head with sweet disbelief while Evan's attention jumped between us, confused.

Chuckling, figured I'd better stop that train that was quickly speeding out of control and do it fast.

"Come on, let's go meet everyone."

Keeping Evan's hand in mine, I tucked my other arm around Hope's waist and pulled her to my side. I pressed my lips to her temple and murmured, "Thank you so much for coming with me. It means more to me than you could know."

Those green eyes found mine. Tender and real. "Just you bringing us here says so many things," she whispered. "I'm honored to be a part of your world. To get to know the people you love most."

Fuck.

This woman had undone me. Unchinked all the armor I hadn't even realized had been there until it toppled to the ground.

An offering at her feet.

Instead of going up the porch steps to the front door, we headed around the side of the house where carefree voices echoed from the backyard, riding on the humidity that was hot and thick and sticky this time of year.

Evan trotted along at my side, continually looking up at me, almost like he was asking for approval, those adorable bug eyes huge behind his thick glasses, wearing that blameless smile that completely destroyed my heart.

Putty in his trusting hands.

We rounded the corner, listening to the easy laughter of my friends, and strode into the grassy, sprawling yard at the back of Rex and Rynna's house that was fenced in by soaring trees.

A big wooden porch ran the back of the house, and a few round tables and chairs sat in the middle of it, covered by colorful umbrellas that stretched out to protect from the searing heat of the Alabama sun.

A built-in grill and outdoor kitchen had been built at the opposite end of it. Smoke already puffed from the closed lid, twisty plumes of white rising into the air, carrying with it the divine scent of grilling steaks.

Hope leaned a little closer to me.

"You're with me, baby. You don't have a thing to worry about."

She peered up at me. "I know. It's ridiculous, but I just always worry when I get Evan in new situations. How he's gonna react and how people are gonna react to him."

I slowed to a stop, tucking Evan to my side before I dropped his hand and turned to take his mother by the face. My hold emphatic. "I would never bring him somewhere he wouldn't be welcome. Would never put him in danger. Not ever."

She blinked up at me, her hands winding around my wrists. "And that's why we're right here, with you."

I wanted nothing more than to drop everything right there and kiss her wild, this woman who'd do anything to stand up for her son.

Protect him.

All I wanted was to hold her and keep her and tell her that

bastard was never going to hurt either of them.

That I'd make sure of it.

That I'd never let her down.

It was getting harder and harder to ignore what was going on in her life. Something I hadn't seen firsthand but saw the same as if I was standing in the middle of it.

Her ex a lowlife fucker I wanted to beat down with my bare fists. Destroy and ruin the way he intended to ruin them.

I shoved the urge back, my voice gruff when I murmured, "I can't wait for them to meet you."

A tender smile fluttered across those full lips, and I hugged her closer before I gathered Evan's little hand back in mine.

Fighting the shudder that ripped through me because I loved the way it felt against mine so damned much.

I led them up the side steps to the porch. Everyone was already lounging beneath the umbrellas, enjoying the Sunday afternoon.

Rynna noticed us first. The second she did, she pushed from her chair and hopped to her feet, all welcoming the way she always was. "I'm so happy you're here."

That chatter quieted to nothing, and about five different pairs of eyes snapped our direction.

Sure, it was unnerving, but it was totally expected.

I knew showing up this way was going to shock the hell out of them. Each of them was doing their best to play it cool when really it was clear their minds were working at a hundred miles an hour.

Because I'd been completely straight up with Hope.

This was a first for me.

Rynna crossed to the edge of the porch where we'd stopped at the top of the stairs. Her sincere gaze moved over us before landing on Evan. When they locked eyes, Evan's hand moved in an exuberant wave.

Her expression grew tender, and she knelt down and signed *HI*.

"Oh," Hope breathed at my side, awe oozing out at Rynna's display of welcome.

It was at the same second that one simple gesture made joy light on Evan's face.

A goddamned sunburst.

Because the kid was so damned sweet.

"I'm Rynna. You must be Evan," she said, her lips moving a little slower than usual.

When I'd called to tell her I was bringing guests, she'd launched into a thrilled-sort of third-degree, badgering me for as much information as she could possibly dig out.

I'd told her about Evan's disability, giving her what I could without revealing too much, telling her he could read lips and not to treat him any different from Frankie Leigh.

Which was ridiculous I'd even felt the need to say it.

Evan gave her one of those enthusiastic nods, his little hand still wound up in mine, swaying at my side.

"Well, it is so great to meet you, Evan. I hope you have a blast at my house today."

With an affectionate touch of his chin, Rynna pushed to her feet and extended both her hands toward Hope. "I'm Rynna Gunner. Welcome to our home. Thank you so much for coming."

Hope pushed the plastic container out in front of her like a peace offering. "Thank you for having us. I brought cupcakes."

Rynna accepted them with a generous smile. "Oh, my goodness, this is exactly what we needed. The only treats my family gets around here are my pies, and I'm pretty sure they have to be getting sick of them by now."

"That's impossible," Hope said.

The girl was so genuine there was no question of her sincerity.

She tucked a strand of that red, red hair behind her ear almost nervously and offered a smile. "I've eaten at Pepper's Pies plenty of times to know it never gets old."

Rynna grinned from ear to ear. "You've been?"

"Of course. Those pies are legendary."

"Well, I can't exactly take credit. They are my grandmother's recipes."

Frankie Leigh suddenly came barreling out the back door with her dog Milo hot on her heels, the screen door smacking shut behind them. "Uncle Kale! Uncle Kale! You came to see me!"

She threw her arms in the air, feet clattering on the planks as she scrambled around the tables, flying for me. She came to a grinding stop when she saw the little boy's hand wrapped in mine.

Her eyes went wide in excited interest.

"Is this mys new friend Evan?" she asked me, looking up at me hopefully.

I knelt beside them. "Sure is, Sweet Pea. This is Evan, and he's really special to me, so I hope you spend the whole day playing with him because he doesn't know anyone else here."

Of course, she would. The kid was a force field of joy.

But I never expected that my Frankie Leigh, my goddaughter and the girl who had always held every inch of my heart, would sign *HI* just like her mom had done, probably more awkwardly than I'd done when Evan had been trying to teach me the alphabet.

But that didn't matter.

Nothing did except that my family had made sure to make this little boy feel welcomed.

Emotion fisted my heart, not expecting to feel this way when I saw the two of them together.

Overcome and a little overwhelmed.

Evan signed with a huge grin, and I looked over my shoulder to Hope. She chewed at her lip, the woman so fucking stunning standing there with the sun shining all around her that I was having a hard time seeing straight. "Wonder Woman," she said, her voice a wisp.

A smile flew to my face, and I looked back at Evan. "Yeah, buddy. This is Wonder Woman."

I turned to Frankie. "And this is my little Hulk."

Mine.

My chest tightened.

All of this was so goddamned new but so goddamned right.

Frankie Leigh giggled like crazy. "I likes the Hulk . . . but he's not as strong as my daddy and my uncles! Thor and Cap'in 'merica."

I felt Rynna staring at me, and I glanced up to meet her eyes.

I'm happy for you.

He's wonderful.

I'm so glad you brought them.

"Wanna play? I gots my puppy and he's so fast and he likes to jump and lick and he's so funny," Frankie Leigh rambled out, pushing the wild, wild locks of her hair from her face with both hands.

Evan didn't even hesitate. He dropped my hand and was rushing down the stairs, clambering behind Frankie and Milo out onto the lawn.

Frankie squealed, dancing all around like the carefree thing she was, and Evan's smile was as big as I'd ever seen it as he tried to follow her lead.

I took Hope's hand.

She squeezed mine back.

Her emotions leaching into my veins.

Gratefulness and joy and that feeling that terrified me kept nudging me more and more.

"Guys, I want you all to meet someone."

All those pairs of eyes that'd been watching us scrambled to their feet.

I introduced Hope to everyone, pointing to them as I said their names.

"Lillith. Brody. That's Nikki, and that little thing sleeping on her chest is my godbaby, Ryland."

Hope gave a tiny wave, still clinging to me with the other hand. "It's nice to meet you all."

Rex, who was grinning as he manned the grill, welcoming her to his home, sending me a bunch of looks on the sly that told me we would definitely be talking about this later.

No shit.

I knew showing up like this was signing myself up to stand in front of the firing squad.

Especially considering the last time I'd been here I'd been claiming my old ways. Certain I didn't need anything more when, really, I'd been lacking everything.

I was ready to face it.

Of course, Hope had already met Ollie. He sauntered up and pulled her into a big, burly, overbearing hug.

Like they were the oldest of friends.

My girl looked like some kind of rag doll when he flung her around, brows climbing to the sky when he peered at me from over her shoulder, silently telling me I had some explaining to do.

So maybe I'd been dodging all his texts and calls for the last two weeks. Didn't show at the bar on either Friday night the way I always did, deciding to trade in a night of carousing and revelry for hanging out with Hope and Evan.

Crazy how quickly things could change.

Finally, he set her on her feet. "So, I see you decided to put up with this asshole, after all."

Hope glanced at me. "Yeah, I guess I did."

Two hours later, we'd eaten, our stomachs were full, and everyone was sitting around talking and relaxing the lazy day away.

Easy.

I had to admit, my gaze was probably a little too eager where I sat on the porch nursing a beer, watching Hope where she was hanging out with the girls over at the far end of the lawn in the shade of a lush, sprawling tree.

Laughing.

Chatting like she'd known them for years.

Ryland was on a blanket, kicking his little arms and legs, and Rynna was propped up on an arm, sitting protectively at his side.

Nikki, Lillith, and Hope had gathered around the little makeshift play area, lounging on chairs and sharing a bottle of wine.

Frankie Leigh and Evan were still racing around the yard,

playing hide and seek, Milo basically giving them away each time, all too quick to sniff them out.

Broderick had to bail to take a conference call with his office in New York.

Rex tipped the neck of his beer bottle out toward the yard. "This is all so very domestic of you," he said, broaching the subject I'd felt coming all afternoon.

He cut me a glance from the side, taking a long pull of his beer as he studied me.

"You about ready to talk about what's going on? Because this is so far out of left field, I'm wondering who you are and what you've done with my friend."

His brow lifted. "You know, the one who's insisted since he finished medical school that he didn't need anyone in his life other than his patients and us. A warm body without a face to keep him company on the nights he wants to get his dick wet right before he goes on his merry way."

He gave a sharp shake of his head. "Then my wife shocks the shit out of me last night by telling me you're coming over with some chick and her kid. That's enough of a one-eighty to make any man's head spin."

Wasn't that the truth.

I drummed my fingertips on my knee. "It's complicated."

Apparently, I had been hanging out with Hope too much.

Rex's expression turned incredulous. "Think you'd better figure out exactly what that means, because there isn't room for fucking around when there's a kid involved."

His words were hard, and there was no mistaking it was fueled by a threat.

He got it on a level many couldn't.

"You really think I'd fuck around with her if I didn't get that?" My tone was a little harsher than I'd intended.

But fuck.

His warning hit me in all the wrong places. In those places where my own terror was held. The worry that I might fail this kid.

"No. I didn't think you would," Rex said with a shake of his head. "Which is why I'm wondering what the hell is going on in that head of yours."

Ollie rocked forward in his chair, leaned his elbows on his knees as he looked over me. "Last time I talked to you, you were still hung up on the past. Thinking you didn't deserve the chance. That you couldn't take it."

His brows drew together. "That neither could she."

My attention landed on Evan, who was in the middle of the yard. His arms were thrown up over his head and he was spinning in a circle as he let the sun rain down on his precious face.

My heart throbbed. Pulsing and pressing and pushing.

"They happened."

A snort puffed from Rex's nose. "Women. When we meet the one, they make us forget ourselves, don't they?" he mused as he sipped his beer.

Ollie scoffed. "Uh . . . no. I can assuredly say I don't know what that's like, man. But this fucker sure seems to have caught the same plague that your sorry ass did." He hooked his thumb my direction.

I smirked at him. "Hey, man, go ahead. Rub it in. Know you're just jealous."

"Fuck no," he said with a laugh, not even realizing his attention immediately drifted to Nikki, who was cracking up in her chair, rocking forward as she clutched her stomach.

Her eyes flashed up to meet his like she felt the weight of his stare.

Just as fast, he jerked his attention back, the way he'd done for too many goddamned years.

Asshole didn't know what was right under his nose.

Or more likely, he just did a damned good job of ignoring it.

Ollie scrubbed a tattooed hand over his face like he was breaking himself from the trance.

I didn't think he knew how he'd gotten there in the first place.

"But seriously . . . are you ready to let it go? Give *her* up? Because you've been clinging to her memory for years. And that girl . . .”

He pointed at Hope, who'd taken Ryland in her arms.

She stared down at the tiny thing as if she were looking on beauty while at the same second it broke her heart.

Ollie's features shifted, not even a remnant of a tease. “She doesn't deserve to live in the shadow of Melody's ghost, man. She doesn't. And neither do you.”

Unease slithered beneath my skin. Melody's face a sequence of flashes in my mind.

Stark, blinding lights. Compression after compression. That fucking flat line.

Smiles and laughter and grief.

Never thought I could love anyone again.

Had never entertained it.

“I'm terrified of it,” I admitted. “That I'm always going to be haunted by her ghost. That I might fail again. But I don't think I can stop this, either.”

Silence fell over us for a beat, my eyes watching Evan as he played. He caught me staring, waved over his head.

This kid.

This kid.

I gulped around the thick emotion that swelled in my throat. “He has a bad heart.”

Rex's attention whipped my direction. “Fuck, man.”

Yeah.

Fuck me.

twenty-five
Hope

held the tiny baby in my arms.

It spun my heart into intricate knots.

Because I could almost remember Evan this way.

The way he'd felt when I'd held him.

Tiny and soft.

But he had been so fragile.

Broken.

While I did my best to breathe belief.

To fill his little soul with it so he'd know he was loved. Cherished and adored. Even though he spent months in and out of the hospital attached to wires and monitors. Even though he'd endured so much pain.

He was loved.

In my periphery, I could see Rynna's smile. "You should see your face right now."

Confused, I looked up at her, blinking.

"With that baby," she sang as if I was ridiculous. It was a soft tease. A gentle coaxing. "Seems you need another one of your own in your arms."

The reality of life squeezed down on that faith. On that hope. I forced a smile that I knew wobbled, my voice more hoarse than I meant for it to be. "No. No more babies for me."

The deepest frown pulled across Rynna's brow, and I could sense Lillith and Nikki shifting forward, as if that minor movement was them standing and taking guard. There for me when they'd barely just met me.

These women were all so different from each other, but each so incredibly kind.

Welcoming Evan and I into their mix as if we'd always belonged.

No wonder Kale talked about them the way he did. The camaraderie and intimacy and devotion they shared.

Ryland cooed and pursed his little lips. He twisted his tiny fingers in front of his face, eyes bulging at the magic of his trick.

I attempted to clear the heaviness from my heart, to shuck the weight from my chest. "Evan's hearing and heart defects were genetic. I can't risk passing that on to another child."

I felt like a hypocrite saying it. Because my son was perfect in my eyes. Yet, I couldn't fathom being so selfish to curse another child to this life.

A muted, whimpered sound wheezed from Lillith.

As if she'd tried to hold it back and it'd bled free anyway.

She inched closer to me. "Oh God, Hope." She splayed her hands out over her heart as if my confession caused her a sharp, sudden pain. She looked over to where Evan played on the lawn. "I can't imagine. He's such an incredible little boy. One smile, and I was in love."

Tenderness had me chewing at the inside of my cheek, fighting the emotion that threatened to moisten my eyes. "He's the greatest gift I've ever been given," I murmured softly.

"But you hate what he's been through," she continued in complete understanding.

No judgment.

Kale was right.

These were amazing, incredible people.

"I completely understand that." She hesitated for a moment

before she asked, "You're the carrier?"

Rynna shifted forward, winding her arms around her knees, listening intently.

I hefted a resigned shoulder. "They deemed my testing inconclusive."

Nikki jolted forward. "Wait . . . you don't know for sure?"

I shook my head. "No."

Her blue eyes widened, and I could tell she was holding it back, fighting a question she figured was out of line. But it didn't matter. I could already see it all over her face, written in big, red, blinking letters.

I went ahead and answered, more comfortable with the three of them than I could have imagined. "His biological father couldn't *possibly* be a carrier, now could he? Not with his dignified Southern bloodline. Testing would be nothing less than an insult to his masculinity and his heritage."

It rolled out in a tirade of sarcastic bitterness and disdain.

So unlike me.

But it'd finally all caught up to me.

The festering mess of anger and disappointment and grief.

It was all doused with the hatred that burned for the fact he could possibly think Evan wasn't worth the fight.

Gasoline to my battling soul.

Finally, I felt ready to face it. Head on.

I didn't know if it was Kale who'd given me the last measure of courage.

Either way, I was so thankful for his promise. That he would be there at my side. That I didn't have to go this alone.

Nikki bit down on her lip, butt shimmying in her seat, before she burst out with, "Oh my God, I can't stand it. Someone please tell me this is where we get to call the wanker names and talk about how horrible he is in bed and how his breath always stinks. Oh, oh, oh, and how he got piss-ass drunk and stepped out in front of a speeding car and now *poof.* Gone. Problem solved."

Her hands made an exploding motion out in front of her.

Lillith smacked at her. "Nikki! I swear. You are always trying

287

to scare the good ones away with that mouth of yours."

She turned an apologetic smile on me. "You'll have to excuse her. This one was never taught that sometimes it's better to hold your tongue. You have to get used to her. She's kind of an acquired taste," she needled a little more, playful admonishment in her words.

Laughter rumbled, and I let my eyes widen conspiratorially when I looked at Nikki. "Oh, there's nothin' wrong with speaking truth where it's due. Unfortunately, all except for that whole speeding car thing was on point."

Nikki squealed in glee. "Oh . . . I like her. I think I just found my new best friend since Lily Pad over here thinks I'm too much to handle." The last came with a feigned pout.

Lillith rolled her eyes. "I can handle you just fine. It's the people around us who I'm worried about. You remember I'm an attorney. I deal with crazies all the time."

"Pssh. Crazy? Who me?" Nikki waved her off, leaning my direction, clear scheming in her tease. "This one just can't stand it that I'm the ultimate matchmaker—that I'm responsible for all the orgasms Brody gives her and she doesn't want to give me any of the credit. They'd still be each other's worst enemies and sending hate emails if it wasn't for me."

A light giggle floated from Rynna. "Watch out, Hope. If you aren't careful, Nikki here will be taking credit for getting you and Kale together. She definitely thinks she set things in motion for Rex and me."

Nikki waved her hands at herself. "Um . . . hello . . . I did set you up with Rex. If I hadn't invited you to Ollie's bar, you never would have hooked up. *And* I was there that night when Kale first saw Hope at Olive's, remember? Of course, I'm responsible. I'm head matchmaker. I just walk through a crowd and all those love-connecting darts start flying out of me, striking whoever I walk by."

"You do remember I first met Brody at Olive's?" Lillith pointed out, trying not to laugh. "It has nothing to do with you. The bar is definitely the tie."

Nikki gasped. "Shut your face, Lily Pad. Stop looking for

solutions when the answer is right in front of you. Head matchmaker." She circled a halo around her head. "Orgasm fairy."

She slanted a knowing grin my direction. "Tell me the last rings true."

Oh.

Redness bloomed on my cheeks.

I was pretty sure I needed to introduce Nikki and Jenna. They had to have been separated at birth.

Lillith smacked her again. "I swear, Nikki."

"What?" she defended, totally innocently before she turned back to me.

Laughing under my breath, I ducked down when I admitted, "It definitely rings true."

Her mouth popped open, and she leaned in closer to me, eyes wide with excitement. "Lovestruck?"

I let my attention slide to where Kale sat on the deck. Evan had scrambled behind Frankie Leigh up to the porch, and my son was now in front of Kale, communicating something to him that I couldn't make out, but he was red and flushed and happy.

So content and free.

My spirit thrashed.

That feeling settled over me.

Because it was true.

I was totally and completely . . . lovestruck.

The day played on in a blur of laughter and joy and easiness. Kale and I sat on the grass with his friends as the sun began to sink in the sky, his arm slung around my shoulders while we watched Evan run through the grass, my son's head tipped back in his silent laughter that I swore I could hear ring through the air.

It was late evening when we said our goodbyes. I accepted all the hugs that were offered and agreed with the girls that we all would hang out together soon.

Joy pressed at my ribs. It was a kind of wholeness that seemed almost foreign where it throbbed within the depths of me.

Kale helped Evan into the backseat of the car and ensured he was buckled before he slid into the driver's seat.

Immediately, he leaned in and kissed me over the console.

In front of Evan.

It felt like a gentle claiming.

A statement.

A promise.

From the backseat, Evan made that scraping, laughing sound, and Kale and I both peered back at him. He was grinning that earth-shattering smile, his cheeks red with a certain kind of embarrassment that manifested the greatest joy.

"Is it okay if I kiss your mom, little man?"

Evan was quick to write on his pad he had on his lap.

You're supposed to kiss her if you're her boyfriend. That's the rule.

I flushed, and Kale leaned his forehead against mine, his voice a murmur. "Then I guess I'm your boyfriend. The kid says it's the rule."

He looked back at Evan. "I'm her boyfriend, and she's my girlfriend. Right?"

Evan nodded vigorously, then his little hand went flying across the paper.

Yep. So, what am I?

Kale stilled, contemplating, before he said, "You're my favorite."

Evan beamed. His entire being lit with a profound joy.

You're my favorite, too.

Every inch of me warmed.

Kale glanced at me as he turned back, a small, adoring smile gracing his striking face. "All right, then. I think that's settled."

He started his car, backed out, and hit the road.

He held my hand as he drove back through our small, quaint city.

A quiet peace filtered through like a murky haze as twilight gathered fast, the moon climbing to the sky from behind the mountain in the distance.

Kale made the last turn onto our street.

We parked at the curb and everyone climbed out.

Rounding the front of his car, Kale swept my son from his feet. "Come here, little man, you look tired."

Evan nodded.

Lines of worry pulled across Kale's brow, and he ran a hand over Evan's forehead. "Are you feeling okay, buddy?"

I watched the two of them, my chest so full as Evan signed.

"He says he's just tired because he had so much fun today."

"Oh, yeah? What did you think about Frankie Leigh?"

A giggle slipped from between my lips when I saw my son's response, my expression so soft when I turned my attention on the man who'd changed everything.

"He said he's gonna marry her."

A grin split Kale's face. "Is that so? You like her that much, huh?"

Evan gave a flourishing nod.

"She's awfully pretty. Seems it's always the ones who are a handful that snag our hearts, isn't it?"

Somehow, I knew he was no longer talking to my son, that smirk washing me over like a slow promise, raking my flesh, making me blush.

Complicated.

Never would I regret letting this man complicate me even more.

I headed up the walk, carrying the empty plastic cupcake container, continually peeking over my shoulder at Kale who trailed close behind, holding my son in the security of his arms.

I balanced the container on my hip, worked the key into the lock, and pushed open the door. I looked back at my son when I did. "We'd better get you a bath and into bed."

Evan pursed his little lips in a pout, and Kale chuckled,

ruffled his hair. "Get your bath, little man, and then we can read that Spiderman story you've been telling me about."

Promise? Evan mouthed.

"Promise," Kale returned, setting him on his feet. Evan took off for the bathroom.

Kale took the container from my hands. "Let me take care of that while you give him his bath."

"You better be careful, Cowboy, or I could get used to this," I teased, though the words were fluttery, my heart and my spirit tied to his.

No longer afraid to hope.

Wanting him a permanent part of our world.

I started to follow Evan when Kale snatched me by the wrist.

Heat sped up my arm, and shock rasped from my lungs when he pressed me against the wall. And the man kissed me.

Softly.

Tenderly.

Stealing my breath.

That energy rose up at our feet, climbing higher.

On a rumbly groan, he dropped his forehead to mine. "I'm such a goner, Shortcake. Don't think you understand the way you've gotten to me."

My eyes dropped closed, the words screaming from the depths of me.

Love. Love. Love.

I didn't say it. I just relished it. Let it surge and dance and swell.

Penetrate those places where it'd last forever.

I heard the faucet turning on in the bathroom. "I better go check on him."

Kale nodded and pressed a tender kiss to my forehead. "I'll be right here."

twenty-six
Kale

From where I stood at the sink washing the container, I could hear Hope through the walls. Her words indistinguishable and ambiguous.

But that didn't matter. I could hear what was important, anyway.

Joy.

There was so much of it. Because that was what these two were.

Joy.

My chest tightened when I realized the magnitude of what that actually meant.

That somehow they had become *my joy*.

My home when I hadn't realized I'd been looking for one.

It should scare me. Terrify me that I had gone into territory I'd sworn I'd never go.

But standing there in the comfort of Hope's kitchen, being all sorts of domestic like Rex had pointed out?

Nothing had ever felt so right.

I'd denied myself even the idea of this.

Family.

Thinking I couldn't have it.

Didn't deserve it.

Old fear trembled in my bones.

I went rigid against it.

Rejecting it.

Because I refused to fail these two. The past was the past and I was leaving it there. Hope and Evan were my here and now.

My future.

After finishing washing the container, I rinsed it and placed it on a dishtowel, drying my hands at the same time.

In my periphery, my sight caught on the stack of mail that rested at the far end of the counter. My head jerked violently in a double take.

I wasn't trying to be nosy. I wasn't. Overstepping my bounds.

But the name . . . the name on the top envelope was all wrong.

Dread sank like a stone to the pit of my stomach, and a freezing cold chill slicked like ice down my spine.

My vision turned hazy, and my eyes narrowed. I swore, my damned heart was beating so hard I could hear the roar of it thundering through my veins.

I inched that direction, my subconscious flailing and thrashing in a disturbed awareness.

The closer I got, the more that distress grew, scraping across my skin like a razor-sharp knife.

At the edge of the counter, I froze, gulping around the knot in my throat that cut off air.

Staring down at the envelope on top of the stack.

I gave an aggressive shake of my head. Like it would clear up the picture.

Because fuck.

I had to be seeing things. Making shit up.

It was all those old memories and regrets and sorrow rising and playing cruel, sick tricks.

Tormenting me with a stark, glaring reminder of my greatest loss. It all pressed down, the soul-crushing fear of losing him the same obscene way.

But it didn't matter how long I stared at it.

All the letters remained the same.

Harley Gentry. Harley Gentry. Harley Gentry.

The room spun. Faster and faster.

My new world crumbling out from under my feet.

Hands ripping at fistfuls of my hair, I stumbled back.

No.

Fuck.

No.

Panic surged. Bouncing from the walls.

Ricocheting.

Gaining speed.

I couldn't breathe.

"What's wrong?" That understanding, tender voice hit me from behind, filled with soft concern.

Slowly, I turned to look at her.

Those green eyes went wide with surprise when she got a look at me, my spine rigid and my face pale.

She took a surging step forward. "Kale? Are you okay? Are you sick?"

Care. It radiated from her like the goddamned sun.

My eyes squeezed closed because looking at all the light hurt. It hurt so goddamned much I felt my stomach clench in a roil of nausea that lifted to my throat.

"Who is he?" I demanded, eyes still pinched closed, not wanting to see her expression when she said it.

Not sure I could handle it.

This couldn't be real. It couldn't be real.

"What are you askin'?" she wheezed, a slip of that country drawl seeping into her worry. "We already talked about this."

I shot across the floor and grabbed her by the outside of her arms.

Her eyes widened. A bolt of fear. A vat of confusion.

"Tell me who he is. Your ex. What is his name?"

"Kale," she pleaded, her eyes searching mine.

"Tell me," I grated, losing my goddamned head.

"Dane. His name is Dane Gentry." It was almost a whimper.

A blow.

A gunshot that rang through the air.

Deafening.

I choked over the confirmation. My hands releasing her like I'd been holding fire.

I had. I had. I had.

I'd been holding fire in the palm of my hands.

My head shook. "No . . . no. Your name is Harley Hope Masterson. Masterson," I almost begged.

She winced. "Masterson is my maiden name."

Sucking for nonexistent air, I fumbled away from her. Panic burning me up from the inside.

No.

Oh, God, no.

Hope reached for me, brow pinched tight. "Kale . . . please don't look at me like you don't know me. I don't understand why you're so upset."

Fumbling away, my back knocked into the kitchen wall next to the arch.

"I . . ." Glass abraded my throat, the raw cuts refusing words.

This couldn't be real.

A plea took to Hope's unforgettable face. "I've been trying to erase him from our lives. You've got to understand that. I told you I would do anything to protect my son."

Hope's explanation became frantic, desperate, the woman edging closer, too close.

So close I could taste her on my tongue and feel her on my skin.

Her rushed words fell on my ears. "I didn't tell you his name because I was afraid you'd do something you'd regret later on. Standing up for Evan and me. Because you're a good man, Kale. Such a good man, and I knew you'd do whatever you thought you could do to protect us. I was protecting you, too. It's just a name, Kale. It's just a name. It doesn't change anything."

But that's where she was wrong.

It changed everything.

"I have to go." It raked from my raw throat.

I had to get out of there.

Run.

Melody.

I squeezed my eyes when I was suddenly assaulted with memories.

Her smile. Her laugh. Her pleas. Gone. Horror. Grief.

I choked.

Hope's face pinched in a brutal kind of pain. "What?"

"I can't do this," I told her, nothing but a coward when I tried to get by her without looking at her face.

Without looking in those earthy eyes to see the beauty that waited there.

The hope and the joy and the belief.

She grabbed me by the wrist.

That roar in my veins cracked.

A thunderclap.

"Tell me what's happening," she begged. "What is really going on?"

I blinked at her, but all I could see was *her* face.

Melody.

Compression after compression. That fucking flat line. "You did this. You did this. She's dead because of you."

Evan's sweet face flashed.

Lifeless.

"I can't do this."

Not again.

Hope tightened her hold, refusing to let me go. "You don't get to do this, Kale Bryant. You don't get to just walk out. You promised."

My eyes squeezed closed again.

Looking at this girl and knowing I couldn't keep her was the most brutal tease I'd ever endured.

Just another fucking failure.

Her words dropped to a wispy plea. "Where did you go, Kale? Where did the man go who is wonderful and generous and kind? The man who ten minutes ago told me he'd be right here, waiting for me? Where is he? Follow me back . . . come back to me . . . because I'm right here. I'm *right* here."

Grief crushed me on all sides.

Pressing down.

Destroying.

Because if I could, I would follow her anywhere.

"I'm sorry," I forced out, because I was. So fucking sorry.

I twisted my arm free from her hold and stepped back.

Her expression twisted.

Horror and grief.

The hurt so blatant.

"You promised," she begged on a breath.

My head shook, and I slowly backed away, looking at her standing heartbroken in her kitchen.

A cascade of red hair, tearstained cheeks, bloodshot eyes.

The girl the best thing I'd ever seen.

I committed it to memory.

What I did. The ruin I inflicted.

Hope had spent years fighting the stigma that her son wasn't enough.

But that stigma was meant for me.

Because I would never, ever be enough.

I spun on my heel and bolted.

Out her door and into the fading light.

I stumbled across the porch. Gasping for a breath, the entire world spinning and the ground canting to the side, crumbling out from under me.

I wheezed, desperate for relief. But all the air had been sucked from the sky.

A hollow, vacant vortex that consumed everything in its path.

twenty-seven
Hope

The walls of the entire house shook when the door slammed closed.

A violent blow.

Or maybe it was just my insides ripping apart.

Collapsing and imploding.

A raking sob tore up my throat, and I bent in two. I wrapped my arms around my waist as if it might be enough to keep me standing.

But it wasn't.

A rush of dizziness swept through me like a landslide, and I lurched forward. My hands barely caught on the counter before I fell to my knees.

A loss so intense pounded through me, and my head dropped between my shoulders, mouth parting in a guttural cry there was no possible way to contain.

"Kale," I whimpered.

Thoughts swirled in my mind. Confusion thick. My emotions had been yanked from the highest high to the lowest low.

What just happened?

I couldn't make sense of the sudden shift.

I didn't know how he could do this to me.

Could do this to *us*.

He'd promised he wouldn't leave.

That he'd be there.

That he'd stay.

After he'd sworn he knew what was on the line.

And he'd left me.

Over a name.

Over that vile, cruel name.

My insides twisted again, my stomach revolting, just the same as my spirit. Because this was wrong.

All of it was so very wrong.

The numbers weren't even close to adding up to the correct sum.

A switch had been flipped, and I had no idea what had been the trigger.

Because I'd grown to know this man in the most intimate of ways. I knew I wasn't just being blind or naïve for the sake of falling for a gorgeous man.

I'd seen him for who he truly was—kind, generous, and devoted.

And that man I'd grown to know was not the one who'd just gone running out my door.

He'd been terrified.

White as a ghost.

A slow dread sank over me like bitter cold.

The horror that had been scored on his face flashed behind my eyes. As if he'd stood right there in the middle of my kitchen and come face-to-face with an apparition.

A demon.

Or maybe the devil himself.

That fear I'd so often seen rise up in him, shuttering that beautiful, unselfish heart, had never been so clear than right then.

He'd demanded Dane's name as if my soon-to-be ex-husband was a disloyalty to him.

As if a name alone held the power to confuse and contort and destroy.

If a name alone were enough to send him running, what would he do when he found out the whole truth?

A thunder pounded on the front door.

Shocked, a breath heaved from my lungs, the sound made up of relief and confusion and deliverance.

Because there was the man, who I trusted implicitly, yanking and pushing. Dragging my fragile heart through the mud.

But I had to realize this was all new to him. I'd asked so much of him in such a short period of time. I hadn't been exaggerating when I'd warned him my life was so very complicated.

As much as I wanted it—craved it—deep down, I knew the man had stepped into a position he might not have been fully prepared to take on.

Maybe he needed some time to catch up. But as much as I knew he deserved that time, I couldn't allow him to go running in and out of our home without thought or consideration of what it might do to Evan.

Of what it would do to me.

When another round of pounding hammered from the door, I straightened and sucked in a steeling breath, preparing myself because Kale and I were going to have to talk.

Really talk.

Lay it out.

It was time the two of us shared our true hopes, fears, and reservations.

I wanted him.

God, I wanted him.

But I could admit we'd been moving fast, and I needed him to be ready before he took that final leap. Deal with the fear that would dim his eyes.

Hurt and a quiver of jealousy staked through my heart.

Maybe . . . maybe he wasn't ready to let her go.

His first love.

Maybe he'd realized he didn't have space for me, after all. The idea of letting him go broke me in two, but I was willing to face that reality if I had to.

Raking my forearm across my bleary eyes, I cleared the moisture, headed down the hallway, and took another deep breath before I turned the knob and carefully cracked open the door.

"Dane." A slick of fear lifted my skin in a clammy sweat when I saw him on my porch.

It mixed with an overwhelming disappointment that it wasn't Kale.

"What are you doing here?"

"I want to talk to you."

There was something new in his eyes that prickled the hairs at the back of my neck and sent a rocket of chills shooting up my spine.

"I don't have anything to say to you."

I went to close the door. I didn't have the capacity to deal with him right then. Not after Kale had left me feeling brittle and broken. His arm shot out to stop it from latching, his voice hard as he pushed open the door. "I said I wanted to talk to you."

I stumbled back, and the door swung open wide. I edged away as Dane stepped into my little home for the first time ever.

It was so wrong with him standing there. Black hair and black eyes and black heart.

"And I said, I didn't have anything to say to you."

"Is that so?"

"Yes." It trembled from my mouth.

He took another step forward. "How about you start by telling me who just drove away from here."

I didn't answer, just took another step back as he took one forward, backing me into the opposite wall. Right in the same place where Kale had had me not thirty minutes before.

Again, my breath was stolen.

But this time it was stolen by the clot of alarm that constricted my throat, my heart beating faster and faster with a warning.

He'd seen Kale. Oh God, he'd seen Kale.

His hot words were venom across my face. "Who the fuck

was here, Harley?"

"No one." The lie cracked on the toxic air. Splinters and shards.

"Bullshit. I saw someone driving away."

Anger fisted my chest. "What does it even matter, Dane. Are you really gonna stand there and pretend like you weren't stepping out on me all along? You think I don't know about all those women?"

I was long over Dane. But there was no stopping the bitterness that came out with accusation.

His jaw clenched, but he angled his head and his voice turned soft. "You know why, Harley. You know why. You didn't have anything left for me since you gave every second of every day to that kid."

Was he serious? He was jealous of our child?

Pathetic.

God, this man was pathetic.

Flinching, I jerked my chin to the side when he reached out and brushed his fingers down my jaw.

Revulsion pulsed through my being.

"None of that matters now. Come home where you belong, and we'll try again."

"Try again?" My eyes snapped back to him, my tone incredulous.

He ran the pad of this thumb over my cheek. "Another baby. We'll start over. Forget everything that's happened."

"You're insane."

Dane suddenly pressed himself against me, planting both hands on the wall on either side of my head.

Gasping, I tried to block out the feel of him. The smell of him. But I was assaulted by a million memories. His cloying cologne. His vicious words. His hatred of our son.

"Don't touch me," I rasped, struggling to push away from him.

He just leaned in closer, his voice turning hard. Malicious. "Did you let another man fuck you, Harley? Touch what's mine?"

"You're disgusting," I spat.

A horrified yelp escaped when he suddenly fisted his hands in the fabric of my shirt and pulled me against his chest. "You think I'm a fool? Is that what you think? You think you can play me? You think I didn't just see that car pull away from here?"

"It doesn't matter, Dane. It's over. You already know this. We're over."

I don't love you.

Thoughts of Kale flooded my mind. His kiss. His touch. His kindness. And I had to wonder if I ever had loved Dane.

"You're my wife."

My eyes squeezed shut. "No."

He crushed his mouth against mine, his hands on my face as he tried to force me to comply. I flailed and struggled against the unwelcome intrusion, trying to fight him off while an avalanche of fear and hate crashed into me.

I drew back my arm, my hand flying out and connecting with his cheek.

The smack echoed through the foyer.

He snapped back, his black eyes glowering before he released a menacing growl. His hands moved from my face and wrapped around my throat. Not tight enough to constrict airflow. But tight enough to exert just how easily he could.

Any coaxing softness he'd worn before had been stripped away, replaced by his true character.

The man I'd fallen in love with completely gone.

As if he'd never existed.

A vile wickedness bleeding free.

His words dropped to a low, vicious threat in my ear. "You really think I'm a fool, don't you, Harley? Why don't you tell me why my attorney can't find a single medical record on Evan for the last year? You think I don't know you're up to something?"

And I'd thought I'd felt fear before.

But maybe I had never really experienced it until right then.

"He's been healthy . . . he . . . he hasn't needed to go in." The lie fumbled from my mouth. Lurching and pleading.

I was prepared to tell a million more when I was struck with a dread unlike anything I'd ever known.

Fear and horror and the undying need to protect my son at any cost compounded and sharpened.

Because all I could hear was the clatter of unaware feet excitedly banging down the hall and through the living room. My little boy thinking he was running out to find Kale and his promise of a story.

Oh, God.

No.

I couldn't let this happen.

It was at the same second Dane bared back down on me, roaring with my answer.

He fisted my dress in his hands and slammed my back against the wall.

Pain radiated through my body, and I cried out, completely caught off guard. Never before had the danger Dane imposed been physical.

He lifted me by my clothing, spewing the words an inch from my face.

"Bullshit, Harley. You think you're going to get away with whatever you're trying to pull? Do you know who my family is? What I stand to lose?"

His statement sent a jolt of confusion tumbling through my mind. I had no idea what he had to lose other than his overinflated pride, but I was too terrified to process it. Too terrified to ask. The only thing I cared about were the feet that rushed across the hardwood floors.

I could feel Evan's presence break the morbid air as he rounded the corner into the foyer.

I felt the second he slammed into shock.

His iPad slipped from his hands and crashed against the floor, and those innocent eyes grew round with stark, cutting fear.

"Run, Evan! Go to your room. Lock the door," I screamed.

But he wasn't looking at me.

Redness blistered across his face, a sort of anger I'd never seen my son wear before. In horror, I watched as he rushed forward. His gangly arms began to fly. He pounded and pounded and pounded against Dane's leg with his little fists.

Scraping, rasping cries jutted from Evan's mouth, and tears streaked from his eyes.

I knew it was surprise that twisted through Dane's furious expression, and the man staggered back a single step, his head jerking down to Evan who continued to wail on his leg.

"No, Evan, no!" I screamed, my spirit begging with him to look at me. To *understand*.

Dane's surprise turned to rage, and he reached out to grab my son.

Blinding fury surged inside me so intense I was sure my blood physically boiled.

I'd never allow this man to hurt my child.

Not ever.

From behind, I shoved Dane with everything I had.

"Don't touch him!" It was a scream that came from the very depths of my soul.

Don't touch him. Leave us alone. We just want to live.

My effort barely moved Dane an inch. But it was *enough*. It was enough to distract him from Evan and set that spiteful, depraved cruelty on me. Terror rippled through the confined space, crawling across my skin like a shivering omen.

Because I could see it slosh and churn from the depths of Dane's eyes.

A wickedness unlike anything I'd witnessed before.

Menace bounced from the walls.

Trembling, I backed away as Dane stalked forward.

Frantic, I found Evan's frightened eyes where he remained across the foyer because I knew, right then, I was in the kind of danger I'd never fathomed.

The movement of my mouth was exaggerated when I shouted for Evan to call 9-1-1.

Evan met my eyes, his fear almost enough to bring me to my knees. But I stood strong, willing to fight for him, the one I'd always been fighting for.

It took only a flash for it to penetrate Evan's mind, and he darted for my purse where I'd left it on the coffee table in the living room.

Dane shoved me so hard it sent me reeling, my feet unable to find solid ground. I flew backward, my head snapping back and smashing against the wall.

A sharp strike of pain blazed across my skull, blurring my vision for a second.

Dane's vindictive voice filled the chaotic air. "He can't hear you, Harley. That little freak *can't hear you.*"

And I knew I would never get through to this man.

But in that moment, while I stood there helpless, sure he was going to end me, I let the years of pent-up hurt and rage pour from my mouth. "He can *hear* me. He's always heard me, just like I hear him. You just refused to listen. To understand him. To *see* him. You're the one who missed out. And now you don't get us, not ever again."

Dane growled an inch from my face, "He was a mistake."

Defiance pulsed through my veins. "He's the best thing that has ever happened to me."

A clatter sounded from the other room.

Dane's attention jerked that way, and his gaze narrowed in shock when he found Evan with the phone, the screen lit and connected, an operator on the line.

Blanching, Dane reared back.

Shock on his face before it was gone and the monster returned. Revulsion curled his fists. "You think this is over? I warned you, Harley. I will find out what you're up to. And you will come home . . . one way or another."

He blew out the door.

A loud sob wrenched from my body, and I slid down the wall to the floor.

It was too much.

The shock and the grief. The hurt and the fear.

Cracks fissuring through my spirit.

Two seconds after Dane disappeared, Evan ran back through the archway with my phone in his hand.

And I swore, I was crushed by his expression when he found me balled up on the floor, sobbing.

No longer able to stand.

His little face was ridden with horror, confusion, and fear. Maybe the worst was that he was looking at me as if he would give anything to have stopped what had just happened.

"Evan," I whispered, and he rushed to me, his precious face a mess of sticky tears.

Arms stretched out for him, I pulled him onto my lap and against my chest. My mouth went to his temple, my lips moving with the promise as I rocked us. "It's okay, it's okay."

He made a scraping sound, and his tears soaked the front of my dress as he clung to me.

"I'm so sorry, Evan," I whimpered, clutching him tighter. "I'm so sorry."

Sorry he had to see that. Go through it. Feel it.

My little man.

My savior.

My protector.

Sirens echoed in the distance, growing louder and louder as they approached. A gasping, relieved breath tore from my lungs when two police officers finally appeared at my gaping door, their guns drawn as they stepped inside to assess the situation.

I pressed Evan's face to my chest to at least protect him from that, hating to put him through any more shock and turmoil.

"We're okay. We're okay. We're okay," I told them through my cries, which only increased as the adrenaline bled away.

As I realized the magnitude of what had just happened.

As I wondered if my telling them we were *okay* was just another lie because I wasn't sure that we truly were.

Dane had just given me ammunition to fight him. An attack that I'd been unprepared for.

But did that even matter when he suspected, knew something was wrong with the records? I held Evan tighter against me as if that one touch might protect him from every danger.

Still, I could feel it slipping away.

Hope.

An officer helped me to my feet, and I carried Evan to the couch, and I continued to hold him as tightly as I could while I answered the officers' questions.

What happened?

Did anything occur to incite the attack?

Were we injured?

I saw it in their expressions when I told him it was my estranged husband.

This was just another common domestic disturbance to them. The same kind of call they'd probably responded to a million times.

Despair settled into the pit of my stomach when they said they would *attempt* to get in touch with Dane Gentry to get his side of the story.

As if the fact he'd forced his way into my home weren't enough.

After an hour of answering their questions, I followed them to the door to let them out, every muscle in my body feeling as if it weighed a million pounds.

The younger officer, the one who'd helped me stand from the floor, paused on the porch and turned back to look at me from over his shoulder, sympathy in the tight twist of his brow. "Make sure you have that door locked up, ma'am."

I gave him a slow nod and followed his instructions.

Though, I wasn't sure it would make a difference, anyway.

Dane had become unstable. Volatile.

And I still couldn't understand why he would continue to press this.

He'd gotten a free card.

A pass.

He could go on and live his life the easy way. Without being tied to Evan. Without being tied to me. He seemed almost desperate for me to return, and that same flare of warning that something was off lapped at my spirit.

I edged back into the living room where my son sat on the couch with his arms wrapped around his knees.

Rocking.

My heart tremored in its confines, the loss and grief threatening to take me over. Drown me in despair.

But I had to be strong.

For my son.

He'd always been my reason.

What I'd been fighting for.

"Come here, my sweet boy."

Gently, I scooped him into my arms, his weight reminding me he wasn't so little anymore . . . that these were the things he would remember. Horrible things that would be etched and scraped into his consciousness.

I wanted so desperately to protect him from that.

Carrying him to his room, I pulled back his covers and nestled him in his bed.

Getting to my knees, I leaned over him and brushed back his red, red hair.

In silence, he stared up at me.

Turmoil in his eyes. So much fear and so many questions I didn't know how to answer brimming in their depths.

I could feel pieces inside me dangling free. Coming apart.

I signed.

ARE YOU OKAY?

His face pinched as if he was upset at me for asking it.

ARE YOU OKAY? His movements were a frantic demand. Angry. As if he wanted to get up and defend me all over again.

Pain clutched my heart, my soul. I swallowed hard, my own movements emphatic as I signed, praying their importance would get through.

*I **AM** OKAY. BUT IT MAKES ME SO SAD YOU SAW THAT. THAT YOU EXPERIENCED THAT. IT'S NOT RIGHT FOR THAT TO HAPPEN. NOT EVER.*

Tears streaked from the corners of his eyes, and Evan sat up in his bed, facing me.

I HATE HIM, M-A-M-A. HE'S NOT ALLOWED HERE BECAUSE HE DOESN'T UNDERSTAND LOVE. YOU CAN ONLY BE HERE IF YOU LOVE. THAT'S THE RULE. REMEMBER WHEN WE CAME HERE? THIS HOUSE IS L-O-V-E.

So upset, his hands flew through the air, his little breaths pants of exertion.

My son.

My beautiful, wonderful, insightful son.

YOU'RE RIGHT. THIS HOUSE IS L-O-V-E. AND I'M DOING MY BEST TO PROTECT THAT. BUT YOU HAVE TO PROMISE ME YOU WON'T EVER STEP IN LIKE THAT AGAIN, EVAN. I KNOW YOU WANT TO HELP, BUT IT'S TOO DANGEROUS. IF SOMETHING IS SCARY OR BAD, I NEED YOU TO GO TO YOUR ROOM. LOCK THE DOOR. CALL THE POLICE.

His head shook frantically. *I HAVE TO TAKE CARE OF YOU.*

NO. NO, EVAN. THAT'S MY JOB. TO TAKE CARE OF YOU.

A fresh round of tears blanketed his face, so much grief in his green, innocent eyes.

BUT IF I DIE, WHO IS GOING TO TAKE CARE OF YOU? KALE WAS SUPPOSED TO BE HERE. WHERE WAS HE?

Oh God.

Crack.

Crack.

Crack.

I could feel everything splintering. Breaking apart. I did everything to hold it together.

YOU'RE NOT GOING TO DIE, EVAN. DON'T SAY THAT.

Frustration and regret sped his signs.

WHERE DID KALE GO?

HE HAD TO GO HOME.

The lies just kept coming and coming. But my lies had always been forged to protect my son. It didn't matter how hard it was, how much *I* hurt, that wouldn't change.

Evan would always be my first priority.

If it landed me behind bars or put me in the ground, he would *always, always* hold that spot.

Evan's face twisted, and a frown pulled at one side of his

mouth. As if he were fighting more tears but was trying to remain strong.

HE WAS SUPPOSED TO BE HERE. HE PROMISED WE WERE GOING TO READ SPIDERMAN. HE SHOULD HAVE BEEN HERE. I WANT HIM TO COME BACK.

He hit his balled fists into his mattress at his sides, so much confusion and sadness in the action tears pricked at my eyes again.

I wondered right then if I'd ever stop crying.

Sorrow shivered through his room.

A new kind of vacancy that had never been there before.

Because Evan could see through it all. My boy always so insightful, clearly knowing Kale hadn't just left, but had run.

Reaching out, I held him by both sides of his face and met his eye. "I want him, too, Evan, but sometimes people are afraid of what they don't understand."

BUT I'M HIS FAVORITE.

His little hands moved like a plea. As if Kale's rejection of him had been his biggest blow.

And I ached. I ached so badly, and I knew my son did, too.

That was the risk of bringing someone into our lives.

Allowing them to complicate us more. We never knew what kind of mess they'd leave behind. But somewhere, somewhere I knew this was bigger than I understood.

"You need to get some rest," I mouthed, and Evan's mouth pursed in reluctance before he relented and settled back against his pillows.

I stayed with him the longest while, running my fingers through his hair as he just lay there, staring at me.

Giving me his own kind of encouragement.

This time, it was my son breathing belief into me.

Time passed before I finally splayed my hand across the steady thrum in his chest.

"My heart," I whispered.

He reached out and splayed his little hand over mine.

My heart, he mouthed.

And mine, it moaned, missing the piece that had blossomed

and bloomed. The piece I'd freely given.

Finally, when Evan had been asleep for a long while, I moved back out into the living room and sank to the edge of the couch, my phone in my hands.

Zero pretension.

Zero pride.

I typed out a message and pressed send.

Me: I need you.

But when I crawled into bed to find a restless, tossing sleep, I'd gotten no response. And when the sun finally struck through the window, sending stakes of glittering light into my room, it still remained unanswered.

And I feared that piece I'd freely given was gone.

Hope shattered.

Maybe it was true what they said. Only fools held out faith.

For the first time in my life, I wondered if that fool was me.

twenty-eight
Kale

Tender hands ran down my bare chest, and giggling lips pressed to my jaw.
"Kale," she whispered.

"Melody," I murmured back, rolling on top of her, pressing her to my bed. "Melody."

I stared down at her. Smiling at her trusting face, wondering how it was possible to feel this way.

Her sweet, sweet face.

It pinched in horror.

In pain.

Everything shifted, my room gone, cement under my feet.

"Kale," she begged from where she stood at her car across the lot, the sun blazing down on her from above. She dropped to her knees on the cold, pitted pavement and clutched her chest. "I need you."

Fear took me whole. Frantically, I ran across the lot and dropped to my knees at her side.

Her eyes rolled back. "Melody!" I shouted.

I searched for her pulse. For her breath.

Screams echoed through the air.

My shouts for help.

"I won't let this happen. I promise, I won't let this happen."

I pressed my hands to her chest and began to pump.

Compression after compression.

Teeth grinding together, I worked over her, begging, "Don't leave me. I won't let you leave me."

I fought and the sun spun out of the sky.

Darkness.

The world canted and tipped from its axis.

Everything shook.

Evan's face.

His little, broken body beneath my hands.

That fucking flat line.

A scream. A plea. Hope on her knees. "I need you. I need you . . ."

A roar ripping from my lungs jolted me upright in bed.

Searching for nonexistent air, I gasped and panted, pretty sure the life was being squeezed out of me.

My eyes darted around the shadowy darkness of my bedroom as the images faded.

My skin drenched in sweat, and my heart beating like a motherfucking drum.

My shoulders dropped when I realized I was alone. That it was just another dream.

Which should have been a comfort, but the awareness of it just sent grief swooping down, shackling me in its chains.

"Fuck," I gritted.

Hand fumbling through the dark, I reached over to flick on the lamp on my nightstand. The muted light broke through the night, and I pushed to sit up at the edge of my bed. The movement sent a wave of nausea crashing over me, sucking me down, taking me under.

Lost in the deepest, darkest sea where voices pleaded and moaned and begged.

I need you.

I need you.

I need you.

I knew I was losing it. Coming unglued. Standing at the edge of a cliff and getting ready to fall over the side into that abyss of nothingness.

Where I'd drown in dreams and torment and screams.

I'd never known a loss like the one I was prisoner to right then.

Losing them.

Hope and Evan.

But at least I'd gotten out before I could cause them more damage or pain. Because God knew, that was all I knew how to inflict. That didn't mean I didn't fight myself every second of every day not to go back to them. To ask for a fucked-up sort of forgiveness that I would never deserve.

If Hope knew what I'd done, the way I'd failed, she'd never look at me the same.

Hell, I knew it'd haunt her the same way that fucking text that had come in just after midnight nine days ago haunted me.

I need you.

I'd nearly succumbed. Broken down and crawling back on my hands and knees like a beggar, groveling, trying to find any excuse in my mind that would make it okay to be with them.

But I sucked it up. Refused the urges and the need and the sorrow.

Because I was staying away for them.

I need you.

Drawn, my eyes peeled open, and my already choppy breaths turned ragged.

By instinct, I reached for the sheet of folded paper sitting on my nightstand, my hand shaking like a bitch and my stomach threatening to spill onto the floor.

I'd found it sitting on the backseat of my car. I'd wanted to think it discarded. Nothing of importance, but I knew the kid had left it there for me.

A message.

Tonight, I unfolded it for what had to be the millionth time because I couldn't help but torture myself a little more.

My chest tightened when I stared down at the drawing.

A fucking fantastic rendition because the kid was amazing.

Clever and talented and smart.

Captain America and a tiny Hulk were holding hands.

My eyes traced what was written at the bottom in the same handwriting I'd come to know so well. Words I heard like a voice.

My favorite.

Regret drove into me like a blunt, rusted knife.

Gutting.

A remnant of Melody's voice clashed with the power of Hope's.

I need you.

I was a goner.

So fucking gone.

And there was no finding my way back.

Every time I'd driven passed A Drop of Hope over the last nine days, I'd gunned my engine and sped by. Refusing to look that way because it brought on more memories and regrets than I knew how to deal with.

But this morning . . .

This morning there was nothing I could do but slow and look that way. Because everything felt different.

An awareness that thundered my heart and twisted my guts in a million knots of need.

My spirit thrashed and screamed.

Because I caught sight of the girl for the first time since I'd left her broken in her kitchen.

Body lush, Hope wearing one of those dresses that drove me out of my mind, the best goddamned thing I'd ever seen.

Considering the fact I was sure my sanity was slipping, I thought for a second I had to be hallucinating.

But there she was. Leaning over and reaching into the back of her SUV to pull out a supply box. That red, red hair whipped around her delicate shoulders when she quickly spun around.

Like she felt me the same way I felt her.

Our eyes locked through the windshield.

The world freezing.

Time suspended.

The two of us lost to a place that belonged only to us.

Grief lined every inch of her unforgettable face, and there was a weight in her eyes that I hadn't ever seen there before.

I could almost hear the plea in the soft part of her full, full lips.

I need you.

Every cell in my body reacted.

Want.

Need.

Regret.

Shame.

The last snapped me back into reality, and I ripped my eyes away from her and floored the accelerator. The coward who had to get away.

It was time.

The way I'd reacted when I'd seen Hope that morning was clear proof of that.

I'd gone astray.

Gotten distracted.

I was pretty sure the second I'd realized Evan was Hope's child, I'd known.

Fate warning me to watch my step. Telling me it'd do me well to take one back.

And I'd just run forward. Careless.

Reckless.

Selfish.

Pushing and pushing for something I wanted, but knew, in the end, I couldn't keep.

The workday had passed in a daze. Every second had been a

struggle to focus. A fucking herculean feat to pass out those damned lollipops like every single one of them didn't nearly drop me to my knees.

I finished with my last patient and stumbled into my office.

I sank down at my desk in front of my laptop.

I had to take care of this.

It'd been a constant nag at the back of my brain. Problem was, it'd been met with so much resistance from my heart and spirit that I'd been avoiding it like the goddamned plague.

Maybe I'd been holding out, thinking I might discover the cure before this feeling became a sickness.

Because that was what I felt.

Sick.

Taking this final step.

Snipping the last thread that tied us together.

I'd already spoken with Dr. Acosta about taking over Evan's care. I'd told her there was a conflict of interest, and I'd be more comfortable with her seeing him for his general visits.

The whole time I'd felt like I'd been committing a betrayal. Not because I couldn't be there for him as his physician. But because I couldn't be there for him at all.

I need you.

My chest squeezed when that voice hit me.

I tamped it down and clicked into his chart so I could write up my final notes on his care and transfer them over. That and send Hope the anonymous note that would let her know her son had the same heart defect that his aunt did, even though I couldn't dig deep enough to find the exact records that would confirm it.

Records that should have been there lost.

Purged or hidden.

I didn't know.

Either way, Hope would finally know.

At least I could give her this.

His chart popped up.

Evan Quinn Masterson.

A shudder rolled through me.

Unease.

A shrinking awareness.

Something was just intrinsically . . . off.

I'd been feeling it for days, a disturbance that flamed and lapped on the fringes of my consciousness. No doubt, part of it was the guilt over just walking out of their lives without giving a reason or explanation.

The guilt that I'd left them thinking it might somehow be their fault when I knew I had to protect them from this. But there was something else. Something just out of my reach.

A light knocking tapped at my door, and my nurse popped her head inside. "I have those reports you were asking for. There is a reprint from two weeks ago that showed it'd been sent from the lab, but I didn't see it come across my desk."

"Who is it from?" I asked, looking at her from over my computer.

"The nuclear radiologist."

"Okay, thank you," I said, reaching out and accepting the small stack of faxes that had been forwarded from the lab and would need to be added to Evan's EHR.

"Anything else you need tonight before I head out for the evening?" she asked.

"No, I'm good. I'm just going to stick around and catch up on some charts."

She paused for a moment like she wanted to say something else. Clearly, she was worried about my state.

But there was absolutely nothing she could do for me to make this better.

I'd brought it all on myself.

She gave a slight nod. "Okay, then. I'll see you in the morning."

She clicked the door shut, and I turned my attention to the printouts, scanning the numbers and tests, trying not to break down in tears like a goddamned pussy.

But fuck.

I missed him.

I missed them both so goddamned much I felt like I was

being torn limb from limb. Stretched so thin there was no chance there would be anything left.

I forced myself to move forward. I scanned one page and then another, moving onto the third.

My heart tripped the second my eyes started to move over the numbers.

It was the report from the nuclear medicine radiologist. The results of Evan's cardiac stress test. The numbers that we should have received two weeks ago.

The walls of my small office started to close in.

While I stared at the numbers on the paper.

They were the only thing I could see.

Only interrupted by flashes of Evan's trusting, sweet face.

The episode of severe shortness of breath at the park. The redness on his neck and cheeks that day at Rex and Rynna's. The way I'd asked him if he felt okay, and he'd said he was just tired.

Tired.

Tired because his transplanted heart was not pumping properly.

His records from earlier in the year had shown the very early signs of coronary artery disease, which was to be expected.

But this?

This was accelerated. Progressing at an alarming, dangerous rate.

Panic shot me to my feet, my chair tipping over and crashing to the floor as I clamored to grab my cell.

Frantically, I dialed the number I'd promised myself I'd never dial again.

In the same second, I flew out the door.

You're my favorite.

That promise roared in my ears.

Deafening.

My favorite. My favorite. My favorite.

Fuck.

This couldn't happen.

I wouldn't let it.

Not to him.

"Answer the phone, Hope," I begged under my breath, agitation lighting a path through me as I listened to Hope's phone ring and ring. On the fourth, it clicked over to voice mail.

That sweet voice hit my ear like a song. Mine was grating and hard when it finally beeped.

"Hope, I need you to call me the second you get this. I know you have to be pissed and confused, but this isn't about us. It's about Evan."

Ending the call, I raced down the hall and out the side door toward my car, feet pounding on the pavement.

Adrenaline surged.

A thunder through my veins.

My car blipped and unlocked as I approached, and I already had the engine turned over by the time I had the door closed. I threw the gear in reverse and whipped out of the parking spot.

The second my wheels hit the road, I floored the accelerator.

I weaved in and out of cars, trying to keep it together.

I told myself we'd caught it.

He'd be okay.

But it was that sense I'd been feeling all week—the one that warned something was terribly wrong—that reared its ugly head.

This dark foreboding that crawled beneath the surface of my skin.

Ominous and grim.

Shouting at me to hurry. That this was bigger than I could see.

I flew by the coffee shop. All the lights were off. It was late enough she'd already be gone for the night, so I took a sharp left turn, tires squealing as I skidded around the corner and headed in the direction of her house.

I floored the gas when I approached a yellow light, barreling through, unwilling to stop or slow, zigzagging between cars, pushing it harder and harder.

I careened around a corner and allowed myself a breath of relief when I made the last right onto their street.

I just needed to get there. Needed to know they were okay.

I slowed when I neared their house.

A disorder rumbled in my chest the closer I got.

An awareness.

An unease.

A sixth-fucking-sense.

I didn't know.

All I knew was the hairs prickled at the back of my neck, standing on end and sending a slow ripple of disquiet skating across my flesh.

It was different from when I'd seen the results of Evan's tests.

This was cold.

Protective and harsh.

A midnight blue car sat in front of Hope's house.

It almost blended in with the deepening twilight sky.

Almost.

All except for the fact it was one of those flashy bits. Not just nice. But the kind that screamed pretension.

The kind of car someone bought because they wanted you to know they were better than you in their own fucked-up, inflated heads.

I couldn't see anyone standing around it.

But I knew. I fucking knew.

My chest spasmed. Heart threatening to beat right through my ribs.

I didn't know how I'd look at him without pounding the bastard into the ground for what he'd done to Hope and Evan.

How I'd remain standing when I'd look at him and see *her* eyes.

This had to be the most savage, ruthless reminder of my failure.

But there was no consideration when Hope's porch finally came into view.

No hesitation.

Because the fucker had ahold of Evan and was dragging him out the front door.

Hope screaming and trying to free her child.

Panic and terror rippled through the dense air.

And there was nothing but the base, fundamental need to protect these two.

twenty-nine
Hope

I sometimes wondered if people were born evil. If they were bred that way. If they had no chance of compassion. No chance of giving love or providing protection.

Or did life's tragedies and disasters seed it, allowing it to grow and grow until it was twisted and vile?

I wondered it as I came to an abrupt stop at the opening of the hall that led to Evan's room and found Dane Gentry standing in the middle of my living room.

Wearing one of his impeccable suits and hate in his eyes.

My heart climbed to my throat and my stomach sank to the floor.

Nothing but fear freezing my veins in shards of ice.

The instinct to protect Evan swelled inside me, and I pushed him farther behind me, my hand on his arm, trying to give him reassurance.

It did nothing to stop the quiver I felt shake through him, head to toe.

I couldn't let this happen. Not again. I had to find a way to put this madness to an end.

"Get out of my house," I warned.

Dane laughed a morbid sound and took a step forward. "Did you really think you could erase me so easily?"

My eyes went wide at the way he phrased it, my already pounding heart taking off at a sprint.

"I don't know what you're talking about." The defense trembled from my mouth. It might as well have been a confession of guilt.

A smirk ticked up at the corner of his mouth. Cruel and biting. "Always so innocent and pristine. Yet, she doesn't hesitate to tell lies or commit felonies."

An alarm sounded inside my head, so loudly I could hear it blaring in my ears.

There was no questioning it then. He definitely knew.

A shudder rocked my spine, and I gulped, lifting my chin and trying to pretend as if he didn't intimidate me when I was shaking so bad I didn't know how I managed to remain on my feet.

"This ends now, Harley. Get your things and get in my car."

My head shook. "You're insane," I told him again. He had to be. Crazy. Crazy for coming here. Crazy to think I'd just jump and do his bidding.

"Come with me now or rot in prison, Harley. Your choice. It seems like a simple one to me."

Or maybe I was the insane one. The one who had thought going down this road was smart. But at the time, it'd felt like the only way.

"I have no idea what you're saying," I maintained, but I knew it was a losing battle.

I knew there was no way to talk my way out of this with the way his eyes gleamed in victory.

Because he knew. Oh God, he really knew, and the true consequences of that were just sinking in when he took another oppressive step forward, coming closer and closer to my son.

My son who he wanted to reject. Do away with. Toss him aside like garbage.

Try again.

"I warned you that you'd regret it if you took this any further, Harley. And you've gone too far. Now get in my fucking car before I drag you there."

Sickness roiled. I was overtaken by desperation. Every nerve and cell in my body flooded with the wild, violent need to protect my son.

I could feel Evan peeking out from behind me. His small frame shook with fear and confusion, his silent questions ricocheting from the floors as if he were shouting them into the air.

He doesn't belong here, Mama.

This house is love.

My little man who thought it was his job to defend me when I would give my life defending him.

I took a step back, herding Evan with me. "Stay away from us or you'll regret it."

Incredulous, his eyes narrowed as he shook his head. "You think I'm going to regret it, Harley? You have it all wrong. You should have known better than to think you could play me. Now tell that kid to get in my car before I make him regret it, too."

"I'll die before I let you get anywhere near him."

I meant it.

But that didn't mean it wasn't the wrong thing to say.

Because rage lit on Dane's face. A match to gasoline. Two quick steps forward, and he had me by the upper arms. As if I weighed absolutely nothing, he tossed me out of his way and went straight for my son.

Panic seized every inch of my body as I flew across the living room.

It was an awareness taking hold. A deep-seated knowledge that I'd pushed Dane over a line. The same way as he'd done to me a year before. When he'd left me without a choice. When there'd been nothing else I could do.

All I'd wanted was to stop the torment.

To give my son the chance to live the life he deserved to live.

And this man was again exerting his horrible, brutal control. This time . . . this time, he was doing it with the force of his hands.

I screamed out as an excruciating pain splintered through my left side when I crashed into the sofa table set up behind the couch.

Frames that showed off Evan's innocent face fell to the floor. Glass shattering as it struck the wood.

Our best memories scattered across the floor.

I tumbled down on top of them. A wave of helplessness took me over. It was never supposed to be like this. I didn't know how to stand up against it. Fight it.

But that helplessness was eradicated the second I saw the horror blanket my son's face when Dane yanked him by the shirt. He started to drag him through the living room and toward the front door.

Evan's eyes went wide. So wide with an overwhelming terror that I scrambled to find my footing, my words screeching from my raw throat. "Let him go! He's just a little boy. Let him go!"

Dane didn't slow, he just issued his command into the air. "You're coming home with me now. Both of you. You no longer make the decisions. Do you understand me?"

Running after them, I grabbed at Dane's arm and tried to break his hold. "Let him go. He's just a little boy. I won't let you hurt him. Not anymore. Not anymore."

Dane spun around. With a single arm, he locked Evan's back to his chest. He stood there as if my son was a pawn. A twisted ransom held between us.

Contempt dripped from his tongue. "What does it fucking matter, Harley? Why are you clinging to nothing? *Nothing.*"

How could he say that? This was a little boy who was made up of flesh and bones and the brightest spirit. Made up of the biggest heart that beat life through his veins. A boy who was everything.

Hopeless tears streaked down my face, my soul fragmenting as I watched Evan kick and flail, frantic as he clawed at Dane's arm.

"Evan," I whimpered.

His feet kept giving out from under him as he struggled to

break free.

His weight held in the palm of Dane's malicious hands.

Dane started backing through my house, his eye on me the entire time as he dragged Evan away. Expecting me to follow. This vile, horrible man using my child as bait.

"Dane . . . don't do this."

"You're out of chances, Harley."

"Why are you doing this?"

My steps were lurching as I moved toward them, and the words flooded from my mouth in a pour of desperation, "Dane . . . please . . . I'm begging you. Let him go. He doesn't deserve your anger. Your hatred. He never has. You are free. We are no longer a burden to you. A worry for you. I don't want anything from you except for you to let us go free. Just let him go and let us live our lives and you can live yours."

At my words, Dane's jaw clenched so hard I could hear his teeth cracking. "I will never be *free*. I will never be free of this."

"What does that mean?" I begged.

For the beat of a second, I wished I could go back to a time when I'd thought I understood this man. When I'd thought our hopes and dreams had been one. Before he'd become *this*.

A monster.

"Please." It ripped through the foyer. Breaking on my pain.

It didn't even touch Dane's rage. He jerked Evan through the door and out onto the porch.

Daylight was giving up its hold. It cast the world in shadows and mist and somehow set everything to slow motion.

A part of me felt detached. As if I were watching it happen from a distance. Removed from the reality that this man was really trying to take my son from me.

It had always been my greatest terror.

But I'd never known how great that terror could truly be until Evan started making these rasping, raking sounds.

Sounds I'd never heard him make.

His lungs brittle. As if my little boy was getting ready to crack.

Still kicking his feet, he stopped clawing at Dane's arm and instead reached for me as if he were begging for a lifeline.

For me to save him.

To keep him safe the way I'd always promised him I would.

"Evan, it's okay. Baby, it's okay. I won't let anything happen to you," I rushed, meeting his eyes, promising him through that connection that I wouldn't allow this to happen. That somehow, some way, I would stop this.

No matter what it cost me.

But Evan's face . . .

It was turning a purpled, beet red. Unnatural. Wrong.

A different kind of panic set in. Stretching out my insides.

Dane spun away and started for the steps. I launched myself onto his back, clawing at his face, screaming in his ear. "You're hurting him, Dane. Oh my God, you're hurting him. Let him go."

I was barely able to see through the haze that clouded my eyes.

This was where we'd come to a head.

Where we imploded.

Where this monster who held a thousand pounds of vile, ugly hate around his heart spiraled into a beast.

"You're hurting him."

I clawed and bit and kicked, but I knew I was no rival for Dane's physical strength.

But that didn't mean I wouldn't fight with everything I had.

I yelped when I was suddenly jarred back, my arms I'd locked around Dane's neck unloosed.

No.

But I was falling. Failing. I crashed onto the wooden planks of the porch.

"No!" The scream tore from my throat as I struggled to get back to my feet.

But it was relief that slammed me when I realized Evan had also been knocked free of Dane's malicious grasp.

It was blinding, cutting relief when I realized it was Dane who was colliding with the ground one second after a fist collided with his face.

A stunned gasp ripped from my lungs.

Kale.

He was there.

Oh, God, he was really there.

Kale dove for him, pinning him down at the waist as he began to pound his fists into his face.

Over and over again.

Shouts and grunts and punches.

Knuckles against buckling flesh.

Dane kicked and grappled. But he was no match for Kale's assault, and his wicked face quickly morphed into a river of blood.

Shocked, I watched wide-eyed and frozen as Kale beat Dane into an unconscious oblivion, my heart thundering so hard and my lungs rasping as I tried to process the scene.

It felt as if it took an age for my mind to catch up.

Kale had come back to me.

He was there.

Saving us.

I finally found a breath for my screaming lungs and managed to tear my attention away from Kale and Dane to look toward Evan. To give him a promise through my eyes.

That even though I'd never wanted him to witness anything like this—violence and bitterness and this savage, brutal war—I wanted him to know he would always be worth it.

My eyes found him where he'd been knocked to the lawn.

The second they did, my heart cracked in the center of me.

Evan was on his hands and knees. His expression was twisted in sheer, confused panic that had him seized.

Locked in pain.

It was one beat before his arms and legs gave.

My little boy fell to the ground.

Face down.

I screamed.

I screamed and screamed. But my screams were silent to my own ears. As if no matter how loud they were, no one would hear. No help to be found.

I crawled for him, half-rolling down the steps as I fought to get there. Everything was weighted, spindly tendrils reaching out from the depths of a nightmare to hold me back.

Because it felt as if I were slithering through quicksand.

Sinking.

Farther and farther away from him with each savage moment that passed.

It was a slowed motion I couldn't breach.

My entire body shivered when I reached for him and flipped him over.

He rolled, completely limp.

I couldn't stop shaking . . . shaking and shaking and shaking . . . when my hand fumbled out to press over his chest.

My heart. My heart.

This time, I heard it.

My scream.

The agony that tore out of me when I could no longer feel the beat of his little life.

My sun and my moon.

I couldn't see.

Couldn't hear.

And I swore, right then, all the stars fell from the sky.

"No," I raked over a sob, my hand pressing harder. Frantically searching. "No. No, no, no. Evan, no. You aren't going to leave me. I won't let you. No. Please."

A cry scraped from my throat when I was suddenly being torn away from where I clung to Evan, hands I'd missed so desperately squeezing me hard for the flash of a second.

Before he'd taken my place.

Kale.

Quickly, the man moved to kneel over my son. He tilted his ear to Evan's mouth then pressed his fingers to his neck.

For the beat of a second, horror struck on his face.

It was the exact same horror I'd seen him wear in my kitchen.

It was the kind of horror that destroyed worlds.

Despairing and desolate.

He started pumping Evan's chest.

My mouth dropped open in another scream.

A plea.

A prayer.

I didn't know.

No. No. No.

Kale's face broke into my vision.

His lips were moving, shouting, but I couldn't hear.

My son, my son, my son.

"Hope. Hope! Call 9-1-1."

Finally, the sound cracked against my ears, penetrating the horrifying daze, snapping me out of my stupor and into action.

I scrambled onto my hands and knees, slipping on the grass before I managed to get to my feet. Clinging to the railing, I fumbled up the steps and raced inside. It felt as if it took a lifetime to get to my room where my phone was charging on the nightstand.

A lifetime flashing.

A tiny infant in my arms.

"I'm sorry, but your son will require a heart transplant. It's the only chance he has."

M-A-M-A, he signed for the first time.

His grin. His smile. His belief.

Love. Love. Love.

Grief fisted me by the throat, and I ripped the phone from the cord and rushed back out, trying to see through the torment as I forced myself to remain steady enough to dial the three numbers.

I was already back outside and dropping to my knees beside where Kale was hunched over Evan when the operator answered.

"9-1-1, what's your emergency?"

"Help, my son. He's collapsed. He's a heart transplant recipient. Please . . . hurry."

I rattled off my address, begging the whole time.

"Ma'am . . . try to stay calm. Can you tell me if he's breathing? Does he have any other visible injuries?"

"No. Just . . . please . . . hurry."

"We have an ambulance in route. Please stay on the line with me."

Kale worked over Evan in a controlled desperation.

Hopefully.

Fiercely.

Grimly.

As if he could pump his own life into my son's body.

While I sat there, helplessly clutching my chest, trying to keep everything from spilling out.

Chills raked down my spine when I felt the shadow looming over us.

It was the evilest kind of darkness.

The man who stared down with animosity and a twisted sort of disbelief where Evan lay on the ground. To where Kale tried to save my son's life.

Then the monster bolted down the walkway and to his car.

His engine roared, and he sped away.

Gone.

The way I wanted him to be.

The sound of sirens whirred in the distance, growing louder and louder as they approached. Red and white lights flickered and flashed through the growing darkness in front of my house as a firetruck and ambulance arrived.

Paramedics swarmed around us, but Kale refused to budge from Evan. He shouted that he was a doctor, making orders, never pausing chest compressions.

Evan's shirt was cut up the middle and a mask was placed over his mouth and nose.

I cringed when an IV was placed in his veins. I hated it for him, how terrified my son was of that specific thing. His fear of needles. The way I'd always wanted to take away all of his pain.

But I'd never, ever been prepared for this.

In a scramble of activity, a defibrillator was set on the ground.

My entire body froze in grief when they set the paddles on his chest and a huge shock jolted his tiny body.

I was certain the entire earth held its breath as we waited for the line on the monitor to blip to life.

But there was nothing.

They administered another.

I could feel all the pieces I'd been trying to hold together fall away when Evan was shocked again and there was still no response. In horror, I watched as Kale went back to compressions as Evan was strapped to a backboard and placed on a gurney.

Kale never stopped his efforts when they moved Evan.

He climbed onto the gurney and straddled my son.

Pumping.

Refusing to give up.

And I prayed. I prayed, and I prayed, and I prayed.

Promising I would never give up hope.

thirty

Kale

Fear took me whole. Frantically, I ran across the lot and dropped to my knees at her side.

Her eyes rolled back. "Melody!" I shouted.

I searched for her pulse. For her breath.

Screams echoed through the air.

My shouts for help.

"I won't let this happen. I promise, I won't let this happen."

I pressed my hands to her chest and began to pump.

Compression after compression.

Teeth grinding together, I worked over her, begging, "Don't leave me. I won't let you leave me."

I fought and the sun spun out of the sky.

Darkness.

The world canted and tipped from its axis.

Everything shook.

Evan's face.

His little, broken body beneath my hands.

That fucking flat line.

A scream. A plea. Hope on her knees. "I need you. I need you . . ."

I bit back the roar that threatened in my throat, a clod of fear and desperation that took up the entire cavity of my chest.

I pumped and pumped and pumped as people moved around the trauma room in a controlled chaos.

I tried to shrug off the hand that landed on my shoulder. "Dr. Bryant . . . you need to step down. We have him. We have him."

"No!" I shouted, continuing to pump through the tears and the cries that raked from my soul.

No.

Evan.

Oh, God, no.

I wouldn't let this happen again.

I couldn't.

Another hand landed on my shoulder, and this time it was Dr. Krane's face that cut into my vision. "Dr. Bryant, we need to move him, and we need to do it now. I will do everything in my power to save him. I promise."

Grief tore through me as I looked down at Evan, to where I was still straddling him on the gurney, the precious little boy's face covered by the mask where one of the nurses pumped the bag.

"We have to move him," Dr. Krane said again in attempt to break through the mayhem that scattered my brain and scrambled my spirit.

No. Evan.

My favorite. My favorite.

Feeling a piece of me rip away, I let two male nurses haul me off the gurney. Knees weak and my arms screaming from the exertion, I slumped forward, sucking for the nonexistent air.

I tried. I tried. I tried.

I would have given anything.

I'd never be enough.

Grief ricocheted from the walls as the trauma room door slid open, and they quickly wheeled out his tiny, broken body and moved him toward the elevators that would lift him to the surgical floor.

Open-heart surgery.

His only chance.

His last chance.

They'd already gotten Hope's consent. I couldn't imagine what she was feeling right then. The devastation she had to be dealing with.

Fuck. I wanted to take it from her. Shoulder it all.

I staggered out five feet behind them. Hopelessness swooped down, winding around me.

Destroying.

Dizzying.

Overpowering.

I tried.

I tried.

They stopped to wait for the elevator, and my attention was captured by the two big wooden doors that led out to the front entrance as it buzzed and swung open.

That awareness was back. Coasting across my skin like an omen.

A chill.

That sixth fucking sense that knotted my stomach and curled my fists.

Dane Gentry strode through, still wearing the suit he'd been wearing back at Hope's place an hour before, though, his crisp white shirt was smattered with blood and his fucking pretentious face, which he'd tried to wipe clean, was mottled with rising bruises and gaping cuts.

And I wished . . . I wished with all of me I hadn't stopped when I did.

That I'd ended the piece of shit the way he'd deserved to be.

Because there was no missing what was written all over Hope who was right behind him. She was screeching and clawing and trying to jump on his back to keep him away from her son.

The one she'd been living for because she'd always been living for the right things.

The best things.

Dane's voice boomed, a vile echo across the linoleum floors.

"Stop what you're doing. That child has a DNR."

Hope screamed. A scream made up of fury and protection. A mother's fight. "He's lying. I would never sign that. Never. Don't listen to him."

Caught off guard, Dr. Krane paused to twist at the waist to check out the commotion behind him. He frowned, confusion and disgust lining his brow. "Excuse me, but I'm afraid I don't know who you are."

When the elevator dinged and the doors slid open, he turned back around and started to move forward, but Dane's voice was bellowing again. "I'm Dane Gentry, Evan's father."

Dr. Krane shook his head. "I'm sorry, but I have no idea who Evan Gentry is. If you'll excuse me, I have a patient to treat."

A blast of hot fury blew through me. I was already moving toward Evan as Dane approached. I'd fight to the end for that little boy.

With everything.

It was all I had left.

What I had to give.

The dickbag had no clue I was there, his attention all wrapped up on one goal. His disgusting ambition that was slowly beginning to make sense.

Those disordered pieces and threads that'd been dangling around me for close to the last two weeks finally coming together.

Seeping into my consciousness.

Dane's words hit Dr. Krane and his team from behind, "If you proceed, I will have your medical license. Your home. Your life. My attorney is on his way, so I suggest you stop whatever she has consented to. This woman's name is Harley Gentry, and that boy's name is Evan Gentry. She perjured his records."

Hope's sweet, sweet voice ripped through the air. Pain. Grief. She tried to scramble around him as she screamed, "No. Don't listen to him. Please, save my son. Save him!"

Her torment pummeled me. Wave after wave, and I didn't know whether to stand guard in front of Evan or rush the motherfucker and make it so he couldn't utter another word.

In the middle of everything, wondering if I would finally truly have something to give.

Because another of those pieces finally took hold. I'd looked through Evan's records what had to be a hundred times. Dane had never been mentioned once.

Not once.

The memory hit me, the plea that had been woven into her tone when she'd told me she'd do absolutely anything to protect her son.

Anything.

This amazing, giving, selfless girl.

Rage churned, and I stepped in front of Dane who was still making his approach.

I didn't give a flying fuck if I lost my medical license. My freedom. Whatever it took.

He tried to keep his arrogant chin lifted, but I saw the way the pussy's knees wobbled, the tremor in his misstep.

I shifted to look over my shoulder at Dr. Krane. "I assure you, Dr. Krane, there is no evidence of a DNR in that boy's file. This man is lying."

It didn't matter if he was or not. I'd gladly go down for this. For Evan. For Hope.

Dr. Krane hesitated, looking between Dane and Evan and me.

"Please . . . save him." I couldn't even manage to get sound into the words. It was just a silent plea.

Issued with every part of me.

Because if I could offer Hope one thing? It would be a chance for her son.

For her amazing, incredible son.

For a moment, Dr. Krane wavered before he cleared his throat and yelled, "Go, get his boy upstairs."

Standing there with my heart battering at my ribs, I watched as they rushed Evan into the elevator. It wasn't until the door closed shut behind them that I sensed the flurry of movement, the whoosh of air before I felt the connection of the fist against my jaw.

Pain splintered across my face and my head rocked back.

But I didn't care.

As long as Evan got his chance.

Hope screamed. Screamed my name so loudly it penetrated my soul, which I swore trembled and shook, stretching out for her.

Wishing it could reach her.

Impossible.

I knew.

But that didn't mean that connection between us wasn't real.

Feet knocked out from under me, I tripped and thudded to the ground. Instantly, Dane was on top of me, going for another blow. Roaring, I caught his wrist just before it connected against my eye.

I tossed him off.

It sent him reeling across the floor. He slammed into a metal file cabinet, head striking against the corner, body slumping to the ground.

I went for him, sitting up high on my knees when I cocked my arm back and let my fist fly. It cracked against his cheekbone. The already fragile skin split and blood poured out.

"Why would you do this?" I demanded, gripping him by the shirt in both of my hands. A new kind of frenzy rose inside me.

Hysteria and turmoil.

A need for Hope. Maybe a need for *me*.

Melody.

I blinked against the images of her face that flashed behind my eyes. That fucking flat line.

"Why? Did you know Melody was sick? Did you know *your sister* was sick?" My own sickness roiled when I thought of the possibility.

Melody falling to the ground, shocked by a pain she never could have anticipated.

I need you.

Hope yelped when I said it. "Your sister? Oh God. Kale. Oh God, the girl . . . your first love who you lost."

No doubt, the girl was catching on to my truth.

The second I'd realized the connection, I'd known the reality would break her in two.

God knew that it'd broken me.

But in the end, she needed to know this more than I did. For Evan. We needed the whole, complete truth for Evan.

I wouldn't stop until we had it.

I could feel her . . . her presence behind me, her cries biting into my skin. Fuck, I just wanted to take it all away. Make it better. Give her back her life.

"Fuck you," Dane spat.

I tightened my hold on his collar, making sure I was cutting off some of the airflow, my teeth gritting as I forced out the low, biting words, "Tell me . . . did you know that your sister was sick? That her heart was bad?"

Guilt streaked across his face before it was replaced with indignation.

He knew. Anger stretched hot across my chest.

"You bastard, you fucking knew." My hands constricted tighter, and his legs flailed, his pathetic hands coming to mine, nails scratching as he tried to break my hold.

"No. You're the one who was supposed to be the doctor. You should have seen it. You should have saved her."

Knives.

They cut and flayed. Slashes across my flesh. Cutting me to pieces.

Because I knew I should have. I should have seen. I should have stopped it.

But I'd ignored all the warning signs. Too busy and too wrapped up in my life to realize their importance until there'd been nothing I could do.

Melody.

My Melody.

"Tell me why, you piece of shit. Tell me."

I cocked my fist back, and he flinched, confession grit from his mouth. "My mother."

Just Dane mentioning Melody's mother threatened to knock me back on my ass, but I kept hold. "Why?"

He roared and struggled to break free.

I curled both my hands around his neck. "Don't assume I wouldn't think twice about ending you. Right now. I've already lost everything. I'd take pleasure in taking you down while I go."

He thrashed, and I tightened my hold, teeth grinding. "Tell me."

His eyes bulged with air loss, his own teeth clenched as he forced out the words. "My grandfather . . . he couldn't know it ran in my mother's family. She had a sister . . . a sister who died from the same thing."

Hope howled.

Dropped to her knees.

The space echoed with her anguished, jutting cries. Horror after horror. "The money. Oh God, the money."

Hope clutched her chest. "It was all about the money, wasn't it? You bastard . . . you bastard, you were gonna let your own son—your own flesh and blood—die over money? That goddamned inheritance? All that talk about your father's prestigious bloodline? It had to remain that way, didn't it? Prestigious and perfect. Without blemish? That's what your grandfather meant? You need a healthy son so you could get your fucking inheritance."

Dane's voice turned almost pleading, the bastard a believer in his own fucked-up, twisted way. "I told you, we could try again."

Hate blistered through my senses.

"You changed his name on his records. You tried to hide his medical records from me." Disgust lined Dane's voice.

Her head shook, lips trembling with the words. "You think I regret that? I'd do it again . . . over and over again . . . no matter what it cost me, so long as it protected him from you."

A sound left Hope.

One of sickened realization.

"Oh, God, you wanted me back because you needed me to have another child. So you could pin the genetic defect on me if you had another child with it?"

Dane's lips pursed.

So goddamned guilty.

But the bastard wouldn't admit it, he only grated, "You'll regret this, Harley," when I jerked him up by the shirt and slammed him down again.

Footsteps pounded around us. It wasn't until then that I realized we were ringed by nurses and bystanders.

Gaping, horrified eyes watched us from the perimeter.

Three security guards and a police officer had busted through the circle and were descending on us.

"Release him," the officer shouted at me, his gun drawn.

I was ripped up from behind.

Arms locked behind my back.

"Let me go," I raged, fighting as the cuffs were locked in place. I needed to get to him. To make sure he could never keep that promise.

End the threat for Hope and Evan once and for all.

Give them something when I could never be enough.

Dane was being hauled up, his knees buckling beneath him when his arms were twisted behind his back. "Twenty-million dollars, Hope. You're willing to let twenty-million dollars go?"

A roar blew from my lungs at his statement.

He said it as if she were the deranged one.

Because the piece of shit couldn't see through his black soul.

Melody.

I gasped over a breath when I realized what it all meant. What they'd been trying to hide.

Hope's face was twisted in the most shocking kind of grief as she climbed to her feet. Her milky flesh illuminated in the lights, glistening with tears.

She took a step toward him.

Red hair flying all around her.

So goddamned strong in her vulnerability.

Her chin trembled, and the words flooded from her mouth. "There was a day I believed in you, Dane. A day when I loved you. A day when I looked at you and I saw the future I wanted."

Her face pinched. "And all you saw was money?"

She blinked, trying to process the blow, before she swallowed hard, gathering herself. "I swear to you, if you so much as think about my son, I will make sure every last person in this world knows who you are and what you did. I will expose you and your disgusting family. I will ruin you, the way you have tried to ruin us."

She took another step toward him.

The girl always standing for what she believed in.

Faith radiating from her.

So damned bright.

"But we *are* not ruined. Not even close. When my son comes out of surgery, because he will—I *know* he will—I will have documents from your attorney relinquishing your parental rights. You will never have a say in his life, or in my life, ever again. Do you understand me?"

His voice was a growl. "You're a fool, Harley."

Mouth trembling, she shook her head. "No, Dane. You are the fool. You were so blinded by greed that you never saw the treasure you already held. The abundant life you could have been given. You are destitute, and I am the one who is rich."

The officer and guards began to haul us toward the entrance doors.

Anger ripped from Dane's chest, and his head jerked back as they dragged him away. "You will pay for this, Harley. You fucked over the wrong person. You won't forget who *I am*."

Just before they pulled me through the double doors, I twisted to look at Hope.

Those eyes met mine.

A mossy, earthy plane. Real and good and genuine.

The best thing I'd ever seen.

In that second, I wanted to promise her a million things.

That Evan would be fine.

That I would protect her.

That she would never hurt again.

Tell her I was so goddamned sorry. That I didn't know. That I would have stopped it if I could have.

That I'd be her hero.

But that just wasn't possible.

Not when I'd already destroyed everything.

thirty-one
Kale

found her in the deserted chapel. Cast in shadows, the quiet space was illuminated only by the candles that had been lit and remained flickering through the deepest hours of the darkest night.

She was in the very front. On her knees. Red hair all around her where she had her head bowed forward.

That sweet body was shuddering and heaving with silent, wracking sobs.

I wondered if any distance could come between us when I might not be able to hear it.

Because I'd *heard* her through those six excruciating hours it'd taken to be released from the small city jail. My charges dropped, my assault labeled defense of a patient.

The whole time I'd felt like I was losing my mind because I'd heard it in my ear. Heard it in my heart.

I'd heard it through time and space and miles.

Her grief thick and profound.

Ingrained in me.

Marked in me.

I took another step forward.

Energy raced across the floor.

Saw it the second it slammed into her from behind. The way her spine jerked in awareness and that feeling rushed out in front of me.

Thick and heavy.

I took another tentative step forward. I might as well have been wading through quicksand, my steps laboring and heavy and slowed.

Going nowhere.

Or maybe I was just wading through honey.

Sweet, sweet heat.

I took another step down the middle aisle, and she jarred forward, bracing her hand on the floor in front of her as she gasped for a breath.

Swore, the flames on the candles shivered where they licked.

Two feet behind her, I came to a stop.

"Hope." Her name was a tortured murmur.

She choked, and all I wanted was to wrap her up. Hold her and make her all the promises I'd wanted to make all along. Knowing if it did, they would only be lies.

She rose on her knees, her hands flattened to her chest like that action was the only thing keeping her from completely falling apart. "It hurts so bad, Kale. So bad."

My throat was clogged, so goddamned tight and thick I could barely speak. "I should have recognized it. Seen it all along. It's my fault."

"No." It left her on a harrowed breath.

"Yes. I should have seen it. Just like I should have seen it in Melody. But I was too caught up, Hope, too caught up in what I felt for you."

Because of it, I'd done exactly what I'd promised myself I'd never do again.

I'd failed.

Old grief slammed me so hard that I rocked forward. Unable to stand beneath it, I sank down onto the front pew off to the side of her, elbows on my knees as I leaned forward, my face in my hands.

I could feel her peering over at me. Could feel the weight of her unwavering gaze. "You were there when we needed you most. You *came back*. Right when we needed you."

Bile swam. "It never should have come to that. I should have caught it the first time he came into my office. Instead, I spent the whole time thinking of touching you."

Wanting her.

Wishing for things I couldn't have.

I could sense her shifting on her knees, turning to face my direction. Disbelief oozed out on her words. "You're really gonna sit there and make that claim? After everything we shared? After the way you treated him? Like he was somethin' rather than nothin'? Like he might be your world the way you became ours?"

Grief stalked my throat, burning and choking. "I wanted to save him, Hope. I would have given anything. And now he's—"

Barely clinging to life.

I bit down on the words. Unable to even say them even though we both knew exactly what I'd meant.

He was barely clinging to life.

I'd gone straight to the ICU when I'd been released. Dr. Krane had just been leaving when I'd walked in. His expression had been . . . grim.

Worse than grim.

He'd touched my arm and promised me he'd done everything he possibly could. He hadn't filled me in like Evan was just another of my patients. His tone had been cautious, filled with sympathy I actually knew the guy truly felt, the jargon slim.

But I knew well enough what lay in his words and Evan's chart.

Evan had little chance of making it through the night.

A panicked regret swelled, constricting and suffocating. I couldn't breathe. "I tried."

I'd tried to save him.

Had tried to save Melody.

And it wasn't enough.

It wasn't enough.

I would never, ever be enough.

Her soggy plea filled the air. "Don't you dare give up on hope, Kale Bryant. Don't you dare. Not when we're finally free."

I forced myself to look up at her.

At this girl who had changed everything.

Green eyes and red hair and dimpled chin striking in the glow of the candles that sent shadows flickering across her gorgeous, unforgettable face.

The best thing I'd ever seen.

And that spark in the deepest part of me, the one she'd ignited, lapped and danced and begged.

I forced myself to stand, my smile weak. "I think you have enough faith for the both of us, sweet girl."

I'd no longer be the one who threatened it.

I swallowed around the misery. "No matter what happens . . . don't ever lose that. Don't ever give up on hope. It's the brightest thing I've ever seen."

I turned on my heel and started up the aisle.

I could feel her pushing to standing, her presence powerful as it slammed into me from behind, her words choked and rasping, "Don't you dare, Kale Bryant. You promised me."

I kept walking.

"I need you."

I need you. I need you. I need you.

Melody's voice twined with Hopes.

Torment.

Torture.

Agony.

I came to a standstill, breaths panting from my lungs.

"Who is it you're running from Kale? What are you afraid of? That the girl you loved was Evan's aunt? Their hearts? Or are you just afraid of lovin' me?"

I tried to stand upright under the crushing weight of the grief that surged and raged and slammed.

I forced myself to look at her from over my shoulder. "I'm afraid of what I've been afraid of all along. That I would never be enough. That I was chasing after something I couldn't have."

Seeing the heartbreak wash over her face, I turned back around and rushed for the door.

Needing to get out of there before I fell at her feet.

Before I begged her to let me try to be that guy I'd been pretending to be all along.

But that guy had only hurt her. Fucked up time and again.

I squeezed my eyes closed when her voice pierced me from behind. "The only way you can fail me is by walking away."

Grief clutched me in its fiery hold. Incinerating. Blistering.

Ash.

When I tore the door open to escape, I knew that was all that was left of me.

Hope

I'd always wondered how many broken hearts one person could endure.

Broken hearts meted out by unexpected tragedy.

Broken hearts delivered by the ones who were supposed to love them most.

True, physical broken hearts that struggled to continue to beat, marred by fate and health and genetic abnormalities.

Sometimes, I felt as if I could endure no more.

Kale had . . . crushed me.

I'd allowed myself to love him so freely. Love him so easily. Because I saw so much greatness in him. So much kindness in his giving, bleeding heart.

Maybe his heart had been broken one too many times, and he knew he could take no more.

I guessed I'd been right all along.

Had seen it coming the night he'd strode across the bar and slid into the stool next to me.

He'd looked like discord.

Chaos with an easy, arrogant smile.

A perfect, controlled disorder.

Just as I thought, the man had looked like a broken heart.

I sat next to my son—my life—in the darkened room where he lay in the middle of the elevated bed. Lights dimmed in the space. He was connected to a million tubes and wires, face covered in tape the same way he'd been as a tiny infant, the machine he was connected to inflating his chest as it pumped life into him.

Where his tiny body fought and fought and fought to conquer another broken heart.

And I knew sitting there, I would endure a million more broken hearts for him.

With him.

I jerked when I felt the presence behind me. I swiveled to look over my shoulder.

Dr. Krane stood there with a cautious smile on his face. "You're still here."

I almost laughed. "I'm not sure you could drag me out if you tried."

Four days.

That was how many days I'd been sitting in this spot, my mama and Jenna bringing me my meals. Keeping me company while I fought the gnawing that ate me from the inside out. Renewing my energy so I could in turn give it to Evan.

They hadn't expected him to make it through that first night.

I'd seen what was written in Dr. Krane's eyes when he'd come to me after the surgery to give me an update, and then I'd gone straight to the chapel.

I'd dropped to my knees and issued up unending prayers.

I'd given all my belief.

Had fallen on my faith.

My heart had always been hung on hope, and I sure wasn't about to give up then. Not ever.

"How is our little fighter today?" Dr. Krane asked.

Tears blurred my eyes. "Maybe I'm just being hopeful . . . but there's something different today. Like I can feel that he's closer. Like his little spirit is right here with me."

Dr. Krane took another step forward. "Don't sell yourself short. I think you know this little guy better than anyone, Ms. Masterson."

He hesitated for only a moment before he angled his attention my way. "I'd like to recommend that we start testing weaning him off the ventilator tomorrow morning. He seems to be gaining strength, and the last blood tests were stabilizing."

I couldn't tell if it was fear or relief that slammed me at his words.

My hope had never been cautious.

But today it was overwhelming.

A landslide of sensation. Because I'd been whittled raw.

Hurt in so many ways I had no idea if I'd ever heal.

My worry for this little boy, who radiated the biggest, brightest life, even from the depths of the coma he remained in, held there by medicines to give his broken body a better chance to rest and recover.

Not to mention, I was still reeling from what I'd learned, that Dane's sister had had the very heart defect Evan had.

I'd never met her. Dane and I had just married when she died, our courtship quick, a whirlwind I'd believed an intense kind of love. He'd said she was killed in an accident in another state and insisted I not attend the funeral. He'd claimed he'd needed his space to grieve, which I'd been confused by, but I'd respected it.

I'd just had no idea he had been pulling a veil over my eyes. Lying and lying and lying from the start.

Yesterday, I'd received the documents I'd demanded. Dane relinquishing his parental rights. Of course, it'd come with the stipulation that if I ever disclosed any information I had on his family, Dane would pursue charges of my falsification of Evan's medical records, the man vile enough to hold the threat of jail time over my head in order to protect himself.

But the truth of the matter was that I was willing to submit to that provision. Let it go, even though it felt as if I were doing Melody a disservice.

Melody.

My heart broke for her. For the greed that had kept her in the dark. Stolen her life. It broke for the man who had loved her and tried to save her and somehow had taken the burden that belonged to the *Gentry name* and placed it on his own shoulders where it never had belonged.

Then those pieces of my broken heart had been crushed when he'd left me. Because he couldn't stay through the grief. Because he couldn't bear any more. Because I'd fallen so hard and I no longer could picture my life without him in it.

But I'd bleed forever if it meant my son would be okay.

"We'll be monitoring him closely," Dr. Krane assured me. "At the first sign of distress, we'll increase him back until we know his heart is ready to beat on its own."

I twisted my fingers on my lap. Almost painfully as I looked at my son.

My heart.

I peeked up at Dr. Krane, the words laden with a plea. "And what do we do if that time never comes? What if he's never ready?"

Sympathy edged across his stoic features. "Then he'll have to go back on the transplant list. But we can cross that bridge when we get to it. Right now, let's cling to the fact he's doing so much better than we ever could have imagined. Could have hoped for. He is a true miracle, Ms. Masterson. I'm hopeful for a full recovery."

My miracle boy.

A single tear fell, and my chest clenched. So tightly. Gratitude and faith and remnants of fear. I reached out and gathered Dr. Krane's hand in mine. Squeezed it. "Thank you . . . for everything you and your team have done for him."

A soft smile edged his mouth. "Cases like this?" He gestured to Evan with his chin. "They're the reason people like us get up every morning to do what we do."

More tears slipped free, and I swiped at them, overcome. "He's going to be okay, isn't he?"

Dr. Krane gave me a slight nod. "He gets stronger every day. That's the only thing we can ask for." Something passed through his eyes. "And you need to make sure you take care of yourself. Get some rest. You'll need your strength for when he returns home."

Home.

THIS HOUSE IS L-O-V-E.

Everything clutched and clenched.

"I'll try."

"Okay, then. I'll see you in the morning." He gave me a soft smile before he moved for the door. He'd barely cracked it open an inch when he paused to look back at me. "You know he saved his life, don't you? We wouldn't be having this conversation if he hadn't made it to him when he did. If he had given up. He fought for him, and he saved him."

My lungs inflated, so light that I felt as if I might blow away. Or maybe I was the most solid I'd ever felt.

"I know."

His lips gave a slight twist at the corner. "All right then . . . I'll see you in the morning. Hopefully come then, we'll get to see this kid's smile."

When the door closed behind him, I turned back to Evan and gathered his little hand in mine.

Love came in so many forms.

For moments and for lifetimes.

Kale Bryant might have broken my heart.

But he'd left me with the piece he knew I needed most.

And that love?

It'd come to us at the exact, perfect time.

"My heart," I whispered.

Evan's eyes twitched behind his lids.

My heart.

This little boy who would forever hold it.

thirty-three
Kale

Blinding light glinted off my windshield. The Alabama summer was in full swing, the sun spraying darts of warmth across the green, abounding earth.

My driver's side window was cracked so I could take in every sense and sound.

Sweet, sweet heat.

Joy.

The brightest light.

Every cell in my body clenched.

Painfully.

Still, it was possibly the best feeling I'd ever experienced.

From a distance where they wouldn't notice me, I watched them.

My heart threatened to jump right out of my chest when Hope slid out of the driver's side and rounded the front of her SUV.

She helped Evan out from the back passenger side.

His homecoming was met with shouts and cheers from the porch where a ton of balloons swayed in the gentle breeze.

Jenna, Josiah's entire family—and a woman who had to be Hope's mother—were waiting.

Their excitement was palpable. Bubbling and binding to the atmosphere.

Hand-in-hand, Hope and Evan walked through the gate of the white-picket fence and up the pathway.

Their red, red hair glittered in the rays of sunlight that poured over them. It appeared like they were being drenched from above.

Saturated with blessings.

I could see Evan grin from across the space.

I'd been wrong that day in my office when I thought his spirit was bright enough to fill the entire room. Truth was, it was bright enough to fill the entire sky.

To light worlds and spark a million dreams.

They headed up the walk.

Maybe I tried to stop it, pretend it didn't exist, that it wasn't real. But that energy flashed, the attraction that had always been alive between Hope and me since the second I'd first caught sight of her.

It sizzled through the air like a crack of lightning.

I saw her spine stiffen in awareness. I thought maybe she tried to fight its existence before she gave and slowly turned to peer over her shoulder.

Like the girl could feel me the same way I swore I could feel her.

I swallowed around the emotion that knotted in my throat.

Intense.

Overwhelming.

Brutal and beautiful.

She stared back at me. The complexity of her expression was almost more than I could handle.

Sadness and overwhelming, stunning joy.

I met those mossy eyes, everything held in them so genuine and real.

I had to curl my hands around the steering wheel to keep myself from flying out the door and running that way.

Because fuck.

I wanted to go to them.

Wrap them up.

Hold them and keep them.

Instead, I sent her all my thoughts, hoping she could hear them. That she would tuck them away, hold them close to her sweet, sweet spirit.

I'm so fucking happy for you and for Evan. For your amazing, incredible kid. For amazing, incredible you. I'm sorry I couldn't have been better. That I wasn't enough.

My guts twisted as she stared back at me.

Brutally.

Because I wanted her. Wished for all the shit I'd been a fool to wish for in the first place.

But seeing them this way?

It was enough.

It was two when I pulled into the gravel driveway of the little house. I killed the engine and then just . . . sat there. Trying to get myself together. To put a goddamned smile on my face.

Tried to remember that this was what I lived for. My career and my friends that were really my family. They were supposed to be all I needed.

Problem was, the only thing I felt was empty.

Dropping my head, I squeezed the steering wheel and drew in a deep breath before I forced myself to open the door and get out. Milo was pawing and yapping at the window, almost as excited as the little whirlwind who came barreling out the door.

Hair flying.

Hugest smile on her face.

She threw her arms in the air.

"Uncle! You came, you came. I 'fought you forgot all abouts me."

Hit with a rush of that love I had for this kid, I swooped her up and hugged her close to my chest. "Forgot about you? What in the world would make you think that? You know I couldn't forget about my favorite girl."

She giggled like she thought it was the best thing she'd ever heard. "I knows that."

Her eyes went wide, and her voice dropped conspiratorially. Like she was getting ready to let me in on a deep, dark secret. "But Daddy told Uncle Ollie they were gonna have to drag your mopey ass over here 'cause yous were gonna ditch us 'cause you been way, way downs in the dumps."

My brow rose. "They said that, huh?"

"Uh-huh."

"Seems to me those two need to stop gossiping like a bunch of girls," I muttered under my breath.

Frankie Leigh made a horrified sound. "Gossip girls? Auntie Nikki loves *Gossip Girl*."

Could this conversation spiral any faster?

"You don't love girls, Uncle? I'm a girl. I 'fought you love me?"

Yes. Yes it could.

A sigh pilfered free. How was I supposed to dig my way out of that one? "Of course, I love girls, Sweet Pea. Girls are the best. I just don't love my best friends who act like the gossiping kind."

"Likes my daddy and Uncle Ollie?"

"Exactly." I ruffled her hair. "And you know you shouldn't say that word."

Her eyes doubled in size. "What? Mopey?"

Rynna suddenly appeared in the doorway, holding Ryland to her chest.

"You made it."

"Of course, I made it. Where else would I be?"

Rynna gave me a look that said I was full of shit, all mixed with a load of sympathy. "We haven't seen you in weeks. We weren't sure you were going to be able to make it."

Her tone held a distinct undertone of concern.

I settled Frankie Leigh on her feet and shoved a nervous hand through my hair. "Been busy."

That sympathy twisted on Rynna's mouth. She knew full well what my definition of busy meant.

I'd thrown myself into work in an attempt to forget.

It was exactly like I'd done all those years ago. But this time, shoving it all down, hiding it in that secret, dead place, didn't seem to work.

It only seemed to emphasize the hollowed-out vacancy that throbbed inside me.

A festering wound that didn't get any smaller the more time that passed.

It just gaped and yawned and expanded.

Growing bigger each day.

Six weeks had passed since I'd sat down the street from Hope's house and watched Evan's homecoming. Thing was, I couldn't help but seem to torture myself. Thinking about them constantly. My car automatically slowing every time I drove by A Drop of Hope because I was desperate for just a glimpse.

To see Evan whole and healthy.

To see the joy etched on Hope's face.

Every patient I saw only reminded me of the brightest smile, those adorable bug eyes blinking at me from behind those thick glasses, fingers flying with silent words that hit me like the sweetest sound.

Didn't know what was worse—that or the nights I spent tossing and turning through the loneliness. Waking up aching, body straining and hard, wanting Hope in a way that was almost depraved.

Desperate and hopeless.

Seconds from sending me over the edge.

"Come on. Everyone's already out back. Oh, and you're officially on uncle duty," Rynna said. Without a whole lot of warning, she was passing Ryland off to me.

I took him in my arms.

My chest grew tight at the feel of him.

Squeezing and pressing and prodding.

Instantly, he calmed, brown eyes staring up at me like he was trying to figure me out.

Mesmerized.

Or maybe that was just me.

It was amazing the way this tiny thing immediately trusted me to protect him. To take care of him. Always do right by him.

I gulped around the shards of glass that raked my throat.

I wasn't sure I knew what that meant anymore.

"You do have the magic touch, don't you?" Rynna asked over her shoulder as she turned and headed around the patio that wrapped around to the back of the house.

Lillith, Brody, Nikki, and Ollie were already hanging out around the patio tables.

Rex at the grill.

I was struck with how similar it felt to that day all those weeks ago. Yet, every-fucking-thing was wrong.

All wrong.

Ollie grinned at me from where he sat at the table, sipping a beer. "Well, well, well, look who's here. Here I thought you'd forgotten all about us."

I sent him a death glare. "So I heard."

Asshole was worse than a nagging mother, getting all up in my business like he belonged there.

But I guessed the dude had earned a free pass since he'd been the one who'd shown up at the police station in the middle of the night to pick up my pathetic ass. He had driven me straight back to the hospital so I could get to Hope and Evan.

The whole way, he hadn't said a word. He'd just allowed me to be silent in my grief, his voice grating with sincerity just as I'd been jumping out the door. *So fuckin' sorry, man. Know what they mean to you. What Melody meant to you. Know what you're going through right now. If you need me, I'm just a call away. Don't hesitate, brother.*

I'd given him a tight nod before I'd bolted out.

Because Ollie got it in a way I didn't think anyone else could.

I took a seat under one of the umbrellas and snuggled Ryland against my chest, lightly rocking him. The kid was out cold in about three seconds flat.

Rynna passed by behind my chair, reaching out to touch my shoulder as she went. "I'm really starting to get a complex over that, you know?"

I forced myself to smile. "Apparently the kid knows when he's in the presence of greatness."

"I think he just knows when he's safe."

A rush of grief threatened to strangle me. Suck me in and pull me under where I'd drown forever.

Lost in just . . . nothingness.

I swallowed around it, telling myself that this was the only thing I needed. My career and the people I cared about most.

I settled into it.

The warmth.

The care.

The love.

I enjoyed the afternoon the best way I could.

Rynna had taken Ryland to his crib so he could sleep, and I tried to sit back and relax. Listen to the conversations going on around me.

Join in.

Clearly, everyone was walking on eggshells. Watching me carefully.

Waiting for me to break.

No doubt, it was time I got over this shit. Put it behind me. Because I couldn't go on like this forever.

Rupturing.

Hemorrhaging.

Splintering, day by day.

I ate my meal as if I didn't have to force it down and then sat back to watch as Frankie Leigh twirled across the lawn, doing all these awkward jumps and leaps, which were so adorable it had my chest clenching again.

I loved that little girl so much.

Found it impossible not to think about her out there with Evan.

He said he's gonna marry her.

Hope's expression flashed through my mind.

Adoration.

Evan's emphatic nod when I'd asked him what he'd thought

about Frankie Leigh.

A wistful smile pulled across my mouth.

Unstoppable.

That feeling I'd been fighting rose so quickly I was sure it was going to demolish me.

Lay me to waste.

That feeling I couldn't afford to name. The one that kept pressing and prodding and picking me apart.

Limb from goddamned limb.

I sucked in a shuddered breath and tried to rein it in.

Rex plopped down across from me. "You ready to talk about that?"

He pointed at my face like my expression was evidence of some kind of crime.

The conversation happening around me immediately fell into silence. Like every single one of them had been waiting for this moment.

All eyes on me.

I shifted uncomfortably in my seat.

Had to wonder if I'd actually been invited over for a barbecue or if this was some kind of intervention.

God knew, Rex had just put me on the spot.

My head barely shook. "Don't see that there's much to talk about."

"Is that so?" His voice was incredulous.

"Yup." It was sharper than I intended.

"Huh, seems awful backward to me, considering you're the punk who never hesitates to set me straight."

I sipped my beer and turned my attention out across the lawn, to the wall of towering trees that blew in the wind. "And what exactly are you setting me straight about?"

From my side, Ollie scoffed. "How about the fact you're fucking miserable, man. Let's start there."

"I'm fine."

"Really?"

"Really."

Nikki's face pinched, her lips pursing together like she was stopping herself from unleashing on me.

But it was Lillith who spoke from where she was snuggled up to Brody at the next table. "You don't seem fine to me, Kale. Not at all."

Ollie pointed at her. "What she said."

I roughed a hand over the top of my head. "Just . . . don't."

It came out a warning. I was about five seconds from jumping to my feet and bolting.

"Don't what?" Rex demanded, leaning in closer. "Make you open your eyes the way you've always done me? Last time I checked, you were zero bullshit, and now you've got bullshit written all over you."

"Told you a long time ago, all I need is you guys and my job. I was stupid to think that'd changed."

"What's stupid is you thinking you don't deserve to love."

That feeling was back. Pushing and pushing into my consciousness.

Too fucking close.

My heart stumbled in its tracks before it took off sprinting.

Regret cinched down on every cell in my body, and my words dropped to next to nothing. "I failed them, man."

"Did you?" he challenged. "Because from what I know, it sounds a whole lot like you saved him."

"I missed it. I was his doctor, and I missed it."

Nikki exhaled, the sound almost pained as she scrambled around so she could meet my eye. "You think you missed it, Kale, but what if you hadn't been his doctor? What if someone else had missed it, too, and they didn't know him the way you did? What if you hadn't gone to them the day you did? What then?"

Sorrow clutched and gripped and bit. My soul feeling like it was being shredded.

What if I hadn't shown up when I had?

I couldn't process it. Couldn't begin to fathom a fate that cruel.

"It never should have happened in the first place."

Ollie's brow pinched, and he tugged at his beard in

frustration. "But it did, man. It did, and you were there, and you saved him. So maybe that's what you need to be focusing on instead of this bullshit excuse that you let them down."

His blue eyes beat against mine. "Unless you were just another asshole with a cold heart who was looking for an excuse to drop some chick and not look like a bastard doing it."

Spears.

Straight through the goddamned heart.

"You know that isn't it."

"You sure about that?" he provoked. "Because I bet that's exactly what that girl is thinking. Hell, she's probably over there thinking you used her up and then tossed her aside. On to the next."

A growl rumbled in my chest.

Rejection.

Anger.

"Fuck you, man, I love her."

I love her.

The heated words were out before I could think through the impact.

A motherfucking bomb that exploded in the air. Decimating me.

Ollie rocked back in his chair. Satisfaction on his face. "That's what I thought."

Unable to breathe, I dropped my face into my hands. Crushed anew. Or maybe I'd been right there all along. Like they thought.

They'd been waiting for me to break.

I guessed they'd gotten their fucking show.

Because I was.

I was fucking broken.

I could feel Ollie leaning in closer, his voice dropping. "You can be pissed at us, man. I get it. Kick my ass if you need to. But I'm willing to take on your wrath if it'll get you to admit the truth."

Bitterness soured on my tongue. "Yeah, and what's that?"

"That you're fucking scared, man. Scared to love again. To

fail someone when you're the first asshole to run in and save them."

I opened my eyes to find Frankie Leigh had appeared at my side. She cocked her head in question. "Yous scared, Uncle Kale? 'Cause Cap'in 'merica is never scared."

She tapped her little finger to her chin like she'd just been struck with an epiphany. "Wait a minute . . . maybe he is scared, and he saves all the people anyway."

She looked to Rynna who was standing just off to the side. "Right, Mommy? That's what brave is, being scared and doing what's right anyway because you love someone so, so much?"

Rynna ran her fingers through Frankie's wild, wild hair. "That's right, Sweet Pea. Being brave is being afraid and doing what is right anyway. Just like when your daddy ran into the fire to save us . . . he was scared, but he knew he would do whatever it took to save us. He came right when we needed him most."

Rynna looked over at me. "Just like your uncle Kale rushed in to save Evan right when he needed him most. I just don't think your uncle knows how very brave he really is."

Frankie started hopping across the wooden planks, singing, "Daddys and doctors are so, so brave! They come to save the day! Superhero, superhero, superhero. And I'm Wonder Woman and I'm brave, too!"

She threw her arms in the air with her silly song that to most would mean nothing, when it felt like it just might mean everything. She turned back to me with the biggest grin stretched across her face. "See, Uncle, you don't needs to be sad any more. You are so brave and you did all the right things. Even if you're scared, you are still Evan's bestest team."

My heart thrashed and my spirit soared.

Because, no, I hadn't done all the right things.

But I knew exactly what I needed to do.

thirty-four
Hope

I rushed out from A Drop of Hope's kitchen, my heels clicking on the floors, my knees feeling a little shaky.

I wasn't sure I'd ever been so nervous in all my life.

Sensing the movement, Evan spun around where he was standing by the inside of the cupcake display case. When he saw me, he smiled a smile so powerful it penetrated right through the center of me.

Moving forward, I grabbed him by either side of his precious face, my thumb swiping across his cheek to clean off the smudge of frosting. "Someone's been sneaking into the display case again."

He nodded in my hold, that smile somehow growing stronger, my little man all dressed up in a suit, and his normally messy hair tamed with product.

Just looking at him sent my bottom lip trembling. "You look so handsome."

His little hands flew between us.

YOU ARE THE PRETTIEST MOM IN THE WHOLE WORLD.

"You think so, huh?" I asked, trying to settle the jittery nerves that scattered through my insides, twisting up my tummy in pride and apprehension.

Jenna popped her head in through the front swinging door. "Are you two ready yet? We're gonna be late if we don't get out of here."

ARE YOU READY? I signed.

YUP!

LET'S DO THIS.

I took his hand and wound us around the front counter and toward the entrance. I clicked off the last light in the shop before we stepped out into the evening, the air still full of humidity and warmth.

Still, a chill skated my skin.

Sucking in a deep breath, I moved for Jenna's car, which was idling at the curb, and helped Evan into the back before I climbed into the front passenger seat.

The second I clicked my buckle, Jenna pulled out onto the street.

"This is so gonna wrinkle up my dress," I said, another dose of that worry injecting itself in my veins.

"Don't even start, Harley Hope. You look gorgeous. You're gonna be the prettiest girl in the whole place."

Funny how I'd never had stage fright for a second of my life. But this felt different. As if I was getting ready to let a room full of strangers view the most sacred part of me. But that didn't mean I wasn't incredibly honored to be invited.

To be a part of it.

I fidgeted with the skirt of my designer black dress, the one Jenna had dragged me out to some upscale boutique downtown to purchase for the event.

An event that was being held at Gingham Lakes Children's Center.

The second I even let the thought enter my mind, moisture was threatening at my eyes. I fought off the tingly sensation that raced my throat.

This was definitely not the time nor place to get lost in that vacancy that echoed inside of me.

I only allowed myself it in the darkest hours of the night. When I was alone, and I was free to let the loss I was dealing with consume me. When I allowed myself to miss him. To ache for him. My body pleading and my heart begging for him through the silence.

I gave myself the time to feel it.

The pain.

The loneliness.

Let the *what-should-have-beens* cry out from my spirit.

Just for a little while.

Then I got up the next morning with a staggering amount of thankfulness.

Told myself, *someday*. Someday I'd find the man who was meant for me. The one who completed me.

The hardest part was Kale had fit every single one of those spaces.

Filled them perfectly.

I gave a little yelp when I was poked in the side.

"There you are, Harley Hope Masterson. Here I was, thinking I was gonna have to crawl around in that head of yours and rescue you from wherever you went. Because you sure seem to be going there a whole lot the last few days."

I choked back the thick clot of emotion. "Just thinkin'."

Clinging to the steering wheel, Jenna glanced over at me and then turned back to the road. "And just what are you thinkin' about? Or more specifically, who?"

I gave her a shrug. "No one."

It might as well have been a shout of his name from the rooftops.

Kale. Kale. Kale.

Because it was always right there.

An echo in my consciousness.

The man carved into me.

"Will he be there?" she asked.

Flinching, I shook my head. "No. I saw the guest list. He isn't on there. I'm sure he knew it'd be too hard on us to see him."

Her jaw clenched. "He owes me his dick, you know? Told him I was gonna cut it off if he hurt you. And that man *hurt* you."

A crashing wave of it hit me from out of nowhere.

Covering me whole.

Hurt.

She was right.

Kale had *hurt* me.

A tear streaked free, and my voice cracked when I whispered, "How's it possible to be so thankful for someone and devastated by them at the same time? It feels like I'm torn right in two, Jenna."

"It would be wrong if you felt any other way, Harley Hope. He saved your son's life, but that doesn't give him a pass for walking out on you."

I wiped the back of my hand across my dampened cheek, trying not to smudge my mascara as a shot of frustration took hold. "That's the problem . . . I want to give him that pass, because he gave me back my world. I just didn't know that, in the end, he'd leave such a huge piece of it missing."

A heavy breath pulled from my lungs.

Weighted.

A thousand pounds of sorrow.

I looked at her. "Does that make me crazy?"

Her head shook. "Of course not. It makes you Hope. Who you are. I just wish he would have seen you for what you are."

My attention shifted away, and I blinked out the windshield at the buildings whizzing by. "I'm not sure him walking out had anything to do with me. I just don't think he could handle it. Seeing Evan that way . . . after going through it with Melody."

A quiver rocked through me when the memories flashed.

Evan collapsing.

Kale right there. Fighting for him. Refusing to give up.

Saving him.

My son.

Emotion bottled high in my throat, and I choked around it. "I forgive him, Jenna. I forgive him, and I refuse to regret loving him. No matter what kind of pain he left behind."

She reached over and squeezed my hand. "Then don't. You don't need to feel guilty for loving him. He's the one who's missin' out."

I glanced back at my son, who was drawing another picture of Captain America on his sketchpad.

He'd been doing it nonstop since he'd come home from the hospital eight weeks ago.

Dealing with his own kind of grief.

The man who'd come to mean so much to him had become his own loss.

Evan's heart on the line, the same as mine.

I couldn't count the number of times I'd found him silently crying. Angry and confused by the fact Kale had saved him and then turned around and left us.

HE PROMISED HE WOULDN'T HURT YOU. THAT HE CARED ABOUT US. HE'S NOT SUPPOSED TO HURT YOU. THAT'S THE RULE, he'd signed, driving another stake right into my demolished heart.

Our kinship so profound because he was a prisoner to the same confusion as I was.

This intense, overpowering gratefulness for a man who'd walked away in the end.

But somehow, I understood he couldn't stay and have to face the same ghosts every day. That it wasn't anything Evan or I had or hadn't done. It just hurt him too much to stay.

And I could only be thankful for what he'd given while he was there.

His time purposed.

Purposed for us.

"Someday," I whispered beneath my breath. "Someday."

Two hours later, I was sitting at one of the round banquet tables up close to the stage.

Balloon bouquets were set up all over the enormous space, twinkle lights were strung up across the ceilings, and extravagant floral arrangements were set in the middle of the linen-covered tables.

Our plates had just been removed after we'd finished the gourmet dinner.

Evan was to my right and Jenna was to my left. Dr. Krane and his wife sat to the other side of Evan, and a few people I'd never met before took up the rest of the round table.

The gala had been setup in a conference room, the collapsible walls opened to accommodate the three hundred guests who'd been invited.

The fundraiser was for Gingham Lakes Children's Center, and while some of the guests were staff and families who'd been helped by some of the center's programs, the lions share were Gingham Lakes's affluent, there to open their pocketbooks to support GLCC Charities.

Minus the Gentry's, of course.

"Thank you for all your support," the chairman of the board for NICU Services said as he completed his speech. Those nerves surged and spun, my stomach growing tight.

I was up next.

I'd memorized the program.

William Wright would speak, then Martha Jiminez, one of the event organizers would introduce me. I clapped for William Wright while anxious wings fluttered and scattered through my entire body. My eyes dropped closed for a moment so I could mentally prepare myself for Martha to step out to take his place.

The clapping died off and a ripple of confusion rolled across the room, a quiet anticipation taking hold to each person in attendance.

Though for me, that anticipation thundered and boomed.

A spark to the air.

I pried my eyes open and gasped when I saw who stood at the podium.

That crazy attraction that climbed to the air. It came alive between us where he stood up there dressed in a fitted black tux.

Potent.

Powerful.

Persuasive.

Kale.

The man was a perfect chaos.

My mouth went dry.

His hair was styled in that immaculate way, every part of him put together.

Commanding and bold.

But I saw beneath that gorgeous exterior. Everything about him tonight was abraded and raw.

So intense I could feel the emotion coming off him like a shockwave.

Under the table, Jenna pinched my leg, her eyes wide when I looked at her. "What is he doing here?" she whispered under her breath.

I gave her a short shake of my head.

I had no idea.

Hadn't expected this.

God, I didn't even know if I could handle it.

He cleared his throat. "I know your programs say Martha Jiminez should be standing up here right now to make this next introduction . . ."

He let a small smirk climb to his full lips. "There's a chance I might have bribed her to let me stand up here tonight, but don't blame her, I've been known to be a little convincing when I need to be."

A small wave of laughter rolled through the room.

Because there stood that cocky, arrogant boy.

A second later, a quiet somberness filled his expression. "But the truth is, I would have paid anything to get to stand up here and make this introduction, because this charity is so incredibly important to me. As a pediatric physician here at Gingham Lakes Children's Center, I have the honor of treating patients with many different illnesses and chronic diseases. There is no better feeling than getting to take part in their care. To maybe have the chance to make their lives a little better."

Those blue eyes locked on me.

Penetrating.

Infiltrating and invading.

A shiver rocked through me, and Evan stirred in his seat, his own surprise coming off him in waves.

"And sometimes, it's the patient who makes *our* lives better. The patient who touches us in ways we never could have expected. The patient who teaches us what true hope looks like."

His voice grew thick, and moisture grew heavy in my eyes.

What was he doing?

Ruining me. That's what. I had no idea how I was going to make it through this. And still, nothing felt more right than him standing up there.

He let his gaze bounce around the room. "I'm standing up here tonight with the great honor of introducing our next charity represented here this evening, A Lick of Hope. A Lick of Hope is a foundation created to support children born with heart defects and their families."

He looked down at the folded sheet of paper he'd brought up with him and cleared his throat before he started to read it.

"A Lick of Hope has raised over two hundred fifty thousand dollars this year alone," he said. "Their mantra reads, 'Anything is possible if you have A Lick of Hope.' After having the honor of getting to know this charity's head and its inspiration, an amazing little boy who taught me exactly what that hope looks like, I am now a true believer of this statement."

My ribs squeezed my heart. Or maybe it was just my heart that was struggling to break out. Desperate for its match.

His head dropped for a moment, as if he were gathering himself, before he looked up and met the crowd. "As physicians, we wake up each day with a huge burden on our shoulders. The health and wellbeing of the little people we get to see and treat. Sometimes that burden can be overwhelming. Wearing. Scary."

Overcome, he sucked in a breath. Finally, he pressed on, "A Lick of Hope was created and is headed by an incredible woman and her son who reminded me what being a doctor is truly about. It's about faith and belief and never, ever giving up, no matter how hard it might be. That even through our losses, our failures, we get up and fight all over again."

My blood thundered through my veins, a torrent of emotion

when he turned that magnetic, knowing gaze on me.

That connection pulsed.

Alive.

Begging and prodding.

"I am so incredibly proud to introduce the heart of A Lick of Hope, Harley Hope Masterson."

A thunder of applause echoed through the room, and tears broke free of my eyes. Overwhelmed, I pushed to standing on my high heels, still caught in the stare of this beautiful man.

Evan was beaming up at me, getting onto his knees on his chair as he frantically waved his hands in the air.

My child unable to hear the sound but no doubt swept up in the vibration.

I touched his sweet chin before I turned and headed for the steps that led to the stage.

Wobbly.

Lightheaded.

Because this man made me that way.

Vulnerable and shaky as he stared down at me as if I were his world.

Hope.

It threatened to bloom in my spirit.

I beat it back and focused on what tonight was all about.

I moved through the intensity that bellowed from the walls.

At the bottom step, I just . . . stopped. Turned around and stretched my hand out for my son.

He was just as big a part of this endeavor as I was.

Truthfully, more.

The inspiration of it.

The lifeblood of it.

And he'd worked his little fingers to the bone helping me make those lollipops.

His grin was magnetic when he saw my invitation. So huge when he scrambled down from his chair and raced for my side.

The room lit up in *awws* and whistles and sweet sounds for my son.

My miracle boy.

I gathered his hand in mine and we moved up the steps toward Kale.

Kale who stepped back and stuffed his big hands in his pockets and stared at us with this adoring, proud, sorrowful expression on his face.

So sincere.

For a moment, we were stuck there, lost to the other, before he leaned in and brushed his lips against my cheek. "I am so proud of you."

Energy flashed.

Ignited.

Chills racing across my flesh.

He ran his knuckle across Evan's cheek before he turned and headed down the side steps and down the aisle.

Barely able to stand, I moved to the microphone with Evan's hand still wrapped in mine.

I swatted at the tears clouding my vision, clearing my throat as I released a nervous laugh and looked out at the still-cheering crowd.

"Thank you all so much for being here. I know A Lick of Hope is a small charity compared to others here, but it means the entire world to me, and I'm incredibly honored to be invited to speak tonight."

I lifted Evan's hand in the air. "And this little boy . . . Evan . . . he's the reason I'm here tonight."

My tongue darted out to wet my dried lips, still feeling the weight of Kale's stare from where he'd moved to the very back of the room at the entrance doors.

"When my son was born, the first thing I wanted to know was if he had ten fingers and ten toes, and when I held him for the first time, whole and perfect in my arms, I'd never been so happy in all my life. I had no idea that we soon would be in for the fight of our lives."

Emotion swam and churned, and I glanced down at my boy, who was still swaying at my side.

It was easy to find my strength in his bravery.

"I'm not sure there could have been anything to prepare me

for learning that he had a severe heart defect. Nothing that could have been said to prepare me for the moment I was told my tiny newborn would need to be flown to another state to undergo emergency surgery to save his life. And there was absolutely nothing that could have equipped me for the devastating news just months later that if he were to live, he would need a heart transplant."

Evan shifted at my side, and I glanced down at him to find him smiling this smile that was so full of love that it nearly bowled me over.

He's the reason I dream.

I looked back to the crowd. "My son might have been born with a heart defect, but it most definitely didn't change the size of it. He's the most genuine, caring little boy I have ever known, and for all the years I can remember since he learned to sign, he's said prayers at night, hoping that no more babies would be born with bad hearts."

I cleared the lump from my throat, so in awe of my child.

For what he'd gone through.

For what he'd accomplished.

For the incredible person he'd become.

"From those prayers, A Lick of Hope was created. And we share that hope with every lollipop we make."

A wobbly, grateful smile pulled to my mouth. "That hope is spread with every lollipop that is purchased and every donation that comes in. Because we will never give up hope that one day, no child will have to go through the pain and struggles my son has gone through. That no parent will ever have to hear the words that their child may not make it through the night. That, through research, congenital defects will be easily repaired, and maybe someday . . . someday . . ."

Someday.

The words stumbled on my tongue and my gaze fumbled to Kale at the very back.

The man just a silhouette.

The most profound thing I'd ever seen.

I finally managed to find my words again. "That maybe

someday they won't exist at all. We couldn't do it without every five-dollar lollipop we sell or the amazing donations and contributions that come in every day. So, thank you . . . thank you for your support. And if you're so inclined, we have some of those handmade lollipops available in the auction tonight. Each one is made with love and our gratitude to you."

I stepped back, and applause broke through the room. But my sight was sealed on the man. On his slow, sad smile. The pride behind it.

Then he turned and disappeared out the door.

And I wanted to hate him and hold him. Scream and drop to my knees.

Instead, I fumbled back to my table.

Evan climbed onto his seat and turned to me, confusion and anger and hope billowing across his precious face. *HE CAME BACK.*

My mouth trembled because I had no idea what that meant. Why he'd done what he did.

But hope, it blistered and radiated and beat.

So intense, I kept shifting on my seat, struggling not to come out of my skin as I listened as the next charity head was introduced then the next and the next until finally the auction was opened. The guests filtered out into the next room to bid on vacations and diamonds and a donated car.

And our small offering.

A thousand lollipops.

As everyone filtered out, I looked to my son, who was clearly growing sleepy. I ran my fingers through his hair before I signed, *ARE YOU READY TO GO HOME, SWEET BOY?*

Yes, he mouthed before giving me a tired grin, and the smile I returned was adoring. Because I was so proud and happy, even though there was a huge part of me that was feeling brittle.

Those broken pieces moaning at the sight of Kale.

The man who'd changed everything.

Who gave me the greatest gift and then stole what could have been.

"Let's go," I said, offering my hand, Jenna at my side. We

said our goodbyes to Dr. Krane and his wife before we headed up the aisle.

Jenna sidled up to me. "Oh, Harley Hope, you are in so much trouble, my friend."

Trouble.

I'd always known he'd be.

"That man does know how to make an entrance, doesn't he, standing up there looking that way. Mmm . . . all that deliciousness. Think that man sent every woman here into a swoon."

She fanned herself. "He does not fight fair. One look, and he knew you'd be nothin' but putty in those big ol' hands."

"Stop it," I scolded her under my breath, stepping out into the courtyard that fronted the conference building. "He just wanted to be here to support A Lick of Hope. That's all. He left me, Jenna. He left us. Let's just leave it at that, okay?"

"How about we don't?"

That deep, powerful voice hit me from the side.

My fragile heart pulsed.

Kale stepped out from the shadows, his hands still stuffed in his pockets.

Moonlight poured in from above, striking against all the curved, defined angles of his beautiful face.

Evan squeezed my hand almost frantically when he realized Kale was standing right there, two feet away from us.

"What are you doing here?" The words were a frenzied whisper.

"Stalking you, clearly." He fought for the joke, but that mouth only managed to minimally tweak up at the side. Too heavy with the sadness that rimmed his lips.

I could feel my son's own turmoil. The questions coming off him as the man who'd rescued us then abandoned us took another step in our direction.

The air grew thick.

Dense and full.

My pulse thrummed.

Erratic.

My breaths turning choppy.

"I'm just gonna . . . go check out the auction items." Jenna's tone was cautious, her eyes searching when she looked at me to find out if that was what I wanted.

If I wanted to be alone with him or if I wanted for her to step in and intervene.

Problem was that I wasn't so sure I knew the answer to that myself.

Finally, I gave her a tight nod while still staring at Kale because I couldn't seem to tear my attention from his face.

When she disappeared back inside, I finally spoke. "What are you really doing here? Why would you stand up there and say all those things?"

It was a plea. A warning. I didn't know.

I didn't know if I should tell him to stop, not to come a step closer, or throw my arms around his neck and beg him to never leave me the way I was aching to do.

He blanched, and all those defined, distinct curves of his face went rigid in stark vulnerability. "I don't have anywhere else to go . . . not when wherever you are is the only place I want to be. Because I meant every single thing I said when I stood up there. You two taught me what it really means to hope."

"You don't get to do this, Kale Bryant. I told you that day in my kitchen, you don't get to come in and make promises and then just walk away. And you sure as hell don't get to walk right back in whenever you feel like it."

And I knew he had his demons. I respected that. But if he wanted a place in our lives, he had to be certain he was all in. That he could handle my son's disability. His old fear.

He roughed one of those big hands through his hair and looked off into the distance as if he were trying to gather himself.

Evan climbed down onto his hands and knees beside me, his notepad on the ground as he began to furiously write across a clean page.

My son nearly broke me when he turned it toward Kale.

You promised you cared about us. That you wouldn't hurt my mom. That she was the prettiest mom in the world. You said you were her boyfriend and I was your favorite. Remember?

And I knew that it broke Kale in some way, too. Because the towering man dropped to his knees in front of my child.

His hands were shaking when he took the pad and wrote out his response.

I did. I was a coward, and I left you. And I know I don't deserve the chance, yours or your mom's forgiveness. But if you can both forgive me, I promise that I will never leave you again. Not as long as I'm living.

Oh God.

My spirit licked and danced and my body swayed.

Lightheaded.

Evan sat back on his heels, his hands flying in front of him.

YOU PROMISED I WAS YOUR FAVORITE. I THOUGHT I WAS YOUR FAVORITE.

Desperation wove into Evan's movements, and his entire face pinched in grief, the remnants of the rejection Kale had inflicted. He lifted his thick glasses, swiping the tears that streaked down his face with the sleeve of his jacket.

Kale gasped over a sob.

Physical, wrenching pain.

He grabbed the notepad, his back heaving as he leaned over to write.

*You are my **favorite**. You are my everything. I'm so sorry I hurt you. I never wanted to hurt you.*

Evan's face was completely blanketed by the heartbreak written all over him, soaking wet with the tears that wouldn't stop falling when he read what Kale had written.

I'd warned Kale what was on the line. Did he see it now? The kind of pure love my son had trusted him with?

Evan sat up on his knees and signed more, anger seeded in

the emphatic movements.

OUR HOUSE IS L-O-V-E. YOU HAVE TO LOVE IF YOU LIVE THERE. THAT'S THE RULE.

Hardly able to see through the bleariness, I attempted to start to translate, but Kale lifted his own hands.

His motions were awkward and prolonged, off half the time, but there was no mistaking what he was trying to say.

*THAT'S GOOD THEN. BECAUSE I LOVE YOU, EVAN. I LOVE YOU SO MUCH, AND I LOVE YOUR MOM. I WANT TO STAY WITH YOU. WITH HER. BE YOUR FAMILY. BECAUSE YOU ARE MY **HEART**.*

He punctuated the last with a fist against the middle of his chest.

I nearly buckled, watching him sign to my son. That he'd taken the time to learn. That he'd listened. That he could *hear*.

Kale looked up at me from where he was still on his knees. "I love you, Hope. I love you so goddamned much, I can't see. I can't eat. I can't sleep."

Slowly, he pushed to standing, his hand still fisted over his heart. "You warned me your life was complicated, that you didn't have any room for anything else, and I pushed my way into it anyway. I wanted to save you. Save him. Be your knight or your hero or whatever you wanted me to be. But it turned out that you were the one who was complicating me. In the best of ways. Waking me up and making me feel, when I'd never thought I could possibly *feel* that way again. All along, you were the one who was *saving* me."

I tucked my trembling bottom lip between my teeth, and Kale came closer. So close I could feel him everywhere. Racing across my flesh, sinking deeper into my heart.

"It kills me, Hope, kills me that I walked away from you that night when you needed me most. I was scared. Terrified. Filled with grief and guilt. But you awakened that dead place in me. That's a gift . . . you and your son are a gift . . . and I don't want to live my life without it."

He took my face in both of his big hands. "I love you, with all of me, and I promise, if you can find a way to forgive me, I will live my life for you. For Evan. For *us*. There might be times when I'm afraid, when I fail, but I will never stop fighting for you. You set me on a path that I don't want to stop walking. I will follow you anywhere."

A soggy laugh jolted free, and I sniffled and reached up to scratch my nails across his jaw. "Cowboy."

He gathered that hand in his, brushed his lips across my knuckles. "Princess."

He stared at me for the longest time before he looked back at Evan who was staring up at us, sniffling and wiping the tears from his face. Kale knelt back down and did it for him. "Do you want me to stay?" he asked, his voice ripping from his throat. "With you? With your mom?"

Evan made that scraping, raw sound as he said, "Stay."

I pressed my hands to my chest. Overcome. Overwhelmed.

Kale smiled at him. Tenderly. With so much love it nearly blew me over.

"Is it okay if I kiss your mom, little man?"

Evan turned back to his pad.

You're supposed to kiss her if you're her boyfriend. Lots of kisses. That's the rule.

"Yeah? And what if I'm her husband?"

Evan was quick to write on his pad.

Then you have to give her a billion.

Kale shifted on his knee and turned his gaze on me, the blue brimming with a sea of promises.

Lust and love and devotion.

He dug in his pocket, and my hands flew to my mouth, a gasp flying free when he held out the little black box.

"What do you say, Hope? Can I give you a billion kisses and all my love, every single day, for the rest of our lives?"

I was frozen, shocked.

Wondering if it was all too much, too fast.

"He bought All. The. Lollipops." I jerked to look to the side where Jenna was hanging halfway out the door and shouting at us. "Say yes, Harley Hope. Don't you dare walk away and not say yes. You deserve this. More than anyone I know."

There was my best friend. Grinning from ear to ear in all her brash, pushy encouragement.

"Yes," I whispered, the word soggy, love sliding free.

Because it didn't matter the circumstances. The path we'd taken to get here. This man had led me exactly where I was supposed to be.

"Yes," I said again, this time laughing with the wave of joy that crashed over me.

He slid the ring on my finger. Diamond glimmering in the moonlight, the man stared down at it.

Awed.

Floored.

Finally, he pushed to standing.

The second he did, I threw myself in his arms.

Kale lifted me from the ground and spun me around.

Round and round.

His face buried in my neck while he clung to me.

He set me on my feet and took my face in his hands. He leaned down and captured my mouth in a dizzying kiss.

Soft and tender and slow.

A promise.

A passionate claiming.

And my unstable world . . . it no longer spun.

It danced.

Clapping went wild around us, and Kale dropped his forehead to mine, grinning against my lips. Redness flushing to my cheeks, I peeked out to the side to see Jenna jumping up and down and clapping her hands.

Dr. Krane and his wife were beside her.

His smile was slow.

Knowing.

Kale looked at Jenna. "You wouldn't mind if I gave these two a ride home, would you?"

Jenna smirked. "Like I'd expect anything less from you, Sir Bryant."

She turned her attention to me. "I just expect all the details tomorrow."

Giggling, I rested the side of my head against Kale's beautiful, bleeding heart. "Of course, she does."

"She's going to cause me all sorts of trouble, isn't she?" he murmured down at me.

"Oh, I think you can count on that."

I stretched my hand out, looking at the diamond glinting on my finger. Giddiness swept through me, head to toe. I peeked up at him, a playful smile taking to my mouth. "A ring, huh, Cowboy? Awful presumptuous of you."

He let that cockiness ride to his lips. "Hey, can't blame a man who knows what he wants."

"Is that so?"

"Mmhmm . . ."

He kissed across my jaw and up to my ear. "Besides, I know my girl. If she knows something is right? Then she's going to jump and trust she lands right where she's supposed to."

"With you."

Kale gathered up Evan's hand. "With us."

He wrapped his arm around my waist and leaned in to kiss me on the temple. "Let's go home, Shortcake."

Home.

I couldn't wait to make one with him.

epilogue
Hope

Laughter roared through the dim-lit space. Downstairs, a band played, the music vibrating through the floors adding to the carefree vibe of the private party happening upstairs.

"Are your eyes closed?" Jenna demanded from behind me. "No peeking, you greedy girl, or I'm not gonna let you have any."

I pressed my hands tighter against my eyes and shook my head. A rush of heat lit me up everywhere. "Are you sure I even want to know what this surprise is?"

She'd basically had my skin the color of a tomato since the second I'd mounted the top step to the second floor, with the games we'd been playing and the drinks she'd been plying me with.

She'd said this celebration was for me, and I was damn well going to enjoy myself.

Funny how she didn't have to coerce me into that anymore.

"Oh, I promise you, you're gonna want this surprise," she sing-songed as she leaned around my side and placed something on the table in front of me.

Whatever Jenna was up to was met with a bunch of giggles and laughed whispers rippling all around me.

Nikki nudged me in the side. "Oh yeah, you are definitely going to want this surprise. All of them. But I'm def taking one for myself. I am the orgasm fairy, after all. I totally earned one of those babies."

"Oh God, now I really don't know if I want to see."

From across the table, I heard my mama's distinct laughter.

Mortified.

Yeah. I was so going to be mortified. Still, I didn't think I'd ever been happier about it in all my life.

"Open up!" Jenna shouted, and I was groaning and bracing myself and simultaneously grinning like a fool when I peeled my hands from my eyes.

Then I busted up laughing.

I was right.

Mortified.

Because there in front of me were at least forty cupcakes.

All of them speared with little stakes that boasted pictures of Kale's face, the writing beneath claiming, "Sex on a stick."

"You didn't," I scolded.

"Um . . . you know I did. With a little help from my new friends, of course," she said, glancing at Nikki, Lillith, and Rynna, who kept busting up in fits of laughter.

"Pass one of those down here," Mindy, one of my old friends, shouted from the other end of the long table. "I want a taste of that."

It was a little surreal that I was surrounded by so many of the faces of the women who'd been out to celebrate Jenna's birthday that fateful night nine months ago.

And now, here we were.

My life now looked so incredibly different.

I'd known I was blessed at that time. No question about it. But it'd also come with a weight so heavy there were some days I didn't know if I'd manage to bear it. Stand up under it.

And now . . .

Joy trembled all the way to my bones as I looked around at

the faces smiling back at me.

With a grin, I pointed at Jenna's accomplices. "All of you are in so much trouble. Hand in those bridesmaid's dresses."

Nikki gasped and pressed her hand over her chest. "Never. You know you love those cupcakes. I mean, look at all that delicious, creamy frosting. Don't you just want to take a big ol' bite?"

Conspiratorially, she swatted at Lillith. "Tell her, Lillith. She loves them so much she's over there squeezing her thighs together and shifting on her seat just looking at them. Mouth watering. Am I right?"

Lillith sent her a teasing scowl. "Always trying to chase away the good ones, aren't you?" She turned her attention to me. "Although, I guess we officially get to keep you."

I widened my eyes. "You couldn't get rid of me if you tried."

"Says the girl who just told us to pass in the bridesmaids' dresses," Nikki said.

A giggle escaped. "Fine. You're right." I reached out and pulled the tray closer to me. "And I want them all. They're mine. I need all the cupcakes."

"Oh no, greedy girl, those are for everyone. You don't want to go and break Maw-Maw's heart, now do you? After I went over there and got her hair done up real nice just for the occasion." Jenna swung her attention to her grandmother who sat right next to my mama. "Right, Maw-Maw?"

Her grayed eyes glinted. "Only reason I came was to get me one of those cupcakes."

My mouth dropped open in mock offense. "Watch yourself, Maw-Maw. I don't share my man."

"That's good, because I don't share, either." The deep voice hit me from behind.

A shiver raced my spine, and this time, I really was pressing my thighs together. Trying to quell the instant ache.

That's the way I felt. Every moment of every day.

This constant desire for a man who stole my breath and filled up all the missing pieces in my life.

The one who stood by me. My support. My foundation.

Because times weren't always easy, and the fear in our lives could never be fully erased.

But he was there to hold me up through it.

"No, you don't, Sir Bryant. Stop right there." Jenna pointed at him. "No boys allowed. Get that perfect ass back downstairs where it belongs."

He shot her one of those heart-stopping grins. "Don't get your panties all up in a twist. Just need to talk to Shortcake for a quick minute."

Jenna's eyebrows rose so high they disappeared behind her bangs. "A quick minute, huh? That all it takes these days?"

"Ouch . . . you really know how to hit a man where it hurts, don't you?"

Crossing her arms over her chest, she quirked a brow. "Oh, you can count on that."

Kale laughed. "I knew you were going to be all sorts of trouble."

His expression shifted into feigned seriousness. "It's incredibly important I speak with Hope immediately. We have some important business to attend to, and it just can't wait."

"Really?" she challenged.

"Really," he said, dropping those blue eyes to me, mirth swimming in their depths.

Love.

It burst from every cell.

I glanced around at the faces grinning back at me. "Well, if you all will excuse me for a second, my fiancé has something important he has to say to me."

Kale wound my hand in his and helped me to stand.

He started us for the glass partition accordion wall.

From behind, we were hit with a barrage of *Ooo's* and teases and taunts, a *brown chicken brown cow* shouted from Nikki, the little punk.

She and Jenna definitely had to have been separated at birth.

I dropped my head in an attempt to fight the rush of heat that flushed and burned and ignited.

He sent me a smirk over his shoulder as he pulled me

through the same gap he'd led me through that night when the only thing I'd planned on giving him was a single *dinner*.

That dinner that had turned into my giving him my body. My heart. My life.

The same way as he'd given me his.

"Oh, Cowboy, I don't know what you have up your sleeve, but I have a party I'm supposed to be attending. Same as you," I whispered through the swell of euphoria that swept through me.

Joy.

I'd never known it could be quite so bold.

Palpable as it surrounded us. Fortified by devotion and loyalty.

He gripped my hand, walking backward as he faced me, watching me with one of those smiles that sent a scatter of butterflies flapping through my belly.

Dominant and persuasive and sexy.

There was my cocky boy.

"Last time I checked, those parties were all about the two of us. Besides, I've got something important to tell you."

He spun me around then pulled me close in an exaggerated, impromptu dance, his arm wrapping around my waist as he tucked me against his body.

His beautiful heart thundered, in sync with mine.

A giggle slipped free, and I stared up at him as he swayed me in the moonlight that poured down from above. "Oh, yeah, and what is that?"

He grinned, but his gaze was soft. "In two days, you're going to be my wife."

I tucked my bottom lip between my teeth, struggled to play along. Because it still blew my mind.

In two days, I would be Kale Bryant's wife.

"Hmm . . . I didn't realize that."

He twirled me again. "No?"

I shook my head. "Must have slipped my mind."

"Slipped your mind, huh?"

Vigorously, I nodded before I was yelping as he dragged me back into the far recesses of the balcony. Right back to that spot that had changed everything between us all those months ago. He hoisted me up and placed my bottom on the table before he plopped down in a chair in front of me.

He gripped me by the outside of the thighs. "Do I need to remind you?"

A tiny moan slipped free from between my grin. "Mmm . . . I think you might."

He shot forward and captured my mouth in a consuming, maddening kiss.

Soft, plush lips and demanding, delicious tongue.

Orange and whiskey.

Smooth.

All man.

My head spun, and my body sang.

Throbbing and needing this man in a way I'd never thought I'd need anyone.

He pushed to standing, and I wrapped my legs around his waist then groaned into his mouth when he pressed his hard cock against my center. "Kale."

"Are you remembering yet, Princess?"

"Almost," I teased, the word both a giggle and plea.

He kissed me deeper.

Passion spiraling around us.

A bind. A bond. Our commitment.

"How about now?" I could feel his smile as he murmured against my lips.

I pulled back so I could look at the defined curves of his face, a perfect silhouette in the shadows. Sobering, I brushed my fingertips across his lips. "I could never, ever forget."

A needy rumble echoed from his chest, all the playfulness gone when he kissed across my jaw and down my throat, words woven in the middle. "Couldn't even stay downstairs for a few hours, knowing you were up here. Only thing I wanted was to get to you. Touch you. I can't believe I've been given this. That in two days, I get to call you my wife. That I get to call Evan my son. Tell me this isn't a dream."

I clung to his shoulders.

Lost to this beautiful, beautiful man.

His devastating body and his extraordinary heart.

"I'm yours," I told him.

Wholly.

Completely.

"I still can't believe it," he murmured, edging back to look at my face as his words rode on the night.

I took him by the face, my gaze locked on his kind, knowing eyes. "Believe it. I believe in us. I believe in you."

Kale had rescued me in so many ways. Filled up all the vacancies. Filled our home with laughter and love.

With security.

He'd worked with his attorneys to ensure Dane could never be a threat to Evan ever again.

And somehow, miraculously, I had received a check for five hundred thousand dollars from the Gentry Trust at the finalization of my divorce.

Almost the exact amount required to cover Evan's emergency heart surgery and ICU stay, plus the debt I'd incurred when I'd made the choice to fight for my son. No matter the cost.

I'd never asked for it, demanded it, my aim only to sever ties with Dane forever. But the truth was, it'd been a lifesaver. Another burden lifted. He'd never admitted it, but I somehow knew Kale had been the one who'd made that happen. How, I wasn't sure. Honestly, I didn't want to know. But I would be grateful for all my days.

He set his big hand on the side of my face. "I love you, Hope. You are my everything. I can't wait to share my life with you. With Evan. Grow our family. I never thought I would get this chance."

I drew in a staggered breath at the thought. I never thought I'd get this chance, either.

Evan would always be enough.

Kale would always be enough.

It almost felt greedy to hope for another child.

Still, that sacred place in my spirit bloomed with the possibility.

But no matter how our family was shaped, I would cherish it.

A tender smile fluttered across Kale's lips and adoration moved across his expression. "I'll never stop fighting for you. Working to protect you and Evan."

"I know that. I love you more than you know," I whispered to him, searching him in the shadows that played and danced across his gorgeous face.

"Princess," he murmured, kissing across my jaw.

"That's queen to you." I let the ribbing weave into my tone before the words softened as I ran my fingers through his hair. "You did say you wanted to be my king."

He released the puff of a chuckle at my neck, chills racing my flesh as he gathered me up.

Held me tight.

"You are my treasure," he whispered.

"And you are my forever," I told him.

My everything.

And I would be the one to treasure every part of him.

Kale had never come to the place where he'd accepted he'd saved my son.

He would tell me it was my faith.

My belief.

My hope that had filled Evan with the strength to fight.

And maybe that was okay.

Because sometimes . . .

Sometimes even hope needed a hero.

And Kale Bryant?

He was mine.

the end

Thank you for reading *Follow Me Back*! Did you love getting to know Kale and Hope? Please consider leaving a review!

I invite you to sign up for mobile updates to receive short, but sweet updates on all my latest releases.
Text "aljackson" to 33222
(US Only)
or
Sign up for my newsletter
http://smarturl.it./NewsFromALJackson

Watch for *Lead Me Home*, coming Spring 2018!

Want to know when it's live?
Sign up here: http://smarturl.it/liveonamzn

More From A.L. Jackson

Fight for Me
Show Me the Way
Hunt Me Down
Lead Me Home – Spring 2018

Bleeding Stars
A Stone in the Sea
Drowning to Breathe
Where Lightning Strikes
Wait
Stay
Stand

The Regret Series
Lost to You
Take This Regret
If Forever Comes

The Closer to You Series
Come to Me Quietly
Come to Me Softly
Come to Me Recklessly

Stand-Alone Novels
Pulled
When We Collide

Coming Soon from A.L. Jackson
Hollywood Chronicles
A collaboration with USA Today Bestselling Author, Rebecca Shea

ABOUT THE AUTHOR

A.L. Jackson is the New York Times & USA Today Bestselling author of contemporary romance. She writes emotional, sexy, heart-filled stories about boys who usually like to be a little bit bad.

Her bestselling series include THE REGRET SERIES, CLOSER TO YOU, BLEEDING STARS, as well as the newest FIGHT FOR ME novels.

Watch for LEAD ME HOME, the third sexy, heart-warming romance in the new FIGHT FOR ME series, coming Spring-2018

If she's not writing, you can find her hanging out by the pool with her family, sipping cocktails with her friends, or of course with her nose buried in a book.

Be sure not to miss new releases and sales from A.L. Jackson - Sign up to receive her newsletter http://smarturl.it/NewsFromALJackson or text "aljackson" to 33222 to receive short but sweet updates on all the important news.

Connect with A.L. Jackson online:

Page **http://smarturl.it/ALJacksonPage**
Newsletter **http://smarturl.it/NewsFromALJackson**
Angels **http://smarturl.it/AmysAngelsRock**
Amazon **http://smarturl.it/ALJacksonAmzn**
Book Bub **http://smarturl.it/ALJacksonBookbub**
Text "aljackson" to 33222 to receive short but sweet updates on all the important news.